You're convinced y
**bona fide psychics. **

   A. Forget about it. \
      your body and you never will.

   B. Beg the man who accidentally hit your car to help
      prove you've just had an "honest-to-God" vision.

   C. Find someone who wholeheartedly believes in *you*
      and make that person your family.

**You've literally just run into the perfect woman,
but she's a certified nut job. What do you do?**

   A. Give her your insurance information and
      run for the hills.

   B. Hang around like a lovesick puppy while she walks
      the freeway overpass to save the poor soul she saw
      in her "vision."

   C. Make love to her *often* to take her mind off the
      vision and place it squarely on you!

If you picked A, it's time you met Opal's indefatigable
Grandma Blue. She's not your run-of-the-mill granny!

If you picked B, start your engine. You just might be
related to Jack Davis, who some say (e.g., Grandma Blue)
is the reincarnation of legendary racing great Dynamite
Davis.

But if you chose C, then you know that when true love
hits like a bolt of lightning, it's *Sheer Dynamite!*

**Other sexy, outrageous reads by
Jennifer Skully and HQN Books**

*Drop Dead Gorgeous
Fool's Gold
Sex and the Serial Killer*

Jennifer Skully

SHEER DYNAMITE

HQN™

If you purchased this book without a cover you should be aware that this book is stolen property. It was reported as "unsold and destroyed" to the publisher, and neither the author nor the publisher has received any payment for this "stripped book."

ISBN-13: 978-0-373-77132-5
ISBN-10:   0-373-77132-0

SHEER DYNAMITE

Copyright © 2006 by Jennifer Skullestad

All rights reserved. Except for use in any review, the reproduction or utilization of this work in whole or in part in any form by any electronic, mechanical or other means, now known or hereafter invented, including xerography, photocopying and recording, or in any information storage or retrieval system, is forbidden without the written permission of the publisher, Harlequin Enterprises Limited, 225 Duncan Mill Road, Don Mills, Ontario M3B 3K9, Canada.

All characters in this book have no existence outside the imagination of the author and have no relation whatsoever to anyone bearing the same name or names. They are not even distantly inspired by any individual known or unknown to the author, and all incidents are pure invention.

This edition published by arrangement with Harlequin Books S.A.

® and TM are trademarks of the publisher. Trademarks indicated with ® are registered in the United States Patent and Trademark Office, the Canadian Trade Marks Office and in other countries.

www.HQNBooks.com

Printed in U.S.A.

Dear Reader,

People often ask where a writer gets his or her ideas. Well, they can come from anywhere. Random thoughts, a story a friend tells you about someone they know. *Sheer Dynamite* was born of a random thought I had as I was stuck in the shadow of a freeway overpass while driving home from work during rush hour. My character Grandma Blue was born the day I sat in a coffee shop with my good friend Krystal, and she told me all about her grandmother. I never met the lady, but I fell in love through Krystal's wonderful stories. (Krystal, I took the liberty of making up a bunch of stuff, as well! Making things up is just in my nature.) The idea for Dynamite Davis came from my husband, who loves scouring the Internet for tidbits about race-car drivers from the early days of racing. Writers store these random thoughts and tales, and one day, miraculously, they all seem to coalesce into one big story that simply has to come out. And *Sheer Dynamite* is the result! I hope you enjoy reading it as much as I enjoyed writing it!

Jennifer Skully

To Janice Beach

For being my friend as well as my sister

Thanks to all the special people in my life!

Lynn Phillips and Saskia Hanselaar,
for listening to my bizarre plot descriptions
during our lunchtime walks.

Jenn Cummings, Rose Lerma
and Terri Schaefer, for all their input.

Christina Ferraro, for reading my work in a contest and
giving me the lift I needed to keep going.
I still have the letter you wrote, Tina!

And Krystal Mignone, for regaling me with
tales of her own Grandma Blue.

My agent, Lucienne Diver, and my editor,
Ann Leslie Tuttle, for all their guidance.

CHAPTER ONE

JACK DAVIS FOUGHT DOWN the air bag and scrambled from the cab of his truck. The woman he'd rammed into was already out of her sporty red mini-SUV and on her hands and knees looking beneath the vehicle.

"What are you doing?" Jack swallowed the epithet he'd been about to use. He'd learned to apply politeness regardless of the circumstances.

Still entranced with the underside of her car, the woman didn't respond.

Standing in the center freeway lane, Jack surveyed the slow-moving traffic on both sides of him. For once, he could appreciate a Silicon Valley rush hour. If they'd been going faster, they wouldn't have made it through the collision without serious injury. Christ. Jack turned to the gold Cadillac that had rear-ended him when he'd slammed on his brakes. The Caddy's driver hadn't moved yet, though his air bag had deflated.

Jack ran back. Squatting by the Caddy's closed window, he shouted through the glass. "You okay?"

No answer, but at least the old man's eyes were open, though dazed, and he'd turned his head. Jack whipped his cell phone off his belt and punched in emergency.

With the call made, he opened the door slowly. The

cars in the commute lane to his left moved over to the shoulder, giving him room. He held the man back against the seat when he tried to move. "Just stay put until the ambulance gets here. They need to check you out. Feel like anything's broken?"

The old man shook his head, but would he really know? His eyes couldn't seem to focus on Jack's face. At least there wasn't any blood. Jack stood.

Then he saw the woman again, the one responsible for the accident. This time her head was under *his* truck, her butt in the air, short skirt barely covering her essentials. "What are you doing now?"

Stalking back, he grabbed her arm and pulled her out.

Still on her knees, she stared up at him with the bluest, most freaked-out eyes he'd ever seen.

"Didn't you see it?"

"See what?" he asked as calmly as possible. She'd started to worry him. He looked for blood on her head, or any sign of trauma.

"The body. It fell off the overpass right in front of me. I ran over it."

She was young, mid-twenties or so. Blond hair that curled softly over her chest, ocean-blue eyes, a healthy bloom to her cheeks and, from his vantage point as she knelt beside his truck, nice…nice everything.

Despite being nuts.

"I didn't see a body flying off that overpass, ma'am." Jack struggled to retain that ingrained politeness.

She bit her lip, then looked through his legs at the Cadillac. "Maybe it's under there."

Jumping up, she tipped sideways on her high heels, leaning dangerously close to the commute lane. Jack reached out to grab her, but she recovered on her own and rushed around him to peer beneath the old man's gold car.

She leaned into the open door of the Caddy. "Did you see a man fall off the overpass?"

The old man shook his head. He still hadn't spoken, and Jack was anxious about him. The gas fumes and the noise started a pounding in his head. "You could have killed someone slamming on your brakes like that."

She sucked in a breath. "Oh, my God, I didn't…are you all right?"

"Fine. Thanks for asking." He didn't point out she should have shown the concern before she crawled under his truck.

She put a hand on the old guy's shoulder. "What about you?"

He smiled up at her blissfully. And nodded.

"I'm so sorry. But the body fell right in front of me."

Jack closed his eyes and shook his head. "There is no body."

She stared at him with guileless eyes. "But I saw it."

He didn't know why he was trying to convince her, but he walked to the front of her car, leaned down to look under it, did the same with his own truck—aw, Jesus, the crushed bumpers and tailgate made him wince—and finally the Cadillac. Then he spread his hands. "Nothing here."

Sirens sounded in the distance. Behind them, traffic was stacking up.

"Nothing back there, either," he said when she looked at the stream of cars with blinkers on, trying to merge around them.

She stared back at the overpass. She'd skidded several feet beyond it. "But I saw it."

He cocked his head. She had that odd manic look, overly bright eyes, flushed skin, like a fever, manic fever. He'd seen it on his mother enough times to know. "You have a name, ma'am?"

She stared at him for a few too many seconds, and he had the gut feeling she couldn't remember.

"Opal," she finally said. "Opal Smith."

Ah, thank God, she knew her own name. Nice name, too. "You have insurance, Opal?"

"Of course. It's illegal to drive without it." She was still staring up at the bridge, and her lips moved. Over the traffic sounds, he couldn't make out the words.

"What'd you say?"

"It was a vision."

He put his finger in his ear, jiggled it. "Come again?"

"I had a vision." She lifted her shoulders and fastened her baby blues on him. "You know. A vision. A premonition."

Oh man. She *was* schizo, a malady with which he'd had far too much experience. Jack looked off down the shoulder lane next to the median where red lights flashed at least a freeway exit away. The ambulance. Or the cops. Another warm June day, but the hot exhaust fumes turned it into mid-August weather. He'd started sweating in his thin T-shirt. Or maybe it was the months of insurance red tape he envisioned. "Don't tell the cops about any *visions* you had."

She tipped her head to the side. "But how am I going to explain about slamming on my brakes?"

"Tell them you saw a dog."

"Jumping from the overpass?"

Jack closed his eyes and took a really deep breath.

He'd never bought the old axiom before, but what they said about blondes might be true. The beautiful ultimate proof stared him right in the face, albeit a few inches shorter than his own six-two. "No," he enunciated slowly as if she were deaf. "You tell them it came from the side of the road."

"We're in the fast lane. Somebody else would have hit it."

He knew he shouldn't have gotten up this morning. Monday. Late for work. The boys at the site were probably sitting on their butts waiting for him to get there. "It was in the median lane, probably got trapped out there, then made a run for it."

"But that would be a lie."

He could see himself repeating this story months from now over *Monday Night Football* at Donahoe's, and he actually had to smile. The poor woman needed help, a lot of help. The most he could do for her now was make sure she *didn't* tell the cops she'd had a vision. "Maybe there really was a dog."

"Dogs don't fall out of the sky."

Neither did bodies. He'd always considered himself a patient man, but he had his limits. "Have you been drinking?"

Her pretty eyes widened with horror. "It isn't even nine o'clock in the morning."

"Head start on Happy Hour?"

She eye-rolled him.

"How about drugs, then?"

She gave him a pressed-lip look. Nice red lipstick.

"If you tell the cops you had a vision, they're going to test you for every illegal substance known to man."

Or, more likely, haul her off to the nearest psych ward. He really did not want to have to call her family to break that news since he knew exactly how it felt. "You have that much time?"

She passed a look from the now-crushed rear of her little red SUV, over his double-whammied truck, to the crumpled front of the gold Cadillac, then to the old man still sitting dazed in the front seat. "All right. A dog." She tipped her head again. "Did you see it? Just in case they ask."

"I didn't see anything but your rear end." Especially when she was peering under his truck. Now that was a vision.

"I HAD A VISION. A REAL ONE." Opal had waited all day for this moment, to make her spectacular revelation.

Grandma Blue's head thunked against the scarred Formica tabletop, her fingers clutching spasmodically at the ceramic coffee cup. The last of the sun's rays shone through the kitchen window making the fuschia blossoms on her muumuu glow.

"Grandma Blue?" Opal had always thought of her grandmother as, well, ancient, though the older Opal got, the less ancient she seemed. Opal's heart thumped. "Are you all right?"

Her grandmother raised her head, her eyes just a little glazed. "No, I'm not all right. I have a daughter who's proclaimed herself 'psychic to the stars,' a grandson who appears on TV calling himself a medium and cavorts with dead people and a granddaughter who gives tarot readings. And actually makes a good living at it." Grandma Blue sighed, world-weary. "You were the only normal one."

Opal had never considered herself normal, at least not in the context of her family. Even her father, who had died almost thirteen years ago—Opal still missed him terribly—had a spectacular gift. Blake Smith had been a world-renowned telekinetic, manipulating objects at will. Each member of her family had a special talent. Opal had been waiting all her life to find her own psychic gift. "Will you love me any less if I had an honest-to-God vision?"

"Won't love you any less, sweetie pie, but I will be losing the only one of you I had anything in common with."

Opal ringed her coffee mug with her index finger. "You know how important this is to me."

Grandma Blue heaved an even deeper sigh, her white hair glistening with blue highlights. "Tell me all about it."

Excitement exploded all over again inside Opal, and the words burst out. "It was a premonition. I saw a man jump off an overpass on the freeway. But when I got out of the car, he wasn't there. There was nothing there. I looked underneath the car, under the truck that ran into me—" She stopped. Oops.

"Someone ran into you?" The glaze had left Grandma Blue's eyes completely. She pierced Opal with her see-everything, know-everything gaze.

"Yes, well." Opal cleared her throat, then took a gulp of her sweet coffee. "I was on the freeway, you see, and naturally, since I thought what I saw was real, I slammed on the brakes to avoid running the man over, and the guy behind me hit me, and another car hit his truck and…" Her voice trailed off. She felt sixteen instead of twenty-eight, trying to explain how she'd wrecked the family car.

If anyone had been hurt in the accident… Opal couldn't bear to think about that. She'd called the hospital to check on the elderly gentleman, and she simply couldn't put words to the relief she'd felt upon hearing he'd been released and was just fine. If he'd been injured, if Jack Davis had been injured, well, her vision would have been a terrible thing. Thank goodness that hadn't happened.

"It was just a little fender bender," she added meekly.

"How little?" Grandma Blue stared her down.

"All right, I had to have the RAV4 towed because there was no way I could drive it, and I won't know for a couple of days how bad the damage is." Then she sat up straight. "But I don't care about the car, if it means I had a psychic vision."

Grandma Blue muted the two televisions she had on high volume in the living room. Opal was so used to the background noise, she hadn't even noticed them. Grandma always had two TVs going, one for stock car racing and one for hockey. Since Dale Earnhardt died at Daytona, she was trying to wean herself off the races. Hockey was supposed to do the trick. It hadn't yet.

Grandma Blue snorted. "You sound exactly like The Mother when she started that 900 number to do psychic readings."

The Mother was Opal's mother. Grandma Blue never called her by her name. In fact, she didn't call Opal's brother Julian by his name, either. The oldest, and the golden child with the weightiest psychic gift, Julian was The Brother.

But Opal was getting off track. "I'm not being stubborn, I just want you to be my witness."

"I can't be a witness unless someone actually jumps off that overpass." Grandma Blue's fingernails tapped her coffee cup. She stared hard at Opal. "*Did* someone actually jump?"

Opal pushed aside the plate of gooey chocolate chip cookies and gripped Grandma Blue's free hand. "That's the beauty of it. He hasn't jumped yet, and I'm going to save him before he does." She sat back, her face feeling all rosy and hot with triumph.

Grandma Blue's hard-edged stare didn't soften. She pushed back her chair, the legs scraping across the worn kitchen linoleum. She opened the oven door and, amidst the cracking of joints and a few grunts, got down on her knees. Her arthritic fingers grappled with a rack, then finally, she stuck her head in the oven.

"Grandma Blue, what are you doing?"

"Turn the oven on, I'm going to gas myself."

"But it's electric."

"Then put it on broil for me, would ya? Hopefully it'll catch my hair on fire and make my head explode." Despite her insistence that she was normal, Grandma Blue had a flair for the dramatic, much like the rest of Opal's family.

"You're going to make your arthritis act up with your knees on the cold floor. Now get back up here and promise you're going to back me up with my story."

Her grandmother eased out of the oven, put the rack back in, and climbed to her feet with a hand gripping the countertop. Opal wouldn't dare think of helping her. Grandma Blue was excessively independent. "Did you have dinner yet?"

Opal's stomach rumbled in answer. "No."

"You should have told me before I put out the cookies. I'd planned on fish cakes."

Fish cakes à la Grandma Blue were to die for. Of course, some people might turn up their noses at such a plebeian delicacy, but then they hadn't grown up on Grandma Blue's fish cakes. "I'd love to stay."

Pulling out a frying pan, Grandma Blue shook it at Opal. "Before I agree to anything, you better tell me about your car."

Opal shrugged. She loved her red RAV4. But the vision was worth the battered back end and the fact that she'd had to rent an ordinary sedan while the damage was being assessed. "It might not be totaled. But I've got good insurance, so everything'll be fine." For luck, she crossed her fingers beneath the table.

The skillet plunked down on the stove with a metal clang. "Not if they find out you caused an accident because of a vision."

The side of Opal's mouth quirked. "That's exactly what the guy who hit me said."

Grandma Blue almost dropped the bottle of oil she'd taken out of the cupboard. "You told some stranger you had a vision?"

"That's canola oil, right?" Opal worried about her grandmother's cholesterol.

"Of course," she answered as she rummaged in the refrigerator, pulling out the plate of fish cakes she'd prepared. "Do you realize what potential ammunition you gave him if there's an insurance battle?"

"I didn't give him anything to use against me. He made sure I told the police it was a dog in the road. The vision thing would only be his word against mine.

Besides, he seemed like a reasonable guy. He was trying to help." Considering the circumstances, Jack Davis had been quite patient. His concern for that poor old man in the Cadillac impressed her, too. And with those dark brown eyes, all that wavy topaz hair—brown with sun-bleached streaks—and bronzed skin, he was sorta cute, when you got past the way he glared. Understandable, though, when she remembered his front and rear bumper damage.

"He gave me his card, in case I had any trouble."

The oil sizzled and sputtered in the pan as her grandmother tested the readiness, then popped four cakes into the hot grease. Opal's mouth watered. They were especially good with a little vinegar and ketchup.

"He's not a lawyer, is he?"

"No." Opal rummaged in the pocket of her purse for his card. "He's a building contractor."

"Construction. Not bad. Shows a man isn't afraid of working with his hands. Let me see that card."

Opal handed over the card, her stomach growling as the scent of frying fish filled the kitchen. "What else are you making?"

"Peas and a cold tomato salad." Grandma Blue tilted her head back to read the card. For seventy-six, she had amazingly good eyesight and could read without her glasses.

The spatula fell from her fingers, clattering to the stovetop, barely missing the oil-filled pan.

"The fish cakes will burn if you don't pay attention." What was wrong now? Opal hadn't seen that look on her grandmother's face since the age of eight, the day Opal's Grandpa Chester had been run over by an inebriated ice-cream truck driver right in front of the house. He'd died a hero, saving two little girls who would have been mowed down by the drunken driver.

Eyes widened in disbelief, nostrils flared in shock, Grandma Blue's breath came in short gasps.

Opal really was beginning to worry about her grandmother's health. No more fried food. "Are you having a heart attack?"

Grandma Blue raised her eyes and hands to the ceiling, the card aloft in her fingers. "It's a sign."

Opal scurried around the edge of the table, grabbed the spatula and flipped the fish cakes before they got overdone. Her grandmother *never* took her eye off the fish cakes. Opal's psychic vision must really have thrown her off balance.

Grandma Blue turned then, her eyes, the exact same shade of blue as Opal's own, glowed maniacally. Opal backed up a step, the spatula clasped in front of her like a shield.

"Do you see this name?" The card shook in her aged fingers.

Opal raised a brow, then whispered, "What name?"

"HIS name." She said it with capitals, almost as if she referred to God.

"You mean Jack Davis?"

Her grandmother's eyes drifted closed and a stream of air, carrying one word, hissed from her mouth. "Dynamite."

Both brows arched this time. "Dynamite?"

"Dynamite Davis."

Mercy. It suddenly made sense.

"We have an honest-to-God sign here." Grandma

Blue threw Opal's own words back at her. "He's got the same name as Dynamite Davis."

"It's just a coincidence."

"Opal Smith, don't you ever say anything concerning Dynamite is a coincidence."

Opal cringed. Grandma Blue never used that tone of voice with her. With The Mother and The Brother, often, but never with Opal or her sister, Pearl.

But then Opal had never before questioned her grandmother's unstinting lust for Jack "Dynamite" Davis. She had been drilled on the intimate details of his life and death from the time she could speak, maybe even before. Of course, Grandma Blue had never met him, but she fantasized about Dynamite Davis. She hadn't driven a Ford since the day he died in the fiery depths of his Ford race car at a North Carolina track back in 1964. No one in the family would dare step on a Ford lot for fear of Grandma Blue's wrath. The first questions asked of prospective boyfriends or girlfriends were "do you drive a Ford, have you ever driven a Ford, would you ever consider driving a Ford?"

Opal secretly lusted after a new Mustang, a red hardtop with a black stripe along the door. Ooh. The thought of sitting behind the wheel of one of those babies made her tingle. The car was so…retro sixties. But Grandma Blue would never survive the terrible betrayal if she plunked down money for a Ford.

Opal was so used to hearing him referred to as Dynamite that she hadn't made the connection to the name Jack Davis.

Grandma Blue really did look as if her head would explode, without the aid of the oven broiler.

"Is he married?" She held the card within an inch of Opal's nose.

Opal tried to back up, but the countertop hit her in the hip. "He wasn't wearing a wedding ring that I noticed."

"How old is he?"

"Early thirties."

"What kind of car does he drive?"

"It was a Chevy truck," she answered instantly, making it up. She hadn't noticed the make, though she'd taken stock of the damage to his front and rear bumpers.

"When's his birthday?"

Opal thought about saying that the fish cakes were getting overdone, that the peas hadn't been set to boil and that she never even thought to ask Jack Davis his birth date. But Grandma Blue just might brain her with the frying pan, hot oil and all, for the slightest infraction. "I don't know—" then quickly added, at the feral glint in Grandma Blue's eyes "—but I can ask."

"What's he look like?"

"Tall. Russet hair, dark eyebrows, nice golden-brown eyes." Just saying plain old brown wasn't good enough.

"Handsome?"

"Yes, yes, tall, dark and handsome would describe him."

Grandma Blue turned on her heel without regard to her arthritic knees and marched from the room. Opal's shoulders sagged with relief as if she'd just faced down a grizzly.

Her grandmother's rubber-soled shoes squeaking on the linoleum signaled her return. She thrust the gold-framed photo in her hand in front of Opal's face, forcing her to stare cross-eyed at it.

"Does he look like this?" Grandma Blue demanded.

Hard to tell from this distance, but Opal had seen the prized photo so many times, she could speak from memory.

Actually, her Jack Davis looked nothing like Dynamite. Jack's dark eyebrows were not one big line across his forehead, thank goodness, and his nose was nowhere near Dynamite's bird-of-prey beak. Noble better described it. Jack's face was fuller, his shoulders broader, and he had one awfully impressive chest. Especially when compared to the slightly built Dynamite.

"Yes, he looks exactly like that." The lie slipped easily off her tongue. She didn't dare say anything else with her grandmother in this Dynamite-induced mania.

Grandma Blue suddenly hugged the picture to her chest. "I've waited, all these years I've waited."

"Would you like me to start the peas and cut up the tomatoes? The fish cakes are done, and I'll just put them in the oven to keep them warm," Opal murmured in an attempt to divert Grandma Blue's zealous fervor.

"Your meeting him is a sign. He's Dynamite, I know he is."

"He's Dynamite?" Opal didn't dare do more than repeat.

"Dynamite's reincarnation."

"Oh." No comment was safe. The grease-laden atmosphere suddenly made her head swim.

"And we're going to prove it." Grandma Blue set the photo on the table, making sure its stand was placed just so. "I've got a plan."

Oh, no. No, no, no. Not that Opal had a choice. Grandma Blue with a plan was an unstoppable force. "What?"

"You're going to ask *him* to help you prove your vision is real. And while he's doing that, you're going to find out everything you can about him so we can prove he's Dynamite reincarnated."

Grandma Blue accused the rest of her family of being abnormal? Jack Davis wasn't going to know what hit him.

AFTER OPAL LEFT, Blue stabbed the mute button on first one remote, then the other. Race cars blared to life. She really had to stop watching stock car races, but it was hard to break a fifty-year habit. Still, she'd taped the entire previous season of hockey games and was now running through them, studying, learning the rules, the players. By the start of the new season, she'd be a fanatic. And she'd be weaned off stock cars for good.

Going back to thoughts of Opal, Blue smiled to herself. That girl was so easily manipulated, it was a wonder Blue adored her the way she did. What Opal needed was a man. A husband. A family. Something that would annihilate her asinine desire to be psychic. For Christ's sake, the girl had slammed on her brakes in the middle of the freeway because of a "vision." Idiotic. A husband and a family would snap her right out of it, give her something else to think about. Something a damned bit more important than competing with her brother.

Not that the competition was Opal's fault. The Mother fostered the rivalry, and she'd started the day that good-for-nothing spoonbender—oh excuse me, telekinetic—husband of hers kicked the bucket in a plane crash on his way to "his bright future" as a TV wunderkind. Opal had been a mere fifteen and devastated at the loss of her father. Julian, at seventeen, with his budding ability to communicate with spirits, suddenly became the rising star in the family. Lillian, The Mother, couldn't live outside the sphere of someone's star quality, as if the glitter somehow rubbed off on her. Opal, poor kid, without a psychic brain cell in her head, got lost in the shuffle. Lillian might be from her own loins, but sometimes, Blue really wanted to smack her upside the head. It had fallen to good old Grandma to make both Opal and Pearl feel loved, wanted and respected.

It was a load she was perfectly willing to share, and Jack Davis offered wonderful possibilities. Tall, dark, handsome *and* a good job. According to the card, the boy owned his own business. Not a bad prospect at all. Opal could get herself mixed up with a psychic, for God's sake, and be forever doomed to feeling second-rate. Jack was the answer to Blue's prayers.

The kicker was that he'd helped Opal despite himself. Now, every self-respecting driver knows the person doing the rear-ending is the one to blame. You were always supposed to leave enough room between you and the car in front so that you could stop before hitting them. He could easily go down as the driver at fault. Still, though the vision thing would have turned the episode in his favor, he'd helped Opal tell a lie about a dog.

The boy certainly held possibility.

Especially since he didn't drive a Ford, and he could be the reincarnation of Dynamite Davis. Which was, of course, as likely as The Mother being Cleopatra the way she claimed. Hah! For now, claiming Jack was Dynamite reborn was enough to keep Opal in close proximity to him.

CHAPTER TWO

"HEY, BABY, YOU CAN WALK all over me with those shoes."

"Honey, wanna help me sink this drill as deep as it'll go?"

A shrill wolf whistle pierced his eardrums. Jack snarled at the hecklers. Though he'd lost a lot of time yesterday dealing with the aftermath of the accident, the crew was making good progress today, considering it wasn't even ten o'clock in the morning.

Correction. They *had* been making progress until this latest distraction. He glanced at the cause of the commotion and did a double take.

Opal Smith tottered toward him across the uneven ground in a pair of spiked heels and a skirt short enough to…didn't she know about construction sites?

Obviously not. "Sorry about the guys, but this isn't a place for a woman dressed like…" Jack tipped back his hard hat, his eyes tracking her shirt, the hem of her skirt and the precarious angle of her heels as she crossed the rugged terrain. "Dressed like that," he finished.

"Whoa, boss, is she yours?"

"Hey, cut the crap and get back to work." The glare with which Jack accompanied the command effectively shut the guys up this time. Not that he could blame any one of them.

Even he couldn't take his eyes off her legs, made even longer by the fact that she wore those stilettos. Which, any minute now, would break her neck if she kept walking on the pitted, broken ground of the site.

She cleared her throat, and he realized he'd been staring at her legs way too long. As he brought his gaze up, his eyes caught on the low-cut, tissue-paper-thin top molded to her body.

Damn, he was worse than his crew. Ogling and whistling after women at a site was not his gig, but blond-haired, blue-eyed, luscious-lipped and long-legged, this woman was the stuff of fantasies. *His* fantasies. Miss Opal Smith was the embodiment of his dream girl. Every guy had one, the girl who got your blood pumping till you were seeing everything through rose-colored glasses—the girl you took home to meet Mama.

Except, in his mom's case, there'd been a chance she'd be having one of her bad days instead of a good one. She'd passed away two years ago. He missed her fiercely in spite of everything, yet when she'd been alive, he hadn't taken women home to meet her. In Opal Smith's case, he might have made an exception. And hoped Mom was having one of her good days.

Jack put a hand on Opal's arm to steady her as she teetered on those impossible heels. Warmed by the sun, her skin looked appetizingly soft and mouthwateringly smooth. Christ, he needed to get himself under control here. "What can I do for you?"

"Well, it's about the accident yesterday."

Ah, yes. He'd given her all his information, including the location of the current site he was working. He dipped his head in invitation for her to continue.

"I didn't apologize to you for doing such a stupid thing."

His equilibrium seemed to tilt. That was the last thing he'd expected to hear, but her remorse seemed too genuine to smack down. "It wasn't stupid, it was just an accident."

She tipped her head. "It *was* stupid. And you're being kind. I didn't think, I just reacted."

Jack didn't sense an ounce of deceit, nor did Opal seem the least bit crazy. At present. Maybe yesterday had been an aberration. He actually wanted to believe it was. "Don't worry about it anymore. No one was hurt."

She bit her lip. "I called the hospital yesterday, and Victor's going to be fine."

Victor Patell, the guy in the Cadillac. Jack had called, too. "They told me he was released in less than an hour."

She removed her sunglasses. "Thank you for looking after him yesterday. I know I didn't seem terribly concerned, and that was awful of me."

Jack had experience with being manipulated, however well-meaning the manipulator was. He wasn't a pushover, but he did recognize sincerity when he saw it. At the moment, Opal Smith was the incarnation of it. The urge to tuck her under his arm for comfort was damn near impossible to resist. If not for his crew, he might have done just that.

"You were in shock, it's understandable." He led her to his office trailer to spare her further wolf whistles, shooting a scowl at the guys to mop up their drool. Opal might be odd, but she was a lady. More, she was woman enough to apologize.

"Thanks for making excuses for me. Even if I don't deserve them," she said as he handed her up into the trailer.

He found himself *wanting* to make excuses for her.

And not because of how she looked. What he felt was more dangerous. He was actually starting to like her.

His so-called office was only marginally cooler than outside. Another hour or two, it would be hot enough to bake bread. He set his hard hat on the drafting table.

"Would you like some water?" His offer had more to do with soothing her than wanting to see her lips all wet and lush. Man, this was not good.

"No, thanks. There was something else I wanted to talk to you about."

Ah. Had she been buttering him up? He tried to believe she had, which would allow him to remain detached, but he could have sworn her concern for the old man had been real. As had her apology. He'd bet on that.

"It's about the dog thing, actually. Well, really, it's about my vision." She held up her hand before he could even open his mouth. "I know you think I'm crazy."

"I didn't say that." He'd only thought it. It didn't make her a bad person.

She dipped her head and gave him an oh-puh-leze expression. "You didn't need to say it, Mr. Davis."

"Call me Jack."

"All right, Jack. Anyway. I know you think I'm crazy, but I really, really need your help."

A ripple in his gut told him he'd be sorry for asking, but he did anyway. Out of politeness. "How can I help?"

A jackhammer went off outside just as she opened her mouth. She stopped, then raised her voice a notch. "I need someone to substantiate what I said out there." She glanced down, then back up, almost nervously. "That is, authenticate that I knew there would be a man trying to jump off the overpass, because you see, I'm going to rescue him *before* he does it. And well, I just need a little independent verification of my vision." She blinked as if what she asked was nothing out of the ordinary. "That's all."

That's all? Okay, so yesterday's assumption had been accurate. She was nuts. Worse, she had damsel in distress written all over her.

Just as he'd learned politeness early from his mama, he'd learned about rescuing. Mom was a damsel, sweet and well-meaning most of the time. Except when she had an episode. That was their polite name for it. An episode, a bad day. Or days. Which ran the gamut from melancholy to delusional, where she might believe she was a princess or a movie star. She'd gotten progressively worse starting after he'd finished college, as if the fact that he was then an adult allowed her to simply give in to her mental illness. Her doctor gave her medication to control the episodes, yet she'd get it into her head that she was better and she'd stop taking her drugs. Since he'd had no family to help out and he couldn't simply abandon her to live in an institution, he'd hired caretakers to look after her when he was at work. But she'd been adept at sneaking off and getting lost or into other trouble. In the end, he hadn't been able to save her, and his failure was something he would live with for the rest of his life.

"I know what you're thinking."

Jack looked in Opal's clear, coherent and not particularly crazy-looking eyes. Nuts or normal? "I don't think you do."

He'd hear her out, which was only common courtesy. But that *was* all he'd do. He'd learned to steer clear of needy damsels.

She bit the plump flesh of her lower lip. "I'm not asking you to go on nighttime TV or anything." Then she perused the fingernails of her right hand. She had long, elegant fingers tipped in a glistening fiery polish that matched her lipstick.

"And?" There was always an "and" or a "but" when a woman started looking at her hands as if she'd never seen them before. He knew he wasn't going to like it.

"I'm wondering if you could be my backup while I stake out the overpass?"

"Your backup? On a stakeout?"

"I know that sounds very cops-'n'-robberish, but I can't think of a better description."

First rule, if you don't want to get involved, don't ask for more details. But, dammit, he asked anyway. "Why don't you start by telling me exactly what you want me to do?"

"Since I had this—" She stopped, looked at him a moment, then went on. "Since I had the vision during rush hour, I think the man will try to jump at commute time." She puffed out a sigh. The sound trickled down Jack's nerve endings. She continued when he didn't respond. "There was something about the sun. It wasn't in my eyes like it should have been. So I'm more inclined to think my vision was of the late afternoon or early evening."

Man. She'd really thought the whole thing through. "So you want to hang around that overpass every afternoon rush hour until you find him?"

She tipped her pert little nose almost defiantly. "Exactly. And I was wondering if you'd be in the park-'n'-ride nearby. Just in case I run into trouble. You can see the whole overpass from there. I checked."

He pushed a hand through his hair, then rubbed the back of his neck. Trouble. Capital *T*. The best thing to do was refuse to help. Then she'd give up the crazy scheme. "I have a construction project to run. I can't take off while there's still plenty of natural light to work by."

"I'm sure it would only be for a couple of days. I wouldn't have had the vision if it wasn't imminent." She suddenly took his arm in a warm grip. "Please. You can't know how important this is to me. I'll do anything."

His brain scrambled with her touch. He felt himself weaken.

"I'll even tell the insurance company the accident was all my fault so you can get your truck fixed right away." Then she fluttered her eyelashes.

His world righted itself. She was manipulating him. "I'm sorry I can't help you. I've got an obligation to the job site, and I can't leave early."

She tipped her head and stared at him, the light in her eyes winking out. "Oh."

Guilt clenched his stomach—a remnant of dealing with his mom where guilt was a constant companion—but he didn't give in to it. "I really am sorry."

She blinked. Then she smiled, a bit sadly maybe but no less heart-stopping. "Well, I thought I'd ask. Thanks for at least listening."

"Sure." But doing the smart thing still made him feel as if he'd refused Opal his hand when she was down for the count.

Leaning against the trailer door, he watched her totter back to her car. He should have been congratulating himself on his miraculous escape.

Instead, he muttered, "You are such an asshole."

JACK'S DAY ONLY GOT WORSE. Correct that. His guilt got worse. He'd called himself a chump, an idiot and every other name for a gullible sucker he could think of. It didn't work.

Along about noon, he'd started making excuses for Opal. And meaning them! She wasn't all that much like his mother. When his mother went off her meds without telling him or her doctor, she retreated into a world of make-believe. She'd watch something on TV, and that would become her reality. After seeing a PBS show on the arboretum in Golden Gate Park, she took the train up to San Francisco where she'd gotten irate when the arboretum attendants wouldn't let her pick the flowers in what she believed was her garden. The scuffle led to her arrest. Opal, on the other hand, seemed to possess only one delusion, which she shared with others. The fact was, lots of people believed in psychic phenomenon, even if Jack didn't. People wrote books about it and actually made pots of money with more ease than trying to win the Lotto.

Still, he shouldn't get involved. Opal presented huge possibilities for messing with his orderly existence. It had taken two years to get his life and his job back on track. He couldn't afford the time—and, yeah, the mental chaos—it would take to keep "rescuing" a potentially unbalanced woman. One rescue wouldn't be the end. One would lead to another, then another. Oh, yeah, he knew the cycle. With his mom, he'd never considered leaving her to her own devices. Absolutely not. But with Opal, he simply didn't have to start the process in the first place. Easy solution.

Then he started thinking about what could happen to

Opal up there on that overpass all by herself. Sometime during the hot afternoon, with the sun beating down on his head—even with the hard hat—he'd convinced himself she *would* go out there by herself. *I'll do anything.* That's what she'd said. He might not get why it was so hellfire important, but she was determined. He'd bet she could be freakin' tenacious when she wanted something. Refusing to give his help wouldn't stop her.

He blamed his uneasy stomach on heatstroke. But the truth was, he'd imagined her dragged from the sidewalk into some guy's vehicle, kidnapped and worse.

The sun was moving across the sky too damn fast. Which meant rush hour was approaching too damn fast. And Jack gave in. It was only a couple of days. It wasn't like dating or marriage. He didn't have to succumb to the next thing she might ask for.

His cell phone was strapped to his belt, but the card with Opal's contact info was in the trailer. As he headed there, a little voice in him snickered. *Chump. Idiot. Sucker.*

Yeah. He was. But he wasn't asshole enough to let Opal Smith hang out completely alone on that overpass.

JACK DAVIS HAD SAID NO this morning. Arriving at her shop, and even now, hours later, the idea still seemed inconceivable. He'd seemed like such a gentleman. Opal had worn her nicest pair of heels and her most stylish skirt to trek across all that dusty dirt. She liked wearing shorter skirts. Her legs were her best feature. Not that her skirt was *that* short. Four inches above the knee. Okay, maybe six. Her heart had started beating faster with the way Jack Davis looked at her legs.

Her pulse had raced looking at *him*. All those muscles bulging as he worked. His broad chest. His sexy hard hat.

But he'd said no! Well, she wouldn't let it bother her. If nothing else, Grandma Blue would tell the family her vision was real. After Opal saved the poor victim. She glanced at her watch. She'd need to leave soon if she wanted to stop by her apartment to change her high heels. She couldn't walk that overpass for a couple of hours in these heels. Not to mention the running she'd have to do if—*when!*—she found her victim.

It would have been so nice, though, if Jack was down in the park-'n'-ride watching out for her.

"I'm never getting married."

Opal jerked up from the ledger she hadn't been concentrating on, meeting her sister, Pearl's, watery blue gaze. Damn. She hadn't been paying attention.

She and Pearl owned the shop, Bedazzled—the name had been Opal's inspiration. In the racks lining the walls and display cases scattered about the shop's center, they sold an eclectic collection of jewelry, crystals, metaphysical books, aromatherapy candles, CDs, and yes, a lovely selection of crystal balls for reading one's future. But Pearl was the cornerstone, what drew people back time and again. Pearl was psychic.

The no-marriage thing wasn't a new refrain for Pearl. She was…transitioning. "Did you have another fight with Ernie?"

That was obvious from the pained expression on Pearl's down-turned lips. "Didn't you hear me say he dumped me last night?"

That's what she'd missed while concentrating on Jack. "I'm sorry, honey, I was thinking too hard and you know how that clogs my ears." Lame, but it was the best she could come up with. Opal leaned across the counter to put her hand over her sister's. "Why didn't you call me when you got home?"

"I did. You didn't answer."

"I was at Grandma Blue's. Why didn't you leave a message?"

"I didn't want you to hear how sorry I felt for myself."

Wouldn't she have heard that if she'd actually been home to pick up the phone? But this wasn't the time to question Pearl's logic. "I never thought Ernie was good enough for you." Pearl had only started dating him on the rebound. "What happened?"

Pearl dealt another spread of tarot on the glass-topped counter before answering. In addition to bringing in a quarter of Bedazzled's revenue, tarot soothed Pearl. She also cast runes and read tea leaves, not that Pearl needed those devices. She used them as a tool, a guide, something to put both herself and her clients in the mood. When they'd opened the shop three years ago, Opal had a special alcove built for Pearl's reading room. Lovely chintz curtains covered the doorway, and when the soft strains of New Age music filled the shop, not one word of Pearl's wisdom could be overheard. Two years Opal's junior, Pearl was amazing. She, in fact, had the very life Opal wanted. Her sister read tarot, read people and saw to the caring of their inner souls. Pearl had a gift.

Opal's talents leaned toward the less spectacular, a head for finance and keeping a good set of accounts. She was proud of those skills, but she'd give them up in a heartbeat to find her one true psychic gift.

Opal pulled herself back to reality as Pearl told the story. "He said he couldn't take going out with a psychic anymore."

"But you never did that stuff in front of him."

Pearl hung her head, her blond hair falling forward to obscure her face. Finally, the truth leaked out. "Once or twice, I did kind of let some things slip that I'd learned when I did a reading on him."

"I thought he refused to let you do a reading."

Pearl's mouth quirked unhappily. "I didn't tell him I'd done it."

Opal couldn't hold back her gasp. "You always said doing a reading that wasn't asked for was violating someone's privacy."

Pearl clucked her tongue. "I know, I know. But he was so closemouthed about himself, I just couldn't help it." She looked near to tears again.

Though the fact that Pearl had done it meant Ernie hadn't been an important part of her life. Pearl didn't read the people closest to her. She didn't want to know. Which was definitely a good thing, especially if it was something she couldn't change.

"You don't know how hard it is being psychic, Opal. I don't know why you wish you were. It's miserable."

"Do you want me to make you a mocha?" A mocha always cheered Opal right up with its rich scent of coffee, semisweet chocolate and whipped cream. She'd bought the espresso machine the first week they'd moved into the shop, used the very best beans and ground her own chocolate. She started every day with a frothingly sweet mocha. Her life wasn't perfect— especially now that her car was wrecked, though that was mitigated by her vision—but with a good mocha, one could deal with almost anything, such as the depletion of the ozone layer, her lack of meaningful dating during the last year or the fact that a neighbor let his dog poop at the end of her walkway every day.

Pearl groaned. "A mocha would probably make me throw up."

"Things can't be that bad."

"I'm never dating a straight guy again."

"Only homosexuals?"

"You know what I mean. I'm never dating someone who isn't psychic."

"And six months ago—" after Pearl broke up with Nile Montgomery, though God help her if Opal should mention *that* name "—you said you weren't dating anyone who *was* psychic. I don't think you have any options left."

Pearl breezed right on as if Opal hadn't spoken. "I don't think I should ever have kids. I shouldn't pass on this curse."

This really wasn't like Pearl. She was usually such an upbeat kind of person, quick to see the joke, always looking for the light before the dark. But she'd changed after being with Nile Montgomery.

Opal was glad Nile was gone. He'd brought Pearl only unhappiness, crushing her bubbly spirit. Her sister had failed to bounce back. She'd lost weight, her willowy figure becoming…well, less willowy and more starkly thin. Now this, calling her precious gift a curse.

Just how was Opal to snap Pearl out of the doldrums? It was on the tip of her tongue to share her vision, just to give Pearl something else to think about. But as much as she loved Pearl, she couldn't jinx this. Instead, she fell on the only other thing she could think of. "I met a really cute guy."

There was one good thing about Jack refusing to be her independent verification. She could date him. Except that he hadn't asked her out on a date, either, after he'd said he wouldn't help her with her vision.

But Pearl brightened, just as Opal hoped she would. "Ooh, want me to see if you're soul mates?"

That was Pearl's specialty, bringing soul mates together through her readings. In Opal's case, so she wouldn't see anything bad she couldn't change, Pearl read the potential soul mate instead of reading Opal. "Umm, well..."

"It's harmless. I won't look at anything personal."

Yes, but knowing a guy wasn't potential soul mate material before you even starting dating him took all the fun out of it, as Opal had found the last three times Pearl had done this very thing. "I think I'll pass this time."

"Spoilsport," Pearl groused with a twinkle in her eye, which was oh-so-good to see. "Well, if you won't let me do that, then I suppose I better have a mocha instead."

"That's the spirit." Opal didn't have much time before she needed to leave, but one more mocha and a little bit of laughter were exactly what Pearl needed.

"So tell me more about this cute guy you met."

Opal told her about the accident, but left out the vision part. Some things were better kept to oneself until just the right time. Namely, once she'd proven her vision was true.

The phone rang just as she was about to ask Pearl if she'd close up tonight.

"Bedazzled."

"Opal?"

Ohmigod. It was Jack. His husky phone voice made her breathe harder. Her heart started to pound and her ears to ring. She just knew he'd changed his mind.

VICTOR PATELL WATCHED Opal Smith's shop from the overhang of a flower shop across the street. Balmy air still circulated beneath the awning, almost but not quite warming his old bones. He'd been in a perpetual state of cold since…well, since Prudence first became ill.

He'd never truly understood how much he'd depended on his wife of sixty years until she was gone. Now, Lord help him, seven months after her death, he missed her with an ache that grew unbearable with each and every day.

He missed Prudence's guidance in so many things. George Whitley-Dorn's daughter had run away last Friday. Victor had known the Whitley-Dorns for years, but it was Prudence who would have been able to provide succor to their dear friends. The most Victor had been able to do was bring in an expert to help in the search for the young woman. Yet he hadn't a clue how to provide the much-needed emotional support.

Victor felt his ineptness like stones laid atop his chest, crushing the air from his lungs.

He'd seen Miss Smith leave a little while ago. He should have approached her then. Something held him back. What, he couldn't say, because after running into her on the freeway with his Cadillac, he had the perfect excuse to talk to her. It wasn't as if he'd arranged the accident. He was an innocent bystander, after all. Except that he'd been behind Miss Smith on the freeway yesterday morning because he'd followed her from her apartment. Yet if he admitted that, she'd think he was a stalker, when the truth was he was just a tired old man who needed her help and didn't have the gumption to ask for it in a straightforward manner.

His hesitancy came from fear and guilt. On her deathbed, Prudence had made him promise to love and take care of their grandson Darius. They hadn't known he existed until a little over a year ago, after Prudence had already become ill. Their daughter Rita had turned to drugs and run away when she was barely out of her teens. They'd learned of her death from a drug overdose seven years later, but her son, Darius, had been swept into a foster-care system without them even knowing Rita had a child. A thirty-three-year-old lost soul, Prudence called Darius, and her greatest desire had been to make up for all the years before he came into their lives. To shower him with love, make him feel wanted and cared for. With her illness, she'd passed her quest on to Victor. He'd let her down. Even from Heaven, she must see how the gap between him and Darius had grown to a chasm he couldn't cross.

If he contacted her in the spirit world, would it be only to find she blamed him for his inadequacy? Victor wouldn't be able to bear it. His stomach was sick with the thought of her disappointment in him.

Yet he would never breach the gulf between Darius and himself without Prudence's guidance.

Thus he'd turned to Opal Smith for help. Though she didn't know it, she alone was his last hope of reaching his dearly departed wife. He'd tried everything else.

AN OLDER WOMAN passed the front of the shop, her eyes scanning the gold letters spelling Bedazzled. Smaller letters underneath the arch of the name foretold psychic readings, tarot and promised crystals, amulets and psychic aides unimaginable.

Pearl loved the shop, cherished its name and adored the gold lettering that sparkled in the late-afternoon sun. In the quiet minutes since Opal had made her mad dash out the door, Pearl had basked in the knowledge that this lovely place was hers, hers and Opal's. The shop was an achievement and a comfort. Without it, she didn't know what she would have done these last few months. She'd told Opal, Ernie was the problem, but she hadn't really become attached to him. His telling her to take a hike had almost been a relief.

No, the problem was Nile. It had always been Nile.

As the thought assailed her, she contemplated making herself another mocha. Opal's miracle beverage. Opal was so like Grandma Blue when it came to food or drink. It was the panacea that cured all ills, physical and mental. Opal enjoyed everything with such gusto. Pearl admired her intelligence, but most especially she envied Opal's lack of psychic ability.

Opal didn't know how lucky she was. She had all the brains. The shop would have sunk into oblivion if it hadn't been for Opal. She'd brought in the jewelry filling the cases—amulets, crystals, the rune necklaces, earrings and bracelets all made by a lady out in Oklahoma. Opal shopped the book outlets, filling their bookshelves with a variety of tomes on various and sundry aspects of the metaphysical. Pearl was just the attraction, the sideshow freak.

She was feeling pathetically sorry for herself. Yuck.

She didn't used to be so self-pitying. But that was before Nile. An invisible net tightened around her heart and tears seemed to automatically pop into her eyes.

He'd left six months ago. Why couldn't she forget him?

Because he was her soul mate. When he left, he took a piece of her with him.

Pearl sucked in a breath and closed her eyes. God, how she loved him. She had from the moment she set eyes on him a year and a half ago. She hadn't needed to do a reading to figure out what he meant to her. She'd just known. She'd attended a seminar on regression hypnosis down in Monterey. When the flyer came to the shop, she didn't understand the urge to attend, but she always listened to her urges. She knew the reason the moment she saw Nile. He hadn't romanced her, hadn't even asked her out to dinner. Instead, he'd driven her to his secluded home in Big Sur and made love to her in his living room. Then on his kitchen counter, the hallway, the shower, and finally the bed.

It wasn't lust, though she'd lusted after him. It wasn't even love at first sight. It was simply knowing the rightness of things. She was meant for Nile and he was meant for her. Two halves living only half a life until they found each other.

She'd thought she'd be able to make Nile believe it, too. Except that Nile wasn't a believer. At least not in the power of love to conquer all.

She knew what it was to be psychic. She just hadn't known what it was like to have Nile's gift. She still didn't truly know. He'd never shared his anguish, she'd felt it only in the ferocity of his lovemaking. Every time she mended a tear in his soul with her love, with her body, his gift would rend another. If he hadn't left her six months ago, she might have drowned in the darkness that surrounded him. She knew in her head that his leaving had saved her. Her heart, though, that was different. Why had she ever thought that dating someone like Ernie could fill the empty space in her soul that Nile had left behind? What Ernie cared most about was other people's opinion of him. When she'd slipped up after reading him, he was afraid she'd embarrass him in front of his friends by going all "woo-woo," as he called it.

Damn, she'd made herself miserable all over again. "A mocha," she whispered. A little of Opal's panacea. She picked up her empty mug just as the door of the shop opened.

A man filled the entrance. He wore a dark overcoat despite the fact that it was mid-June.

The mug fell to the carpet from her numbed fingers.

She'd know that silhouette anywhere.

Pearl's heart picked up its tempo, her tummy tumbled, her palms perspired and she couldn't hear over the sudden roar in her ears. Why now? Why after she'd just turned her heart inside out thinking about him?

She'd never struggled so hard to sound calm and serene, even as her eyes ached with the memory of all the tears she'd shed. Later, she knew she'd never even remember what she said. She'd remember only how awfully steady and bland her tone sounded. As if she didn't care.

"What do you want, Nile?"

CHAPTER THREE

"YOU'RE NOT ACTUALLY going to wear that outfit on the overpass?" Jack glanced over his shoulder, assuring himself his crew couldn't see Opal out here in the parking lot.

As if she didn't have a single clue as to why he'd object, Opal looked down at her clothes, the same she'd worn that morning when she'd come by the site. "I like my outfit."

So did Jack. Too much. So would every man driving by.

He scratched the back of his neck just to keep his hand busy. "Wouldn't you be more comfortable in jeans?"

"I was at the shop. I didn't have time to change." She gave him a pretty pout of her red lips. "I was running late."

On second thought, tight jeans were probably a bad idea. He sighed. "Get in. I'll drive over."

She closed the door of her rental car and waltzed to his truck. For tonight's trip, they'd leave her car parked with his crew's vehicles. He had yet to hear back from the insurance company on the damage quotes he'd submitted this afternoon, but the truck still ran, though Jack did a mental cringe every time he noted the damage.

"I really am sorry." She must have followed his gaze.

Holding the truck door open for her, he waved a negligent hand. "Don't worry about it. It'll get fixed."

She stopped him just as he was about to hand her up into the cab, her touch warm, searing straight to his extremities.

"I mean it." She held him with that bright gaze of hers.

His pulse raced. Oh, man, he was a goner. "I know you do."

She smiled. "Why did you change your mind?

Because he was a chump, an idiot and a sucker, but not an asshole. "I decided it wasn't a good idea for you to be out here by yourself."

"Well. Thank you for helping me." She squeezed his arm.

He thought he'd expire with the wave of heat that rushed through his body. "Up you go." A moment longer, one more squeeze or another bat of her eyelashes would be his undoing. He'd probably do something irreversible. Such as kiss her.

On the other side of the truck, he climbed in beside her and shut the door. Her delicate perfume filled the cab. Women always smelled so good, especially Opal. Made it hard for a man to think rationally.

He rolled down his window and searched for something to take his mind off her perfume and her legs. "You work at a shop?"

"My sister and I own it, actually."

An entrepreneur, like himself. He'd rather think of her as a kooky blonde, just to keep his sanity around her, but he knew there was more to Opal than that. Most crazy people—at least the ones he'd come across—couldn't hold down a job, let alone manage their own business successfully. Opal was bright in more ways than one. Jack started the engine and backed out.

Opal pulled a notebook from her oversize purse. "Can I ask you a few questions?"

"Questions?" Uh-oh.

"They're for my grandmother."

Her grandmother was getting involved? Not a good sign. "Why?"

She settled the notebook on her knee, which unavoidably drew his attention to her legs again. He almost missed the stop sign.

"Well, I've already told my grandmother about you and my vision. Then, after we save the man before he jumps, that's when you can verify it for the rest of my family."

"Your family? I'm supposed to tell your family?" Oh man. *See?* There was always something else. First a woman wanted this, then she tacked on that. Until a man was embroiled with no way out.

"Well, yes, who did you think we were going to tell?" She gazed at him innocently.

He *hadn't* thought. That was the problem. Then again, he didn't believe some guy was going to try to jump off the overpass, therefore he wouldn't have to independently verify anything for her family. A couple of days, a few whiffs of Opal's sweet perfume in his truck, and it would all be over. The funny thing was, Opal seemed normal enough to accept it when her vision didn't come true.

"All right. Your grandmother, what does she want to know?"

"Grandma Blue has this idea…that…"

He wanted to tell her to spit it out, the suspense was

killing him. But it was her legs that were killing him while her scent fogged his mind. He made a left and hit heavy street traffic. Damn. The drive would be longer than he'd anticipated. He'd be brainless by the time they got to the overpass.

"Grandma Blue thinks you're the reincarnation of Dynamite Davis, and she wants me to ask a few questions, for verification and all." The words rushed out, a bit breathless, and his wayward mind wandered once again to places it shouldn't go.

He wanted to laugh. Maybe a little hysterically. She was yanking his chain. First a vision, now reincarnation?

"I know it sounds a little odd, but…"

He glanced at her face and found her staring at him with those big eyes, waiting, expecting. She was odd, her grandmother was odd, probably her whole family was odd. Then he lost himself in her gaze. Seconds, minutes, maybe hours ticked by. At least that's what it seemed like in the crawling traffic.

He was such a chump for blue eyes.

Well, in for a penny, in for a pound, wasn't that the old saying? Besides, he liked the way Opal looked at him, her eyes vivid. Her gaze made him feel…important. His business was important, building his professional reputation. But there was something elemental about having a woman look at you that way.

It shouldn't feel this damn good. But it did. Damn.

But what the heck? How could answering a few questions hurt after what he'd already agreed to?

"Shoot." He probably should have asked who Dynamite Davis was, but…better not to know more than he had to.

She smiled, and that mouth was a sight to behold. "Well, first Grandma Blue wants to know when your birthday is."

"February twenty-fifth."

She made a little ooh sound that reached right down into his abdomen. After jotting a note in her book, she asked, "How old are you?"

"Thirty-four."

She didn't ooh, and he prayed he'd get it right the next time. "Where were you born?"

"Florida."

Praise the Lord, she aahed, the sound slipping from her lips. He shifted in his seat, trying to get comfortable.

"Have you ever been married?"

"No."

A little hmm. The sounds Opal made in her throat should be outlawed. Especially when a man was trying to drive. By the time he pulled into the park-'n'-ride, his upper lip was sweating, and he was under Opal Smith's tantalizing spell.

Man, he had it bad. He wondered what else the woman could get him to agree to?

"WHY ARE YOU HERE, NILE?"

He advanced into the shop, the overhead lights encircling him like a spotlight, casting shadows across his lean cheeks. He'd lost weight. Though six feet, Nile had never been a big man. Now, a strong wind might blow him away. Pallor accentuated by his overly long black hair, he looked as if he hadn't seen the sun since the day he walked out on her. He'd aged in the past six months. He'd always made her heart race, but now, the need to soothe the new lines from his forehead and the strain from his mouth beat inside her. Pearl drove the impulse away. Nile had never allowed anyone to feel sorry for him, least of all her.

"I'm staying with…a friend."

Did that hesitation mean it was a woman friend? Pearl tamped down the jealousy. She couldn't afford it.

"I'm helping him look for a missing girl," he went on.

Darn that flush of relief that his "friend" was male. She searched his face for an emotion. None. She knew Nile's special psychic gift. He found missing people. But, sometimes, he didn't find them quickly enough. A man who held that much pain inside, never sharing what he saw, never even admitting how it tore him apart, fell into a shadow world. Nile lived in shadows and darkness. He always would.

"Tamara Whitley-Dorn. She's twenty-three and disappeared last Friday. Her family wants her back." There was a wealth of unexpressed emotion in those few short sentences.

With Nile, that emotion would forever remain constrained. That had been the biggest part of her problem. Their problem.

"What about the police?" Though calling in the police had never eased Nile's burden.

He shook his head. "The police can't do anything. She packed a bag. As far as they're concerned, she ran away."

"Maybe she doesn't want to be found." She wasn't sure she believed that any more than Nile seemed to. She sighed. "I hope you find her. But I wasn't asking why you're in town again. Why are you here?" She tapped the glass counter with her fingertip.

He tipped his head, regarding her with his dark eyes, tired, empty eyes. Eyes that never revealed his inner soul. "I want you to do a reading for me, Pearl."

"You know I could never read you." Nile had too many barriers, too many walls that kept her out.

"I need you."

She closed her eyes. She'd prayed for those words every night since he'd left her, and long before that. But nothing had changed for him. His torment covered him like a too-thin blanket, never keeping him warm, simply giving him the illusion of comfort. Nile basked in his anguish, agony that had grown tenfold in the months since she'd last seen him.

"I can't go through it again, Nile." Not just the end of the affair, but the brooding silences, the black-as-pitch nights that seemed to emanate from his soul. She was twenty-six, he was thirty-six. At first she thought it was the age difference, until she'd realized an entire lifetime couldn't have draped her soul with the same depths of despair in which Nile lived. The glimpses she'd endured had been unbearable.

"I never meant to hurt you." He moved to the counter, placing his hands on the glass. She knew he wouldn't leave a mark. His hands were too cold, too dry. Nile didn't perspire. "I was trying to protect you. From me."

"I knew that. It didn't make it hurt any less."

He smelled of summer rain in a deep forest. He'd always smelled earthy to her. Beneath the black coat, he wore a navy sweater and black jeans. She shivered as if she were underdressed in her strapless cotton sundress and the temperature outside wasn't over eighty.

He raised his head and scented her as if he were

some primal animal. "I sucked you dry, didn't I? Took every bit of light and laughter you had."

There was no use denying it. "I haven't gotten it back." Maybe he'd been right to protect her. She'd thought about that, too, in her darkest moments.

Nile's departure had been the best thing for her. Eventually, she'd have lost vast pieces of herself never to be regained. When he left, she'd thought with time she'd make her way back into the light, especially around Opal's effervescent personality. Instead, Pearl lingered in twilight, neither daylight nor full night. She'd never stopped loving him. The urge to reach out and cover his hand with hers was irresistible.

His flesh was cold the way she'd known it would be. While Nile had been busy sucking the life out of her, something had been oh-so-busy sucking it out of him. His jaw tensed, his teeth grinding behind his closed lips. He wanted to say something. But he wouldn't. He'd keep it inside as he always had.

"I've changed, Pearl."

She smiled as gently as she could. "You haven't."

He gave a short, self-deprecating laugh, almost a snort, but the grief lay deep in his eyes. "You're right. But I want to."

She raised a hand to his forehead, gently traced the new furrow there. His eyes drifted closed against her tenderness. "Even if you do, I'm afraid it might be too late." As much as she loved him, she wasn't sure she could survive being with him.

He said nothing.

She trailed her palm down his cheek. "Don't come here again, Nile."

He swallowed, his Adam's apple seeming to bob with difficulty. Looking down, he splayed his fingers on the glass counter, staring at them for long moments. Then he reached in his deep pocket, pulling out an unmarked ivory envelope. "I need you to read this."

He laid the letter on the counter, pushing it until it touched the tips of her fingers. The contact sent something electric and terrifying zapping through her body. She jerked her hand back.

"What's in it?"

"Everything you ever wanted to know and I wouldn't reveal."

She read people, not inanimate objects. That was Nile's forte. He received his visions through touching things. So it wasn't a sixth sense that made her petrified of his letter. It was intuition, something she'd learned to rely on where Nile was concerned. Pearl knew that envelope held something terrible, not a declaration of undying love nor an explanation for why he left her, but something she'd be better off not knowing.

The breath she took hurt her throat. "You wrote it all down in a letter?" She was afraid to ask what "it" was.

He shook his head, the shaggy length of his hair rippling at his ears. "No. I didn't write what's in there. But once you read it, you'll know exactly what I live with every day, every night. You'll understand why the things I see haunt me." His midnight gaze pierced her. "I don't think you really know what you asked for." He pushed lightly with his fingers and the envelope skittered across the glass top. "And I'm sorry that you'll find out, but I need your help."

She'd asked for Nile's revelations. She'd even

believed she wanted them. It was akin to Opal wanting to find her psychic gift. Opal hoped and prayed and wanted and needed, but the day she found it, she'd realize she'd also opened other doors she'd rather leave tightly locked.

If Nile had shared himself instead of leaving her, maybe Pearl could have read what he'd given her with much greater ease. If she hadn't had months to reflect that his departure was devastating but perhaps necessary. If, if, if…

The ivory envelope sat on the counter long after Nile's departure. It sat there as Pearl counted out the register and closed up the shop, as she walked to the back door. She was to her car before she changed her mind, rushing back, unlocking again and shoving the letter into her portfolio.

She wasn't ready to read it.

But she wasn't ready to throw it out, either.

OPAL FELT UTTERLY EXPOSED walking back and forth on the College Avenue overpass. She'd been out here a little over an hour and already six cars had stopped, the assorted miserable occupants asking her if she wanted to go for a ride. And not just any ordinary ride.

They thought she was a prostitute. Jack had been right about the short skirt and high heels attracting the wrong kind of attention. She really should have gone home to change first. But when Jack called and said he'd help, she'd been afraid he'd have too much time to change his mind, *again,* if she didn't get over to his site right away.

Still, she was a dork. Her scrunched toes were absolutely killing her. How was she supposed to run after her victim when the need arose?

But the way Jack stared at her legs gave her the most wonderful feminine thrill. She liked him a little too much, which could get in the way of her mission. She needed an impartial witness to prove her psychic ability to her family. Potential boyfriend material would not work on them.

The light at the opposite end of the overpass turned red, and the cars started queuing across the bridge. Opal headed back toward Jack. Safety in the park-'n'-ride. The farther away he was, the less secure she felt. To this point, she'd obeyed his instructions to the letter, never going farther than the middle of the overpass, in case she got into trouble and needed him.

Which wasn't improbable considering the nefarious traffic traveling the roads.

A black-and-white vintage Chevy pulled to a stop beside her, all chrome, wings and red leather seats. Men were animals. Teenagers were the devil incarnate.

"Hey, baby, wanna go for a ride?"

"I'm not into premature ejaculators, thank you very much." Grandma Blue would be proud of her. Of course, if she were really a prostitute, she'd probably appreciate a premature ejaculator. The service period would be much shorter.

She beat a hasty retreat, back toward Jack, in deference to that rather ill-advised comment. But really, who did those little pipsqueaks think they were? A woman had a right to walk anywhere she wanted dressed any way she wanted.

"Ma'am?"

The man was suddenly in front of her. Since he was barely above five feet, she'd almost missed him in her beeline for the park-'n'-ride. With four inches of heel and probably six inches of extra leg, she towered over him. What he lacked in height, he had overabundantly in girth. "Yes?" she prompted to the bald spot encroaching on the top of his head.

"I know you're probably busy."

He spoke to her breasts. She was afraid the little guy might strain his neck if he tried looking her in the eye. "What can I do for you?"

"Well, I wonder if you'd like to have dinner with me."

If it weren't for that bald spot, she'd think he was in his teens for all the reticence in his voice. Then again, maybe he usually anticipated rejection. Sympathy trimmed her voice. "I'm sorry, but I can't. I'm…" She struggled to think of a lie that would save his dignity. A date? No. Drinks with the girls? No. It had to be a circumstance she couldn't get out of. "I have to work tonight."

"I don't want you to think I wouldn't pay you. I would, I really would. Just for dinner. I don't expect anything else. Except maybe another night. After we get to know each other. But I intend to pay you for every moment you grant me the opportunity to be in your presence."

She'd had enough, first cars full of teenagers, now this man. Opal was tempted to shoot him down in much the same manner she had the carful of randy teenagers. But then she noticed the red stain spreading across his bald spot, and she took pity. Stomping on him would be tantamount to kicking a dog when it's down. He wasn't insulting her, so she couldn't squash him. "I'm really sorry. I can't. But thanks."

She left him at such a pace that he wouldn't be able to catch her even if he ran, and she was out of breath when she reached the driver's side of Jack's truck. He'd rolled the window down, catching the cool breeze. My, he looked good in a T-shirt, his tanned arms dark against the white material.

She was reminded of that Coke commercial with the hunky construction worker.

"They thought I was a prostitute." She glanced back at the overpass, the little man who'd solicited her now shuffling away.

"I know," Jack said. He slouched in his seat, all comfy and delicious-looking.

She jammed her hands on her hips and eyeballed him with her best I-can't-believe-you-said-that Grandma Blue look. Scads of pithy comebacks careened through her mind, not the least of which was the freedom of dress issue. What popped out of her mouth was something else entirely. "Then why didn't you come get me?"

"You wouldn't have appreciated it." He took a slug of his soda, and Opal knew how the office workers in the Coke commercial felt.

She huffed. "I appreciate everything you've done so far."

"What I mean is that when a woman gets it in her head to do something, there's not a man on earth who's going to be able to stop her. All we can do is watch from a close enough distance so there ain't no violence." He affected such a slow, sexy drawl, her mouth went dry.

She had to admit he was right. She had always learned the lesson more quickly and surely as a result of making her own big fat mistake. The crux was that she couldn't see an alternative to her present course.

"What am I supposed to do? I can't stop my…victim if I'm busy fending off men's advances."

Jack flashed an appraising glance down her legs. He didn't linger, but the look made her tingle nicely anyway.

"If your victim thinks you're a hooker, he's not going to be too worried about you prowling his intended overpass. It therefore works in your favor." He shooed her with a flap of his hand. "Now we've got another hour before dark."

"But Jack, these shoes are killing me." She should have gone the tennis shoe route.

"That'll teach you to wear something more comfortable tomorrow night."

Well, that wasn't very sympathetic. Except that it did indicate he'd be with her tomorrow night. She glared at him anyway. "You're punishing me, aren't you?"

"Why would I want to punish you?" Jack said, innocence personified.

The only one being punished was him. Watching Opal stroll back and forth in high heels and a short skirt was pure torture.

Not to mention his reaction to the occupants of the cars driving by her. A couple of times he'd been ready to jump out of the truck. Yet he'd realized that coming to her aid would be an insult to her self-esteem. She'd handled the little guy who'd approached her at the end. She'd taken care of herself without help. Still, Jack was sick and tired of watching her from afar.

Which was why he was employing a little reverse logic. If he told her to get back out there, she might just pack it in because she didn't like him telling her what to do.

If it didn't work, he had another hour before dark. He wondered if he could survive an hour observing her perfect...her lips were moving, and she gave him a look.

"Did you hear what I said?"

Busted. "Sure, but let's talk about it later."

She tipped her head to one side, not convinced. But with a sigh, she let it go. "I'm thirsty."

"Have some soda." He handed the Coke through his window.

Ah, man, that was a mistake. By the time she handed back the can, he was light-headed.

"You know, it seems to me that I can watch the overpass just as easily from the cab of your truck."

Not on your life. Sitting next to her, breathing her in, having her close enough to touch, that would drive him over the edge. "You wouldn't be able to get to him fast enough if he's on the far side of the bridge."

"You could do it."

She looked down at him with a trusting look, as if he were Jack the Giant Killer. Or maybe just Dynamite Davis. "I hate to disappoint you, but I wasn't a runner in high school."

She pursed her lips. "Okay, I admit it, my feet can't take it anymore. And since there's only an hour or so of daylight left, I don't think tonight's the night anyway."

Ah, reverse logic wins! Smiling, he leaned across the seat and opened the passenger side door. She circled the hood, climbed in, took off her shoes, then pulled her feet up onto the seat to massage them.

"Want me to do that?" The offer issued forth with a

very strange, oddly strangled sound. He never even thought about leaning forward to look up her skirt. *Really.*

"No, that's okay. You're driving."

He didn't care if he was a rock star with an audience of twenty thousand waiting on him, he'd still take the time to ease the ache in her abused toes. She just smiled, happy go-lucky and massaging her feet. Didn't she feel any of the pent-up tension vibrating in the cab?

He started the engine like a good boy, but rammed the truck into gear too hard. They didn't have far to go, but getting out of the park-'n'-ride with a left-hand turn was a sonuvabitch. The wait didn't improve his situation. Mostly because she was humming. He felt that hum right down to the tip of his...

Man, did he ever need to get his head screwed on straight. She'd asked him for a favor. He'd agreed. Opal was not offering anything else. And he was only volunteering a few days. He took advantage of a break in the traffic flow and surged across.

"You know, you really are a nice man."

Sweet and nice were not usually adjectives a man liked to associate himself with. From Opal, they seemed the highest praise. He actually wanted to preen like a peacock. "Thanks."

Damn, he was getting out of control on too short an acquaintance. After all, he'd rammed her rear end because she'd had a vision. She was not all there.

Opal was a little odd, but then who wasn't in their own way? If you grew up in a family that believed in reincarnation, you'd believe in the same things, too. That didn't make her incapable of taking care of herself.

She ran her own business. Her credit rating was decent enough to allow her to rent a car.

So she believed in visions and reincarnation. That wasn't such a big deal. But he knew he was rationalizing, struggling to find a way out of viewing the whole thing with that same helpless sense he'd had every time his mom...

"Would you like to meet my grandmother?"

Hitting the brakes a little too forcefully as he pulled into the parking spot next to her rental car, Jack put out a hand to hold her in her seat. His fingers rested on the soft upper flesh of her arm, too damn close to her left breast. He jerked back as if she'd burned him.

"Your grandmother?" Shock, fear and soft, feminine flesh played havoc with his vocal cords.

"Don't you want to know more about Dynamite?" She gave him a sweet smile.

No. Then again, maybe if he met the grandmother, he'd figure out the granddaughter. And if he didn't like what he found, he was man enough to run like hell. "All right."

She offered a final inducement despite the fact that he'd already agreed. "She bakes the best chocolate chip cookies in the whole world. As long as she doesn't eat all the cookie dough first."

"No one can eat a whole batch of cookie dough."

She raised one eyebrow. "Tried it, huh?"

What man—or woman—hadn't gotten a cookie dough stomachache at least once? His had been earned with the store-bought kind.

"Well, Grandma Blue can. She can do anything she sets her mind to. You'll understand when you meet her."

That had an ominous tone. "Sounds...great." He

gave her a smile that he was sure looked more desperate than congenial.

"Good. You can follow me over. Now I don't expect you to stay a whole long time. You just leave when you're ready, and don't let Grandma Blue get her hooks in you."

She climbed from the truck, then turned to beam at him.

Her grandmother's hooks in him weren't the ones he was worried about.

CHAPTER FOUR

THE BOY LOOKED shell-shocked, to say the least, Blue thought. His eyes glazed over as she told him Dynamite's history, which had taken over half an hour. His hand started to shake shortly after she'd coaxed out that he had a thing for blue-eyed blondes. The girl he'd had a thing for in high school had been a blond-haired, blue-eyed cheerleader. Good, very good. By the time Blue asked him his annual income, he hadn't batted an eyelash. Hadn't answered, either, but then men could be uptight about that kind of thing. Blue shoved a fourth double-shot chocolate chip cookie beneath his nose and filled his coffee mug for the third time.

"Dynamite always took his coffee black, too. Thick as molasses and black as tar." Not that Blue knew a damn thing about how Dynamite drank his coffee, nor did she care.

"I don't think that proves anything, ma'am."

Hmm, polite, too. Blue couldn't count the number of times he'd called her ma'am in the hour he'd let her grill him. That certainly proved intestinal fortitude. He'd have to have it in spades to put up with the family.

"Let's review the evidence." She smoothed a wrinkle from her Day-Glo orange muumuu, starting the inter-

rogation over as if she hadn't reviewed the evidence
with each refill of his coffee. Anything to keep the boy
where he was, facing Opal, getting an eyeful of the
girl's rosy complexion and shapely attributes.

They sat around Blue's old scarred kitchen table, Opal
on her right, the boy on her left. The pleasant aroma of
her fried dinner lingered in the air. Opal was nursing her
second cookie, breaking off tiny bites and savoring them
as if they were pieces of the last treat she'd ever have in
her life. Blue savored the way the boy watched Opal's
lips every time she licked them. He certainly wouldn't
kick her out of bed for eating cookies in it. The boy had
a healthy case of lust. Blue could work with that.

"First, you both were born on February 25th."

"Dynamite was born in 1929 and died in 1964. If I
was his reincarnation, I should have been born the day
he died. But I wasn't."

Blue closed her eyes remembering the scene of that
fiery crash. It still had the power to move her to tears.
"You don't know much about reincarnation, do you?
Opal, tell him."

Her granddaughter snapped to attention. "Reincarnation doesn't happen the day a person dies. We all come
back with many of the people we knew in that previous
life. That takes time. In fact, we've been coming back
with the same souls populating our lives for thousands
of years. It's all about learning certain lessons, and if we
don't learn them in one life, we have to come back to
try again."

"Sure must take the human race a helluva long time
to learn anything then," the boy grumbled into his coffee.

Definitely a nonbeliever. Exactly what Opal

needed. A man who wouldn't give a damn if she never had an "honest-to-God" vision in her life. Blue continued her cross-examination. "What about your mother? Dynamite adored his mother. She was the apple of his eye."

"My mother's dead."

Flat tone, thin lips, not good. His reaction was the first unsettling thing she'd heard the entire evening. A boy needed to love and respect his mother. Then again, maybe he was still grieving. "We're so sorry to hear that, aren't we, Opal?"

Blue relished being older than dirt. Old people could get away with so much that younger people couldn't. Age let you dare anything. "When did she die?"

"Two years ago." He squirmed in his seat, and that dazed look faded from his eyes.

"Was it the cancer?" Horrible death, that was. She'd seen many a friend suffer the terrible fate.

"No."

No elaboration. There was something there about the mother then, but it wasn't any of her business. Even Blue knew when to steer away from a touchy subject. "What about your dad?" She wondered if that was a safe topic.

"My parents were divorced when I was young."

"And you haven't seen him since?"

"No."

Hmm. The topic of parents was a tricky issue. But didn't the boy have anyone? "How about brothers, sisters, aunts, uncles or grandparents?"

"I was an only child and my grandparents are gone." Jack drummed his fingers on the table. "I thought we were reviewing the evidence."

So he was alone in the world. That meant he really needed Opal.

Despite being a nosy old bag, Blue went back to reviewing. "You were born in Florida. So was Dynamite. You've never driven a Ford." And of course, there was the pièce de résistance. "Opal, get the picture."

Obediently, the girl rose and slipped into the living room to the treasured spot.

Blue watched Jack's eyes follow her granddaughter's lovely behind. "She's something to behold, isn't she?"

"Yes, ma'am, she is."

Opal would die of mortification if she knew Blue was about to extol her many fascinating and extraordinary qualities. "Well, let me tell you—"

"Grandma Blue."

Darn, Opal moved too fast. Giving her old Grandma a glare to flay flesh, she bent down next to Jack's ear as she held the gold frame in front of him. The boy's eyes glazed again, he swallowed with difficulty, then a sigh slipped from his lips. Blue knew the signs. Definitely a sexual tingle going on there, with Opal breathing in his ear.

"Now that's Dynamite. I'd say you're a dead ringer."

The boy didn't look a damn thing like Dynamite, but his reaction would be telling. Would he lie to please an old woman?

He stared at the picture a long time as Opal took her seat opposite. Finally, "I admit there's a resemblance..." His voice trailed off, he looked up at Opal, and something special and silent passed between them. The girl smiled.

Jumping Jehosaphat. He was lying for little Opal. This was even better than she'd hoped. Sweet enough to fib to make Opal happy, strong enough not to let Blue's insistence cow him, but kind enough not to crush an old lady's hopes, even if they did sound utterly preposterous.

"Now, we'll need to do a séance to determine the truth."

His eyebrows damn near vanished beneath his hair. "What?"

"A séance," Opal whispered, a hint of terror in her eyes.

"Yep," Blue carried on. "We'll do a séance to see if we can contact Dynamite's spirit. If he's in you. Of course, we could also try hypnosis and regress you back."

"No," Jack said emphatically. "No hypnosis."

Blue slapped the table. "Then a séance it is."

His breath rushed out of him. He got that terrified I'm-surrounded-by-a-pack-of-marauding-females look in his eye. Then he swallowed, looked at Opal, blinked. And bit the bullet. "All right. When?"

Yeehaw! Doing a séance wasn't necessary at all. Just the fact that he agreed was all Blue wanted. Yeah, the poor boy had it bad. Things were going perfectly according to plan. "I'll ponder that and let you know."

He breathed an audible sigh of relief. She knew he was hoping she'd forget.

Blue had one last test to determine if he was the perfect husband for her granddaughter.

She excused herself, ostensibly for the bathroom, but instead she picked up the phone in her bedroom and called Dynamite's future mother-in-law. If he survived The Mother, then he was definitely the one for Opal.

HALF AN HOUR LATER, Grandma Blue's doorbell rang, and the little lady took her sweet time answering it. Surveying her living room, Jack was sure it hadn't been redecorated since the early seventies. The sturdy American Colonial style sofa was done in a yellow-and-brown plaid, the coffee table, though dust free and polished, had definitely seen a few boot heels planted on its surface, and the carpet was a recently raked shag of indeterminate color showing every footprint. Two eighties-vintage TVs on trolleys flanked the wall—was that hockey and stock car racing? No, no, he wouldn't ask. Grandma Blue would embroil him in another bizarre discussion.

Opal, standing next to him, gripped his arm as if it were a lifeline. "It's my mother," she whispered close to his ear.

Damn, he wished she'd quit doing that. She smelled too good, and the puff of air against his ear fried his brain cells like a raw egg laid out on bare rock in the midday desert sun.

First the grandmother, now the mother. Meeting a woman's family was serious stuff, enough to strike terror into the heart of most men who were basically just interested in one thing. But this was about—what had Opal called it—independent verification of a vision. He had nothing to worry about. Right?

Somewhere, he heard the sound of his resistance being sucked down the drain. Two hours in Grandma Blue's company, not to mention scenting Opal like a hound dog, was all it took. *Chump.*

But damn if he didn't feel sort of…at home in Grandma Blue's outdated living room. *Double chump.*

"Now remember not to call her Lillian Smith, because she only goes by her stage name of Lillian Fontaine." Opal looked up at him with big blue eyes.

"Not that it's a 'stage' name, as if she's putting on an act. She just believes it gives her clients more confidence in her abilities than plain old Smith."

She was overexplaining. Jack smelled a rat, and it wasn't Opal Smith's perfume, which was something temptingly sweet.

"So, when am I supposed to talk about your vision?" Best to get things on track immediately. He was here for only one thing, independent verification. Oh yeah, and to sit patiently through Grandma Blue's nonsense. Just a few days, that was all.

If only Opal didn't smell so good. If only there wasn't a direct line from his arm where she clutched him to the crotch of his jeans.

Her nails dug into his flesh. "Don't say *anything* about it right now. Not until after we save that poor man."

But who was going to save poor Jack?

Lillian Fontaine entered with the regal posture of a queen, a snazzy black handbag dangling from one arm, a white Persian cat cuddled in the other.

"This is Shitake," were the first words out of her mouth.

"We just call her Little Shit for short," Grandma Blue informed him.

"Mother." Halfway between shock and admonishment, Lillian's lips thinned.

"Well, that's what you get for naming it after a mushroom."

Jack had had enough chocolate cookies to fell a lumberjack and enough coffee to make his eyeballs float. Grandma Blue was a steamroller. No one could stop her once she got going. Jack had known her all of two hours, yet he understood that without a doubt. It wasn't that anyone said no to her, just that things rolled off her tongue without any internal censor—or external, for that matter.

Opal was right. Grandma Blue would do whatever she set her mind to. Such as eating a whole bowl of cookie dough without getting sick. Or prove *he* was Dynamite Davis reincarnated.

Yep, she was a queer bird. Opal's mother, however, was something altogether different. Jack just hadn't figured out what.

Opal's resemblance to her was nothing short of remarkable. Except for the pinched disapproving look, something Lillian probably did often if the lines fanning out from her lips were any indication. Though somewhere in her mid-fifties, her upswept hair was still the same blond as Opal's, a mixture of platinum and gold that, on Opal, shone like a halo in the sunlight. On her mother, it appeared to be nothing more than a fairly decent dye job.

"And who is this young man?" She turned to Opal for the introduction.

"Jack."

"Dynamite," Grandma Blue amended.

"As in Dynamite Davis?" One elegantly arched eyebrow rose.

"We've concluded that Jack is Dynamite's reincarnation," Grandma Blue acknowledged.

Lillian didn't even flicker a heavily gooped eyelash. All she said was, "Mother," the pinched look on her mouth again.

Opal's mother glimmered in an elegant blue St. John suit, not that Jack would admit he knew a St. John from something off the rack at a discount department store.

St. John had been a favorite of his mother's. She'd bought two suits when she thought she was a princess. But since she wasn't a princess and she didn't have a charge card, the purchases had ended up on his account. He'd made sure she didn't get access again.

"Mother is *the* Psychic to the Stars," Opal announced, eyes on her mom, a worshipful expression glossing her features.

"But I don't bandy that about the way *some* people do."

Jack wondered who did. He decided the moment called for enthusiasm. He mustered what he could. "That's…uh…great."

"She works with all the big names." Opal beamed like a gemstone. "But it's against Mother's ethics to reveal names."

It might also have made her liable for lawsuits. "Amazing."

They all turned, three pairs of blue eyes drilling him, and he wondered if he'd let a little sarcasm seep through. Not a good idea in a room full of women.

The cat suddenly jumped from Lillian's arms, ran across the faded living room carpet and sank its claws into his jeans.

"Shitake."

"Little Shit."

"Mushroom." The last from Opal as she rushed forward to grab the monster, shooing the cat away.

"Shitake never did like Dynamite." Obviously, Lillian subscribed to the same beliefs as her daughter and mother. Well, duh, she *was* "psychic to the stars." Could it be group mania or was it just a matter of how one wished to view life?

Jack knew the haze fogging his brain probably afflicted his voice, but he couldn't help himself. "If Dynamite died over forty years ago, how could Little Shi—" Lillian felled him with a glare. "How could Shitake know him…me?" Or whatever.

"It's a matter of her reaction when she sees his picture." Wicked satisfaction creased Grandma Blue's lips as she delivered her final blow. "She tries to piss on it every chance she gets."

"Mother, please, you know I hate that word."

Eyes sparkling, Grandma Blue covered her mouth like a little girl. "Oops, sorry, I meant she tries to *pee* on it."

"Mother, can we please mute those TVs? They're giving me a headache." Lillian put two delicately manicured nails to her temples.

The volume on the two TVs had not been overly loud, but Opal reached for the remote and did the deed. Though she said nothing, a glower marred Grandma Blue's face.

"Opal dear, I've got something in my purse for you."

"Yes, Mother?" Opal's eyes lit up.

Lillian opened her black bag and pulled out an overstuffed brown envelope, the corners crumpled from being shoved into the undersized purse. "I'd adore it if you could just look over these few little documents and give me your advice."

"Don't do it, Opal," Grandma Blue warned. "You know what happened last time."

"Mother, this is between Opal and I. Please butt out."

"It's all right. Of course, I'll look at it." Opal turned to her mother, took the envelope, shoving it inside her own purse which was sitting by the coffee table. But something in that big brown envelope had dimmed the light in her eyes.

Lillian moved to the plaid sofa, bent down to brush away some lint. "Mother, where are those plastic slipcovers I gave you to keep the sofa clean?"

"My butt stuck to them so I threw them out."

"If you didn't allow people to eat on the couch…" Lillian closed her mouth, obviously considering it another argument lost. Perching on the edge, she crossed her feet daintily and patted the seat beside her, staring at Jack. He went over and sat like an obedient dog. Best not to rile the woman for any reason. At least not with Opal and Grandma Blue watching.

"Opal, dear, would you fetch me a cup of tea? I'm parched."

Grandma Blue grunted. "I made coffee. You can drink that."

"Mother, you know how coffee stains the teeth and corrodes the digestive system."

"And tea's any better?" Animosity sizzled off Grandma Blue.

Opal jumped between them as if she were used to mediation. "There's still some of those herbal tea bags left over from last time. I'll make you a nice cup."

"Thank you, dear. Now, Jack, tell me how long you and Opal have been dating."

Opal's cheeks turned a pretty shade of pink. "Mother, we're not dating."

"If you're not dating, why on earth would you bring him to meet Grandma Blue?"

Opal hung in the middle of the living room floor, taking first one step toward the kitchen, then one back toward her mother. "Well, you see, I had a little accident, and Jack—"

"I rear-ended her," Jack stepped in to save the day, realizing too late the sexual connotation the words took on.

Lillian's eyes widened, and she sucked in a shocked breath.

"On the freeway," he amended, which didn't seem to make things better. "A traffic accident. Completely my fault. I was tailing too close." And why was he taking the blame for it? Ah, hell, because it was the right thing to do in the situation.

Grandma Blue's dancing gaze found his. He heard that drain-sucking sound again.

"And you came to my mother's house to…?" Lillian left the question hanging, looking at Opal.

"To discuss insurance issues," Jack jumped in, damning himself all the while. "Neutral territory."

"He hit your car, Opal?" Her mother deliberately cut him off with a steely-eyed look at Opal.

"I'll make your tea, Mother."

"Just a minute, young lady. What happened to your car?"

Silence reigned for a moment longer than necessary. "It's still at Sil's. He'll have damage estimates in a couple of days."

Embarrassment tinged her cheeks as her mother berated her like a child. In front of a man.

Jack put his foot down right in the middle of it. "While Opal makes your tea, Ms. Fontaine, I would really love—" he gulped at the word "—to hear more about what you do. It sounds very…" Very what? "Intriguing."

Which seemed the most innocuous and the closest to the truth.

Grandma Blue looked about ready to dance a jig, Lillian Fontaine preened beneath his glowing interest, and Opal's eyes sparkled as if he'd just climbed a mountain for her.

Opal was sweet, beautiful, caring and, for the most part, radiated amazing pluck and determination. He'd never met a woman like her. And the smile of gratitude on her face made him feel…as if he actually wanted to be Dynamite Davis. For her. Which was far too powerful an emotion. As if being needed was something he'd missed in the last two years. Yet with Opal, he didn't feel strangled by the prospect.

A voice piped up inside him. *Run, run like hell, dude.*

He feared it was too late for that.

"YOU DIDN'T HAVE TO LET my mother talk your ear off, you know."

Opal stood in the V of her open door, Jack a hairbreadth away with his hand braced on the roof of the car. She'd parked just beyond the direct glow of the streetlamp, the relative darkness almost intimate, his closeness jangling her nerves. He was all coffee-and-chocolate scented, her favorite combination.

"No big deal." He gave her an endearing aw-shucks look. His eyes were coffee-and-chocolate colored, too. A delicious but deadly combination.

"But it *was* a big deal. I know you're not a believer."

"You don't have to believe to play along."

Yeah, well, he hadn't met some of the guys she'd dated. Not that she was putting him in the same class with a date. He wasn't. He was her independent verification. She didn't even think of him as a man at all. Not that he didn't have the nicest set of shoulders in that white T-shirt. She wouldn't have been a female if she hadn't noticed the way his jeans hugged a very tight end, even if he hadn't played football. There was something in the intent manner he watched her lips curve that sent a tingle straight up from her toes.

All right, she *did* think of him as a man. He was so scrumptious, any normal woman would. Independent verification, she reminded herself. "Well, at any rate, you were a good sport acting like you were really—" she raised a brow "—intrigued."

He laughed. "What makes you think I wasn't? Your mother's a very…intriguing person."

Right. And Jack was the absolute best fibber. She'd seen his hackles rise a few times, but he'd kept his cool. "Anyway, the whole evening was sweet on your part. Thank you."

His eyes seemed to darken in the shadows just beyond the lamplight. "I'm not sweet."

"Of course you are." She smiled, patted his arm, her fingers lingering a moment too long on the hard muscle. "You're a very nice man, you know."

"You said that before. But you should know I'm definitely not nice." There was the tiniest edge to his voice now.

Opal wondered what she'd said wrong. "Of course you are, and that's why I'm thanking you."

"Then stop thanking me like I'm noble or something."

Opal's breath caught in her throat. His head blocked out whatever light reached down from the streetlamp.

Her voice dropped to a whisper despite herself. "Well, in a way you are."

"Not considering the thoughts I'm having right now."

He was looming over her, but there wasn't the slightest thing menacing about it. In fact, it was exciting. Her heart picked up its pace.

She shouldn't ask. Because she wasn't so dense that she didn't know the answer. She shouldn't be playing with her unbiased witness this way.

Except that she couldn't help herself. "What is it you're thinking about?"

His gaze fell to her lips again, and his breath caressed her cheek. "I'm thinking of showing you how really not nice I am."

Now would be the time to put a stop to the risky game. She hadn't intended to start it. All she had to do was put a hand on his chest and push. He'd give, she knew it. He was a gentleman.

Instead, she pulled her bottom lip between her teeth and looked at his mouth.

Chocolate and coffee, that's all she could think of when he pulled her into his arms. Chocolate and coffee and how badly she wanted to taste him. His lips were surprisingly soft and his tongue surprisingly agile. She didn't so much open her mouth to him as let him invade her. He cupped the back of her head with one hand and molded her to his chest with an arm across her back. She wound her arms around his neck. And then she was in free fall. His mouth slanted across hers while his tongue teased and his teeth nibbled. He sucked on her lower lip.

When he backed off to drag in a breath, she somehow managed to speak. "Well, I think that qualifies as nice."

She'd planned for his reaction. This time, he held her face in both hands and attacked her lips. No softness now, just his unrelenting mouth doing something totally marvelous. She felt the lick of his tongue straight down to her belly. Oh, no, it was not a nice kiss at all.

His breath was harsh when he let her go, his eyes glittering down on her despite the fact that the light was behind his head. "No more thank-yous and no more calling me a nice guy, okay," he said against her lips.

Her brain felt all muddled, her legs squishy and her lips hot. "Thank you for being such a nice guy," she whispered.

He laughed, then groaned. "We're standing in front of your grandmother's house, and if I'm not mistaken, those curtains are moving suspiciously. Don't push your luck."

She wanted to push, because it was obvious that, on top of being her unbiased witness, he was most definitely a potent male.

NILE SAT IN HIS CAR outside Pearl's apartment long after her lights had gone out. A night breeze rustled over him laced with the hint of flowering bushes. He was nocturnal, preferring to sleep in the day. The truth was, he couldn't sleep at night, with only the sound of night creatures and the occasional bark of a dog to break the silence of a quiet suburban neighborhood. The silence kept him awake, kept him thinking, brooding. He'd given up trying, sometimes staying up thirty hours until his body shut down, and his mind with it.

The glow of his watch said 3:00 a.m. He pictured Pearl in her silly fuzzy lime-green pajamas. She looked like a snow cone and made him want to lick her all over. Then. Now. Forever.

Not that he could ever tell her that. What she said was true, he'd never shared a damn thing with her except a bed, and sex—sex so good and hot that it burned every thought, every image, every shred of darkness from his soul for those few brief moments he lived inside her. She was light, he was darkness. He knew he was stealing her brilliance, her warmth, even as he hoarded every moment with her. He'd left before he dragged her into his world. Before he destroyed her completely.

Should he have told Pearl the truth today? Would it have made any difference? His gift was gone, its departure emasculating him. Yet a small hungry place inside of him was so damn grateful he could no longer see.

That was the truth. He used his gift to help people find their missing loved ones, but he was glad the blight was gone because he knew he'd die if he had to tell one more parent, one more brother, sister, uncle, son or daughter that their loved one was dead. He'd die if he had to see one more dead body.

Nile leaned his head back against the seat. Not to see. God. His visions came to him when he touched objects. Images, thoughts and feelings of the people who had touched it, owned it. He'd been in control of his ability, able to turn it off during his everyday existence in order to avoid the bombardment of a million small details contained in something as ordinary as, say, a can of tomato soup at the grocery store. Twenty-eight days ago, his gift had deserted him. Put simply, he couldn't turn it back on again. For almost a month, he'd seen nothing, and the sense of freedom rushed through him like the taste of Pearl on his lips. Twenty-eight days without seeing a single death. A blessing.

Yet a curse. The lack of sight—even though a part of him believed the cause was a mental block of his own subconscious creation—stole his very essence. He didn't know who he was without it. He had no identity.

And he couldn't find Tamara Whitley-Dorn. He'd felt for Cecelia, the grieving mother. He'd wanted to give her hope. When she'd shown him Tamara's room, she'd stood in the doorway watching as he touched her daughter's things, waiting for him to pick up a clue from one of the items. Yet not one image of the girl had come to him.

As much as he basked in his new freedom, he couldn't stand the look in Cecelia's eyes or the guilt of knowing he wasn't doing a damn thing to help her. He couldn't stand the impotence any more than he could the thought of finding Tamara's body.

He'd come to Pearl one last time for succor. He'd shared his body with her and found immense comfort. If he shared his soul the way she'd always asked, might he be able to reclaim his accursed gift? Not that he wanted to, he had to. For Tamara and her family. Pearl had always been the answer for him, the karmic key. If he gave her a glimpse of his inner turmoil, he nurtured the hope she would bolster his spirit in the same way she soothed and rejuvenated his physical body. No, more than a glimpse was necessary. She had to know exactly how the gift ripped holes in the fabric of his heart and mind. From the first moment he'd seen her, he'd known she was his other half, and instinct told him the only way to mend his broken pieces was to open himself to Pearl completely. To become one in body *and* soul. The letter shared what he couldn't share with words. Once she knew the final event that had caused the gift to desert him, he would reveal to her the essence of his life, his torment. And the shoring up of his psyche could begin.

It's what she'd asked for, but he knew she'd be sorry, so sorry, once she read what was in that envelope.

CHAPTER FIVE

"EXCUSE ME, MISS, I'm looking for Opal Smith."

The elderly gentleman, dressed in a natty three-piece suit complete with tie clip and pocket watch, leaned on his mahogany cane as he approached the cashier counter filling the left corner of the shop. A pure white snowcap of hair topped his head, wire-rimmed glasses perched on his nose and tiny red lines meandered across his weathered cheeks.

"I'm Opal." She closed the office supply catalog and stuffed it beneath the counter. Opal had a fetish. She loved office supplies, colored binder clips, neon Post-it pads and pens of all colors, sizes and types. It boggled the senses.

She should have been looking at the statements her mother had given her last night. Her mother had a bad habit of asking for financial advice, then doing the exact opposite of whatever Opal suggested. When it didn't work out, she still blamed Opal. But without a psychic talent, the only thing Opal had to offer her gifted family was her financial common sense.

"My name is Victor Patell. I did think that was you, but the eyes just don't see like they used to—" he tapped his wire rims "—even with double bifocals. I can't decide whether wearing them helps or makes things worse." He removed them, popping them in his breast pocket.

"Oh, my God, you're the man in the gold Cadillac." She looked at his cane, something akin to horror chilling her bones. "I didn't do that, did I?"

"No. It's just a helpmate." He tapped his cane on the carpet. "Getting old is a pain in the patootie." His mouth twisted wryly. "And everywhere else, too."

Ooh, Grandma Blue would love him.

"I'm sorry about the accident. I was really dumb."

"It happens to the best of us, dear. Don't fret about it."

But if it wasn't about the accident, why was he here?

The soothing scent of aromatherapy candles and the low murmur of voices drifted through the chintz curtain covering the doorway to Pearl's sanctum, where she performed her readings. Though the words weren't distinguishable, Opal dropped a low-volume CD into the player. They'd discussed putting Pearl in the front window of the shop, but had both decided privacy lent legitimacy to her work. The amazing things of which Pearl was capable shouldn't be displayed like some sideshow act.

So they used the little bay window at the front of the shop for coffee time. "Can I make you a mocha, Mr. Patell?"

"Why, I'd love one."

A good mocha always cleared the air, put people at ease and helped the energy flow through the chakras. Unless… "You don't have any medical problems where you shouldn't have coffee or chocolate, do you?"

"My doctor tells me coffee and chocolate will help me live to be a hundred. It's the cigars I'm supposed to give up."

Chocolate and coffee made her think of Jack. And that kiss. Her cheeks flushed. "Just take a look around for a few minutes, and I'll be right back."

A mocha with Mr. Patell would take her mind off her mother's messy finances. Opal was back lickety-split with two steamy, whipped-cream-laden mochas in white ceramic cups. Mr. Patell had already found the comfy seat in the front window and didn't show the least compunction about being stared at by every passerby. Opal liked to think seeing a cozy chat in the window actually helped bring in potential customers.

He sniffed appreciatively. "That smells marvelous. My wife used to mix the most wonderful coffee concoctions, too."

"I really am sorry about your car, Mr. Patell."

"Please call me Victor. And don't worry about the car—" he waved a hand "—it's taken care of."

"Are you sure you're okay?" Even having a vision wouldn't have been worth it if she'd hurt someone in the process.

Victor took a sip of his mocha, closed his eyes and sighed. "Not a scratch, my dear. My doctor's a crotchety old crow and wanted me to stay overnight. I think he was trying to line the hospital's pockets. And his own." He wagged a finger. "But I didn't let him get away with it."

"Well, it was nice of you to stop by just to…say hello?" She let her voice end on a question, a not-so-subtle hint. Not that she didn't enjoy spending time with anyone who enjoyed her mochas as much as he seemed to.

"You're probably wondering why I'm here."

"Actually, I was." The sun was warm on her arm, the

whipped cream and chocolate fragrant, the hum of street noise lulling and the memory of Jack Davis's kiss sweet. Sometimes, when she felt this good, she wondered why she so desperately needed a psychic gift to make her feel whole.

"I'm looking for a psychic."

His words snapped her out of her reverie. "Whatever for?" Which was not what the entrepreneur of a thriving psychic-based business should say.

"I need someone to contact my wife for me."

"Yes, well, I…" Opal wasn't quite sure why she stumbled over the words. Shock perhaps.

"Come, my dear, don't be modest. I admit I was a trifle dazed right after the accident, but I did hear you talking about your vision with that nice young man."

"He doesn't like to be called nice," she said without thinking. Actually, with too much thinking, about that wonderful kiss. Victor heard her talking about her vision? Very interesting. Maybe *he* could provide independent verification.

"It's the Kiss of Death, you know."

She stopped, the cup halfway to her mouth. "Excuse me?"

"When a woman calls a man nice, it means he'd make a nice pet, but she wouldn't want him muddying up her bedsheets."

Goodness, she'd have to tell that one to Grandma Blue. Yes, yes, her grandmother would simply adore Victor Patell. "I'll have to remember not to call him nice again. Now, about your wife, why don't you tell me a bit more? And, by the way, I'm sorry for your loss." She patted his hand.

Expressive gray eyes misted a moment. "Thank you, my dear. My Prudence passed on last year. Thanksgiving Day."

"Oh, I'm so sorry."

"No, no, it was like a present. She'd been so ill and in so much pain. It was the perfect day to say goodbye." Despite the sentiment of the words, his liver-spotted hand trembled on his cup handle. "We were married sixty years."

Opal loved a love story, and the shine in his eyes spoke of something that hadn't died with his wife's passing. "She must have meant a lot to you."

"She was my life. I really thought God would take me in those first months after she was gone. But the ticker just keeps on ticking." He tapped his chest, then met Opal's eyes with an intent gaze. "Which is why I need you."

"Me?"

"I need you to contact Prudence for me. I want to talk to her. I want to make sure she's okay."

"She's in Heaven, Victor. Of course she's okay."

A sheen passed over his eyes, and his coffee cup lay forgotten in favor of a strong grip on her hand. "I *have* to talk to her."

Her heart ached for him, but her own desire to be something she wasn't—yet—couldn't take precedence over this man's sixty years with his wife. Why, that was over twice as long as Opal had been alive. "I'm not a psychic, Victor. I wish I were."

"But you had that vision."

"It was the first vision I've ever had." Though she'd had a lot that turned out to be totally false. "I haven't even validated it yet." She decided right then that Victor couldn't be her verification. It wouldn't be fair to ask him when he was still grieving over his wife. She covered his hand, speaking gently to deliver the blow as easily as possible. "Even if I did have an honest-to-God vision, that doesn't mean I can communicate with your dead wife."

Pearl's talents didn't extend to contacting the passed, either. But her brother's abilities did. Julian, however, with his newfound fame, jealously guarded his off-TV hours. She couldn't offer *the* Julian Smith, syndicated medium, to Victor Patell without asking first. And she couldn't give Victor hope in case Julian said no.

"I'm sorry to let you down."

The intensity of his gaze didn't lessen. "But I need someone I can trust."

She tipped her head to one side. "I wrecked your car. I'm not sure that makes me someone you can trust."

"No, but it makes you independent."

Sort of like independent verification. "I'm not sure I understand."

"I approached you, you didn't approach me."

She knew she was still staring at him blankly.

"It's about money, my dear. I have a lot of it. The mediums I have talked to are much more interested in the size of my pocketbook than they are in my wife."

"That's terrible." Though of course she was aware there were charlatans out there. She wanted, oh she wanted so badly to tell the man her brother was Julian Smith, whom, if he was medium hunting, she was sure Victor would have heard of. But her loyalty had to reside with her own family. Julian would kill her if she promised without his permission. Not to mention giving Victor false hope.

"I need your help, my dear. There's nothing more important to me in the whole world than contacting my wife."

Opal knew all about important things, like how important proving her vision was.

"You understand, don't you, my dear? Nothing is more important than talking to my Prudence." His whole soul seemed to be reaching out to her. Moisture shimmered in his eyes.

She took a deep breath. How could she *not* help him? The idea was unconscionable. "I think I can find someone."

"Someone you trust implicitly?"

She might not always see eye-to-eye with Julian—he could be stubborn—but she believed in his abilities unconditionally. She feathered another stroke across the elderly man's hand. "I wouldn't ever send you to someone I didn't have faith in."

"Thank you. I knew I could count on you."

That was odd. He didn't even know her. "Why?"

Victor smiled like the kindly old gentleman he was. "Because you were so kind to me the day of the accident. Just as that young man was."

She sat in the window long after Victor Patell left.

Somehow, some way, she had to get Julian to help. Opal left her brother a syrupy-sweet message to call her right away. If she was lucky, he'd call her back.

VICTOR PATELL CROSSED the street to his Lincoln, which he was driving while the Cadillac was in for repair. He saw now that he'd parked the boat of a car at an odd angle, making it impossible for the vehicle beside to back out. Where was his mind these days?

Such a silly question. His mind, such as it was at eighty-three, was working voraciously on a seemingly unsolvable problem.

He climbed in his car, then rested a moment. He'd move before the occupant of the other vehicle returned. In a moment, after a little rest. His heart was heavy with the fact that George and Cecelia's daughter was still missing and he had yet to contact Prudence for guidance concerning Darius.

Up to this point, he'd tried everything he could think of. Opal Smith was his last resort. But merciful heavens, he felt guilty using the poor girl. The only way Victor could bury the guilt was to remind himself his actions were all to a higher purpose. Which was how he'd gotten over his indecisiveness about approaching her since the previous day.

He knew far more about Opal than he'd let on, the most important fact being that she was Julian Smith's sister. He'd called the medium's TV station several times, attempted to follow all the appropriate steps to be granted an audience with the man. To no avail. Mr. Smith, in the form of his staff, had turned down his every request, forcing Victor to find another avenue. That avenue was the man's sister. He'd debated telling her that he'd already gone through the proper channels and been refused. In the end, he'd decided it was too big a risk. That fact might give her a reason to turn him down. But if she thought it was *her* idea to go to her brother…Victor could only pray he wasn't making a miscalculation. The tear in his eye there at the end had worked. Probably because it was so very real.

He needed Prudence. Last night Darius had left the

house again. What did he do on these all-night excursions? Victor had asked often enough, but Darius had given him a look. *Mind your own business, old man.* His grandson would never actually say something so rude, but Victor knew the meaning of those raised eyebrows. How was he to help if he didn't know what Darius was up to during these odd late-night sojourns?

Sometimes, in his darkest moments, he wished that Darius had never come into his life.

An awful guilt assailed Victor, making him feel every one of his eighty-three years and then some. That's why he needed Prudence. She had loved the boy without reservation. And she would show Victor the path to loving him, too.

Yet he feared that simply wasn't possible.

JUST BEFORE THE EVENING rush hour, Jack crossed the uneven ground of his construction site to where Opal waited by her rental car. He eyed her red skirt and tennis shoes and all that bare leg in between. Even without her usual high heels, his mouth went dry. It was going to be another long evening.

"I'll drive this time," she offered.

"No, I'll drive." Jack had his truck keys out and the passenger side door open before she could say yea or nay. He tried, really tried not to look at her legs as she climbed in.

She caught him anyway despite his best efforts.

"Don't say a word about my clothes."

"I wasn't going to say anything."

"I even wore tennis shoes in case I have to run."

Yeah, but the skirt, though only a few inches above

the knee, left him visualizing the parts he couldn't see. But wanted to. "I said I wasn't going to say anything."

And Jack didn't, not even after he pulled himself into the driver's seat, started the engine and headed toward the freeway. Nope, not even then. In fact, he didn't even look again. No siree. Looking was off-limits after that kiss last night.

Kissing her messed with his mind. Kissing her made him think of doing more than just kissing. Kissing her made him lie awake all night fantasizing about doing those other things, when all he'd really been trying to do was show her—and himself—that he was *not* her Mr. Nice Guy.

Oh man. He had it bad. And he couldn't afford it. Opal's safety depended on his complete concentration. Not on her short skirt, her long legs, her kissable lips, but on her safety.

Hello, Jack, get a grip, dude.

Tonight, he had one job. To make sure anyone else looking at her on that overpass didn't get close enough to touch so much as a hair on her pretty head.

Damn. He sounded…protective. Nice guy aside, lust was one thing. But feeling protective, that was more dangerous to a man who wanted to remain uninvolved. Protective was *involved*.

"What are you doing?" she asked as he climbed out of the truck with her once he'd parked in the overpass lot.

"I'm waiting on the bridge with you." He only had to act the protector part for a few days. After she realized her vision wasn't real, their association would be…over. He didn't like how that thought made him feel.

Opal stopped, jammed militant hands on her hips and glared at him. "You are not coming up there with me."

"I am." He imitated her stance.

Irritation sparked in her eyes. "You'll ruin everything. He won't come if he sees you." Timid with her family, she could be a real spitfire with him.

And damn if he didn't like it. A lot. So, he ordered her around some more, just to see what she'd do. "Or else I'll drag you back into that truck and tie you down until your little witching hour is over." There, that was firm and decisive.

She gasped. "You wouldn't dare."

"I would." You bet he would. The image sort of punched him in the face. Or rather the groin. He almost wished she'd push him so he'd have to act on the threat.

She breathed, her breasts rising and falling beneath the thin striped sweater. She hadn't bothered with nylons, probably due to the heat. He wondered if she'd bothered with panties.

Get a grip here, Jack.

He put a stop to his runaway thoughts. They were in the middle of a parking lot with a steady stream of cars passing the entrance. They were attracting attention. Or rather she was attracting all that attention in her too-sexy skirt. It was like waving a red flag in front of a bull.

Which is why he would be out there with her on the overpass no matter what she said. It was the right thing to do.

She tipped her head. "All right."

"All right?" Her submission took him by surprise. "Does that mean what I think it means?"

"You can wait out there, but you have to stand at the

end of the overpass. I don't think anyone should know we're together."

"Why?"

She chewed her bottom lip, driving him crazy. Again. "I'm not sure."

"If you don't have a good reason…"

She pulled her purse strap up over her shoulder, slammed the truck door and started up the steps to the overpass. "I don't have to have a good reason. I'm a woman."

"A truer statement was never made." He followed, taking the steps two at a time and reaching the top before she did.

"I will not let you ruin this. It's my vision, and it's my save," she said from two steps below, not seeming to care about his height advantage.

Though he did like the view, right down her low-neck sweater. She suddenly became aware of the direction of his gaze and pulled up on the sweater, which only emphasized the roundness of those pretty breasts. Then she marched up the last two steps.

"Stop ogling my breasts."

"I'm a man. That's what we do. Ogle."

She stopped then, her mouth relaxing. "Why are we arguing?"

"Because you won't let me protect you in a manner that makes me feel secure." It was about the way she made him senseless. With worry. And lust, and a bunch of other stuff. He shouldn't have kissed her last night. His mind wanted a step back, but everything else wanted two giant steps forward.

"If it's about protecting *me*—" she stabbed a finger

to her breastbone "—then why do *you*—" another stab, this time at his chest "—need to feel secure?"

"I need enough time to get to you before someone can do any serious damage, if they intend to. I can't do that from the front seat of my truck down in that damn parking lot. What if that little guy last night had a knife hidden somewhere?"

She rolled her eyes. "Oh come on, he was harmless. He just wanted a date."

"He *seemed* harmless." Jack had to agree the guy was the least dangerous-looking animal he'd seen out there. But in all conscience, he didn't want Opal letting down her guard.

She crossed her arms over her chest and tapped her foot. "All right."

She did it again, agreed and took all the wind out of his sails.

"You stay here—" she pointed at the stairs "—and I'll walk back and forth across the overpass. Then you can see me."

"Okay. But don't go past the middle so I can still get to you fast enough."

She smiled, hitched her purse strap over her shoulder once more, then waggled her fingers at him.

She might not be crazy, but she needed someone to take care of her. Then it hit him like a one-ton girder falling on his head right after he'd removed his hard hat. God help him, he *wanted* to be the one to take care of her. It made him feel like Jack-the-damn-Giant-Killer. And he freaking *liked* it. Damn, damn and damn again. He wanted to feel…necessary. But he'd probably end up feeling helpless. Again. After two years of being worry free.

The catcalling started before she even made it to the middle of the overpass. Yep, it was going to be one damn long evening.

JACK REALLY WAS a nice man. But she didn't like the bickering, even if it was a way to keep him from kissing her again. Kissing was a bad thing for independent verification, but squabbling was beneath her. She could keep him at arm's length without treating him like trash. After all, he'd gone out of his way to help her even though she'd been the one to cause the accident in the first place.

Besides, she liked the idea of him looking out *for* her just as much as she liked how he looked *at* her. If she was honest, she'd dressed in a skirt, rather than shorts or jeans, for Jack.

Except the tennies ruined the whole effect. Oh well, her vision did have to come first.

"Hey, baby, need a lift?"

She felt Jack come abreast of her. "No, she doesn't."

"You're not supposed to know me," she hissed as the car rolled on with the line of traffic.

"That's only for anyone walking. They weren't."

"You were supposed to stay over there." She gave him a little push down the hill.

An hour later, her feet were getting tired despite the tennis shoes, the glare in Jack's eyes would have roasted a small animal, and the smell of exhaust fumes had started to make her head pound. She was ready to call it quits.

"Ma'am, I hate to bother you."

The little man sneaked up on her. Her shoes had three inches less heel than her pumps of last night, but the man was still shorter. From this angle, the growing bald spot on his head gleamed in the setting sun's glow.

"I'm really busy," she told him.

"I'd like to take you to dinner. And a movie. That's all, I swear."

She wanted to be nice, despite the ache in her feet and her head. "I'm sorry. Really I am. But no means no."

"The lady said no." Jack's fingers grabbed her upper arm.

The little guy stared up at Jack's six feet plus and blanched. With one last look at her breasts, which were almost at eye level, he dashed off to the far end of the bridge.

Jack didn't let go. "We're outta here."

"But—"

He propelled her forward. "No buts."

She forgot that a few minutes ago, she was the one ready to quit. "We've got half an hour of daylight left."

"But I'm out of patience." He dragged her along with him. Opal barely managed to keep her footing on the stairs.

She tugged against him at the bottom of the steps. Not that it stopped him from dragging her across the parking lot to his truck. "What is wrong with you?"

"I'm tired of looking at guys looking at your legs."

"But—"

He cut her off again, his hand still on her arm as he dug in his pocket for his keys. "He's not going to be here tonight."

The rest of that sentence was in his eyes, even if he didn't say it. Her quarry wasn't going to be here at all. Ever. She was crazy, and he was just humoring her. Oh yes, she saw all that in the flare of his nostrils and felt it in the way his fingers kneaded her arm.

"He *will* come. And I'll save him from jumping off the overpass. And if you don't want to help me, I'll find someone who will." Like her grandmother. Or someone.

"Get in the truck, Opal."

He unlocked the door, yanked it open and practically shoved her up into the seat.

"I don't appreciate being manhandled," she blurted when he finally climbed in beside her.

"Yeah, but you don't mind every Tom, Dick and Harry begging you to get in their car so you can—" This time he cut himself off. Scrubbing his hand across his face, then back through his hair, he turned to look at her. "I think I was better off watching from inside the truck."

"I told you to let me do it on my own."

"Is that how bad it was last night?"

She shrugged. "Pretty much." Wearing tennies hadn't made a lick of difference to the number of whistles and comments.

Jack slumped in his seat. "Then I'm sorry I let you do it."

How tired he looked. His eyelids were at half-mast, and the grooves along his mouth were deeper.

She'd kept him up late with her mother and grandmother and had him standing on the overpass for what seemed liked hours. "I'm sorry."

He quirked open one eye, which had closed in the time she'd been staring at him. "Christ, I hate it when women say that."

"But I mean it."

"Yeah, I know you do. That's the problem."

Such a wealth of bitterness tinged the words, she knew he was referring to far more than just the last couple of hours.

Without another word, he started the engine, rammed into gear and shot out of the parking spot with a squeal of the tires.

I'M SORRY.

Damn. Why'd she have to say that?

Watching Opal's progress along that overpass had been like reliving all the games Jack had played with his mother. Watching out for her. Bailing her out of jail. Picking up the pieces. The endless round of apologies she made until she was hoarse. Only to have her lose her grip on reality all over again.

That wasn't the worst. The worst came when she cried, the sound so utterly sad it broke his heart. He hadn't been able to do a thing to help her then. He was the one who was sorry, for never having the right words, for never taking the right action, for being totally inadequate when she needed him.

"Jack?"

He was speeding, he knew it as he flew by the other cars, weaving in and out dangerously, idiotically. He slowed down to save both their necks from his memories.

Opal wasn't like his mom. He'd told himself that a thousand times as he watched her. Back and forth. Back and forth. Until he thought his head would explode. He knew he was overreacting, but he hadn't been able to stop himself.

He couldn't pinpoint when he started to boil over. One too many catcalls asking her to do despicable things. Unless she was doing those things with him. Jealousy had a lot to do with it. So did impotence, because no matter what he said, he knew Opal would not give up her scheme.

"Jack, talk to me."

He punched the accelerator when the light turned green, and blew away the car sitting next to him.

He didn't have hope for Opal's happy ending. He wouldn't let anything happen to her physically, but for sure, when her vision wasn't validated, she'd be crushed, depressed, melancholy. And if she made it past that, the cycle of craziness would start all over again. How in hell was he supposed to help her then?

"Jack, you missed my car."

"I would have hit it if I was trying." Shit. At the end of the block, he had to back up to pull in next to the rental.

She stared at him openmouthed, as if she actually believed he might ram her car, then said, "You know, Grandma Blue can help me. If I do find the man, she can tell my mother and brother and sister that I was right."

Not on your life, baby. He would not let an old lady do his job for him, no matter how much the thought of Opal crying herself sick ripped him apart. "I'll meet you tomorrow, same time, same place."

"But Jack—"

"Same time, same place tomorrow evening," he repeated between gritted teeth. Dammit, he couldn't get the image of Opal's tear-streaked face out of his mind.

She scrambled out of his truck, climbed into her rental, locked the doors, buckled up and pulled out of the parking spot. Maybe he should follow her to make sure she got home safely.

Not necessary. She'd make it just fine. In a host of ways, Opal was nothing like his mother, who, when she lost her hold on reality, couldn't have found her way home if she was standing right outside her own front door with her house key in her hand.

Opal's car disappeared around the corner.

He liked her. He wanted her. He even had a growing soft spot for her wacky grandmother.

What bothered him was actually having to admit that "saving" Opal somehow gave him back a purpose in life. As if he hadn't had any purpose at all after his mother died. It was tantamount to saying he needed Opal Smith more than she needed him. She was his atonement for failing the last time.

That idea was infinitely more terrifying than the prospect of being Dynamite Davis reincarnated.

CHAPTER SIX

JACK HAD PRETTY MUCH tossed Opal out of his truck. Two hours later, it still wrangled her insides like an overdose of triple-shot mochas—sometimes there was too much of a good thing. Opal couldn't figure out what she'd done wrong. Or rather, she couldn't decide which thing she'd said or done set him off.

Not to mention that Julian hadn't called her back after umpteen phone messages on both his home and cell phone. How was she supposed to help Victor, who desperately needed help?

Opal collapsed on her sofa, the portable phone in one hand. She'd closed the blinds, made herself a cup of tea—food was the furthest thing from her mind—and exchanged her skirt and tennies for a pair of flannel shorts and flip-flops. The best thing she could do now was hit Memory One on her phone and wait for the pickup.

"Grandma Blue, can you help me tomorrow night?"

"What's wrong?"

"I need you to go with me to the overpass so I can look for my vision."

There was the briefest of sighs. "What about Dynamite?"

"We had a fight."

"Opal, you've known him two days, how can you have a fight?"

"He's not really interested in helping me find the guy that's going to jump off the bridge." He'd told her he'd meet her tomorrow night, but he'd used that snippy tone, which made it really hard to tell whether or not he'd be there.

"Now, Opal, you listen to me. That man is interested."

"Grandma Blue, *you're* not listening to me."

"Opal, he practically sucked your face off last night out by your car."

"You were spying on me!"

"I'm illustrating the point that the boy is interested."

"He's not anymore. I irritated him." Maybe it was her brief display of attitude because he kept picking on everything she did. But he'd deserved a little attitude.

"Your mother irritates. You merely obfuscate."

"If you don't help me, I'm doing it alone. I'll probably get kidnapped by one of those horrible men driving by, and you'll never forgive yourself." She didn't feel the least bit guilty. She'd learned extortion from the best, Grandma Blue herself.

"Blackmailer. You need more respect for your elders."

"Please, Grandma Blue."

"Have you really screwed things up with that boy?"

"I think so." She reminded herself she'd known him only two days, two inconsequential days. Except that her time with Jack didn't feel inconsequential. It felt momentous.

Grandma Blue was silent. She knew that after a few moments of dead air Opal would cave and tell her everything.

And Opal caved. "He gave me the silent treatment all the way back from College Avenue, then he practically threw me out of his truck." His behavior was like a sliver rooted in her finger. If she didn't get it out, the wound would fester.

Grandma Blue snorted. "Sounds like a male snit. Did you refuse to sleep with him?"

Opal gasped. "He didn't ask me to."

"Aha, that's it then."

Sometimes her grandmother made her head spin.

"He was expecting you to ask him. And you didn't. Men are very sensitive creatures."

They certainly were. But not for the reason Grandma Blue was purporting. "He's in a snit because he thinks I'm out of my mind."

"Ah well, chickadee, he'll forget all about it by tomorrow."

"I don't think so." He'd had that I've-got-to-get-away-from-this-female-or-jump-off-an-overpass-myself look in his eye. He'd kissed her last night. Then today he'd run as though the devil were on his tail with a flaming pitchfork.

"Stop feeling sorry for yourself, sweetie. Jack will be back. I guarantee it."

Maybe. Probably not. But she could hope. "You have to promise not to push the Dynamite séance thing. If he does come back, that is."

Grandma Blue snorted. "It'll be fun."

"No."

"Party pooper. I'll make a deal. When he asks you to marry him, then we'll do the séance."

Oh, my God. Her grandmother was way ahead of

herself. Way ahead of Opal. And way ahead of the prospective groom. But since Jack was only going to be independent verification—if he ever called her again—then why not make the deal with her conniving grandmother. "You're on."

"Now what time are you picking me up?"

"Four o'clock." Opal would have to leave the shop early.

"You didn't rent a Ford, did you?"

"You know I'd never do that."

"I'd disown you if you did."

Opal managed to smile. Grandma Blue was good at getting a girl to smile no matter what. "I love you, Grandma Blue."

"Don't go getting all sappy. And you better come early so you can set my VCR for me. I don't want to miss that race while I'm gone."

Grandma Blue knew perfectly well how to set her own VCR. "I thought you were weaning."

"I am, but I've been mainlining stock cars so long, it's going to take a bit longer than I thought."

Could one kiss be considered mainlining? Opal wondered how long it would take to wean herself off Jack.

PEARL KNOCKED TENTATIVELY on Opal's apartment door, despite the lateness of the hour. She thought if she stayed in her own apartment all by herself one moment longer, she'd do something drastic. Such as try to find Nile. She simply couldn't allow herself to do that. So here she was at Opal's.

Her sister opened up only moments later. "What are you doing here? It's after ten."

"I need to talk."

Opal pulled her inside. "You're a mess. What's wrong?"

Pearl agreed she was a mess. She'd tried applying makeup to cover the dark circles beneath her eyes, but then she'd started crying, and she didn't think she'd gotten all the residual off her eyes before abandoning the attempt and driving to Opal's.

She couldn't sleep, she couldn't eat.

"You need some tea."

Even as Opal was dashing to the kitchen, Pearl nodded agreement. She needed to wrap her fingers around something warm.

"Sit down," Opal called. Water ran, the teakettle clanked, a cupboard door slapped shut, then the fridge whooshed open and closed. Snuggling into the print cushions on the sofa, she knew Opal would take care of her. Opal took care of all of them.

Pearl loved her sister's apartment, a one-bedroom on the second floor of a modest apartment building. Trees shaded the parking lot, and flower boxes lined the walks and landings. Opal's living room flowed over with carefully tended plants and always smelled fresh like springtime. Especially after watering when the combined scent of damp earth and new blossoms permeated the whole apartment. Even the print on her couch was a jumble of flowers, yellows and oranges against a green background. And lots of pillows. Pearl hugged one to her chest.

Pearl had never had the green thumb that Opal did, and she came here when the world was biting at her heels. Like now.

"Here you go. And some of your favorite lemon bars."

Smiling, Pearl kicked off her sandals and tucked her

feet beneath her on the sofa. Just like Grandma Blue, Opal showed her caring with food. The tea was hot, the cup searing warmth into her palms.

"All right, now talk," Opal said.

Pearl hadn't talked about him in so long, but the words just seemed to spill out now. "Nile's back in town."

"That dirty rat bastard. What does he want?"

Pearl breathed deeply, letting the tea's steam soothe her cheeks. Her sister's unconditional backing warmed her as much as the hot tea did. "He said he wanted a reading."

"No way. It's just a ruse." Opal sipped her own tea, then pursed her lips. "What do you think he really wants?"

Some of her tension seeped away as Pearl snuggled deeper into the cushions. Nile's defection all those months ago had nearly crushed her. She hadn't thought she'd survive the nights alone in her bed. If it weren't for Opal, she might not have made it. Opal hadn't asked any questions, hadn't tried to make her talk. She'd simply been there. Pearl needed her again. "I think he wants to say he's sorry."

"And then he'll ask you to take him back?"

Pearl sat for a moment, listening to the sounds outside, a few cars on the road, and closer, the cheep of crickets. "I don't know. He said he's in town looking for a young woman who's missing." What was her name? It was bad not to remember the name of someone who was in trouble. "Tamara. That's it," she said. "Tamara Whitley-Dorn. Twenty-three years old. She's been missing since Friday."

Opal pressed Pearl's hand. "Let's put it out to the universe that he'll find her safely."

It was like praying, since God was the universe. They held hands for Tamara. Pearl added a prayer for Nile.

"She'll be found," Opal asserted. "When did you see him?"

Pearl blew on her tea. "He came by the shop after you left yesterday."

"Yesterday?" Opal's pitch rose a notch. "Why didn't you tell me today?"

"I didn't want to bother you with it." She'd needed to mull it over for a while on her own, just as she'd mulled over her broken heart for six long months. All that mulling hadn't helped, not since the day he left, and not now that he'd returned.

"I knew there was something wrong." Opal tapped her forehead. "The old sixth sense, you know."

Pearl laughed for the first time in over twenty-four hours. "You're such a liar. You didn't notice a thing."

Opal's lips drooped in a frown. "I'm sorry. That was pretty selfish of me not to notice something was bothering you."

"You don't always have to take care of us, Opal. Sometimes we have to take care of ourselves." Though Pearl had to admit she hadn't been doing a very good job for herself.

Opal tipped her head. "What do you want me to do for you? I'll help. Just tell me what you need."

Pearl hadn't cried, not when Nile walked into the shop yesterday, not when he walked back out, not even last night as she lay alone in her bed and remembered all the nights he'd lain beside her. It had taken twenty-four hours for the tears to come. Now her eyes ached. "He gave me a letter."

"What did it say?"

"I haven't read it. I'm afraid." It was an awful thing

to admit, that she was afraid of an envelope and what it contained.

"Why?"

Pearl sipped her tea, hoping the hot liquid would give her courage, at least enough to tell Opal what was bothering her. "There's something in that letter I don't think I want to know."

"Like an explanation of why he walked out on you?"

Pearl tipped her head. "Yes." Then she grimaced. "No." And finally sighed. "I don't know. I spent all my time with Nile wanting him to share his innermost thoughts and feelings." She bit her lip. "But now I don't think I can handle knowing."

"So you think the letter's going to reveal all that?"

Pearl put the warm mug to her cheek. Just thinking about what Nile wanted made her feel cold. "It's something to do with his gift. The things he sees. What they do to him. His gift tears him apart."

"You sound like you're awfully close to feeling sorry for him." Opal's mouth turned militant. "The universe has given him something special. He should appreciate that."

Opal couldn't understand that being psychic wasn't always a magnificent gift granted by the universe. Some people actually didn't want it. But what was the point in saying that again? It would just be a repeat of the conversation they'd had yesterday in the shop. "I'm not feeling sorry for him."

Opal leaned over to touch her hand. "Want me to read the letter for you?"

"God, no." If she couldn't handle it, how could she expect Opal to do it for her? Pearl reached into her purse where she'd dropped it by the side of the couch, pulled out the thin envelope by the corner as if it were a scary spider and set it on the coffee table. "I just want you to hold it until I'm ready."

"What will make you feel ready?"

She sniffed. "When I think I can read it without losing myself."

Then her very intuitive sister asked about the other thing Pearl had been wanting to avoid. "Do you want to take him back?"

Pearl quirked her mouth. "Maybe." Then a tear slipped over the rim of her eye. "Pretty stupid, huh, a guy walks out after giving you the most incredible orgasm of your life and just never comes back."

Opal gasped and covered her mouth. "He did what?"

Dipping her head, Pearl stared into her half-empty mug. Afraid of what she might see, she was glad Opal had used a tea bag instead of leaves. "He came back after one of those trips." One of those awful trips where he arrived on a scene far too late to help the victim. She'd known it was bad, felt the darkness trying to steal over him, steal him from her. "He made love to me. I don't think I've ever felt anything quite like it. I thought all he had to do was touch me and it made everything better for him."

"What happened?" Opal's voice was just a coaxing whisper.

The darkness won. "He was gone in the morning. He left a note." She bit her lip. "All it said was goodbye."

Opal squeezed her hand. "Dirty rat bastard," she whispered. "Repeat after me."

"Dirty rat bastard." Pearl sniffed. "Evil slimy worm."

"That's my girl." Opal picked up the plate of lemon

bars and waved them under Pearl's nose. "At least you got the incredible orgasm before he left. Some men skip that part altogether."

Pearl laughed for the second time that night. Opal was interjecting Grandma Blue humor. Another person might have thought the comment callous. But her sister was the furthest thing from callous. She simply knew that laughter was the best healer. Coming to Opal had been the best thing to do. Pearl felt herself opening up after all these months rather than slipping deeper into a morass of self-pity.

"Somehow, Opal, you always know just the right thing to say so I don't feel like bawling anymore."

Opal tapped her forehead again. "Old sixth sense, you know. And I'll keep the letter for you until you're ready."

Pearl wasn't sure she'd ever be ready. But she wouldn't be completely over Nile until she read whatever was in it.

PEARL, AFTER ANOTHER CUP of tea, half a lemon bar and a hot bath scented with lavender, had slept in the other half of Opal's queen-size bed. Opal couldn't let her sister go home in that overwrought mental state. But a good night's sleep had done wonders. Or maybe it was getting it all out last night. Whatever, Pearl's step seemed to have an ounce more bounce when they'd opened the shop this morning, and right now, she'd dashed off to the post office before it closed.

Speaking of closing time, Opal glanced at her watch. What was taking Pearl so long? In half an hour, Opal had to pick up Grandma Blue for their trip to the overpass, and she needed Pearl to close up the shop. She could only hope Nile didn't come while Pearl was alone.

All day, Nile Montgomery's letter had screamed at Opal from the depths of her purse. She was glad the dirty evil slimy rat bastard worm had sealed the envelope or she would have read it. And probably gone postal. As it was, she definitely thought about ripping it to shreds.

Focused intently on the image of tearing Nile Montgomery limb from limb if he put one foot inside the shop, Opal startled when the phone rang. Then she pounced. Jack! The immediate reaction showed subconsciously how he'd been in her thoughts all day right behind her guilt over Pearl and anger with Nile.

"Yes, I'm here." *I'm dying to see you tonight.*

"I'd like to speak with Miss Opal Smith."

Not Jack. The male voice was soft, a little quivery, suggesting old age and uncertainty. "This is she."

"Dear, this is Victor Patell. I was just wondering if you'd had a chance to talk to—" he hesitated, then plunged on "—to find someone to help me with my séance."

Julian hadn't returned her messages, and she'd forgotten all about Victor while dealing with Pearl. She should have called again last night before going to bed because Julian never got in until after eleven, at least not on weeknights. First there was taping the show, then the L.A. nightlife he couldn't resist.

"I'm so sorry, but I haven't yet." Niggles of guilt twisted her insides.

"Oh." Something deflated in his voice. "Oh."

"But I haven't stopped trying, Mr. Patell."

"Call me Victor. Please." His tone distracted, his words sounded automatic. "Well, if you could let me know as soon as possible…" His hope seemed to trail off with his words.

"I promise. I'm going to make some calls right away."

He sighed. Moments passed. "Thank you." Something more hung in the odd, breathy silence. "I'm truly counting on you, my dear. I don't think you can know how much."

Guilt, guilt, guilt. Victor was surely worrying about mortality, with losing his wife only months ago, then being involved in an accident, hospitals, doctors…. "I'll do my best," she promised.

"Thank you."

"I'll call you as soon as I know."

"You're very kind."

His soft goodbye and the click of the phone in her ear sounded so desolate, it tore at her heartstrings.

This time she left Julian a dire message. "I know what you did, Julian, and you better call me back or you'll be sorry."

Cryptic but effective. He'd have to call back now just to find out what she was talking about. Then she'd get him up here to contact Victor's wife, even if she had to resort to blackmail. Such as refusing to monitor his stock portfolio.

VICTOR RUBBED HIS CHEST right over his heart.

The entry hall clock chimed the half hour, its tones reverberating through the marble foyer. One after another, his many windup clocks followed suit. Purposely he'd timed them all to trail each other so that the entire process took over five minutes. He'd wanted sound filling the empty mausoleum of a house once Prudence was gone. And winding his clocks was the only thing he managed to do effectively these days.

What was he to do without Prudence's advice? How was he to decide the best course of action on his own? Victor's body shuddered with anxiety and indecision.

"Is something wrong with your heart, Grandfather?"

Jolted, Victor slammed his knee against the side drawer of his leather-topped desk.

Darius. The chimes had masked his footsteps on the marble hall's floor.

"Not to worry. I'm fine." Victor let go of his chest, but there was something wrong with his heart. Very, very wrong. He was failing Prudence in the worst way. Because even now, looking at Darius, he couldn't find it in himself to love the boy.

Though he wasn't a boy. At thirty-three, Darius was a man full grown. Still, there was something fascinatingly youthful about his blond good looks and unlined face. The features of an angel, the slender build of an artist or a musician.

It brought to mind Oscar Wilde's *The Picture of Dorian Gray*, where all Dorian's sins had been reflected on his painting instead of his face.

Oh, traitorous thoughts. Why did he have these awful feelings about Darius? Why couldn't he care for the boy, his own flesh and blood?

"You were thinking of Grandmother again, weren't you?" Darius pulled out the leather chair opposite, sat, hitched his trouser leg, then crossed his legs. "I'm so sorry. I wish there was something I could do."

Victor searched for some emotion in his grandson's pale blue eyes. But his gaze lacked emotion just as his forehead was devoid of lines. Darius had spent the months since Prudence's death trying to console him.

Yet the harder Darius tried, in that odd detached way of his way, the more Victor was repelled.

"I've never known the kind of love you had, Grandfather. I can't imagine what it would be like to lose it."

How could Victor explain? He wasn't sure Darius would recognize it even if it came to him. In his heart of hearts, he honestly believed the boy had arrived on their doorstep a year ago because he'd learned his grandparents had money. A lot of money. How did you help someone like that? How did you make them understand love when they'd never known it? Yet with his promise to Prudence, he couldn't abandon the boy.

Because they *were* flesh and blood. Upon Darius's return, Victor had insisted on the test despite Prudence's objections. She'd simply wanted to believe.

"I do miss her. But I have you and that helps." It was a lie, but he'd been mouthing platitudes since the day the boy came home with the story that he'd searched the Internet for his birth parents, but had found his grandparents instead.

Victor was never sure how the Internet had scrounged up the information, but Prudence wouldn't allow any questions. Not after the test had proven the blood relation.

Darius leaned forward to cover Victor's hand with his. Victor felt a chill to his marrow.

"You're such a good man, Grandfather. But I don't know how you go on. I really don't."

Neither did Victor. He so needed Prudence. Prudence had loved the boy unconditionally from the moment he rang their doorbell. She would tell *him* how to love Darius.

"If only she hadn't died." Victor didn't realize he'd

spoken aloud until Darius squeezed his hand. It was meant to be comforting, but it ached in his old bones.

"I'd understand if you just couldn't take it anymore. I really would. You must want to be with her so badly."

Be with her? He did want that badly. But Darius couldn't mean really being with her. That would necessitate…suicide, something Prudence would abhor. No, his grandson was just offering sympathy, something he obviously hadn't learned how to do well. Though he didn't want to, he patted Darius's hand. "I'll survive this. We both will."

Darius glanced at his knees. "I'm here for you, Grandfather, to help you in any way I can."

But Darius hadn't helped in any way he could. When Victor had suggested they do family counseling, Darius said he didn't believe in shrinks. When Prudence was alive, the situation was tolerable. Then, in the first few months after her death, Victor had grieved so inwardly that he hadn't paid attention to Darius. Now, he remembered his duty to Prudence, his promise.

Perhaps if he saw it from Darius's point of view. But when he thought about the life the boy must have led, he felt only his own guilt. He'd allowed his flesh and blood to be abandoned to God only knew what. He didn't know what, but he should have done something, looked more into Rita's death, into Rita's life, something that would have revealed she had a child. Darius had never really said what his life had been like. He seemed polished, charming and strangely well-bred despite having been raised in foster homes. He claimed to have worked his way through college, but he'd been very vague about his work history. Since coming home, six months before Prudence died, he hadn't looked for a job. He'd said it was so that he could be there for Prudence, and Prudence had been ecstatic to have him. He'd eased her passing in some indefinable way. Victor had been grateful for that.

"You were the best thing that happened to Prudence since..." He couldn't finish the sentiment.

Prudence had had such tragedy in her life, losing Rita, their only daughter, wondering what they'd done wrong that she'd turned to drugs. She'd only been twenty-two when she ran away. Then there were the years of constantly contacting psychics and private detectives to find her. Prudence had tried everything. For seven long years, she hadn't given up hope.

Darius sighed. "I know how Tamara's disappearance must bring back the awful memories of the time my mother ran away."

God. How, even in his own misery, could he forget poor Tamara even for a second? When George had called last Friday begging his help, he'd felt his closest friend's anguish as if it were his own. Yet he'd been unable to give George true comfort. "Yes, yes, it does bring it back."

"It must make you relive it all. I don't know how you can bear it."

"Only with your understanding." Another lie to heap upon the many he'd told. He'd called in Nile Montgomery to help. With Victor's prayers, the young man was now out searching. Just as Nile's father Franklin Montgomery had searched for Rita.

Their daughter had run away almost thirty-five years ago. For seven years, they'd searched to no avail. Then

Prudence discovered Franklin Montgomery, famed for finding missing loved ones. If only she'd come across Franklin earlier. Perhaps they would have found Rita before it was too late, before she'd died of that drug overdose within days of Franklin's tracking her down. Lord, that day would forever live in his mind.

"Grandfather, are you all right? I'm sorry. I shouldn't have brought it up."

He tore himself away from the memories. "No, no, my boy. I appreciate your concern for Tamara."

Victor still didn't quite understand why Franklin hadn't found the boy, too. Upon Darius's miraculous appearance, Nile had surmised that his father had been tuned to Rita and Rita's debilitated drug state had precluded her own son. In other words, Rita had been so involved with her own misery that she had nothing to spare for the boy, not even a thought or image for Franklin to pick up on.

It had taken Prudence years to recover from their loss. The wasted years. The awful, terrible wasted years.

Then Darius had arrived.

"You were the light of her life in those last months." He wasn't seeing the room or Darius, only Prudence's soft grateful smile, as if Rita had finally come home. "I can't thank you enough for that, my boy."

Which was why Victor would take care of his grandson, he would love him, he would keep his promise to Prudence.

He owed that to his wife and daughter. And to his grandson.

CHAPTER SEVEN

JACK KNEW HE SHOULD HAVE called Opal earlier to confirm he'd meet her as usual for her trek across the godforsaken overpass. She'd gone there without him. Worse, she'd gone with Grandma Blue, who now sat in Opal's rental car watching the overpass. That alone was serious torture.

"This is Opal's gig, boy. If you wanna hang around this overpass, you gotta hang with me here in the parking lot. Not out there with her."

Grandma Blue's militant glare made him hesitate. Jack crouched down by the open passenger side window and began to reason with the little lady.

"She was going to meet me at the construction site just as we did the other two nights, but she didn't show like she was supposed to." Nor had she answered her cell phone when he realized she wasn't coming. He nearly had a freaking brain meltdown racing to the park-'n'-ride thinking she was all alone. Not that Grandma Blue constituted protection.

Grandma Blue smirked. "The way I heard it, you got snippy with her, and she didn't think *you'd* show up."

Guilt spiked through his chest. Snippy was as good a description of his conduct as any. "I work at the site. I have to show up."

She waggled her eyebrows. "Don't get hoity-toity with me."

He sighed. Arguing about who said what to whom wasn't getting him where he wanted to go. He needed an ally in Grandma. Maybe together, they could get Opal to give up her vision quest. It was as good a solution to protecting her as any that had occurred to him. "You do realize that every car out there is chock-full of guys trying to hit on her."

She raised a barely visible white eyebrow. "Not *every* car. Every other one. She's a mighty fine-looking girl, so of course, they're admiring the view. I would expect no less of my granddaughter. Especially in shorts."

He followed Grandma Blue's gaze to Opal in a butt-hugging pair of shorts. Thank God they didn't actually show her cheeks. Now that really would have given him meltdown. "Holy Hell."

"You can say that again," Grandma Blue sighed with satisfaction. "I used to have a butt like that, you know. My dear departed, God rest his soul, married me for my butt. Isn't that sweet?"

Jack ignored the unimaginable image and tried again, with the extreme patience he hadn't had the foresight to use last night. "Haven't you given any thought to the idea that perhaps one of those guys might pull Opal into his car and kidnap her?"

Grandma Blue pulled down her wraparound sunglasses and eyed him over the rim. "Why are you talking to me like I'm a retard?"

"I didn't think I was."

"Well, you are, so cut it out. And think about this,

chum. It's the middle of rush hour, there's at least twenty-five cars on that bridge, and even if someone did grab her and pull her in their car—which I seriously doubt they'd do—they *ain't* going anywhere." She pushed the glasses back up her nose. "So get your head out of your butt."

He didn't know whether to laugh, cry or beat his fist against the roof of the car. "But what if I wasn't here, and it was just you and Opal?"

She had him again, lifting her modular cell phone up in front of his face. "Bet my cell phone's smaller than yours."

Damn, the old lady had him on every count. Nothing left to do but take his head out of his butt, as she suggested. Even if Opal was grabbed, no one was taking her anywhere in all that traffic, not before he could drag her back to safety or Grandma Blue could call 911.

So much for protection being his motive for meltdown. That left just idiocy or jealousy. And the unrelenting fear that he'd arrive too late. Hell and damnation. His meltdown was as much about saving himself from another catastrophe as it was about doing right by Opal.

Grandma Blue suddenly shoved the door open and banged him in the knee. "Oops, sorry. Didn't realize you were so close."

Jack stood, resisting the urge to rub his kneecap, then held out a hand for Grandma Blue.

"Do I look decrepit? I can get out on my own." And she did, quite nimbly. Her blue-flowered muumuu billowed in the breeze. At a little less than five feet, she barely reached his armpit, and from this angle, the glint of sunlight on her blue hair damn near blinded him. Then she looked up, her wraparounds much too big for her face and turning her into…a space alien.

"Let's sit in your truck. It's higher up, and I can see better. Plus you managed to find the only tree in this lot."

Jack had parked two spaces closer to the stairs. "Sounds good to me."

"Besides, I've always loved those Dodge Ram trucks. They're just so…" She cocked her head, searching for the right word. "Sexual, that's it."

If he'd been eating or drinking, Jack would have choked. "Yes," he finally managed, "I've always thought the same thing."

"Opal finds 'em orgasmic, too."

He tried to show no reaction to that one, since reaction was exactly what Grandma Blue wanted.

She turned abruptly, peering through the wraparounds. "Guess she hasn't told you that yet, though, has she? That girl's always been reticent about revealing licentious thoughts."

"But you?" He let the question hang, while his mind flirted with the licentious things he'd like to do with Opal.

Grandma moved down between the cars and waited at the passenger side for him to unlock it. "Well, I suppose in my youth, I did watch a little bit more what I was saying." She patted him on the arm. "But there's one really nice thing about growing old…" She paused dramatically.

Jack filled in the gap for her. "And what's that?"

"You don't give a damn what you say or who you say it to. You don't even care what other people think anymore. It's very liberating. Sort of like passing gas in a five-star restaurant, pointing to the guy at the next table, saying 'he did it' and waiting for the fallout."

Well, there certainly was something to be said for not caring about what other people thought. Jack unlocked the door, then looked down at the length of Grandma Blue's legs. Even with the running board, there was no way she'd make it.

She looked up at him. "I'm not missing my chance to sit in a Dodge Ram," she said mutinously.

"Let me think."

But Grandma Blue wasn't giving him a chance to back out. "Okay, I'll put my foot there, then I'll hang on here, then you put your hand on my butt and push when I tell you to."

The thought of putting his hand on Grandma Blue's rear made the blood rush to his head. But the lady was a force to be reckoned with.

And she was counting down. "Okay, one, two, three, push."

Jack did, and Grandma Blue, being far lighter and stronger than he'd expected, flew into the front seat of his cab, her head coming perilously close to the dash.

"I'm in." She gave him a beatific smile exactly like Opal's. With all her outrageousness, she charmed him. She made him wish he'd had a grandmother—or a mother—just like her. She made him wonder what it would have been like to be part of a normal family, despite the fact that Grandma Blue was anything but normal.

Before shutting the door, he looked at her. "Do you think your granddaughter's going to be like you when she gets to be your age?"

"That girl will be worse."

"Then I think I just might ask her to marry me as soon as she gets off that damn bridge."

Grandma Blue pinched his cheek. "I'd marry you myself if you weren't young enough to be my grandson." She put a hand over her heart. "Oh, what Dynamite missed when he didn't find me in his last life."

Yeah. Poor Dynamite.

JACK WAS BACK! That fact had buoyed Opal for at least half an hour.

But that half hour had ended an hour ago.

Now Opal was tired, she was cranky and the platform shoes Grandma Blue had insisted she wear would not be easy to run in. Upon arriving at her grandmother's house, the running shoes she'd had on were nixed in favor of four-inch platforms.

The refrain went something like this. "No self-respecting granddaughter of mine with legs as gorgeous as yours is going to cop out to comfort, especially while wearing those tightie-tight shorts." It wasn't as if they were *short* shorts, but Opal had given in. She always gave in to Grandma Blue.

Now, however, she just wanted all those leering pimply teenage boys in their lowrider cars to disappear from the face of the earth.

Oh thank goodness, no one could eavesdrop on her thoughts. Except God, of course. But then He knew she didn't mean it.

He also knew that the only thing that kept her from marching down off this bridge was the fact that Grandma Blue was sitting in Jack's truck. Even more than verifying her vision, this whole thing had become about staying power. Or who's right and who's wrong. Or the whole woman-on-top thing. Jack thought he knew what was best. Jack didn't. Simple as that. She had not lost it. She'd had a vision.

"Hey, baby, how much to—" expletive, expletive. Very bad expletive. Not that she hadn't used the word before in one of her more than mildly irritated moods, but still... She needed to resonate positive energy and rid herself of all these negative vibes. Opal believed in the metaphysical premise that you created your own reality by the thoughts and feelings with which you resonated. Okay, resonate with tolerance and love. She kept walking with her head held high.

The other thing bothering her, of course, was Pearl. If Nile Montgomery had stepped into the store, Opal would have blown him away with her Uzi. If she'd had an Uzi. He was damn lucky she didn't. Her own homicidal tendencies didn't help Pearl's problem. Nor did telling her sister she better not take the dirty evil slimy rat bastard worm back under any circumstances seem like the smartest thing to say. Men.

"Hey, girl, love the shoes."

The universe didn't work in mysterious ways. It was almost predictable. Resonate with love and you attracted lovely ladies such as these admiring her shoes. With identical saucer-size hoop earrings set against big, *big* hair, and shorts that were far shorter and tighter than Opal's own garb, the three women crowded around admiring Opal's footwear.

"Where'd you get 'em?"

"My grandmother's closet. She saved them from the seventies." Retro shoes. Did the teens of today know the seventies had already invented bell-bottom pants, platform shoes and ugly lime-green sweaters? Or was that the sixties? Personally, she thought the forties had the cream of the crop. The suits those women wore were classic and sexy all at the same time. And they did wear short shorts, believe it or not, albeit without going so far as to reveal their butt cheeks.

A police car rolled by in the opposite lane, then disappeared on the downside of the hill. So cops weren't above giving a girl the once-over, either. Her gaggle of ladies skedaddled in the opposite direction. Hmm, could they be…? Yes, they probably were.

"Hey, baby, you swallow?" Why did these—she sighed, thinking of the kindest description—nice young men all call her baby, as if the title had somehow been stored in the universal knowledge banks? If Jack called her *baby*, that might be nice, but with these rotters it was more like calling her a… Resonate with tolerance, she reminded herself.

"Swallow what?" Probably not the best thing to ask, but luckily the light changed and the car moved on.

Resonate with love. Another police car passed, moving at far less than the posted speed limit as the two young cops gave her the once, twice and thrice-over. She tried smiling, thought about waving, then decided against it and resonated with more love and tolerance instead.

Did anyone really know how difficult that was when your platform shoes seemed to be made of hardwood instead of nice soft suede and cushiony rubber soles? And if she really thought about it, this was all Jack's fault.

Resonate with love and tolerance.

It was his doubting energy that was making it take

so long for the vision to come true. It should have happened in a couple of days. First he'd messed up her energy by kissing her, thereby making her lose sight of the goal. Then last night, with his grumpiness, he'd squashed her positive energy with his negative.

Resonate tolerance and love.

On this smog-infested overpass? She was trying, really she was. She simply didn't have the patience of either a saint or Grandma Blue.

"Miss?"

Oh, please, no. Not her little friend again. She looked down, and yes, there was that familiar bald spot.

Tolerance and love. With firmness. "Sorry, not tonight."

"Tomorrow night?"

"Not then, either."

"When?" He scratched the top of his head and displaced a very bad last-minute comb-over that did not work in any way, shape or form. Hmm, he hadn't had that the other two nights. Had he been working on ways to impress her?

Good Lord. She gritted her teeth. Tolerance. Love. Okay, she'd be happy if she could at least maintain a civil tone.

"I'm afraid the answer is never." There, that was civil. It wasn't the little man's fault. It was all the others that came before him.

"Do you think you'll change your mind?"

Why couldn't a girl just say no without having to explain?

He waited, his feet in brown penny loafers—she didn't know they still made penny loafers—and guilt got the better of her.

"Look, it's not you personally."

"It's because I'm short." He said it without looking up, which, of course, made him look even shorter because all she could see, all she'd ever seen, was the top of his head.

"I love short men. But I'm working with a different goal here, and you just don't…fit it," she finished lamely, wishing she'd never started explaining at all. Because saying he didn't fit in had to be something the little guy had heard all his life.

And so, she'd crushed him. So much for resonating with love. Or even tolerance.

"I REALLY DON'T LIKE that little guy," Jack muttered, watching the short fellow once again approach Opal. He put his hand on the door. "What's he want?"

Grandma Blue grabbed his arm. "Get real, bub. He's about as dangerous as a baby with poopie diapers. Besides, she's handling it."

Where did she come up with these analogies? Jack wasn't swayed and narrowed his eyes at her. "I don't trust him."

"She told me about him. He's just a sorry man who wants a date. If you go charging up there, you'll damage her sense of independence."

"He could be carrying a gun or a knife or a—"

"Are you PMSing, Dynamite?"

"Women PMS."

"Then it must be SRH."

"SRH?"

"Semen retention headache."

Just when he thought Grandma Blue could no longer

shock, she threw out a zinger. He spluttered, but not a word came out.

"He hasn't got a knife, and he's harmless."

Maybe it was his own need to slay giants for Opal that had him wanting to rush to her side. But Blue—and Opal—were right, the guy wasn't a giant he had to bring down. So he pushed the button to unroll his window and Grandma Blue's to let the warm breeze flow over him. It didn't help his muddled mind, though it did feel good. Like Opal's fingers lightly brushing his skin.

But he was here to work on Opal's behalf, not fantasize about her fingers on his flesh. "Grandma Blue, we've got a problem, you and I." It seemed you always moved closer to your own goal when you made it someone else's, too.

"And what's that, Dynamite?" She lowered her glasses and fluttered nearly nonexistent eyelashes at him.

"You and I both know that Opal isn't going to find her vision up there on that overpass."

"We both know that?"

He glanced from the little lady's blue tint to Opal and back again. "Yes, both of us." He paused dramatically. Grandma Blue believed he was Dynamite Davis. So why *wouldn't* she believe in Opal's vision? Except that somewhere deep in his gut, something suggested the old bird was pulling a scam.

"I'm listening."

"When her vision isn't proved, she'll be heartbroken."

Grandma Blue's lips twitched. "Yeah."

"If we find a way to make her forget about this vision and get her down off that bridge, we'll save her all that heartache."

It would have been nice if the little lady took off the alien glasses so he could gauge her expression, but she didn't. She could have been staring at Opal, who'd reached their end of the overpass once again, or she could be scrutinizing him. The back of his neck prickled as if someone had walked over his grave. Having Grandma Blue try to see inside his head was downright terrifying. But he remained just as he was.

Then she smiled, and Jack didn't know if he'd won her over or he was about to be snookered big-time.

"I have an absolutely marvelous plan brewing," she crooned.

If it saved Opal, he'd do it. "What's your idea?"

"Hold it, hold it." She closed her eyes and massaged her temples beneath the sunglass stems. Then she flashed him a wicked smile. "I've got it. You have to get inside my granddaughter's bloomers."

Just about now, a sane man might start bashing his head against the steering wheel. But he wasn't sane— being here was proof of that. "And that will make her forget about her vision…why?" He spread his hands.

"Hot nooky makes a girl forget everything."

He eyed her wizened cheeks. "How old did you say you were, Grandma Blue?"

"Young enough to remember lust and old enough to talk about it."

"I just didn't think women of your—" her frown said watch-it-pal "—generation thought like that."

"*Every* generation thinks that way. Why do you think there were babies born out of wedlock?"

Not to mention that she freely admitted her husband had married her for her butt. "All right. Hot nooky is the plan."

He'd already tossed out the idea of bashing his head on the steering wheel, and he knew he was no longer sane. So what the heck? Getting pointers from Grandma Blue might be a good idea.

Eyes on Opal's delectable rump up there on the ramp, he went for broke. "Just how would you suggest I get in her bloomers?" Whatever it took to get Opal's mind off her need to prove her vision. All right, there was a lascivious side benefit.

"You got any chocolate?"

"No, sorry."

"I feel like some chocolate ice cream."

"You can have ice cream after Opal's done up there."

"With those little colored sprinkles on top?"

"Wouldn't be an ice cream without 'em."

"You buying?"

"My treat."

"Okay. First, you gotta stop telling her what to do."

"I haven't told her what to do."

Grandma Blue lowered her alien sunglasses so he could see her roll her eyes at him. "Men disapprove with a look. You know, that long-suffering sigh accompanied by a sort of half-masted eyelid thing."

Hmm, that seemed genuinely female to him. Especially the sigh. "So, don't tell her what to do."

"And stare at her breasts."

"I thought women hated that."

She gave him the above-the-glasses eye roll again, then pushed the glasses back up her nose for punctuation. "Women love it. They're just not ever going to admit it."

"Okay, one, don't tell her what to do. Two, stare at her breasts. What's next?"

"Oh and remember, when you're staring at her breasts, get all sort of dreamy and salivating."

Salivating. He could do that. He'd already done that. A lot. "Got it."

"Then, tell her she's smart, and *don't* tell her she's milquetoast with her family."

His eyes seemed to jerk from Opal's pretty butt to Grandma Blue's alien wraparound glasses. Did the old gal think she was psychic, too? A mind reader, maybe, because he sure as hell couldn't remember voicing that thought aloud to Opal last night.

"Don't worry, you never said it. But I'm seventy-six years old, and you don't get to that age without being able to read the looks on people's faces." She harrumphed. "Besides, it's true. She is milquetoast." She turned and wagged a finger at him. "Which is exactly why you shouldn't tell her that. Women don't want to hear the truth."

"You know, Grandma Blue, I'm having doubts about you. Women always say they want the truth. It's their biggest complaint when they dump you."

She flashed him a sly smile. "Been dumped, have you?"

His turn to roll his eyes. "A time or two."

"Well, take my word for it, they want the truth, but only if it's not about them."

"Okay, don't tell her the truth. Check."

"And finally, keep kissing her the way you did out front of my house the other night."

Now *that* he could do.

"WE'RE GOING FOR ICE CREAM." Grandma Blue seemed to bounce on the front seat of Jack's truck like a child.

Opal wanted to sag against the door, but she reminded herself to resonate with energy. Besides, Grandma Blue seemed to be having the time of her life.

And Jack was staring with something dark, seething and volatile in his eyes. With Grandma Blue between them, Opal couldn't tell whether it was anger or something else.

"I didn't expect to see you here, Jack." In her heart of hearts, she was so glad.

"Find anything?"

He knew she hadn't. This was his way of turning the tables on her. She gave him a bright smile belying the ache in her feet, her head and her exhaust-numbed nose. Really, how did ladies of the night do it? "Nothing yet, Jack, but thank you so much for asking."

"Will you two quit fighting? I want ice cream. Dynamite's buying."

"We're not fighting." Opal wasn't sure what they were doing.

Opal spared a glance for Jack, who gave an imperceptible nod, and suddenly she wanted that ice cream more than anything else in the world. At least until she went back out on the overpass tomorrow night, at which point, she'd pray her vision jumper would attempt to make his jump, because she just wasn't sure she could make it through another night out there.

"Come on, Grandma Blue, we'll follow Jack over."

Grandma Blue pursed her lips militantly. "Dynamite doesn't know where my favorite ice-cream shop is. I've got to give him directions. Besides, I've never driven in a Dodge Ram before. It's like driving as high up as a bus. Bet he can see right down onto the laps of ladies sitting in the passenger seat and wearing short skirts." She turned to Jack. "Can't you, Dynamite?"

Jack didn't even bat an eye at the outrageous question. Which meant he'd probably gotten an earful of Grandma Bluisms over the last two hours and was inured to the effect of them. He merely smiled and said, "You'd be surprised how far a short skirt will ride up. And at what some of the ladies *aren't* wearing."

Was that level look meant for her? Opal thought maybe there was a certain sizzle there that sent an answering shiver straight to the tips of her toes.

"Let's go." Grandma Blue bounced once again in her seat.

Pulling her keys from her bag, she wondered what Grandma Blue had up her sleeve this time.

Opal knew where they were going and got there first. The shop was crowded due to the warm June evening. She pulled a ticket, then cased the counter to see what she wanted. Barrels and barrels of every ice cream imaginable. She almost knocked over a little kid who got in her way. His dad pulled him back with a sharp look at Opal.

The hair ruffled at her nape, and she smelled Jack, some woodsy cologne and warm male skin. "What are you having?"

Your-lips-on-my-neck double scoop, please. She almost closed her eyes and sighed. He barely touched her, but she felt him down the length of her back, her thighs and everywhere in between. Gee, with Jack so near, the ache in her feet didn't seem quite so bad.

"Butter pecan."

"Like the nuts, huh?"

She glanced over her shoulder to find his lips dangerously close, and that was definitely not anger in his sizzling-hot chocolate gaze.

Whatever bug he'd had up his hind-end last night had certainly worked its way out.

She almost missed their number. "Over here."

Grandma Blue ordered first. "Single scoop double fudge chocolate caramel swirl on a sugar cone with sprinkles on top. And don't be chintzy with the sprinkles, either."

Opal got her butter pecan, and Jack ordered vanilla.

"Just plain vanilla?" Grandma Blue demanded.

"I like vanilla."

She eyed him, looking like a little gnome. "Dynamite's favorite was vanilla."

Opal wanted to laugh and suddenly the oppressive energy of the last two hours lifted. She was sure Grandma Blue hadn't a clue what flavor ice cream Dynamite Davis preferred.

Once outside again, the sun was going down, but the heat still rose from the concrete, warming her legs.

Without warning, Grandma Blue elbowed Jack in the stomach.

"Oomph." He almost lost his ice cream off his cone. "What?"

A look passed between them, one Opal couldn't assess due to the heavy tinting of Grandma Blue's glasses.

Then Jack was staring at *her*. At her breasts. As if she were a scoop of ice cream. Honestly, how could a woman stay angry when a man melted her with a look like that?

CHAPTER EIGHT

"I'LL COME IN WITH YOU, Grandma Blue." Opal turned to Jack, an easy smile on her face and a sparkle in her pretty eyes. "Thanks for the ice cream."

"You will do no such thing, Opal. I don't need a nursemaid making sure I get in the house all right."

"But—"

"No buts." The sunglasses had been stowed in the pocket of her muumuu, and Grandma Blue sent Jack one of those significant looks. All he did was smile. Which only made Opal seem to seethe.

"Now give me a kiss, dear." She raised her cheek for Opal's kiss. The weathered skin was dusted with a coating of powder a couple of shades too light for her skin, which added to that alien look she had going.

Then she shot him another glance. Outside the ice-cream store, it had meant "stare at Opal's breasts and salivate." Obedient to a fault, he had. He still was. Now her look meant, "kiss Opal."

He wasn't sure if Opal would have anything to do with him after his SRH attack last night.

Grandma Blue scurried up her walk, and once inside, set about closing all the blinds along the front rooms of the house. Supposedly to give them privacy. He'd bet his last dollar she'd peek through one of those closed-up windows just to make sure he was following her "absolutely marvelous plan."

Opal still stood on the sidewalk, one hand in her purse as she searched for her keys. The last of the light faded from the sky, and for just a moment, they were cocooned in the warm, fragrant June night.

"There'll be hell to pay from your grandmother if I don't kiss you."

"She told you to kiss me?"

"Among other things."

"What other things?"

"She told me you liked to have your breasts ogled."

Her hands went protectively to the cited objects. He salivated just the way Grandma Blue wanted him to, but not because she'd told him to. He simply couldn't help himself. Opal was edible.

He took three steps toward Opal, maneuvered her beyond the fall of light from the streetlamps in a replay of two nights ago. "Get in my truck."

"Why?"

"Because the windows are tinted, and she won't be able to see whether I kiss you or not."

Opal sucked in a breath. "*Are* you going to kiss me?"

He closed his lids, longer than a blink and less than a nap, and thought about the taste of butter pecan on her lips. "Oh, yeah, I'm going to."

"You know, that really isn't a good idea."

"Get in my truck."

"You said yourself that I'm crazy." But she climbed in when he opened the door for her. He thought about putting his hands on her behind, just for a little help.

She was still talking when he climbed in the other side. "We really have nothing in common."

"Come here."

"And you don't have to kiss me just because Grandma Blue told you to."

He grabbed her arms and pulled her halfway across the seat. "Shut up and kiss me."

Her eyes darkened to a sultry midnight blue, then she parted her lips.

Butter pecan and crunchy cone, all sweet and luscious and rich. She ended up in his lap, her arms wrapped around his neck like a limpet, and he let her take over the kiss. She nipped and tugged and licked, then made a tentative tongue foray into his mouth. A fire built low in his belly, and he twisted her to straddle his lap. Ah, God. She felt so good. He pressed himself between her legs, and with her sharp intake of breath against his lips, he knew she felt his hardness. Then she pushed down to meet him. His fingers found her magnificent breasts beneath that tiny tight top, and her nipples pebbled beneath his touch. Another sharp inhale, a hint of a moan, and she attacked his mouth, grabbing his head by the ears and holding him captive. She wriggled in his lap, then suddenly let go of his mouth and arched back, her breasts thrusting into his hands.

"Are you sure Grandma Blue can't see this," came out as almost a hiss and a moan.

"I'm sure." He rolled her nipple between his fingers and was rewarded with another healthy moan and the grind of her hips against him.

Suddenly getting her to give up her hopes for her vision was the furthest thing from his mind. He went up in smoke, pushing her back against the steering wheel and feasting on the column of her throat with lips and tongue.

The horn went off like a siren, and he didn't know if he'd sat on his car alarm or if that was a fire engine come to douse the flames.

Opal scrambled off his lap back into her own seat as he fumbled in his pocket until he found his key alarm and shut the damn thing off.

He looked at the dash. Three minutes. He'd almost lost it all in three minutes of being devoured by her.

"I think I killed some brain cells with that one," she said, and she could have meant the blare of the horn in her ear or the fire that had almost consumed them.

He swiped his hand through his hair and tried to slow his breathing. "Let's go to my house."

"No," Opal answered. Sure. Definite. No hedging.

Jack looked at her as if he couldn't possibly have heard right. "No?"

He'd heard right. Opal just wasn't absolutely sure she could stick by her determination for long. "It was just some weird aberration. I'm not sleeping with you."

"I don't want to sleep."

"You know what I mean."

"I know what you meant when you were kissing me."

Ooh, boy, this was a pickle. Why on earth had she jumped him like that? "I haven't had sex in over a year." She really didn't mind telling the truth. "And I forgot myself."

He looked at her as if she were a Martian. "A year?"

"I don't sleep around. He and I broke up a year ago."

Light sparkled in his eyes. "Serious relationship?"

"I thought so, he didn't." She had gotten over it

quickly, which meant she hadn't been so serious about him after all.

"Sorry." Jack exhaled a heavy breath. "That especially means we should go to my place."

"No." She didn't think she could say no too many more times without giving in. And ooh, boy, she wanted to give in badly.

He sighed, then put his head back against the rest, a wry smile curving his lips.

"Why are you smiling?"

He lifted his head and gazed at her. "I feel good."

"Why?" She looked pointedly down at the bulge in his pants.

"Because when you do finally decide to come home with me, it's going to be one helluva night."

She felt her eyes widen involuntarily. "But I just told you I'm not going to sleep with you."

He looked at her and didn't even bother to call her a liar. They both knew. Opal could only wonder what on earth she was resonating now.

BLUE CLOSED THE GAP in the blinds feeling all dreamy inside. The boy didn't want Opal's heart to be broken if her vision didn't pan out. And he'd sure jumped at Blue's absolutely marvelous idea to make the girl forget about her vision by getting inside her bloomers. No doubt about it, he was hooked.

Opal had gotten in her own car and driven away. But, what with the way that truck had rocked and rolled and the car horn screeched into the night, it wouldn't be long before her granddaughter was dynamite in Jack's hands.

Jack might not look like Dynamite, and he might not

be Dynamite's reincarnation, but with the look on that girl's face when she stumbled out of his truck, Jack Davis was nothing less than explosive.

NILE SHOWED UP when the clock struck midnight. Pearl knew it was him before she even opened her apartment door.

"You can't come in." She wanted to let him in so badly, her throat tightened up on the words.

"Let me talk to you, Pearl. Just for a little while. I promise I won't touch you."

Unless she asked him to. Unspoken, the words hung between them. They both knew what happened when he touched her. He'd always known just how to touch her physically even if she'd never known how to touch him emotionally. In that respect, Nile was unreachable.

"I need you, Pearl."

He didn't plead with his voice, but his eyes were like black holes in his face. If she wasn't careful, she'd lose herself in the emptiness there, just as she had before.

Her head told her to slam the door in his face and hide in her one-bedroom, one-bath, one-*person* apartment. Her heart made her open the door wider and let him in, the full sleeve of his black overcoat brushing her breast as he passed.

"Did you find Tamara?"

Something shuddered down his spine. "Not yet."

"You will, Nile." She had faith in his psychic ability even if she didn't have faith in his ability to love her.

He didn't turn, didn't accept her platitude.

She used another banality to ease her own tension.

"Coffee?" It would keep her busy for at least a few minutes while she marshaled her thoughts and her resistance.

He faced her, one hand in his coat pocket. "Brandy."

"You never used to drink."

"You just never saw me."

Wasn't that the crux of the problem, her problem? There were so many things he'd kept tightly locked inside, so many places he'd never let her go.

"Have a seat." She indicated the couch. When she sat, she'd take the wing chair, separate from him.

He removed his coat, throwing it across the back of the sofa. Beneath it, he was dressed completely in black. Nile always dressed in dark colors. On anyone else, it would have been pretentious. On Nile, it was simply a reflection of his personality. He sat on the sofa, putting one booted foot on top of the opposite knee. A relaxed position for most, but with Nile, it was only a facade.

She handed him a small brandy snifter, half-full, then took the wing chair. She'd poured herself a Baileys Original Irish Cream, allowing a few uncomfortable moments of silence, long enough to coat her lips and tongue with the sweet liqueur before she couldn't stand the quiet anymore. Her living room was small and with the beige curtains closed, she felt trapped with him.

"What do you need, Nile? Money?"

He gave a short bark of laughter, swirling the amber liquid in the glass before he answered. "I've always made my own way."

He had a trust fund from his father. All his time and energy went into his searches. She'd only asked the question as an opening. Or maybe to make him angry enough to leave her alone. "Then I'm at a loss."

"You haven't read the letter, have you?" He watched with dark predatory eyes. She'd always felt like Little Red Riding Hood beneath that wolflike gaze.

"Opal's holding it for me."

He assessed the liquid in his glass once more. "Why are you afraid of it?"

"I don't know." Which was not really a lie. There were so many reasons, she couldn't put her finger on any particular one.

He stood then, moved to the side of the couch, stroking the lace she'd thrown over the lamp to give the room a soft glow. Flicking the curtain, he closed a slight gap against the night. Her fireplace dominated the room, an array of brightly colored scented candles decorating the hearth. Pictures of her family adorned the mantel. There was still one of Nile and her at his house in Big Sur that she'd never taken down. He prowled the room like a big sleek cat, touching the brandy bottle she'd left on the cherrywood sideboard, lingering over a wildly flowered print she'd hung to pretend to the green thumb she didn't have.

"What are you doing, Nile?"

"Remembering."

She was afraid to ask. "Remembering what?"

"How much younger you are than me."

"Only ten years."

"At times, it seemed like a hundred." Between them, the difference had been vast. He turned abruptly. "Teach me how to be twenty-six and young again."

"I don't know if I remember myself, Nile." After a year spent loving him, she'd aged two decades.

He turned, looked at her, a thought softening his features. "I know I did that to you. And I'm sorry."

"It wasn't your fault." The darkness was simply his nature.

He covered the space between them in two slow strides, then towered over her beside the chair. She wanted to shrink into the cushion, and only with effort managed to remain just as she was. His fingers hovered along the planes of her cheek, a bare millimeter short of touching. Her heart raced, and her breath seemed to lodge in her throat.

"I didn't leave because I didn't love you. I left because I saw us dying, saw *you* dying."

"Don't be so melodramatic." But it was nothing short of the truth. His leaving had been the best thing for her. So what did his coming back mean?

He arched a dark brow. "That's me, Mr. Melodramatic." It was the closest Nile could come to a joke, a mixture of sarcasm and self-derision.

She still didn't know what he wanted, but heat sizzled between them. She was either going to scream, cry or throw herself at him.

He went down on his knees beside her, setting the now-empty brandy snifter on the coffee table. Taking her face between his palms, he ran a finger across her lower lip. The caress sparked a shiver deep inside.

"Make love to me, Pearl. Like you did the first time."

The first time. God. She'd given everything, and he'd taken. They'd both found pleasure, exhausted themselves with it, so much that they'd slept away the following day. But while he immersed her in a seductive, erotic world she'd never imagined, he'd also drained something from her, fed on her. It had always been like that with them, until she had nothing left to give, not even to herself.

His finger rubbed hypnotically, his dark scent filling her, his palms, their hold light yet still trapping her.

He dipped his head, and his lips took over where his finger had been. He sucked the sweetness of the Baileys from her mouth, until all she tasted was the headiness of brandy and desire. She wanted to put her arms around him, but almost as if drugged, she couldn't seem to move except to part her lips for him. And he fed on her, like a vampire, sucking the will from her. She'd do anything he wanted, for as long as he wanted, for...

He was gone, a cold seeping into her cheeks where his fingers had been.

His gaze above her was impenetrable. Her blood sang, her only thought to be back in his arms, to hold him deep inside her.

"That's what I really want, Pearl, your lips, your body, your heart, your soul. I shouldn't, but I can't help myself."

He sounded very much like the devil.

He trailed a fingertip across her jaw, leaving a path of sparks in the wake of his touch. "But this time I will give you something in return."

"What?" Her voice seemed to crack on the word.

"What you wanted. All the things I wouldn't give you before. All the things you begged me to share."

A fist squeezed her heart. She'd asked for something she was afraid she couldn't handle.

"You have to open the letter first."

It frightened her more than ever. "What's in it?"

"The darkness of my soul."

DARIUS HAD LEFT the house at 7:00 p.m. He still hadn't returned. At a little past one in the morning, Victor sat at his Queen Anne dining table, a steaming bowl of chicken noodle soup in front of him. Prudence bought the dining room set on their twenty-fifth wedding anniversary. He could have purchased her something much more expensive, elaborate, certainly something a cut above ready-made furniture from a department store. But Prudence had always shopped for the bargain. She'd done that when the most they could afford was a one-room walk-up. She'd done it after he made his first million. Prudence had done it almost to the day she died. You didn't live through the Depression and ever forget the meaning of frugality.

He'd give every cent he had just to talk to her again.

He'd been to more psychics than he cared to admit, but he'd never believed they were talking to Prudence. They said all the right words, almost verbatim what he told them, which was the problem. They didn't tell him anything he didn't already know. He might be old, but he wasn't senile. Some were slick as oil on a duck's back, some had excellent intuition, but the fact remained that he'd spoon-fed them all the answers. Prudence had never been there.

The front door opened. Victor stiffened. Then Nile appeared in the dining room doorway, and Victor's tension evaporated.

"Any luck?" Hope didn't flare in his chest. Nile didn't look as if he had good news.

And indeed, he shook his head. "I would have told Tamara's parents and informed the police if I had." His coat hung on his frame, his dark hair lay limp against his head. He looked…wilted.

"Where did you go?"

"San Francisco. The Tenderloin. I didn't see her."

Victor's heart tumbled. Nile was Tamara's only hope. George had called the police Saturday morning when Cecelia found that Tamara hadn't slept in her bed. She'd gone to bed early, supposedly, but in the morning she was gone. Clothing and her suitcase were missing, but the kicker came when evidence of drug use was found in her room. Though the police had courteously said they'd do everything possible to find Tamara, they'd probably thrown the report in the round file. In the ensuing days, Victor called the lead investigator several times to check the progress but nothing had moved forward. It was like Rita's disappearance all over again.

"Do you want some soup?" Victor rubbed his neck where a muscle had begun to tick. "There's some left in the kitchen."

"No, thanks."

When did he eat? Victor hadn't seen him do so. And if he didn't miss his guess, Nile had lost weight since Prudence's funeral seven months ago. Concerned about getting Nile over to the Whitley-Dorns house as soon as possible after he arrived on Saturday, Victor hadn't paid attention to the subtle changes in the young man.

"I'll try again tomorrow."

"You'd better get some rest."

Nile nodded and turned to the stairs. He'd been staying with Victor while he searched.

Victor was beginning to worry about him. Nile seemed to have lost something intrinsic. If he didn't know better, he'd say Nile suffered from the same paralysis of mind with which he himself was afflicted. Victor closed his eyes, feeling a sob rise to his throat.

He knew exactly how George Whitley-Dorn felt when his daughter went missing.

If he could contact Prudence, perhaps she'd have news of Tamara.

God help him. So many things in his life seemed to hinge on Prudence. *Please, God, help me talk to her.*

Maybe he'd be better off praying to God outright. But Victor had prayed for them all, Prudence, Rita, even Darius. It hadn't helped.

OPAL WOKE the next morning with wild excitement. Today was the big day; she knew it, she resonated with it, soared to the beautiful blue sky with the knowledge. Which was why she dressed in her favorite teal skirt.

Jack couldn't help but notice the shortness of the skirt—another reason she wore it. Not the only reason, of course. Teal was her color, made her cheeks glow and her hair shine like gold. It was a happy color, a feeling she had to exude for Pearl's sake. A battle color, too, in case Nile showed up.

"Do you have the letter?" Pearl wanted to know the minute Opal walked into the shop.

"It's in my purse. And I didn't open it."

"Good. Put it on the counter next to the coffee machine."

Opal did as instructed. "Why?"

"I want to get the sense of it whenever I walk by." Pearl's cool blue gaze gave nothing away.

"Let's burn it." Damn Nile Montgomery.

Pearl shook her head, and each time she went into the back room, Opal knew she sniffed the universe with her psychic senses for a clue as to the letter's contents.

Of course, Pearl could have just opened it.

Minutes then hours ticked away, Nile didn't show—a bit of a disappointment to Opal's fighting mood—Pearl gave four readings, and Opal made a killing in metaphysical book sales.

But she struck out with her brother, Julian. She'd left another umpteen million messages he failed to answer. Why hadn't threatening worked? She'd even called her mother to find out if she knew what was up with Julian, but Lillian didn't know a thing. Dammit. Poor Victor would have to wait another day.

Finally, it was time to leave for Grandma Blue's house. She'd insisted on coming along today.

"Take the letter," Pearl insisted.

Opal made no move to retrieve the envelope from the back room. "Will you be ready to read it tomorrow?"

"I'll meditate on it tonight."

"Don't let him in if he shows up."

Pearl merely stared with another unreadable gaze.

"I'll beat you black and blue if you let him in."

Finally, a smile creased her sister's face. "Why have you been leaving early the last few days?"

"What's that got to do with Nile and his letter?"

Pearl's smile reached her eyes. "Nothing at all." Then she tipped her head to the side and her focus seemed to fade.

"Don't you dare try reading me, little sister."

"I don't have to read you. Even a layman would know you're dressed up for a man. Hunky Construction Guy?"

"I am not dressed up for anyone." Opal tried for impassive. "At least not in the way you mean."

"Liar, liar, pants on fire," Pearl chanted softly.

So she hadn't fooled Pearl. She also knew after an hour on the overpass, she'd regret the platforms. But Grandma Blue was right, she couldn't cop out for comfort where impressing Jack was concerned. Darn. She wasn't supposed to want to impress, but facts were facts, she wanted him to drool.

Lest Pearl should see *that* written all over the universe, Opal grabbed her purse from the desk drawer and ran.

"Wait," Pearl called.

"I'm late." And she dashed out the door.

It wasn't until she was halfway to Grandma Blue's that she remembered Nile's letter, which she'd left on the back counter. Too late to go back, Pearl would have to deal with it. Maybe that was for the best.

"Now that's an outfit to seduce a man if I ever saw one," Grandma Blue quipped as she clambered into Opal's car fifteen minutes later. She'd dressed in a fresh muumuu right out of the plastic bag, the neat package folds still creasing the lemon-yellow flowers.

"I think you're dressed for seduction yourself. Have you got a crush on Jack, Grandma Blue?"

A loud harrumph emerged from her wrinkled lips. "An old woman can have her fantasies, too, you know."

When they arrived at the construction site, her eyes lit up like blue flames when Jack strode toward them in black jeans, black T-shirt molded to his mighty-fine chest and big leather work boots. A workman called his name. He stopped to give instructions, gesturing with his hands.

"I admire a man with authority and a nice ass," Grandma Blue said, already opening her door. "I'll drive with him."

Jack leaned in Opal's window. "You'll both drive with me."

Opal liked a man with an air of authority, too, especially accompanied by his very nice ass. She tingled in all the right places as his gaze dropped to the way her skirt had ridden a little too high on her thighs.

"I get to be in the middle." Grandma Blue skipped around the front end of the car as Jack opened the driver's door for Opal to get out.

His fingers skimmed Opal's arm. "So, are you ready for whatever may happen tonight?"

He felt it, too, the sense of something immense about to explode into the atmosphere, the independent verification of her vision. Opal wanted to skip the way Grandma Blue did. Maybe he actually believed her.

Then again, with the way his gaze raked her from her lips to her breasts to her bare legs below her skirt hem, maybe he wasn't referring to her vision at all.

Opal started resonating with something altogether different.

CHAPTER NINE

"Now that I've got you all to myself, Grandma Blue—"

"Call me Blue. That way, if I'm not looking in a mirror, I can pretend I'm thirty-something again and sitting in the front seat of Dynamite's white Corvette."

"Your Dynamite had good taste in cars." Jack was a truck man himself. See, he *couldn't* be Dynamite's reincarnation, though he didn't say that out loud.

Blue sighed. "He had good taste in everything. That's why it's such a shame he never met me."

"A downright crime against nature," he agreed.

The little lady shook herself, then gave him the most ridiculous imitation of a coquettish gaze, pouty too-red lips and big blue eyes in a garishly made-up face. She'd ditched the alien wraparound glasses tonight.

She batted monstrous fake eyelashes she certainly hadn't had affixed to her eyelids the night before. "Now, about you having me all to yourself…"

She hadn't worn those extensions for him, had she? Scary thought. He'd found a nice shady nook near the front of the park-'n'-ride, one with a clear view of Opal's grand apparel. Which did nothing to bring down the temperature inside the cab. It only made him think of last night. Her tongue in his mouth and her breasts against his palms was heaven on earth. He was in danger of setting off his alarm all over again.

Unrolling both windows didn't bring him the breeze he was dying for. Periodically, he'd turn on the engine to run the air-conditioning. It also did nothing for the heat in his jeans. He needed something to take his mind off Opal strutting her stuff along the overpass. Or Blue's unthinkable innuendos.

"Tell me why she calls you Blue. Something embarrassing, right?" It was probably nothing more than the tint of her hair.

She wagged a knobby finger at him. "Maybe, maybe not. I'd rather talk about those steamed-up windows in your truck last night."

"My windows weren't steamed up."

"Something was."

She was right about that. Watching Opal prance around in that itty-bitty teal skirt up there on the overpass made him believe in self-immolation. But he kept his mouth shut.

"Did you take her home with you?"

He drew his head back and stared down the length of his nose at her.

She remained unintimidated. "Well, did you?"

"I don't believe that's any of your business, Blue."

"Of course it is, she's my granddaughter."

"Then you'll have to ask her yourself."

She patted his hand on the console he'd pulled down between them after Opal had scrambled out. "Spoken like a true gentlemen. Dynamite wouldn't have told, either."

"Now, weren't you going to tell me about your nickname?" Actually, if silence were to reign in the cab of his truck, he could concentrate on Opal's petite figure and remember the feel of her tush in his hands last night.

Blue flashed him a grin. "Maybe it's my real name."

"You're pulling my leg."

She waggled her eyebrows and opened her mouth.

"Jesus, don't say it." He knew she was about to make a sexual innuendo and that would be...beyond the pale.

"Killjoy." Then she patted the top of her head. "My hair turned white with this weird sort of blue tint thing going on. Opal was just a little mite when I went through the change, and that's what she started calling me. Grandma Blue."

"I knew it! What's your real name?"

She batted those false eyelashes once more. "Godiva."

"Fibber."

"I'd show you my birth certificate, but then I'd have to kill ya so you don't go spreading around my real age."

"You mean you're not really—"

She shoved her palm at his face. "Talk to the hand."

He'd never met anyone like her. Young at heart didn't begin to describe the old lady. Maybe there was something to be said for being a little nuts. And Opal had the little lady's same joie de vivre. Except...he glanced at the overpass just as Opal made another turn. There was an edge of desperation to Opal's need to prove her vision real which made his gut roil.

"Are you going to lie for her about her vision?"

He did *not* believe the old lady had just read his mind. "I thought I was supposed to distract her by getting in her bloomers."

"What if she still won't give up?" A veteran eye-twinkler, there wasn't a trace of twinkle in the lady's eyes.

He couldn't answer. He'd never once encouraged his mother's delusions. He'd always tried to talk her out of them.

"She wants someone to believe in her."

"I believe in her." Jack beat his index finger against his thigh. "That doesn't mean I believe in her fantasies."

"Maybe that's what she really needs."

"She needs someone to accept her just as she is. Without all the hocus-pocus."

Blue pursed her lips as if to say he just didn't get it. "She needs someone to believe without making her prove anything."

Something slithered down his arms like a snake in the Garden of Eden. What would have happened to his mother if he'd simply told her he believed all her stories? Every single one. He'd never had that kind of unconditional acceptance in him. Nor, on second thought, did he believe it would have made a difference. "I'd rather convince Opal being psychic doesn't matter."

"That'd be like trying to convince a puppy not to chew up your slippers." With a mighty harrumph that shook the yellow flowers on her muumuu, she turned to stare through the windshield at her granddaughter. "Well, she's going to be disappointed tonight. And you better make it up to her."

Making it up to Opal seemed like a helluva tall order. "How am I supposed to make up for a lifetime of wanting to be something she's not?" Getting in Opal's bloomers wasn't going to be the answer.

Blue shot him a piercing blue glare, and he wondered

if that look was really the reason they'd nicknamed her Blue. "Tell her what she wants to hear."

"It's her family she wants to hear it from, not me."

"That's just an excuse. Dynamite never made excuses."

She hadn't even known Dynamite Davis.

"I need some air." He shoved the door open and stepped out into the sultry evening. Still no breeze, but it was better than the stifling cab, better than listening to Opal's grandmother asking *him* to become something he wasn't. He didn't believe. He would never believe. Believing was dangerous.

HER FEET SHOULD HAVE BEEN killing her, and the wretched fumes should be making her barf all over the roadway. But Opal bounced on her toes, fresh as an unused dryer sheet, because tonight was the night. She'd resonated with victory all day. The universe simply couldn't ignore her. She'd glowed with enthusiasm all evening.

With the first, "Hey, baby, wanna blow on my exhaust pipe?" she'd smiled and replied, "Your car needs a tune-up," then gave a pleasant wave as the car rolled down the hill to the light.

Bounce, bounce on her toes. Tonight, she'd prove to Jack that she wasn't crazy. And prove to her family that she, too, was gifted. Fighting-happy in her favorite teal skirt, she took on yet another vehicle loaded with scraggly-haired teenagers.

Why did they all seem to think she was a lady of the night just because her skirt was short? Whatever, nothing could bring her down. Besides, all the attention she was getting might make Jack a little jealous.

She was even polite and decent to her short friend,

the second time he showed up within the last half hour. Before he spoke, she smiled brightly and said, "I'd love to, but I can't."

"You're busy again?"

"I have a boyfriend." Jack wasn't her boyfriend, but what was a small lie to preserve the man's dignity?

"I only want to take you to dinner. We can be friends."

"I'm sorry. He's the jealous type and wouldn't understand." She smiled and turned her back. Goodness, was that a sniffle she heard? She whirled around, but he was already walking away, a speedy shuffle his short legs belied.

After passing her, a dented Nissan pulled into a gas station at the bottom of the overpass by the stoplight and two men got out. Were those bills they were waving at her? She flapped her hand dismissively and headed back toward Jack on the opposite end of the bridge as rapidly as her platform shoes would carry her. Not that she was afraid in this crush of traffic, but she decided she'd stick a little closer to him. The Nissan took off with a screech of tires followed by the aroma of burned rubber.

Jack's dark head appeared outside the truck, and Grandma Blue's hair gleamed blue-white in the sun as its rays meandered down on her. Her bodyguards. A girl couldn't feel any safer.

She couldn't fail, she just couldn't. She loved Grandma Blue more than anything, but her grandmother didn't understand how important this was to her. But the old gal was a doll for sticking by her in the still-hot early evening.

And Jack...well, Jack all gussied up in black was as hot as the summer day had been. How could she ever justify wrecking his beautiful black Dodge Ram—the repair of which the insurance company had still not authorized—if she didn't save a man's life?

Something tugged on the hem of her skirt. She squeaked and jerked around. The little guy gazed up at her hopefully. "I'll give you double your going rate."

"Please stop. I told you I'm not for sale." Really, she did have a perfect right to walk on this overpass without everyone thinking she was…trolling. A police car rolled by in the far lane. "I can call a cop, you know."

"I'm sorry. But this is really important to me."

She knew all about really important things and getting a girl you'd seen loitering on a sidewalk to have dinner—not to mention have sex—with you wasn't one of them. "I understand, but you have to stop doing this."

"But you *don't* understand."

She decided not to debate the point. "Don't you have a job or a wife or some friends, somewhere you're supposed to be?"

"Triple your usual rate?"

"No. You can't be asking women you meet on street corners to have sex with you." She thought about telling him that she was here only to save a man who would climb the overpass fence and try to jump to his death. But he wouldn't believe her about that any more than he believed she wasn't a hooker. She wasn't even sure Jack believed in her vision. And she didn't think telling the little man *her* goal would make any difference to *his* goal.

"All I really want is dinner."

Right. "That's what all men say. Now please, go away."

"Please, please."

There was nothing left but to crush his feelings completely. Only the blunt truth would keep him from coming back. Again and again. For his own sake, she had to put an end to his self-humiliation…with more humiliation.

"Look." Realizing she'd been stooping to make him feel better, she pulled to her full height plus several inches of platform. "I'm going to have to have my boyfriend beat you up if you don't leave me alone." Guilt made her eyes water.

He stared at her. Oh, God, were those tears in his eyes?

"Understand?" It felt bad to be so nasty, but it had to be done. She had a mission. She couldn't let him interfere. A man's life was at stake.

He nodded, but his feet seemed frozen to the concrete.

The times called for drastic measures. "Look. I wouldn't have sex with you even if you—" what would be sufficient to finally and truly make him give up "—offered a million dollars."

This was terrible. She pointed down the hill. "Go."

She really hated herself for being so harsh as she watched his slumped shoulders disappear beyond the corner gas station. Tough love, this was definitely it.

Another car, another offer. One of the scuzzbuckets threw a dollar at her. Of all the dirty tricks. It was like leaving a waitress a penny tip. She flipped him the bird.

Where oh where was the man in dire need of her help? She resonated a caring, loving energy, raised her face to the pink-and-orange glow of the sun as it spread a profusion of color across the sky. She was one with the caring universe.

"Hey, lady."

She snapped to attention. The man stood between her and her view of Jack. Cropped brown hair, faded jeans, dirty white T-shirt. He didn't smile beneath his mustache.

"Excuse me?"

"I been watching you out here, and I like what I see."

This wasn't her pathetic suicidal victim. He wasn't even her persistent short guy. He was sort of... menacing. Where had he come from? Unlike the Nissan, she hadn't noticed him pulling his car over to park. She should have been watching more carefully.

She resonated bravery and courage under fire. Made all the easier by the fact that Jack was close by in the park-'n'-ride watching out for her. "Thank you for the compliment, but I'm not interested."

He snorted. "What, you don't like the way I look?"

She willed him away, resonated with his turning around and walking back the way he came.

But he didn't go. "I've got something burning a hole in my pants." He waggled his fingers in his jeans pocket.

She didn't think he was talking about money. For one unconscionable minute, she doubted the universe. She stared at this cold, hard man, his hands shoved in his pockets and his lips pinched in an unfriendly line, and wondered if the universe was playing some horrible joke on her—giving her a vision, then ripping the reality of it right out from under her.

"Four nights, I've been out here four nights. My feet are sore, my head aches, my eyes are about ready to pop out of their sockets from the exhaust. My face is probably going to break out tomorrow from all this smog. I even crushed that poor man's spirit like he was a bug. And for what?"

The guy eyed her with beady eyes, snakelike eyes. "You tell me, lady."

She narrowed her eyes. He just didn't get it. He needed to be taught a lesson in the worst way. "I don't think you can afford someone like me."

"Are you actually admitting you're a streetwalker?"

"This is a street and I'm walking."

He paused, his beady black eyes roving over her as he thought up his next line. "And you think I can't afford you because…what, you don't like my jeans or something?"

She looked at the frays across his knees, very fashionable at a high school, but… "Actually, it's the spaghetti stains on your T-shirt that offend me. I *know* you can't afford me."

"Try me."

His persistence called for something totally outrageous to put him in his place.

"How about a million dollars?"

He gave her a nasty little snarl, but he didn't go away. "Yeah, right. Let's get real here."

So, outrageous didn't work. Fine, she'd be more realistic, but still way above his holey jeans price range. "It'll cost you…five thousand dollars for the whole shebang. And I don't, under any circumstances, swallow." God. Had she really said that? Yes. That was her story, and she was sticking to it.

He laughed. "You've gotta be kidding me."

"I'm not." And that should send the baggage on his way lickety-split.

"One last chance, you sure that's how much it'll cost me to have sex with you?"

How dare he laugh at her? For a day that began with so much exuberance, it had certainly gone to the dogs now. "You heard my price. What, you think you'll get a cut rate by asking nice?" Now, surely now, he'd rush off in a male huff.

"No, ma'am, just getting the story straight for my report." He pulled out a wallet—God forbid he actually had the money—then flashed her a gold-plated badge.

Suddenly he was right up in her face. "You're under arrest for prostitution." He turned her around and slapped the cuffs on her wrists. "You have the right to remain silent…"

Oh my God, she was being Mirandized.

JESUS CHRIST. What the hell was going on up there? Jack bounded up the parking lot's stairs three at a time in his haste to get to Opal, leaving Blue behind yelling a blue streak.

He hadn't liked the looks of that guy, but the damn handcuffs scared the shit out of him.

"Get your filthy hands off her." He grabbed a shoulder, came away with a handful of T-shirt, but it was enough to whirl the guy around.

"Jack. Wait. Don't."

Jack plowed his fist into the pervert's face. The bastard went down. Hard. And he didn't get up.

Sirens blared close by. Thank God. The light at the bottom of the hill changed, and the sea of cars moved forward. A black-and-white pulled up, red lights swirling.

Two uniformed cops jumped out.

He pointed to the prone figure on the ground. "Arrest this guy. He attacked my girlfriend."

"Jack." Opal's voice was a harsh, not-so-soft whisper. "You don't understand."

The taller cop nudged the guy with his toe. "You all right, Zeke?"

"Is he all right?" Jack couldn't believe his ears. "He just tried to kidnap my girlfriend."

The creep on the concrete stirred, sat up, put a hand to his bloody nose and looked from one cop to the other. "Must be her pimp. Came out of nowhere. I didn't have a chance."

"Pimp?" Jack's gaze started to blur around the edges.

Opal pursed her pretty red lips. "That's what I've been trying to tell you, Jack. He thinks I'm a hooker."

"Bloody hell."

"You're under arrest for assaulting an officer."

He couldn't believe his ears, but he could believe the cold metal the second cop latched around his wrists after none too gently pulling his arms behind his back.

Looking at Opal, Jack shook his head, but all he really saw was his mother's face. His mother's tears. He'd have liked to be pissed at Opal, but he'd wanted to do better for her than this, shades of Blue's whisperings in his ear about how believing in Opal's delusions was all she needed.

The only thing believing in a delusion brought was cuffs chafing Opal's wrists. Jesus, he'd really fucked up this time.

"You let go of Dynamite."

No. God, please no, not Blue, too. Jack closed his eyes and turned his face to the fading light of the sun.

"Ma'am, you need to get your foot off mine."

"Let him go, you swine."

Jack didn't bother to open his eyes, saying only, "Blue, back off. Now."

"But, Dynamite—"

"I. Said. Back. Off."

"Ma'am, please. Step away from the prisoner."

"We'll sue your blue butts off for false arrest." But the crackling voice now came from a few steps behind him.

Jack opened his eyes to find a snarl of traffic surrounding them on one side. Gawkers, laughing, pointing, jeering. Below them, the rush of traffic. Gas fumes and dirt rose up to blind him to everything but Opal. Failure beat against his eyeballs like the achingly bright glare of a hot afternoon sun.

"Why do they think you're a prostitute?" It was obvious, but asking the question was better than yelling at her.

"It's all just a misunder…" She faltered under his hard stare. "Okay, I told him it would cost him five thousand dollars to have sex with me." She glanced beyond him to her assailant. "I just wanted to teach him a lesson." She arched one fine eyebrow. "But I guess it sort of backfired."

The woman was a study in understatement. Five thousand dollars for sex? No, no, he wouldn't think about that part.

"Get 'em in the cruiser." His arm was grabbed. The tall one tugged Opal, at least a little more gently than the hand on his own arm.

"Where are you taking them?" The concrete shuddered with the force of Blue's stamping foot. Or maybe that was a semi rumbling across the overpass.

"Pine Street Station, ma'am."

"I'll have your heads for this." Blue, drama queen, shook her fist, her muumuu billowing, as the cop shoved Jack's head down and pushed him into the backseat of the squad car.

"Dynamite, I'll call the best lawyer I know, and don't worry, I won't drive your truck," Blue shrieked to be heard, then finished off with, "Now where the hell's my cell phone?"

Opal's sweet perfume assailed him as she, too, was ushered inside with a gentle push. Pulling herself upright, she blinked twice, then flashed him a brilliant smile that under other circumstances would bring him to his knees in worship. "Well, I'm glad my vision verification is done for the night. My feet were really starting to kill me."

"Opal, we should bow our heads and pray."

"Why?" She gazed at him as if he'd gone completely insane. Which he had.

"I think we should be thanking the Lord my hands are cuffed. Otherwise, I'm sure I'd be strangling someone right now."

That someone would be himself.

CHAPTER TEN

NILE MONTGOMERY HATED police stations as much as he hated morgues and hospitals. People would be surprised at the diversity in police stations. No two were alike. Big cities usually housed noisy, rank-smelling warehouses full of detectives, phones always ringing, people always shouting. Small sheriff's offices could be as quiet as the morgue itself. And empty, especially late at night, sometimes little more than a couple of rooms in a rented space. Next door you might find a software company or a publisher of technical manuals.

The only thing that was the same were the faces of the grieving, frightened parents, the grimness of the overwhelmed cops, and the frantic scurrying like rats in a maze.

The Pine Street station house was a cross between big-city police and small-town sheriff—fewer cubicles, smaller holding cells, the faint smell of waste from an inadequate sewer system leaking into the offices. And the noise. Earsplitting. Deafening. Each separate source indistinguishable, melding together inside his brain, turning it into chaos.

Nile prayed his head would explode from it.

Because he couldn't stand the pain on the stark,

white, worried faces of Tamara Whitley-Dorn's parents, ages and features obscured by a heavy mantle of fear and anguish for twenty-three-year-old Tamara, who had disappeared a week ago without a trace.

Tonight, they'd called and asked him to meet them down at the station. They were still hopeful. Nile wasn't. He didn't need a psychic ability to know that Tamara wasn't coming home. In his experience, good girls from wealthy families who fell into bad hands didn't come home again. They disappeared into drug-infested hell-holes never to be seen again.

But he hadn't left Big Sur for the Bay Area to tell George and Cecelia Whitley-Dorn his own statistics. He'd come to help them find their angel, because Victor Patell had called him in desperation. And to give her parents some kind of closure.

Except Nile knew he was no longer capable of providing those things. He couldn't tell Cecelia one way or the other. That fact chewed holes in his gut.

Sergeant Guthrie, so far, had done most of the talking, leaving Nile to sit quietly, leaning forward in the stiff chair, elbows on his knees. They were in a small cramped office space so that Guthrie could close the blinds, saving the Whitley-Dorns the interested ears and the prying eyes. Rubbernecking happened even in a police station.

If they hadn't been rich, Nile didn't think Cecelia and George Whitley-Dorn, let alone their daughter, would rate the office or even the time Guthrie had so far put into them.

A fringe of gray roots trimmed the woman's blond hair as if she'd aged from the inside out in the last week. They hadn't been there when Nile first talked with her the previous Saturday. Though middle-aged, certainly over fifty, she was well-preserved—manicured hands, regularly facialed skin. But no amount of pampering could hide the new lines of strain. Just as no amount of money could erase the anxious furrow from her husband's brow as he clung to her hand with a white-knuckled grip.

"As I told you before, Mr. Whitley-Dorn—" the officer's mouth curled around the rich, hyphenated sound "—since there's no indication of foul play or kidnapping, we can't do much beyond..."

Guthrie's patient voice droned on, detailing, for perhaps the hundredth time, all the police couldn't do for them, since, as far as the authorities were concerned, Tamara walked out of the house last Friday under her own steam. The drug paraphernalia found in her frilly pink room didn't change anything for the investigators. It merely added corroboration that Tamara had gone of her own free will, probably in search of her next fix.

"And we're very glad to have Mr. Montgomery here...."

Not. The police tolerated him, at least in this small suburb. He could never be sure of his reception. The best Nile got was tolerance. But Cecelia Whitley-Dorn had brought him in, with Victor's help, and no cop was about to tell a frantic mother that a psychic didn't have a chance in hell of finding her daughter alive any more than the police did.

The woman pulled her fingers from her husband's tight grip. "Would you please give Mr. Montgomery the necklace?" Her voice was soft, musical, cultured, as befitted her elegant clothing, but determination glowed in her hazel eyes.

Without looking down, Guthrie ran a finger beneath the open envelope flap, once, twice, as if using the time to make up his mind, then he picked it up. "The Whitley-Dorns received this earlier today. We've run it through tests, along with the mailer it came in. You're free to touch it." Without words, it was clear in Guthrie's harsh tones that the supposed tests had revealed nothing.

Holding the envelope three inches in midair, Guthrie let the gleaming pearls slide out onto the scarred wood.

Nile rested his palm against the desk without touching the necklace. Electricity arced between his outstretched fingers and the double, choker-length strands. "Tell me about it."

Guthrie answered. "It came in the mail, brown padded envelope, computer-generated label. No note, no message. Just the necklace." He glanced at the mother. "I'm sorry, but it still isn't evidence of foul play."

Those weren't the details Nile wanted to know. He raised just his eyes and met Cecelia's gaze.

"We gave her the pearls on her sixteenth birthday."

Sweet sixteen. His gut clenched at Tamara's innocence. How much of it had been lost in the ensuing years? "Did she wear them often?"

"All the time. Even after she started…"

After she started using drugs. Though Cecelia didn't finish, Nile made the educated guess.

Stretching slightly, he let his hand crawl across the desk toward it. Hooking his index finger inside the clasp, he dragged the strands closer, closer, but felt nothing. Not even the arc of electricity that had come when he'd first put his hand on the desk.

Then the pearls were in his hand. He didn't hold them, but let them dribble from one palm to the other, the beads softly snicking against each other. Again. A third time.

"Are you done?" Guthrie asked, his nerves had obviously worn thin.

A single tear slipped down Cecelia's cheek. Her husband's hands fisted, knuckles cracking, but remained on his knees.

"What do you see?" Cecelia whispered, almost mesmerized by the creamy pearls in Nile's palm.

The girl had spent seven days and six nights away from home because of his failure. It was as if his subconscious had gone into lockdown and his conscious mind had thrown away the key. Images frothed on the edge of his awareness, but he couldn't bring them into focus. He in fact feared letting them in with every cell inside him.

His gift was gone. Perhaps in his own anguish, he'd tossed it away himself.

Whatever the true reason, his mind couldn't face seeing one more dead body. Not to save Tamara's parents from another night of anxious waiting. Not to save Tamara herself from another night out there alone, even in death.

Nile could no longer save himself.

The need on Cecelia's ravaged face sliced through his flesh. If he'd known how to get past the lockdown on his own, he would have. By everything that was sacred, he would have done it, for Cecelia's sake. He'd pinned all hope on Pearl being his key, that by understanding his anguish, sharing it, soothing something deep inside him, she could untangle the shackles binding him, but he feared even that wouldn't work.

"I'm not seeing anything." Then he added, because he couldn't wrest all hope from the woman's desperate eyes, "Yet. I need time. May I keep them?"

Nile looked to the mother; she looked to Guthrie. The sergeant nodded. Nile knew he was being granted possession because the necklace didn't mean a thing to the police. The girl could have sent them herself as a symbol of goodbye. To her parents, to her old life, to her innocent childhood.

Cecelia popped the snap on her designer handbag and pulled out a small felt bag. "You can put them in this. To keep them clean."

Clean and safe for when her daughter came home. He took the bag, employing the same reverence with which she offered it.

Held by the clasp, the pearl string fell to full length, then he let it slither inside the green felt. Finally, he pulled the drawstrings tight to keep the delicate burden safe.

"We'll call you just as soon as we hear anything," Guthrie said as he rose. Like puppets, the Whitley-Dorns rose with him.

Cecelia looked at Nile. "How long does it take to…see something?"

"It usually takes hours for the vision to completely form," he lied smoothly. When he opened his mind to an object, he saw immediately, as if the vision were a hatchet cleaving his brain in two and filling the empty space. He had no such feeling now, but he'd always been a great liar. "I'll let you know just as soon as I see something," he finished lamely. He would never see anything.

The Whitley-Dorns passed through the door, shrunken husks leaning on each other. The sudden silence in the office screamed in his ears. He opened his briefcase and laid the bag containing the double strand of pearls on top of the photos he'd taken of Tamara's room. Pink comforter, white lace, stuffed animals, as if she were perpetually sixteen, or as if her parents never wanted her to grow up. In contrast to the frilly exterior lay the folded bits of paper that had once contained cocaine, the powder's residue licked clean. Why had she saved the homemade envelopes?

"I don't like your kind, Montgomery." Guthrie stuck an unlit cigarette between his lips, dragged on it. "Don't trust the lot of you farther than I can throw you." He exhaled, puffing out a smokeless stream of air. "But I will grant you this, ya don't give 'em false hope."

Nile looked through him. "There is no hope to give. You know as well as I do that when, *if* you find Tamara Whitley-Dorn, you won't find her alive."

Guthrie looked at him for a long moment. "Why do I get the feeling that bothers you?"

It tore his insides out. "Haven't got a clue."

Another long stare. "If you were for real, I'd say your job would get to you the way a cop's does."

"Except I'm not for real, am I." And a cop didn't spend every day of his life flying to godforsaken parts of the country looking for people—daughters, sons, brothers, sisters, parents, lovers, wives or husbands—he knew he'd find dead. So few, so very, very few had he found in time.

Pearl had asked why he didn't share. How could he

share with her the horrors he'd seen? Why would she even want to know?

Whatever he'd been looking for, Guthrie seemed to find written in the weary lines of Nile's face. "I'll walk you out, Montgomery, while you tell me what you aren't telling the family."

The grip on Nile's arm was no-nonsense.

Nile chose to turn the question back on the sergeant. "If I figure out where she is, I'll call you. Then you can finally decide if a crime's been committed."

Guthrie's voice dropped to a growl. "You think I get off sitting behind a desk telling people I can't do a *fucking* thing? That their daughter's just another rich bitch kid off on a lark and who gives a damn if she's snorting shit up her nose while she's doing it? That she'll come home in her own sweet-ass time or we'll call them when she hits the morgue, but sorry there isn't any evidence of a crime that we can act on right now?"

It was the most impassioned speech Nile had heard from the man in the many days he'd visited the station. The law might not care, but Guthrie was a human being, and he cared deeply.

"You think I want to tell them chances are she's already dead? Or if she isn't now, she will be soon." The words were Guthrie's but the anguish in them was Nile's own. The cop was as powerless as Nile himself.

"No. I don't think you want to tell them that, Sergeant. I think you'd move heaven and earth if you thought it would help."

They both knew it wouldn't.

The hopelessness of it swamped Nile, blurred his vision to the gray linoleum floors, the scratched and dirty institutional white of the walls, swathed his head in cotton to drown out the voices, the yelling, the emotional residue of ruined lives.

By way of an apology, what Nile had offered wasn't much, but the burn in Guthrie's eyes eased. "I asked what you know."

"Thought you didn't believe in what *our kind* does." A delaying tactic. Because he couldn't admit he'd fed that distraught couple a pack of face-saving lies.

"I don't." A hint of a smile sparked in Guthrie's craggy face. "But I've seen a helluva lot in my time. Doesn't make me a believer. Just makes me willing to use whatever I get no matter where it comes from."

They stopped just inside the double doors leading out to the processing room. The metal handles battered the wall every time a cop barreled through, leaving twin holes in the Sheetrock that had been patched and rescarred innumerable times.

"If I knew something, I'd tell the parents. And you. That's my job."

"Your job?" Guthrie coughed and looked like he'd spit on the floor at Nile's feet. "These people paying you?"

"No. I work pro bono." And to do that, he lived as simply as possible on his dad's trust fund. His father *had* charged for the use of his accursed gift, but Nile never would.

"God. You sound like a frickin' lawyer." Guthrie snorted and opened the door to pandemonium.

For a small department, the processing room was packed. Sweaty bodies, bad breath, the stench of vomit and voices one on top of the other raised to the level of cacophony.

Nile wanted to close his eyes and cover his ears. See no evil, hear no evil. But the evil seeped into his mind through everything he touched, even through the fetid air across his skin. The black coat he habitually wore couldn't block it out.

"If I suspect for one moment you know more about this case than you're telling me, I'll make sure you fry."

Nile had fried long ago. He'd also become used to suspicion and threats. He looked down at Guthrie's hand on the sleeve of his coat. The man cared. For all his anger, blunt speech and almost brutal hold, the thing Nile felt most was his impotent emotion for one young woman he couldn't help.

"I'll give you whatever I have." Which would be nothing if he couldn't somehow open his mind and see. If unburdening himself to Pearl would somehow be the balm his soul needed to restore his gift, he would do it. He had to.

Guthrie dropped his arm, and the noise in the room almost pushed Nile to his knees. Yet there was one voice above all others.

"My granddaughter is not a prostitute. Release her immediately."

Grandma Blue. Pearl's grandmother.

The old lady seemed a foot taller wearing that voice. Ubiquitous muumuu, hair bluer than he remembered, and a tone the size of the Empire State Building.

"Nile Montgomery." Her voice suddenly became a gravelly, scratchy screech that drowned out every other sound in the room. "Nile, you tell these men that Opal is no hooker."

"A hooker? Opal?"

There she stood, a pretty thing. Pearl had always thought her sister outshone her when of course, the exact opposite was true. Still, Opal was a pretty thing, especially in that teal skirt and the handcuff jewelry.

"You know these people, Montgomery?" Guthrie had not left as Nile thought.

"Know them isn't exactly the right word. A she-devil, Opal might be. A hooker, she's not. She's my girl-friend's sister." He omitted the ex in Pearl's title.

"Is that a she-devil you want to leave to her fate or a she-devil you want me to step in to save?"

"The latter."

Guthrie, beside him, sighed. "Let me see what the hell's going on."

"Thanks." He didn't stop to ask why the sergeant would bother helping him or anyone he knew.

Approaching the desk, Guthrie took charge. Grandma Blue bounced over to Nile in her orthopedic shoes. She hadn't changed, she would never change no matter what her age. He believed she'd looked just this way for an eternity.

She pulled on his arm to force him down to her height. "It was entrapment. Opal and Jack didn't do anything wrong. Well, except for when Jack slugged the cop. But he didn't know he was a cop. The slime had his hands all over my girl, and Jack was trying to protect her. He's Dynamite's reincarnation, you know."

Tall, darkish hair and an even darker scowl, the man in question stood close to Opal, his hands secured behind his back. They wore matching handcuffs. Charming. His arm rested against Opal's protectively, his body tensed to pounce if anyone dared harass her.

Though he wasn't smiling now, laugh lines bracketed his mouth, making the scowl incongruous.

Nile didn't ask about Dynamite, Grandma Blue's favorite fantasy man. He didn't even inquire how or why Opal could have been mistaken for a prostitute. "Who'd he hit?"

"That man." Blue indicated a guy in torn jeans holding a handkerchief to his nose, now talking to Guthrie. Two uniformed policeman flanked him.

"Did you call a lawyer?"

"Lawyers? We don't need no stinking lawyers."

Which meant she didn't know any lawyers to call. She actually brought the smallest of smiles to his lips, though he thought they might crack under the pressure. "Blue, I can honestly say I think I've missed you."

She scrutinized him, wrinkles stretching out from the corners of her eyes. "You *think?*"

He knew if he said another word, he'd open himself up for one of her famous double whammies. He did it, almost gladly. "I'm *sure* I've missed you."

"Then when are you going to do Pearl? That girl hasn't had a good lay since you left. You know what celibacy does to a body?"

Ah, her insanity swept over him like a calm sea wind. "Whether I say yes or no, I'm sure you're going to tell me anyway."

"Causes constipation."

He actually laughed, the unfamiliar sound hoarse and gritty in his throat. "Pearl's going to kill you for saying that."

"Then don't tell her I said it." She shook a finger at

him. "Which should be damn easy for you since you don't reveal anything to anyone anyway."

"Have I ever told you I love you, Blue?" He'd never meant anything he'd ever said to the old lady more.

"Only when you wanted something. What do you want now?"

A family. Her family. Pearl. "Help me get her back."

Blue shot a look to Opal. "It won't be easy. The Mother always hated you, not to mention The Brother. And Opal, well, maybe, if you get her and Dynamite out of this little fix they're in…" She turned back to him. "Take it from an old lady, constipation's real bad. It's liable to stop up an entire body if it's not taken care of. Gets all impacted, and well, I've heard of people dying of that kind of thing. Sort of like a broken heart."

"What do I have to do?"

She stared up at him, eyes clear and piercing, and dropped the constipation metaphors. "Tell her the truth."

"I'm not sure what the truth is."

She pushed aside the lapels of his overcoat and tapped him in the center of the chest. "You know what it is, you're just afraid to see it."

Despite what every other member of the Smith family believed, Grandma Blue was the most profound psychic of them all.

OPAL STALKED Nile Montgomery across the parking lot of the Pine Street Police Station. "I don't care if you did help us get out of there, you're a dirty rat bastard worm. This is for Pearl." Jumping in front of him, she kicked his shin for punctuation. "And this is for the stupid letter you've gotten her all worked up about."

Jack grabbed her arm and pulled her back before she could kick the dirty rat bastard anywhere else.

Tired down to her bones, every body part aching from standing too long on hard concrete and sitting too long on wooden benches which had not been properly formed to her rear end, Opal almost took a swing at Jack. She was that worked up.

"Anyway, it wasn't you, it was that nice Sergeant Guthrie who got those silly policemen to see reason. You—" she shook off Jack and stuck her index finger right in Nile's dirty rotten chest "—didn't even open your mouth."

The parking lot, well lit, was still almost full even at one in the morning. Sergeant Guthrie had gotten them released, but not until after she'd explained herself hoarse and the policeman Jack had hit suggested she be admitted to a psych ward. Nasty man. If she'd been thinking properly, she would have told him she wouldn't have sex with him if he was the last man on earth. Her scheme for the night was totally shot, and an inkling of doubt about the vision's veracity was creeping into her mind.

To make everything the worst it could possibly be, she'd have to ask Nile for a ride because they didn't have a car.

"If I was a violent woman, why I'd…get violent with you right now." It was so much easier to take her disappointment out on Nile. Especially after the way he'd treated Pearl.

"You already kicked him, Opal," Grandma Blue reminded her.

"I'll kick him again." She pulled her foot back to do just that when Jack yelped.

"Is that my truck?"

His black Dodge Ram with its crumpled tailgate gleamed in a pool of lamplight at the end of the row of cars.

He whirled on Grandma Blue. "You said you weren't going to drive it?"

"I lied." It was simply amazing how tall Grandma Blue could appear when she wanted to. "I didn't want you to worry about that while you had other troubles on your mind. You can get the dent in the passenger door fixed when you have the bumpers done. The insurance company will never know."

He choked. Or was that a sob?

Opal was suddenly cold, and, horror of horrors, she smelled bad. The stink of the police station clung to her clothes, her hair. Or maybe the stench was just stuck in her brain for all eternity.

Except for one very bright and wonderful spot. Jack had rescued her. He'd come charging along that overpass like an enraged bull. For her. That fact alone warmed her. Jack warmed her. She could actually get used to having him around. He was the sweetest most caring nonbeliever she'd met since...well, gosh, ever.

Grandma Blue took charge. "Jack, you can drive us back to Opal's car. She'll take me home." She wagged a finger at them both. "Sorry, no kissie face tonight. Here's the keys."

She fished them out of her deep muumuu pocket. Opal's face flamed, and she was glad to be standing just beyond the ring of light from the overhead lamps. A little kissie face might have made her feel better. Much better. In fact, besides kicking Nile in the shin again, a little kissie face with Jack, and his arms around her, was the thing she'd like most right now.

Jack. Her hero.

"And you," Grandma Blue was now wagging that finger at Nile. "You know where you're supposed to go."

Opal's blood boiled again. Nile could go straight to hell. That was no more than he deserved for what he'd done to Pearl.

CHAPTER ELEVEN

OPAL'S RENTAL CAR was the only one left at the park-'n'-ride when Jack pulled in. Blue, that sneaky lady, had grabbed Opal's keys from her hand and darted to the car, slamming the door hard to let them know they'd have a few minutes of privacy.

How long, Jack wasn't sure, just as he wasn't sure he could stand Opal's lackluster gaze. Any moment, she'd break down.

"Are you mad at me?"

"Mad is not the word I would use to describe how I feel about slugging a cop, getting arrested and having your grandmother drive my truck." This was serious business. Rather than gather her in his arms, he needed to read her the riot act.

"You shouldn't have left your keys in it."

"I didn't think she could reach the pedals. Besides, I thought I'd be right back after I dragged you off that overpass." That was a lie. He hadn't thought of anything at all except that guy's hands on Opal.

"After you rescued me, you mean." Opal didn't break down. Instead, she smiled, with her lips and her eyes.

Jack's knees seemed to weaken. He was supposed to give her a talking-to. Things would be much easier if he could be angry with the woman, but Opal didn't inspire anger. She was too damn sweet for that. She left him tongue-tied.

"You've known Grandma Blue for almost a week, so you know there's no way she'd stay behind in the truck and wait for you."

"You're right. I must have been suffering from temporary insanity." He rolled his eyes. He was letting her distract him from reprimanding her over *tonight's* insanity.

"There's no reason to be sarcastic."

There was every reason to be sarcastic. Defense mechanism. She was standing less than five inches from him, and she'd just freshened her cherry-red lipstick.

He gave up the idea of scolding completely. She was like a powerful vortex sucking him under. "Five thousand dollars?" He'd heard the whole overpass incident repeated verbatim. Over and over. Ad nauseum. The really insane thing that had been going through his head the entire time was whether she meant it about not swallowing. He'd jumped to her defense, he'd gotten them both arrested and, still, he lusted after her. Ah hell, he'd lost his mind, finally, totally, irrevocably.

"It was the most extreme thing that came to mind at the time."

It had been extreme, all right. He should be yelling at her for her foolishness. He should be feeling sorry for her. He should at least be admiring her pluck and ever-positive attitude. After tonight, her vision walk was over—she'd agreed, as a condition for getting out of that police station, that she'd never "troll" the overpass again—but instead of crying over the loss of her dream, she'd taken on her sister's ex-something like a Valkyrie riding in on her white charger. Or whatever the Valkyries rode. She had not broken down at all.

Maybe her pluck and sincerity and *extreme* way of thinking were what had him lusting until he couldn't see straight. He needed to get his mind elsewhere. "Why do you hate your sister's boyfriend so much?" The question seemed a better idea than strangling her, kissing her or begging her to come home with him.

Opal's vigilante eyes narrowed. "Nile is not her boyfriend. He's her *ex*-boyfriend and he treated her like… like…" She fumed so hard, but she couldn't seem to come up with a despicable enough word. "And not only that, he's a body-finder."

"Uh…okay. What's a body-finder?" Had to be something really bad, like those guys who worked on the FBI body farms measuring insect growth rates. He really had no desire to watch a repeat of that show.

"He's got the sight to locate missing people. But Nile, he almost always finds them dead. He's Mr. Bad News all around."

Maybe that was why the guy looked pale as a ghost and hollow as a dummy in a wax museum. Not that Jack believed Nile was psychic, just that he probably had good instincts. Or not so good if he couldn't locate his quarry before something bad happened to them. "You think that's why he was there tonight? Looking for someone."

"I know it was. Pearl said he's in town searching for a young woman named Tamara. She's been missing since last Friday."

Jack felt sorry for the guy. His job or gift or whatever he had didn't seem to make him terribly happy. A more sorrowful guy Jack hadn't seen since the Raiders left Oakland the first time. All right, bad analogy. The guy looked used up and washed-out. "I hope he finds her before it's too late."

"I do, too. Then I hope he rides out of town on his broomstick."

One thing about Opal, when someone misused someone she cared about, she was a hellcat. He admired her unconditional loyalty.

What would it be like to have her go to the mat for him? He started to contemplate the feeling….

Just then, Blue honked the car horn.

Opal touched his arm. "I have to go. Will you call me tomorrow so we can thoroughly discuss what happened tonight?"

Discuss which part? The details behind the five thousand dollar "whole shebang"? Christ Almighty. He'd never survive *that* conversation. "There's nothing to discuss." Unless he yelled a lot about her getting arrested, which he realized wouldn't do any good.

"Yes, there is."

She didn't get it. He thought about spelling it out, that for some insane reason, all he could think about were the sexual ramifications of what she'd said to the undercover cop. But then he might be incapable of keeping his hands, or his lips, to himself. She'd had a long night. He'd had a long night. Tomorrow, the true impact of the evening's events would hit her, because he also didn't think she'd gotten *that* part. Her vision hadn't been real.

As much as she wanted it and needed it, Opal wasn't psychic.

OPAL COULDN'T SLEEP. Nothing had worked out tonight. She'd had to promise the cops she wouldn't "troll" the overpass. Though that didn't mean she couldn't sit in Jack's truck and *watch* it, she couldn't be sure Jack would help her tomorrow night. And the worst? He hadn't kissed her goodbye.

She wouldn't let any of that stop her. Her vision *was* real. She *would* rescue the jumper. And Jack *would* kiss her again. She practiced resonating with those thoughts when the phone suddenly chirped on her bedside table. She jumped on it.

"Did I wake you up?"

Her brother, Julian. In all the excitement, she'd forgotten about him. Lord-love-a-duck, she'd forgotten about poor Victor Patell, as well.

"It's—" she glanced at the clock "—almost two in the morning. What do you think? Why didn't you call me back?"

"I *am* calling you back." He didn't wait for her to contradict or say it was one helluva long wait. "How did you know I screwed it up again?"

"Sixth sense." She didn't have a clue what he was talking about, though she had left that cryptic message hinting that he'd better call her, or *else*. She'd been hoping he'd *have* to call back to solve the mystery.

"Mother told you."

"Did you tell her?" Hmm. If he'd questioned Mother, it must have been about his finances.

"No, I didn't talk to Mother, but her sixth sense is better than yours."

"Not when it comes to money," she singsonged.

"I tried to do what you told me to, Opal, but it was so boring."

Aha, she was right. Finances. Which put her in the one-up position for asking her big favor. "It's not boring when you watch your net worth grow. Tell me what you did."

"I only started with a small amount. And I was doing phenomenally well—"

"What did you do with it, Julian?" This time she used a harsher tone.

"You know that buddy of mine, Harper Hall, the spoonbender."

"Father would have hated that term. Telekinesis was an art form to him, a special gift he prized above all others. He was *never* a spoonbender."

"Well, Father might not have been, but Harper is definitely a spoonbender. He hasn't even graduated to forks."

"And you took his advice when he can't even bend a fork?"

"Just because he can't get beyond the spoon phase doesn't mean he's a bad guy. Opal, you're really classist sometimes."

"Can we get back to the advice part? How much?"

"I started small. But that stock just took off and—"

"You bought some more, then lost it all."

"Not all of it." There was a slight whine in his voice.

"How far back did you put yourself, Julian?"

"Ummm, to, like, maybe…the year 2000?" Okay, he was definitely whining now.

And well he should. It wasn't her money, but she still felt her stomach drop clear to her toes. "But Julian, that was before you even got the show." She almost couldn't breathe thinking about all the money he'd lost. The stock market had *ruined* people back in 2000.

"I know. Don't yell. Just tell me how to fix it."

Fix it? If he lost it all, it wasn't fixable. Then again, her brother was a bit of a drama king and prone to exaggeration. "Fax me your statements. I'll look over everything. And you have to promise to do exactly what I tell you to do."

"I promise."

"And in return you have to do me a favor. When are you coming up to San Francisco next?"

Ah, it had all worked out so well, at least for getting that little favor for Victor Patell. She didn't even have to fall on Julian's mercy. He had to fall on hers.

"I hadn't made plans. What do you need?"

She closed her eyes and said a prayer. "Just a teeny-weeny séance for a friend of mine. He needs to contact his wife."

"I can't get away right now. Maybe at the end of August."

Victor seemed too desperate to wait two months. "Couldn't you just come up for a night? I'll look at those statements." She dangled the promise in front of him.

"Sorry. No can do, sweetcheeks. Not now."

Her heart sank. "Julian, he needs you."

"Tell him to call my producer and get on the show."

That would take forever. "He needs you now."

"Opal, I absolutely can't make it now. Your friend will have to wait. You know how important what I do is for millions of viewers around the world."

Yes, she knew. Julian was a very important man. But

what would she tell Victor? *How* would she break the devastating news?

"But you'll look at the statements for me, won't you?"

She should say no, but she couldn't. Her mother would have a fit if Opal didn't fix things for Julian. "Yeah, I'll do it."

Julian was still talking. "And I'll be up in August. Promise. Gotta run."

Dead air hummed on the phone. Opal had a terrible feeling August would be far too late for Victor.

She had to do something for him now. She *would* do something.

She just had to figure out what that something was.

NILE DROPPED HIS COAT and briefcase on a chair beside the ornately carved antique desk. The old wood chair creaked beneath the heavy weight of Tamara's pearls. Nile's head pounded beneath the weight of their responsibility.

Grandma Blue's voice had eased the tension but for a few minutes. He could no longer remember how or why she'd made him laugh. The moment seemed aeons ago instead of mere hours. His shin still throbbed where Opal had kicked him, almost a pleasant sensation if only because it meant he could still feel. Feel enough to know that going to Pearl tonight would be a bad thing, might always be a bad thing. If he couldn't live with his gift, making her privy to its horror was unconscionable. Yet, without her, Tamara's parents were doomed to forever wonder what had become of their daughter.

To know or not to know? Nile had no answer for that.

But Pearl had told Opal about the letter. Did that mean Pearl had read it? If she had, she'd have contacted him, he was sure. Was he wrong to give her the letter? His initial thoughts had been that once she'd read it, she'd have to ask for more. She'd be forced to call him. He'd be compelled to tell her exactly what his gift had done to him over the long, grueling years. His soul's torment would be revealed, and the very act of sharing that experience with Pearl, his other half, his spirit mate, would begin shoring him up, pulling him back together.

But his desires had been selfish. He'd always been selfish where Pearl was concerned. Taking. Never giving anything back.

Whatever he should have done, Pearl had the letter now. She would read it or she wouldn't. It was out of his hands. The thought made him feel like Pontius Pilate washing away his accountability.

Something scraped the bedroom door. He held his breath, waiting, as if it might be a hound from hell. The sound came again, this time he could make it out as a soft knock.

"Come in."

Victor Patell's face was scoured with age, but his eyes sparked with alertness despite the lateness of the hour. "Did you see anything tonight?"

The burden of the pearls, Tamara and the whole damn world suddenly made Nile collapse. He managed to find the edge of the bed before he fell flat on his face.

"Not yet, Victor." He'd been saying it to everyone for a week now. Soon, Victor would stop believing in him the way Nile had himself. The pearls had provided no clues, and the police weren't making any headway, either. According to Guthrie, they hadn't even found a credit card transaction or an ATM withdrawal. Tamara had simply vanished.

Victor gave him a tired smile. "That's all right, old boy. You'll find her in the end."

The end. Tamara's end. *She's dead, Victor. I can't save her.* The words slid from the back of his throat to the tip of his tongue, but Nile didn't say them.

He didn't need to speak aloud. Victor heard what he didn't say and bowed his head. "Is time running out, Nile?"

It ran out days ago. Fated before the girl even went missing.

"Nile, I can't watch it happen again. I just can't."

Victor's daughter's story had been much the same as Tamara's—drugs, sex, bad men. Niles's own father had done the search. Even then, failure was the Montgomery family's middle name. Rita wasn't found in time, and Franklin hadn't picked up a single psychic clue that Rita had a child. Over the years, his failures had driven Nile's father to drink, which eventually killed him. Now, Nile gave in to despair.

And Victor? Too much pain rode the old man's shoulders.

"Where's Darius?" When he'd pulled into the driveway, he'd noticed the guy's new car, the one Victor had bought him, wasn't in the driveway. Nile didn't particularly care what Darius was up to, but asking a question was better than telling Victor that Tamara's so-called savior was a fraud.

"I don't know. He went out again. I worry about him."

Nile worried more about Victor's need to keep Darius around than about Darius himself. When he'd miraculously returned, Nile had gotten a bad feeling about the guy. There was something wrong about Darius. During one of his periodic visits with Prudence and Victor, Nile had offered to touch one of Darius's belongings and to give whatever impressions his gift revealed, but Prudence had gone…guess the only word was ballistic. She'd been a petite, fragile lady, but her anger that day had turned her into a mother grizzly protecting her young. She hadn't wanted to contemplate that there could be anything amiss with Darius.

With Prudence's passing, Victor hadn't asked and Nile hadn't offered again, as if even after her death, it was sacrilege to go against her wishes.

After being in the house this week and witnessing Victor's tension, Nile longed to offer some kind of relief, to present Victor with some insight that would help in his dealings with Darius. That meant finding his gift again. And sacrificing Pearl in the process. He knew he'd have to push her harder.

Once she read the envelope's contents, Pearl might understand what his gift had done to him, but she would never forgive him for making her face it.

JACK SAW THE FLOWER TRUCK before the rest of the guys did. The driver must be lost. The sun was blazing at only ten o'clock in the morning, he was tired from lack of sleep, his head pounded as if he had a really bad hangover, and he was paying the guys overtime to work on Saturday. The only good thing he could say for the day so far was that when he'd gone over every inch of his truck that morning, there wasn't a single new dent. Blue had been teasing him.

The flower guy had opened the back of his van, pulled

out an enormous vase of red roses all tied up in a yellow bow and begun a trot through the gate of the site.

With a consultation of his clipboard, he said, "I'm looking for Jack Davis."

She wouldn't. She couldn't. Jack's heart sank down to the toes of his work boots. She had.

The perfume of the roses carried on the hot breeze. His guys had stopped work, and a hush fell. "No one here by that name," he said. "Can't you see this is a construction site? You must have the wrong address."

"The lady told me it was a construction site. And this is the right address."

"Well, there's no Jack Davis here," he lied to save face.

"Oh, Jack." A male voice singsonged from a girder thirty feet off the ground. He'd forgotten the way sound carried to higher levels.

"Oh, Mr. Davis." Another voice, another guy he'd have to deck.

"Are you sure there's no Jack Davis?" the delivery guy queried as innocently as the witch bribed Hansel and Gretel with the promise of treats.

His mind wrestled, his mouth worked and finally, "Okay, now I think I know who you're talking about." He was loathe to touch those flowers. Only girlie-men received flowers. "Why don't you just put them in the trailer over there?"

It seemed like a mile to the office trailer while every eye followed the progress across the dusty lot.

"Get back to work," he yelled, but the taunts went on.

Like an oven, the inside of the trailer would have those flowers dead as a doornail before noon. Then he could dismember them and carry the parts out in separate trash bags. No one would ever know what happened to them.

"Sign here, please."

Jack penned with a flourish, handed back the clipboard and hustled the guy out the trailer door in less than thirty seconds.

"There's a card in there, too," was the man's parting shot.

"Yeah, yeah, I saw it, thanks." *Now get the hell out.* Standing on the stoop, he watched the back end of the truck to make sure it disappeared around the corner without coming back.

His relief was short-lived.

"Gonna read the card to us, Jackie Boy?" The shout floated down from fifty feet above him.

"Didn't I just tell you assholes to get back to work?"

"We can't. Come on, Jack, the suspense is killing us."

"You're all fired," he shouted, the sun blinding him as he looked up for the voice's source.

"Oh, Jackie Poo."

Christ. The only safe place was in that hothouse trailer. With the damn flowers.

Inside, the heat had somehow tripled the scent. Did they spray the things with extra perfume? He coughed, his eyes watered. A pink envelope attached to a clear plastic trident nestled in the middle of the array.

Yep, there was his name. Clearly printed.

He picked up the phone and dialed her number at the shop.

"Bedazzled. Opal Smith speaking."

"Are you doing okay?" was his first question,

prompted by his own visions of her coming to terms with her lack of psychic ability.

"Jack." She didn't *sound* all broken up. "Did you get my little thank-you gift?"

He got it all right. The catcalls were still filtering in through the trailer window despite its being tightly shut. He had to be firm. Some things just weren't appropriate. "Do not ever send flowers to a construction site."

"If I'd sent them to your home, they would have died in the heat before you got there."

He ignored that. "I will not make it home now. I can't leave the trailer."

"Why not?"

"Opal, how do you feel when a bunch of construction workers are whistling at your butt in those short skirts?"

She was silent a moment. "Well, it's kind of embarrassing because you know they aren't really complimenting you, they're just acting up for their friends. I mean, if they really meant it, well, that would be…" Her voice trailed off. "It seems to go on and on. They don't quit. Until you walk away."

"You're right, they don't quit. Now, imagine what they're like when their boss gets a bunch of flowers." He tried not to grit his teeth as he spoke, because the woman was cute even if clueless. "And he can't just walk away."

She gave him a tiny little, "Oh." A pause. "I'm sorry. You know, real men can receive flowers, too." She paused again when he didn't react. "Did you read the card?"

"I didn't get that far."

"Then how did you know they were from me?"

"I'm psychic."

"Oh." She was saying that a lot. "Well, then, I guess I'll see you at four like usual."

"What are you talking about?"

"We have to watch the overpass."

He was sure his head was going to pop in the heat of the damn trailer. "You promised those cops you wouldn't go near it."

"I promised them I wouldn't loiter on it. We're going to watch from the cab of your truck."

Sitting with her in the cab of his truck was like being entombed with these roses, her perfume went to his head, made him dizzy, crazy, ready to lose his grip and do something really stupid. Like dragging her back to his apartment to seduce the idea of being psychic right out of her heart. And then to seduce her delectable body.

He could do nothing more than groan into the phone.

She took that as a yes. "Good. I'll see you at four. But read the card, okay."

This time he grunted in answer. A noncommittal, slightly Neanderthal grunt.

Hanging up, he pulled out the pink envelope. He was totally inept. He couldn't convince Opal to give up her dream. He couldn't even read the little pink card. *Be a man, open it.*

He did, barely suppressing a cringe.

To the sweetest, kindest, nicest man. Thanks for all the help.

Ah, shit. Sweet. Kind. Nice. He was going to have to force on her the realization that her vision was crackpot, then watch her smile crumble to dust when she finally got it. And she was *thanking* him. A trickle of sweat rolled off his brow, and it wasn't due to the ovenlike temperature inside the trailer. Nice guys didn't squash a lady's last hope.

He ripped the card into miniscule pieces as if they would somehow erase the vision of his complete helplessness, then turned on the radio to cover the noise of the shredder as he fed it the scraps.

"And in other news, last night, a local man tried to jump off the College Avenue overpass into oncoming freeway traffic."

Jack slammed off the shredder and stared at the radio.

"A police department spokesman said he might very well have been able to accomplish his task if not for the fact that police had been patrolling the area heavily in recent days due to an increase of prostitution activity."

"Holy shit," he whispered.

Opal's vision had come true.

CHAPTER TWELVE

"I CAN'T BELIEVE IT."

"It's there in black and white." Jack tapped his finger to the newspaper he'd spread on the countertop.

Opal stared at the printed words, then looked up at him, her eyes oddly misted. "Do *you* believe it?"

He straightened, backing off from the question. When he'd rushed out to get the newspaper, then raced over to her shop, his only thought was to please her. Which was damn scary all on its own. But did he actually believe she was psychic? He saw the incident for the weird coincidence it was. There was nothing psychic about it. Of course there wasn't. Yet he couldn't dash Opal's hopes. He'd rather receive a hundred vases of roses than crush her. He didn't actually have to believe, he just had to get her to believe he believed. Why did that sound convoluted when he tried to wrap his mind around it? Whatever.

There was a bright side. Telling her what she wanted to hear meant she wouldn't be out on that damn overpass ever again.

"It says right here he was trying to jump." Turning the paper so he could read, Jack repeated it for her. "He was despondent because the prostitute he'd tried to pick up turned him down four nights in a row. That was you."

Opal sucked in a breath, put a hand over her mouth. "How terrible. It was that little man. I never should have said those awful things to him."

Ah, good distraction from her question. "What awful things?"

She looked at him, her eyes limpid pools. "They're too shameful to repeat. Oh, this is all my fault."

Jack spread his hands. "Because of you, he got the help he needed. You saved him."

The lines at her mouth eased slightly. "Do you think so?"

He didn't know what to think, except that her odyssey would be over. But if it was over, then Opal didn't need *him* anymore. The thought drove right up under his rib cage, but dammit, he needed to concentrate on Opal. He'd think about what this all meant for him later. "I know so. You did it, sweetheart." The endearment seemed to roll right off his tongue.

Opal beamed.

In the back corner of the shop, he saw a woman sweep the flowered curtain aside and step out of the enclosed cubicle, followed by another lady. Jack had been aware of the low murmur beyond the wall, but was too intent on Opal to care.

"Thank you so much, Miss Smith. I didn't know what on earth to do. It was driving me crazy. But now…" The older woman, middle-aged and matronly, spread her hands, the sleeves of her white blouse ruffling with the expansive gesture. "Oh, my dear, I just don't have words."

"I'm glad I could help. And you can do what has to be done." This one was younger, her voice a sweet melody. She had Opal's blue eyes and blond hair, but the resemblance ended there. Slighter, with an air of fragility, a puff of wind through the open door might have knocked her down. She looked as tired as Jack had felt before hearing that radio news bit. Dark circles beneath her eyes spoke of more than one sleepless night. Opal was lush like a garden, her sister, though with the potential for beauty, was nothing more than a young sapling bent by the wind.

"Let me walk you out." After giving Jack a once up-and-down survey, the sister took the lady's arm and walked her to the front door of the shop, murmuring further encouragements.

He leaned into Opal, sniffing gently at her delicate perfume, letting it swirl inside his head. "Is that Pearl?" Though he knew before he asked.

"Yes. She reads tarot, and she's good with runes."

The former he knew had to do with cards, the latter, he didn't have a clue about. "Did you tell her you kicked Nile last night on her behalf?"

"No. I didn't even tell her I saw him."

"Then I won't mention it." He zipped his lips.

"Thank you." Opal's eyes sparkled her gratitude.

It knocked him sideways. Her smile was the reason he'd rushed over here, armed with a newspaper detailing the event. The desire for her smile made him toss aside his good sense.

"Are you going to tell her about this?" He tapped the paper once more, unwilling to use the word "vision."

"No." She gave a decisive shake of her head, a lock of hair falling forward from behind her ear. He wanted to stroke it back in place. "I want to tell all my family at once," she announced.

"When?" He shouldn't have asked, dreading what would come next.

"Tonight. At Grandma Blue's. I'll have to start making arrangements right away so that everyone's there, and Grandma Blue has time to make yummy things to eat. Will you come over?" She leaned closer, her scent setting him off-kilter once more. The sister was coming back, her footsteps softened by the carpet. "Independent verification and all," Opal whispered. "Please."

How could he even consider saying no when she uttered *please* with that pretty little pucker?

She pulled back before he could find his voice and folded the newspaper to cover the brief article. "Pearl, this is Jack."

Pearl tipped her head the same way Opal did. "Jack?"

"Jack. The guy who hit me."

That deserved a glare. He gave Opal a stern one.

"I mean, the person who rear-ended me when I so foolishly slammed my brakes too hard on the freeway the other day."

"Ah, the one who wrecked your car." A hint of a smile curved Pearl's lips. Opal's smile was much more devastating.

Jack let Opal off the hook. "I'm here about the insurance stuff." The excuse had worked easily enough on Opal's mother the other night.

"So you haven't heard from your insurance about your estimates yet?" Opal queried, as if that had been the topic Pearl interrupted. "His bumpers got a bit mashed," she explained for her sister's benefit.

That very sister was eyeing him speculatively, her gaze flicking to Opal, then back to him.

"I haven't heard about the truck. What about *your* car?"

"Sil, my auto guy, called to say that someone had been in to evaluate it yesterday. They pretty much agree it's totaled, a bent frame or something."

He felt a ridiculous surge of jealousy at the casual way she referred to her auto guy. *My* auto guy. "That's too bad," he sympathized. A bent frame was definitely bad. Thank God she hadn't been hurt. He looked at the sister looking at him, then checked his watch. "Better go."

"I'll walk you out." Opal rounded the counter, tucked her arm through his. "Grandma Blue's. Eight o'clock," she whispered in his ear as they reached the door. Did she have any idea what that did to him? No, because she went on with barely a breath between sentences. "I've got to make sure Mother will be there. She can be a bit difficult with last-minute arrangements."

Yet Blue had accomplished it the night he'd met Lillian. "I'm sure you can wrap her around your little finger." Just as Opal had him wrapped around hers.

She snorted, which was kind of cute. "My mother does the wrapping, not me."

He could have shown her exactly how badly he wanted her wrapped around him, but they were framed in the front doorway and the sister was staring with a knowing gaze.

"Eight o'clock," Opal repeated in a breathy voice that sent his blood into perpetual motion.

"I wouldn't miss it." What harm was there in supporting her? Once her family believed that she was psychic, she could stop trying to prove herself. He could stop worrying about her.

It was only out in the bright sunshine that he had his

epiphany. If *he* didn't believe in her vision, how was he going to make her family believe?

IT WAS A MIRACLE. She was psychic. Opal was breathless, light-headed and tingly all over. Even her fingertips hummed. She'd gotten less than five hours sleep last night, but she felt totally energized. This must be what it felt like to skydive. Or climb to the top of Mount Everest. Or enter King Tut's tomb after it had been sealed for three thousand years. It was also a bit like being on the Titanic just before it sank. What if something went wrong?

"You're mooning over him."

Pearl's voice pulled her out of her reverie. Opal was still standing by the front door. Jack was gone. But life was good. Closing the door, she smiled like a movie heroine after the first kiss. "I'm not mooning." Which sounded like something one did bare-assed for a joke.

"And he was mooning over you."

"He was not." But she liked thinking he had been. Jack was oh-so-marvelously wonderful. He believed!

Pearl tilted her head, a knowing smile creasing her lips. "Right. If it was 'insurance stuff' he wanted, he could have called you."

"He was in the area."

"Likely excuse."

"It was business."

"That little tête-à-tête by the door didn't look like business. If I hadn't been here, I think the guy would have grabbed your tush."

Opal rolled her eyes. "You sound just like Grandma Blue."

Pearl crossed her arms over her chest, drummed her fingers against her elbow and arched one brow. "And just when did he meet Grandma Blue?"

Damn her own big mouth. If she told Pearl how Jack met Grandma Blue, then she'd end up spilling her guts about last night and how she'd kicked dirty rotten Nile in the shin, though he had deserved it. Then the whole vision thing would come out before she was ready. Better to keep quiet about everything. Opal busied herself straightening books on the shelf. "This place really needs a cleaning. Where's my feather duster?"

Pearl sauntered a couple of steps closer. "He is awfully handsome, just like you said. And *you* have the hots for him."

Putting her thumb and forefinger together with barely an inch between them, Opal said, "Just this much. Nothing serious."

Besides, he was her *unbiased* witness. Her stomach turned over anew with the miracle. It was happening for her, it really was. She didn't think she could dust, she didn't think she could stay cooped up in the shop all day. She wanted to dance.

"What?" With her thoughts of dancing, she'd completely missed what Pearl said.

"You might think it's nothing serious, but he's got other things on his mind."

"You're exaggerating." But Opal's heart leaped.

"Come on, Opal, you've got to admit there's something going on between you two."

The phone rang. Opal rushed the distance to the counter and pounced on it before Pearl could. "Bedazzled?" In her relief, it came out almost like a question.

"May I please speak to Opal Smith?"

Oh, no. She knew exactly who it was. "This is Opal."

"My dear, it's Victor Patell. I was just calling to see if you'd had any luck finding a medium for me." He was breathless, as if he'd been running. But eighty-something-year-old men didn't run. Maybe it was his anxiety about contacting his wife. Opal's stomach headed south with a queasy sensation.

"I need a little more time." What oh what was she to do? "Can you call back tomorrow?"

There was a lengthy pause as if he were trying to keep from bashing his head with the receiver because she was *so* useless. Yet his answer, when it came, was extremely polite. "Why, of course, my dear. What time?" She had the feeling he'd call at five o'clock in the morning if she let him.

Victor oozed with worry. Opal soothed her guilt with the thought that his wife's spirit wouldn't be gone tomorrow or the next day. She'd still be there in August if that was the best Opal could do with Julian. The thought felt like a cop-out.

"I'll call you, since the shop isn't open on Sunday," she told him.

"That's fine, just fine." She could tell by the quiver in his voice that it wasn't. "What time?"

How long was long enough for her to figure out what to do? "How about ten?" Still not long enough, but she couldn't stall the poor man forever. Maybe she needed to rag harder on Julian. Or perhaps she'd have a brilli- ant idea tonight after she told her mother about the vision. If she proved she was psychic, well then, she'd have much more clout in the family.

"Let me give you my number."

But she wasn't listening as he rattled it off. Her vision was real. She was psychic. Maybe she could… "I'm sorry, I didn't have a pen. What was that again?" This time she wrote even as her mind reeled with possibilities.

She *was* psychic. Maybe *she* could talk to his wife. She'd watched Julian do it enough. She could copy what he did.

"Tomorrow then, Miss Smith." Victor paused long enough for Opal to feel uncomfortable again. "Thank you."

Finally, he was gone, but her mind still whirled.

"Who was that?" Pearl asked at her elbow.

"A dear old man who needs a medium to contact his wife." She could do it. She had to at least try. Maybe she should take a couple of books home on the subject.

"Why don't you get Julian to do it?"

"I tried. He can't come up until August." Opal tapped the pen against her lips, thinking, thinking.

Pearl misunderstood. "Well, don't look at me. You know that's not my gig."

No, it wasn't Pearl's gig. But since Opal had never tried it—except with a Ouija board when she was thirteen and that failure didn't count because her brother was manipulating the board—there was no reason not to give it a try.

"So, how about coming to Grandma Blue's tonight?" Where she'd break the wonderful, stupendous, unbelievable news about her psychic gift. "I feel the need to binge on the appetizers she's got in her freezer."

Then Pearl said, as if she had a psychic hint about what would be happening tonight, "Wouldn't miss it."

Which is exactly what Jack said. Opal felt the entire universe supporting her.

She pulled the newspaper closer as if it were a signed, sealed, delivered certificate from the Academy of Psychic Professionals.

Once she'd earned her family's respect tonight, she'd invite them all to Victor's séance. They couldn't refuse.

OPAL LEFT EARLY. AGAIN.

Pearl could only be thankful that her sister, in the wake of this new man in her life, seemed to have forgotten all about Nile's letter. Pearl was tired, grumpy and she'd had two too many double-shot mochas. The envelope was still in the back room by the side of the espresso machine. Waiting for her.

Coward. She was hanging in inner space. She had to cut the cord. Or take him back. She had to stop giving that damn letter supernatural powers.

The phone rang at her elbow. Pearl jumped as if a spider had dropped on her head.

"Bedazzled. How can I help you?"

"Open it."

The command set her nerves jangling worse than the mochas had. "How do you know I haven't read the letter, Nile?"

She could almost hear him clamp down on his teeth. "You wouldn't be so calm if you'd read what's in there."

Now *that* shot shivers of alarm along her scalp worse than the thought of spiders tangled in her hair. "You were always so secretive. That's one of the things that bugged me." When they were face-to-face, she empathized with him. Now, he just made her angry.

"Secrecy is a hazard of the job."

"Your job is about revealing things to people, Nile, not keeping them in."

He was quiet a long time. "I've lost it, Pearl. I can't read objects anymore."

She felt the words crawl through her mind. As much as she hated being different sometimes, hated the outcast complex, hated it when she couldn't help someone the way they needed, to be without her gift…she simply wouldn't know who she was anymore. Her gift defined her.

"I'm sorry, Nile." For him, it might actually be a blessing.

His voice, when it finally came, was barely above a whisper. "I've prayed for this, you know, to lose it. To be free of it. But not this way. Not when someone's family needs me again."

"You mean Tamara's family?"

"Yes. That's exactly what I mean. Help me find my gift again. You're the only one who can."

Her anger rose once more in a wave. "Don't you dare put this on me, Nile. It isn't my problem."

"I can't find her," he whispered. "I need you."

"I don't have those kind of capabilities, Nile. I can't find her for you."

"No, but you can help me find the thing I've lost."

"Nile, I could never help you with anything." All she could do was love him, and that had never been enough.

"Only because I never let you see what it was like."

"Because you would never share anything with me." Not his greatest triumphs nor his deepest fears. She was sure he didn't have a clue how much that had hurt. But she also suffered a fear of his revelations that she hadn't known when they were together.

"I'm willing to share now, Pearl. Open that letter and you'll know exactly how it feels to be me. You don't even have to be psychic to understand."

The anger was blinding. She wanted to hurt him, to rend his soul the way he'd shredded hers. "Opal's right. You're a dirty rat bastard. All you do is take, Nile, expect, need."

"And give nothing in return. I know. I just need to take from you this one last time. For Tamara."

"And you're an extortionist, too."

She slammed the phone down, then wanted to rip it from the wall and send it flying through the front window.

Damn him. Slamming through the bead curtain to the back room, she stopped by the counter. And damn the damn letter, too. Grabbing it, she crumpled it into a ball and threw it into the trash can.

She wouldn't fall for his crap this time, she just wouldn't, but her fingers flexed impotently.

The bell over the front door tinkled. She peeked through the curtain. Two teenage girls. Gigglers. They laughed and covered their mouths as if they'd walked into a sex shop.

"Can I help you?" Pearl asked, entering the front part of the store with the sweetest smile she could muster. It probably came off looking more like a grimace.

From the back room, the letter called to her like an incubus in the night. She should have ripped it up or burned it.

Because in the end, she knew she had to read it. For the missing girl, if not for Nile.

CHAPTER THIRTEEN

IT WAS A PARTY! Grandma Blue had pulled out baking sheets full of homemade hors d'oeuvres from her double-door freezer in the laundry room. Filling the kitchen were the scents of sausage rolls, sweet-and-sour chicken wings, potato skins, cheese puffs, crab-stuffed mushroom caps and more. Opal made spinach dip, her mouth twanging with anticipation.

"How should I tell them?" She really wished Julian was going to be here, too. For now, she'd have to content herself with telling Pearl and her mother.

Grandma Blue slid hot cheese puffs onto a cooling rack, licking the crumbs from her fingers. "Don't get your hopes up."

Too late. She was already flying. "This is the biggest thing that's ever happened to me. I deserve to be excited." Finally, she would be just like the other members of her family. The *psychic* members. She could barely contain her exhilaration.

"Remember that genealogy project you worked so hard on?"

Opal dipped a piece of French bread into the spinach mélange, then closed her eyes to savor the delicious concoction. Who invented spinach dip? "Grandma

Blue, that was the sixth grade. And it wasn't the same thing at all."

"You were sure you'd get an A plus. Instead you got an F."

Opal could still remember the horror of it. She'd flunked. The only time in her life. She snatched a sausage roll off the cooling rack and popped it in her mouth. Flaky pastry with delicious, greasy, bad-for-your-arteries sausage. Wonderful. So what if she got an F in the sixth grade?

"It taught me a big lesson, Grandma Blue."

"What, that you shouldn't tell your teacher your mother was Cleopatra in another life?"

"No. That genealogy means different things to different people." Mmm, the smell of mushrooms, crab and Parmesan cheese made her taste buds go wild.

Grandma Blue slapped her hand. "Quit eating that stuff until the family gets here."

"What difference does it make whether it goes into my stomach now or later?"

"Don't do it because I told you not to do it."

Opal leaned over to kiss her cheek. "Spoken like a true grandmother who doesn't know the answer."

Grandma Blue nudged her aside. "All right, dammit, now tell me about your lesson."

"Oh." Opal licked the finger she'd just run around the spinach dip bowl. "Well, some people think a genealogy is your family tree. Or it's a history of your family. Rich snooties might even call it their pedigree. But…"

She paused for drama. Grandma Blue shot her a quelling glare.

"It's so much more than those mundane things. It's

like the universe, endless, boundless. It isn't just biological. It's this wondrous thing that explains why you are who you are." Opal spread her hands, waving the wooden spoon in the air before licking the last remnants. "Which is why I had to put in there that Mother had once been Cleopatra. We come from a long line of magnificent rulers."

"As I recall, Cleopatra got power hungry and had to feed herself to a bunch of snakes."

Opal pulled her shoulders back regally and tossed her hair with a flourish. "She was a queen."

Grandma Blue pulled another baking sheet from the oven. More delicious aromas filled the kitchen. "The only thing your mother was queen of was the bathroom. She spent hours in there picking her face and curling her hair. Cleopatra she was not."

Opal slumped, put her elbows on the counter and her chin in her hands. "Well, all I know is that teacher didn't have a creative bone in her body. My family tree was unique—"

Grandma Blue snorted. "I'll give you that, all right."

"—and thought-provoking. It didn't deserve an F."

"But you got crushed. Which is what I'm trying to say about tonight. If you keep your expectations low, you can't be hurt."

Opal stared at her grandmother with wide eyes and open mouth. "Why, Grandma Blue, I've never heard you say such a horrible thing in my whole life."

"Contrary to popular opinion around this dump, I've got my feet on the ground."

"But what about Dynamite?"

"Dynamite was a fantasy. I always knew that. You have to learn the difference, Opal."

This *couldn't* be Grandma Blue talking. "But my vision…"

Slamming the oven door shut, Grandma Blue switched off the heat. "There, we're ready. I'll do another couple of batches later. Now where's that no-account family tree of yours?"

Opal looked at her watch, letting herself be distracted. Fifteen minutes to eight.

The doorbell rang. Opal jumped. It had to be Jack. Both Pearl and her mother would have walked right in. Her fingers suddenly shook with nervousness.

"Go answer the door, girl."

Opal almost skipped. With excitement and stress. She'd be a basket case by the time she made her momentous announcement.

Maybe she'd have Jack give her a big, fat, sloppy kiss for luck. Her lips were practically puckered as she opened the door.

"Julian! What are you doing here?"

"Your grandmother threatened to disinherit me if I didn't attend your little soiree." He didn't smile. His finances were in worse shape than she feared if he flew up from L.A. on a moment's notice to make sure he remained in the will.

She dragged him inside. "You've lost weight."

"Working hard. You look—" he patted her cheek "—like the cat that ate the canary."

She certainly did. And while he was here, she'd get him to do that little séance for Victor. Oh, the universe was certainly working in her favor today.

JACK'S HAIR STOOD ON END, and, yes, that clicking sound had to be his teeth chattering. The Smith family was something to see. Blond, beautiful and completely nutzoid.

Pearl, the sister, was a stunning waif, but definitely moody if the downward curve of her lips was any indication. Lillian, the mother, played the heavy-handed queen bee, signaling her children with a flippant wave of her hand whenever she wanted something. The brother, Julian, obviously assumed he was Apollo the God material. Tall, blond and good-looking in a wimpy aristocratic way.

When channel surfing in the past, Jack had seen him briefly. Very briefly. Though he might not have made the connection if Julian hadn't managed at least five times in a three-minute conversation to insert the fact that he was a famous TV personality.

"Opal, you're acting a little more manic than usual." Julian shoved a greasy sausage thingamabob into his mouth and spoke around it. "Did Pearl screw up your runes again?"

Opal shot Jack an impotent look. The sniping had been going on almost since he'd arrived forty-five minutes ago, and now he just wanted to pop the asshole brother one in the kisser. Julian somehow managed to insult both sisters in one fell swoop, even if Jack wasn't exactly sure how. "I think her runes look great."

Julian eyed him, an indulgent gleam in the contact-enhanced depths. "You would."

Jack figured he hadn't said the right thing.

Opal figured that, too, because she started defending herself, or rather, her sister. "Julian, you know Pearl doesn't read the people she loves, not even with runes."

No one seemed to care.

"Opal, I think you might have put a tad too much mayonnaise in the spinach dip." Lillian was a percher, sitting on the edge of the sofa and pulling her head back to stare down her nose at the dip-laden French bread. "Did you use the light kind?"

Blue didn't give her granddaughter a chance to answer. "Opal used my recipe, so it's perfect."

Lillian was also a brow-archer. "Mother, you don't have a recipe for spinach dip."

"Had one since before my first tumble in the hay with your father." Blue gave Jack a twinkle. "Premarital, of course."

Lillian sniffed delicately. "Mother, you're embarrassing Opal's guest."

"I'm not embarrassed," Jack stepped in. "And you can call me Jack." After all, he'd earned a first-name basis since she'd "intrigued" him for an hour describing her star-reading.

The woman took a deep breath, straightened her already impossibly straight spine and gazed down her nose at him. "I'm so glad to hear you have a thick skin, Jack." Distaste rolled off her tongue.

The brother dusted off his fingers and jumped into the middle of the fray. "All right, Opal, what's this favor you want in return for getting my finances back where they should be?"

Opal opened her mouth to answer Julian, but got no further than, "I—"

"And next time, you need to keep a closer eye on them so they don't get so 'mucked up,' as you put it."

"But it's not—"

"I'm not blaming you. I'm just saying it would be easier on both of us."

Jack started gnashing his teeth. He couldn't stand the pompous ass. "Perhaps you should get a financial planner you *pay* to do that kind of thing."

Julian's blond eyebrows shot to the top of his forehead. "Why on earth would I pay someone when I have Opal?"

Jack bared his teeth. "Because—"

Opal coughed. Loudly. "Jack."

She idolized these people? Wanted to be psychic just to impress them? Wanted to *be* like them? Jack managed a deep breath, controlled his tongue and searched for something inane to say. "Blue thinks I'm the reincarnation of Dynamite Davis."

Blue rose from her recliner as regal in her lime-green muumuu as Lillian was in her designer suit. "Don't you think he has Dynamite's—" Blue's gaze dropped pointedly below the belt of his khaki trousers "—physique?"

Pearl stifled a snort of laughter, the first sound she'd made the entire evening. Julian outright guffawed. Lillian closed her eyes, accompanying it with a long-suffering sigh. At least she hadn't brought Little Shit with her this time. His pant legs were safe from cat claws, if nothing else.

Opal's eyes bugged out, her skin burned an apoplectic red and he was afraid she'd swallowed her tongue. Blue slapped her on the back, and she sucked in a shaky breath.

When it came to her family, he sure did suck at figuring out the right thing to say. Or do.

"Dynamite," Blue commanded. "In the kitchen. Now."

He beat a hasty retreat, guilt at leaving Opal defenseless moving his feet faster. Get in, get out, be back a moment later.

In the kitchen, the little lady handed him two pot holders and opened the oven door. The family had pretty much plowed through what she'd prepared, and she was into her second batch. "They're ready," she announced.

He bent down, the heat rolling like a wave across his face. "You didn't ask me in here to take snacks out of the oven."

"They're crucifying her, Dynamite. We have to do something."

"I am." He put the two trays of steaming appetizers on top of the stove.

"I mean something besides verbal rapier thrusts with The Mother and The Brother." Blue carefully slid a spatula under each tidbit, then moved it to a rack.

"How about just throwing them out of the house?"

"Nope, Opal won't go for that." The wizened flesh of her face creased in thought. "She wouldn't have minded that they were picking on her except that you were there, and she was trying to impress you."

Opal didn't need to impress him.

"But she thinks she does."

His eyes moved to her without the slightest turn of his head. "I didn't say that aloud."

"Of course, you didn't. But you need to work on developing a poker face. You must lose your shirt playing cards. Not that I'd mind seeing you without a shirt."

He realized they were whispering. And Blue was making those horrific innuendos again. The sound of Opal's voice carried, explaining about…he didn't quite get it. Something about Julian doing a séance and contacting the spirit essence of the wife of a friend of hers.

And Julian's refrain: "Sorry, no can do, sweetcheeks. Your little shindig is costing me time away from all those helpless souls who need me." Julian deserved a good fistfight.

Then Lillian got in on the act. "Opal, you know how important your brother's work is."

Maybe they both deserved a good knockout. Not that he would ever hit a woman.

Determination flowed through him. "All right. What do you want me to do that I haven't already been doing?"

"You gotta tell them about Opal's vision. But don't mention the prostitution thing. That'll just give The Mother another thing to gripe about."

He almost choked on one of the too-hot goodies he'd stolen from the tray. "Me?" He stabbed a finger to his chest.

She added a poke, too. "You're Dynamite's reincarnation, and that's what he'd do if he wanted to get into a girl's pants." She'd lowered her whisper to a dramatic hiss.

"I wouldn't defend a girl against her family just to get in her pants."

"Then why *are* you defending her?"

Because Opal needed him. Because her so-called family ripped the sparkle from Opal's eyes with every nitpick. He couldn't stand it. But he wasn't going to tell Blue that. "It's the right thing to do. They're making mincemeat out of her."

They stood nose to nose, or rather nose to damn near navel with Blue being so many inches shorter than him.

"And why do you care?"

She knocked him upside the head with that one. He did care. Too much. Just as he *liked* looking after Opal too much. He straightened, letting Blue feel his full height. "I don't like it when people get ganged up on."

"She's used to it." She flashed a thumb over her shoulder. "This ain't nothing." She went back to arranging her trays. "All right, if you won't do it, I'll have to."

He had visions of Blue, drama queen extraordinaire, describing battered bodies annihilated beneath the tires of Opal's car, how Opal walked the bridge until she'd worn through the soles of her five-inch platform shoes, how she'd...

He'd handle it. "It should be something short and sweet. I'll take care of it."

Blue blinked, wiped her hands on a tea towel and smiled. He'd been had, and he knew it, but he could live with it.

He carried the tray into the living room. Lillian still perched like a bird, Julian scowled and Pearl ran her fingers across the top of a rumpled envelope she held in her hands.

"I'm sure you're wondering why Opal asked you here," he announced dramatically.

Julian didn't wonder. "She wanted to blackmail me."

Jesus, everything was about *him*. Get a life. "This is about Opal, not you."

They all stared at Opal as if she'd suddenly become a newly discovered variety of bug. All right, maybe not the sister—who'd mesmerized herself with that envelope.

"Do you need a letter opener or something?"

Pearl jerked at his question and shoved the letter

down between the seat cushions. "No. I'm fine. You were saying?"

"Opal asked you here to announce—" What? Her vision? Her psychic gift? Saving the little guy from the bridge?

"Oh, God, she's pregnant," Lillian moaned, then dabbed a starched lace handkerchief to her lips.

"No."

"She's going to marry *you,* a construction worker?" Lillian Fontaine could muster a degree of disdain that would reduce a fifty-ton girder to scrap metal. Jack was made of stronger stuff.

But was Opal? For the first time, he glanced at her. His heart jumped in his throat. She was staring at him with the sparkle back in her eyes and the most hopeful smile on her lips, as if she thought he really was Jack the Giant Killer.

And the words that were stuck in his throat suddenly gushed out. "Opal had a vision."

Julian harrumphed as Blue shoved the newspaper, folded back to display the article in question, into Jack's hands.

He held up Opal's proof for all to see. "Opal knew this guy was going to try leaping off the bridge. And she saved him."

Lillian leaned across the coffee table to snatch the newspaper from his hand. Everyone started shooting questions around the compact living room.

"How on earth—"

Opal had all the right answers. "That's why I had my accident."

"What accident?" Julian asked.

"The one where Jack rear-ended me. I thought I ran over a body that fell off the overpass. And then…" Opal laid out the whole story for them, glowing with the telling of it.

"Let me get this straight," Julian began his paraphrase. "You saw a body in what you thought was a vision, during which Jack here totaled your car, then you waited on the bridge, you talked to the guy several times, insulted him and finally saved him when he tried to climb the fence and jump onto the freeway."

Beneath the probing eyes of her mother and brother, Opal stumbled. "I didn't exactly stop him from doing that. The police did." Her eyes flashed to Blue's fingers as they pressed to her ancient lips. "They were…"

"They were what, Opal? Dear?" Lillian's endearment didn't come off sounding very endearing.

Opal turned a frantic gaze to Jack, and he took over the explanations. "The police were worried about Opal's safety up there on the overpass. They were there because they were watching out for her."

"Why would they do that?"

"Because." The stern look Jack shot Julian surprisingly shut him up.

"There's the proof in that article," Blue supplied.

Lillian's blond head bent over the newspaper. "It says here they were looking for prostitutes."

"That's why they were worried about Opal being up there," Jack invented. "The unsavory element."

"It also says here that the Poor Lost Soul—" Lillian's teeth gnashed over every word "—was insulted by one of those prostitutes." She looked at Opal. "Did he think you were a prostitute?"

Jack slashed a hand through the air to shut them up. "You're missing the point here. Opal knew this man was going to jump off the overpass into freeway traffic before he ever even tried it. And because of her, he was saved."

Julian sat down again, hiking his trouser legs up to accommodate his knees. "You've got that wrong, chum."

"How so? It's there in black and white." He really had to beat the guy up fairly soon.

"If this article is correct, and Opal confirms that it is—" Julian glanced at Opal now sitting silently in the chair Blue had vacated "—then this is a case of Opal creating her own reality."

Lillian smiled. Jack sensed a touch of malice to it. "You're exactly right, Julian. She's created her own reality."

Jack, still standing, jammed his hands on his hips. "What the hell does that mean?"

Julian did the honors. "It means that Opal so believed in her own *vision*—" he double quoted his fingers for emphasis and maybe a little ridicule "—that she created a person who would fit the bill."

"You mean she deliberately went up there four nights in a row and insulted some poor slob so that he would jump off the bridge just to prove she'd had a vision?" Jack's hands fisted at his sides now. "Maybe you think she bribed him to do it, too."

Julian spread his hands expansively. "No, no, no. There was nothing deliberate. It's just that she resonated her desire for the *vision* to come true so loudly that the universe created it as reality for her."

Opal stared at her hands.

"What are they talking about, Opal?"

She spoke to her hands. "Julian's right. I never thought of it that way. But if I hadn't been there to insult the poor man, he wouldn't have had any reason to jump off the bridge. So rather than what I saw being a vision, it was merely a daydream that I turned into reality."

Jack turned to Blue. She raised her eyebrows and hands at the same time in a what-do-you-expect-me-to-do gesture.

A sudden shriek tore the room in two. Pearl, on her feet, fists balled, the telltale edges of the letter crumpled in her hand, fire-flashed her audience with a ferocious glare. "Why don't you all leave her alone? Let her have her vision, give her a big kiss and a hug, whatever. What difference does it make to you? Can't you, for once, be supportive?"

Then she burst into a flood of tears, grabbed her purse, dashed through the front door and disappeared into the darkness.

Blue, a gust of wind ballooning her muumuu, closed the door. "Now that's what I call having a bug up your ass."

Opal laughed, the sound a note off true. Jack wanted nothing more than to gather her in his arms. He knew a crushing blow when he saw it. All her hopes, all her dreams, the most important thing in the world to her...

Julian slapped his hands on his knees. "Well, now that we've got that settled, I just wanted to mention, Jack, that I see a presence hanging around you."

"A what?"

"I sense a mother figure. Has your mother passed?"

Passed what? Gas? Jack's head felt as if it were floating in ether. "She's dead, if that's what you mean."

"I'm getting an M name. Martha, something like that?"

Margaret. Jack's muscles turned to steel, his jaw clenched and he couldn't have gotten a word out even if he'd wanted to.

"She wants you to know that she's safe now. You don't have to worry about her anymore, and she was always so thankful you were there when she needed you. And—" the asshole made some sort of swirling motion with his hands "—she wants you to know that she's sorry about the Tinker Bell thing." He turned to Jack with a brotherly, caring, totally phony smile on his arrogant face. "Does this mean anything to you?"

Jack saw red. He wanted to smash his fist into Julian's smug face. Both fists. "Don't ever try pulling that shit on me. I'm *not* one of your viewers."

"Ooh, hit a sore spot, did we?"

He itched to pound Julian Smith's pearly whites right down his throat. He might have done it, too, except for the gentle hand on his arm. Opal. Sweet, soft Opal.

"Julian, leave Jack alone right now."

The ass gaped at her. "I wasn't—"

"You were. So just stop it." And she glared.

Jack hadn't known her blue eyes could muster such a hard edge. His heart gave an odd lurch. Milquetoast-with-her-family Opal was going to bat for him. Against her star-quality brother. Jack had always picked up the bat on behalf of someone else, usually his mother. But this time, Opal was defending *him*. He'd wondered what the phenomenon would feel like, but now, faced with the reality, he wasn't even sure. Only that it felt good. Damn good. Maybe too good. A man couldn't let a woman fight his battles.

Except for this one. Because as much as Opal was

going to bat for him, she was also standing up for herself after the way Julian the star had trounced her earlier.

Opal pulled on his arm. "Come on, Jack. It's time to go."

Way past time. Jack was still pissed, but smashing the guy's teeth in wouldn't feel as good as having Opal stand up to her brother on his account.

Being with Opal was starting to feel too good all around.

BLUE GLARED AT The Mother and The Brother, clasping her hands tightly behind her back to keep from jumping with glee. If that fierce protective look Jack had given Opal meant anything, the boy was hooked but good.

But now to the task at hand. "That was shameful."

Lillian, the little whelp that had come from Blue's very own loins, pursed her overly ripe red lips. "Oh come, Mother. You know Opal didn't have a vision."

She knew no such thing. "Pearl's right. You should have let Opal have her moment."

Julian cleared his throat. "Grandma Blue, I think you blew that one when you stared at her beau's crotch." He covered his mouth to giggle like a child of ten.

Blue pointed one of her bony, arthritic fingers at him, the action almost painful. Damn the old fingers anyway. "And you, playing your hocus-pocus on the unsuspecting."

Julian shrugged. "I'd be remiss if I didn't tell him his mother was nearby watching over him. I don't know why you and Opal are so upset about it."

"You just wanted to cut the rug out from under him."

"You're so melodramatic." The Mother always

stepped in to defend her perfect baby boy, whether the boy was wrong or right.

Blue socked it to them both. "You want melodramatic? I'll give you melodramatic. You're both cut out of my will."

They stared at her with similar aghast expressions.

"You don't mean that."

"I'm leaving it all to Opal and Pearl."

"But, Mother—"

"But, Grandma Blue—"

She held up a gnarly hand. Goodness, her hands looked old. "Not another word. And get out. Or I might never change my mind."

Thanks to Chester, her dearly departed, much-loved husband, and the settlement the ice-cream company paid for his wrongful death, Blue's estate was nothing to sneeze at. She hadn't necessarily wanted the money, but after Chester lost his life saving those kiddies, well, she just had to make sure that ice-cream company *never* let another drunk behind the wheel of one of their trucks. Of course, these days, ice-cream trucks were few and far between. See, her plan had worked!

At her threat, the two scoundrels shot out the front door like balls out of a cannon.

Now for Pearl. Blue tried the number, but it merely rang and rang until the blasted machine picked up. Oh, she hated machines. Especially since they always made her sound stupid. It was just that she couldn't find the right joke if there wasn't somebody standing in front of her to appreciate it.

Blue tried anyway. Someone had to try for the girl.

"I've got one word for you, Missie. Nile. Now get cracking."

She was sure Pearl would understand.

Turning on both TVs, she punched the volume up, sat back in her favorite recliner and hit the play button. Ah, last Sunday's race, and there was that nice hunky driver all dressed in lovely Viagra blue ready to get into his Viagra-sponsored car. "Go Viagra," she cheered. She'd wean next week.

Right about now, Dynamite should be getting into Opal's pants.

CHAPTER FOURTEEN

JACK HAD NOT MADE IT to the zipper of Opal's jeans. He hadn't even made it to the buttons of her blouse or the clasp of her bra. In fact, he hadn't even tried. Much to Opal's disappointment. Things had gone so wrong at Grandma Blue's. A nice little escapist orgasm or two right now would be perfect.

"Tell me how I can help you, sweetie." Jack stroked her back as she half lay across his lap in the cab of his truck.

In Grandma Blue's house, Jack had been mad as a skunk-sprayed wasps' nest. She'd seen such a thing once, and it had indeed been a scary sight. Not to mention the smell. Julian really shouldn't have mentioned his mother. She'd been honor-bound to come to Jack's defense, though she should have stepped in a few minutes earlier. Having sensed there was something about his mother that bothered Jack, for a little while there, she'd thought Julian's comments might be good for him. On Julian's show, people found such relief in hearing from their departed loved ones. It wasn't that way for Jack. She actually thought he might punch her brother. At some point, she should get him to talk about his mom. Only now wasn't the time.

Right now, she wanted to wallow in her *own* misery.

Opal burrowed her face against his throat. Such a hero, he'd insisted on driving her home after her disappointment—though somehow they hadn't made it inside her apartment—and even offered to drive her back to Grandma Blue's in the morning to pick up her rental car.

Did he mean to spend the night? Not a bad idea.

She sniffed for effect. "Don't call me sweetie."

"Fine, no more sweeties. But what can I do so you'll stop crying?"

"I'm not crying."

Her eyelashes dripped, her nose had an attack of the sniffles and her voice had developed a nasal twang, but no, of course she wasn't crying.

He tucked a finger beneath her jaw and tugged her chin up. "You know, I believe in your vision."

Her lips felt all quivery, and she could barely see him through the watery sheen misting her eyes. But she wasn't crying. "They're right. I created it all myself."

Jack snorted, and she wanted to hug him for being on her side despite the fact that he was a nonbeliever.

"Your family isn't right about everything. And they're wrong about this. You take what they say too much to heart."

"They're my family. Of course I take what they say to heart."

"Yes, but—"

She put a hand over his mouth. "I can't help it if I want them to believe in me." She spread her hands as if that could express everything she felt. "They're my family."

He sighed. "Well, at least let me ask you this. How could you have the ability to make some guy try to jump off a bridge?"

She dipped her head. "It was that thing I said to him."

"Which thing?"

She hadn't told Jack the other night, but she had to now, to show him how she'd created the whole situation. "The one about how I wouldn't have sex with him even if he paid me a million dollars. And that I'd have my boyfriend beat him up." The words brought back the shame of what she'd done to that poor man.

"Aw, honey, that's really not all that bad."

She felt Jack's smile as he leaned over to kiss her forehead. Holding her against him, the unmistakable shudder of his shoulders confirmed his laughter.

Opal pulled back, braced her hands on his chest. "You're laughing at me."

"Never. I'm in full commiseration of your disappointment."

"You mean failure."

"I mean disappointment that your family didn't accept it."

"I have to face that I'm not psychic. I never have been and I never will be."

"You saw a vision of a body, then some guy decided to jump. No matter why he decided, that's psychic."

"Anyone could have done that, Jack. Even you."

Giving her an indulgent smile, he pushed her head back down to his shoulder. "You're not giving yourself enough credit."

She could have stayed that way, breathing in his heady scent, sinking into the gentle stroke of his fingers through her hair. She *could* have stayed like that forever, but she had to make him understand. "The universe gives you what you want if you open yourself up to the possibilities. That's what I did." Tipping her head back to look at him, she smoothed her fingers over his chest. "It's like going to an interview for a job you want badly. You put your best foot forward, doing whatever's necessary to make a good impression. And you get the job."

"Except that with a job interview, you have control over your own actions."

"That's it exactly. You control the outcome." She beamed at him. He was getting it.

A car passed, its headlights flashing across his face, illuminating the set of his jaw. Okay, so he wasn't getting it. His patient tone proved it. "Opal, in a job interview, *you* don't have control over whether the person you're interviewing with is actually going to give you the job. And you didn't have control over what that guy's reaction was going to be."

"I'm not explaining it right."

"There's nothing to explain." He slid back a lock of her hair, lingering for a delicious moment on her ear. "You had a vision. I believe you. And screw what your family said. You don't need them."

She liked lying in his arms with the quiet intimacy of the dark surrounding them. She liked his manly defense of her. It pushed back the enormity of what had happened tonight. Maybe she wasn't psychic, but she sure had an ability to create her own reality, and she wanted to do a little creating right now.

Kiss me. She didn't say the words, just looked at him. And he did exactly what she wanted him to do.

His fingers curved against her scalp, and his head blotted out all the light as he slipped his tongue along her bottom lip.

"That's not kissing, that's licking." But, oh, such a nice lick. She wanted more and opened her mouth.

He delved with his tongue, stroking hers, angling her head for better access. Opal moaned, wrapped her arms around his neck and pressed herself to his chest.

She wanted his hands on her breasts, and her nipples peaked against the hard wall of his chest muscles. She rubbed, and things responded, a bulge at her hip, his hand sliding down to her butt, squeezing, yanking her closer so that her body seemed to surround him. Then his fingers up her side and finally, his thumb finding the nub of her nipple. Heat rushed down to her legs as he teased the peak with his nail. She squirmed, adjusting so that her breast filled his hand. His tongue devoured her mouth.

The buttons, she wanted, needed him to undo the buttons of her shirt, push her bra aside and put his hot, hot touch to her bare skin. With another wriggle, she made him groan and forced his hand into contact with the buttons. His quickened breath heated her flesh as the buttons popped open. And then he was inside the lacy cup. Oh, the wonderful feel of calluses abrading her nipple. Unique, erotic sensations spiraled down until moisture pooled between her legs. He tugged on a taut peak, and an electric shock shot straight to her clitoris.

Please, please, an orgasm. His mouth tugged from hers, and he bent his head to the nipple his fingers had worked. He sucked, licked, nipped. She held him fastened to her, her body undulating to the rhythm of his incredible mouth. Oh. Yes. She arched, throwing her head back, a sound halfway between a moan and an outright cry fell from her lips. Her tension built, threatened to bubble over beneath his touch. He cupped her,

pressing the heel of his hand against the hot, oversen-
sitive flesh between her legs. Just a tiny bit more.

She tangled her fingers in his hair. A thousand little
electric lights exploded behind her eyelids. Her body
bucked against his hand, against his mouth at her breast,
his tongue and teeth still clamped to her nipple. She rode
the luscious wave as it crashed over her.

With the ebb, she realized he'd crushed her to his
chest. All smooth and fluid and relaxed, she nuzzled his
throat, sighed against his skin.

"What the hell was that?"

"I had an orgasm."

"Jesus, I didn't even get your jeans off."

"Wasn't necessary."

"Are you always like that?"

"No. I was trying to prove a point."

His breath came out in a gust. "What point?"

"I wanted an orgasm so I created my own reality."

"*I* gave you that orgasm," Jack said.

"*You* didn't even get my jeans off."

"Doesn't matter. My hand was down there."

"And don't forget where your mouth was."

"See, you're admitting I was the one who did it."

"Okay, you helped," Opal admitted. "But I never
even asked aloud."

"You didn't have to say anything aloud. There is
such a thing as body language, you know."

She pulled back and gave him her best militant stare,
eyes narrowed, lips pursed just like her mother's.
"You're a tough nut to crack. There I go, giving you a
perfect demonstration of creating one's own reality, and
you have to scoff."

"You're a nut." But he smiled when he said it.

She hoisted upright, putting several inches between them and bracing her right hand on his left thigh. "All right. How about you trying it? Maybe you'll get the whole process then."

"You want me to create my own orgasm?"

"Yeah. Without saying one word."

"You've got to be kidding."

"No, I'm not." And to prove it, she straddled him. "Come on, let's give it a try."

He grabbed her hips, holding her in place when she wriggled. "I am not coming in my pants to prove something to you."

She pouted. "Don't you want an orgasm?"

His eyes darkened, his fingers clenched against her jeans. "No. Not here. Not now."

But it was obvious he did. With his erection pressed between her legs, she couldn't help herself, she rubbed.

He squeezed his eyes shut, a small groan passing his lips. "Stop that."

She put her hands on his shoulders for leverage, and this time when she rubbed, he was helping her, pushing her down, his hips rising to meet her. His head fell back against the seat.

"See, Jack, it's so easy to create your own reality."

"Uncreate it, then. I'm not coming in my pants like some teenage jerkoff. Please, Opal, not like this. It's too goddamn embarrassing. We're in front of your apartment building, for God's sake."

The tendons at his neck corded, his lips thinned with tension and his eyes seemed to plead with her even as his body rose between her legs and started another fire burning in her.

"I could swallow it all if you wanted. Would that make you feel less like a teenage jerkoff?"

His eyes went dark and luscious. "I thought you didn't do that under any circumstances."

She smiled. "For you, I'll make an exception."

Opal didn't have to offer twice. In two seconds flat, she found herself off his lap, back on the seat beside him, and he'd already worked his buckle free.

"Goodness, you're beautiful."

"Guys aren't beautiful." Jack's snort of laughter ended in a choked groan as she leaned over and swiped her tongue across the tip of his penis. Delicious. He gripped himself in his hand for her feast. He was big, filling her mouth as she slid him in and savored the exotic, salty taste of him. Against her arm, light tremors rippled through him. He let go of his erection as her fingers took over, then he fisted his hands in her hair. He was so hard, and when she dipped down to cup his balls, she was sure he was almost ready.

He wrapped locks of her hair around his hands, stopping just short of pain. She took him as deep as she could, her reward the strangled oath that filled the cab of the truck. Withdrawing, she sucked, hard, squeezing him with her hand as her mouth slid away. Then back down. It was all he could take, his body doubling over as his taste flooded her mouth. She laved lightly until he calmed, slowing rising the length of him and licking him clean. Then she zipped and buckled and patted him down.

Collapsed against the seat, his brown eyes sparkled obsidian as he stared at her.

"Don't ever do that again." He shook himself. "At least not in the truck." He licked his lips. "Or your car. Or anywhere outside in the open."

"I didn't do it, you did. You were almost ready to come before I even went down there. That's what I meant about creating your own reality."

"Well, don't ever create it in my car then."

"You have a truck."

"You know what I mean."

"Is this like not ever sending flowers to a construction site?"

"Exactly like that."

"You have to learn to lighten up, Jack."

He raked an unsteady hand through his hair. "God, why do I hear your grandmother's voice when you say that?"

"Because she'd say it, too."

"I think you've made me totally crazy."

"Jack?" She leaned forward and kissed his cheek, then nuzzled his ear.

"What?"

"Thanks for making me forget about what happened at the party." She really did feel better, much better. Even if depression might hit her later on.

He looked at her, and all the tension that was surely robbing him of a truly fantastic afterglow seemed to melt from his features. "Is that what this was about? Making you forget?"

She tipped her head to one side. "Is that a bad thing?"

"I'm not sure. If I were female, I'd probably feel like you used me."

"I'm sorry."

"But I'm not female, thank God. I'm a guy."

"And guys never feel used?"

He smiled, white teeth in a dark face making him look wolfish. "Not after what you just did to me."

"Besides—" she smiled in return "—I'll come up with something else to prove to my family that I'm psychic."

She knew just what that would be. Victor Patell's séance. If she created a vision, she could create a séance, too.

"WHAT ARE YOU talking about?" Jack's mind had ceased to function around the time Opal went for his zipper. There had been only the slide of her lips down his flesh and the incredible sensations of her mouth on him.

Afterward, he'd almost begged her to let him into her apartment, into her bed, but she'd gone off like a butterfly, babbling something about having to read, read, read. Something about texts on talking to spirits. Did she plan to try raising the dead now?

He wanted her, hell, he even liked her, but what she was saying now failed to make sense in his sex-fogged brain.

"I said that I think I can contact Victor's dead wife for him." Opal wore the most guileless expression and a sparkle in her eye from the lamplight two cars down.

Jack jiggled his finger in his ear. "Something's not making sense here." Maybe it was him. "Why do you want to contact Victor's dead wife?"

She doe-eyed him. "Because Victor's miserable without her. He told me all about it a few days ago when he dropped by the shop after the accident. I have to help him speak with her. She died of some dread disease on Thanksgiving Day—isn't that terrible?—and talking with her will give him relief."

Right. It was something a charlatan—like her brother—would do to bilk an old man out of his money. Opal wasn't like that, but she *was* too sweet for her own good. She wouldn't be able to take it when her séance failed. "Let your brother do it. That's his job." Jack let derision drip from his voice. He felt himself getting pissed at the guy all over again.

Opal missed the sarcasm completely. "Julian is going back to L.A. tonight, so he can't do the séance. I'm going to do it." She smiled eagerly. "I'll use the same energy that I used to create my vision."

This was a bad idea. A *really* bad idea. He'd told her he believed in her vision, a nice face-saving fib. And he'd created a monster. She was in for a world of hurt when her séance didn't work. If only he could convince her it wasn't worth it. "No one can contact—" his voice croaked "—dead people."

"But Julian did it tonight with your mother." Opal had open blue eyes that revealed everything going on in her mind. She'd gone up against her brother for him, and now she wanted him to *talk.* God forbid.

A crimp in his stomach twisted tighter, and he once again felt that overpowering urge to smash something. "He did not."

She leaned forward to put a hand on his thigh. "I'm sorry."

"It wasn't your fault. He was yanking my chain. That's all." His jaw hurt from trying to speak and not clench.

She rubbed his thigh, oozing compassion. He wanted to back away from her touch, her sympathy. But then she'd get an inkling of how his guts roiled with his mother's intrusion into the truck's cab.

"Do you want to tell me about your mom?"

"No, I do not want to tell you about her." He didn't look at Opal's face. He knew she'd be crestfallen.

In Grandma Blue's house, he'd felt good about Opal sticking up for him. *Too* good. Here was the "too" much part of it. In return, she wanted him to open his past to her scrutiny. Women always thought talking accomplished something. It accomplished nothing, except to remind him that Opal had a whole bunch of craziness in her life. Maybe *she* wasn't exactly loony, but she sure as hell knew how to get herself into trouble. And ask him to help get her out of it. Been there, done that, for too many years.

"It's time for me to leave," he muttered. She messed with his mind. He couldn't think properly with her scent filling the truck and the aftereffects of an incredible orgasm still thrumming through his body.

"I understand."

She didn't understand a frickin' thing. And he wouldn't burden her with tales of his mother. It was a painful subject better left unopened.

"Tomorrow," he said. "I'll pick you up and take you back for your car." By driving her over here, he'd had some off-the-wall plan about making her feel better by getting in her bloomers. Blue's idea. But sex wouldn't fix anything.

"You're so sweet. Are you sure you're going to be okay?"

"I'm fine."

She curled her feet beneath her, rose up on her knees and leaned over to gently brush her lips to his temple. "Thanks for everything," she whispered.

Ah, man. Was there anything sweeter than this woman? "Welcome," he whispered back.

She slid out, the door snicked shut as if she were careful not to slam it. Minutes later the lights flipped on in her apartment, she flicked the curtain and waved at him.

He could breathe now, he could think, unencumbered by the feel of her in his arms.

Was she crazy? Or did she just want to measure up to a very bizarre family standard? She needed to belong with an intensity that made her do seemingly crazy things, but she wasn't anything like his mom. Opal was sweet, lovable, caring and funny. Not to mention smart and the owner of her own business, albeit an unconventional business. For Christ's sake, she'd actually defended *him* against her brother. His mother's state of mind precluded even being aware of other people's problems. Opal didn't need looking after 24-7 to make sure she didn't hurt herself. She was quirky, but far from delusional.

She wouldn't suddenly start believing she was Tinker Bell with the ability to fly off the roof of his apartment building.

Not like his mom. If only she hadn't once again gone off her medication without telling him. If only her caretaker hadn't gotten sick the same day the building inspectors had scheduled his sign-off at the site he was working. If only he hadn't told himself mom would be fine for a short couple of hours. If only...

How could Julian Smith have known about his mom and Tinker Bell?

And what the hell did it matter now? His mother was gone, but Opal was still right here.

Watching the light in her window, finally able to *think* despite her lingering scent in the truck, Jack suddenly got an inkling of her importance to him.

Maybe Opal was his second chance. He might not have saved his mother, but he could save Opal from the heartache brought on by trying to be something she wasn't. He could hold her, easing the disappointment when her latest scheme failed. He could dry her tears, stroke her body and help her "create" one of those fantastic orgasms she'd enjoyed so much. He could do so damn much for her.

If he was completely honest, Opal could do so damn much for *him*. And really, that wasn't such a bad thing.

Jack's heart rate calmed, and his stomach settled as if he'd coated it with a gallon of Pepto.

Yeah. He had a good plan. And there was no reason he couldn't get a jump on things by giving Opal a few more fantastic orgasms tonight. Sex didn't fix things, but making love was a whole different remedy.

PEARL HATED HER FAMILY, she really hated them. Julian could be such a…dick. And Mother. Well, nothing was ever good enough for Mother.

She didn't know how Opal took it, sitting there in serene, almost perfection. But then, she'd had Mr. Jack Davis there to fight for her this time. Besides, Opal had her financial gift. And Grandma Blue had her acerbic wit. Pearl had nothing to impress, entertain or even irritate them with. She didn't think her mother or brother knew she was there until her outburst.

With too much residual energy coursing through her, she took the stairs to her apartment two at a time. She should meditate. Or exercise. At a time like this, something physical was the only answer. She'd change into her shorts and go for a speed walk. So what if it was dark, she'd tuck a key into the palm of her hand. It could gouge out an assailant's eye. She might be a little on the skinny side, but far from helpless.

Ten minutes later, her feet pounded the pavement with each stride. Her legs pumped, and she found that peculiar, hip-rolling rhythm she thought she could keep up for hours. Following her usual route, she let her mind slip into a nirvanic state. She did her best problem solving in that almost trancelike condition. Her feet knew the way, turning the corners, rising to make the curbs. Her mind could wander or focus as it chose, people didn't exist, and the day's heat retained in the sidewalks formed a wavery rising cloud. You had to be attuned to the universe to see it.

She didn't see or hear anything else until a hand jerked her off her path.

"It's after ten, Pearl. Anyone could have been out here in the dark waiting for you."

Nile's breath caressed her ear as he pressed himself to her back.

"I have my key in my palm," she huffed out on a harsh exhale. "I would have poked his eye out."

"He would have had you down on the ground and your shorts around your ankles before you even noticed he was there."

"So I was concentrating. Big deal."

He had an erection, she felt it in the crease of her buttocks. His hand slid through the sheen of perspiration covering her arm. His touch didn't do anything about slowing her breathing.

"Concentration killed the cat." His fingers found the soft bare skin of her belly between her sport top and shorts.

"I think that's curiosity. And take your hands off me."

"You're breathing hard."

"I was exercising."

He dipped his head to her shoulder, running his tongue along the curve. "Mmm. Salty. Did you read it?"

If he'd asked if he could follow her back to her place, if he'd simply pushed her into the bushes lining the sidewalk, she'd have begged him to take her. Or said nothing and simply ripped at his clothes.

Instead, she jammed her elbow into his ribs and pulled away, turning on him with all the fury that had been building in her since he'd come back. Not to mention the adrenaline his touch had shot through her veins.

"You want me to read it? Fine, I will. But it's not going to change my mind about wanting you out of my life. And I do, Nile. Your leaving was the best thing that ever happened to me."

He hadn't doubled over, but he did rub his belly where she'd jabbed him. "I know."

She whirled on her tennis shoes and found her way back to the parking lot of her building. God, she'd been walking for almost forty-five minutes. He was right, she'd been a sitting duck for any whacked-out creep in her path. She squelched the fear, crossed the too-dark lot, and bounded up the steps. Hers was the second door. The key slipped in her grasp, but she managed to unlock the door.

Leaving it open for him to follow, she marched to the phone table in the corner and rummaged through her purse.

"Here it is." She held it aloft, anger vibrating through her, making her hand shake.

Still wearing his damn infernal black coat, Nile stared at her out of his equally black eyes.

She tore the end off, the rip of the paper loud in the quiet apartment, louder even than her own tortured breathing. Two sheets of creased copy paper yielded to her grasp and slid out. She unfolded them and read the first line.

"My Final Words for My Loved Ones."

CHAPTER FIFTEEN

OPAL'S APARTMENT seemed dark and dreary without Jack in it. She'd been hoping he'd spend the night, but she'd obviously scared him off by being a tad too forward in the truck. Or maybe she shouldn't have mentioned his mother. He'd been doing fine before that.

She changed out of her jeans into a loose, comfortable skirt, then headed back to the living room to search for the books she'd need.

The phone rang on the end table. "Hello?"

"I'm sorry to wake you, Miss Smith."

"Victor?" She glanced at the dining room clock. It wasn't eleven yet, but didn't old people go to bed early? Unless they were Grandma Blue, who never seemed to need sleep.

"Yes, it is I."

"I should have called you earlier." She'd only just come up with her brilliant plan, and she still felt the weight of her failure to illicit Julian's aid. "Please forgive me."

The elderly man didn't answer. But for the sound of his harsh breathing, she'd have thought they'd been cut off.

He cleared his throat. "Do you have any news for me?"

"Actually, I do." She could only hope he would like it.

"Oh Lord, thank you. You've found someone to help me."

She had a number of contacts in the metaphysical community, but once the idea of doing the séance herself came to mind, she couldn't give it up. Putting a hand to her chest for bravery, she blurted out her intentions. "*I'm* going to do your séance."

He gasped, then coughed. "But what about…" He didn't finish.

She knew what he was thinking. Why didn't she volunteer herself when he told her he needed a medium? She couldn't tell him Julian had refused to help. First, he didn't know who Julian was and second, it put her brother in a bad light that he'd denied an old man in distress. Maybe she should have had Grandma Blue threaten Julian's inheritance again. But an unwilling medium leading the séance was as bad as a nonbelieving guest.

She realized Victor wasn't saying anything. Just breathing. "I've got it all planned," she told him. At least she would after she read up on it tonight. She had an extensive library on a number of metaphysical-related topics, but was sad to say she hadn't found the time to read most of them. As for the art of talking to spirits, she'd seen Julian do it enough to get the gist, but her brother had a gift and didn't require props. Spirits just gravitated to him like…well, she couldn't say flies on a dead body because that was gross, but still, it was apt. Opal knew she'd need to go the more traditional route.

"That's very nice of you to offer, Miss Smith, but I can't put you out that way."

"It's the least I can do after causing that accident the other day."

"You needn't worry about that. Really, I couldn't bother you. You must know someone. I'd be willing to pay."

"Victor, you just put payment right out of your mind."

"But—"

"I won't hear another word. It's my greatest wish to do this for you."

After a few silent seconds, he acquiesced. "When shall we do it?"

She would make sure he didn't regret it. "Tomorrow night. After dark. Does that sound okay?"

"Wonderful." There was far less excitement in his voice than the word suggested.

Opal bit her lip. "I know this may be a painful question, but did your wife pass in the house?"

"Yes, Prudence died here under hospice care." His voice was terribly weak.

She felt his pain. But she *was* going to help him. "Then we should set up in your home."

He seemed to think about that for a moment. "Couldn't we do it at your shop?"

She hated to push the issue when he was obviously in emotional pain. "It's best to do these things in the dwelling where the spirit passed." The room itself would be even better, but that would be too much for Victor.

He sighed. "If you think it's necessary."

"I really do, Victor."

"Well then, I bow to your superior knowledge," he conceded graciously. Victor was a trooper.

"Do you have a round table? Things always go more smoothly with a round table."

"I'm sure I can find one that will work." Then he let out an immense sigh as if he couldn't take one more question. "Do you still have my card from the other day?"

Somewhere. But only the universe knew for sure. "Why don't you give your address to me again?" She rummaged in her purse for a pen. "I'd like to bring my grandmother and Jack, if that's okay." As witness and moral support.

"The more the merrier," he said with forced brightness. "Is Jack that nice young man I ran into?"

"The very same."

"Well, I can make a spot of supper for us to eat while you're setting up."

"That's not necessary, but very nice. Now, the address?"

He gave it. Opal wrote it on the back of the TV Guide, which was all she could find. She'd use MapQuest to find the directions and save Victor the trouble. Once he'd hung up, she stared at the receiver in her hand.

Victor's cheeriness those last few minutes seemed overdone. He was disappointed she hadn't found a real medium. She could understand that, but she wouldn't let it get her down. Nor would she let him down.

She had such a lot of reading to do. Books just popped themselves from her shelves into her hands. She might not have read everything she had, but she knew where every volume was.

Could she really do it? *Please, please, please, let me do it right.* She didn't like all this internal doubting.

The doorbell rang and she almost dropped her books on her toes. At this time of night, Pearl was the more likely candidate after the way she'd rushed out of Grandma Blue's.

But Jack stood on her landing, his hands in his pockets and his gaze on the books clutched to her chest.

Oh, my. Oh, wow! Jack was back and he was here to help.

Then again, she wouldn't mind if he was here for something else entirely.

MOISTURE CLOUDED his vision, and Victor sagged in his chair.

God had conspired against him. He'd made a tactical error in approaching Opal Smith. Or perhaps he should have been honest with her, told her Julian Smith's representatives had turned down his plea and *begged* her to convince her brother. Now, short of telling her that he'd been following her and had lied to her, there was nothing he could do but allow Miss Smith to attempt to contact Prudence.

But how was he to keep it secret from Darius when they would do the performance right in the house? His only chance was that Darius would once again vacate the premises for whatever it was he did on his evenings out.

And what of Nile?

Victor almost laughed. It was a moot point anyway. The chances of the inexperienced Opal Smith finding Prudence when no one else had were zero.

OPAL'S APARTMENT WAS SO…girlie, Jack thought. Pillows lined her flower-print sofa, pastel watercolors adorned the walls and a rocker with whorls and curlicues sat by the window. The place even smelled like her, a wealth of sweet, flowery scents to fog Jack's brain and make him stray from his goal.

What was the goal? Oh, yeah, to take her focus off her psychic abilities. To fog *her* mind so that she wouldn't care if her latest scheme failed.

"What are you doing here, Jack? I thought you'd gone home." The smile on her face confirmed her pleasure, but she hugged a load of books to her chest as if she still needed reassurance.

"I just wanted to make sure you were okay after…your night didn't go as you planned." He wanted to touch her. Now.

She blinked, then her smile grew. "Thanks for asking, but my night went very well."

Yeah, it had. In his truck at least. That just went to show that Opal could be distracted from *her* goal. But judging from the stack of books in her arms, he had more distracting to do. "What ya got there?"

She turned and spread the books out on her coffee table, pushing aside an empty glass of wine.

Séance Made Easy, The Buddy Séance System and *How to Idiot-Proof Your Séance.* Ah, hell.

"I was going to bone up on my skills."

Man. The sexual image in that statement was overwhelming.

"This one's my personal favorite." She pointed. "Talks about the whole process in layman's terms."

How to Idiot-Proof Your Séance. Christ, he wanted to laugh so badly his temples throbbed trying to keep it in.

She clasped her hands as if she were nervous or hopeful. "Do you want to help me make up a shopping list?"

Her blond hair hung over one shoulder. She flipped

it back with an absent gesture, her breasts moving subtly beneath her shirt. Under his gaze, her nipples peaked.

"What kind of shopping list?" he managed to ask.

She crossed her arms. "Oh, you know, candles, incense…and stuff." She paused long enough to make him wonder if her mind had wandered to other things just as his had.

"Sure, I'll help." Why not? They'd have plenty of time to create orgasms after her shopping list was done.

She just stood there as if she couldn't believe he'd agreed. "Paper? Pencil?" he murmured, and steered her in the direction of a small, antique rolltop desk on the other side of her four-seater dining table. The living area was one long room, with a door on the left presumably to the kitchen, and her dining area on one end. While she rummaged in the desk, Jack sat in the middle of her flowery couch, his butt sinking into the soft cushions. He thought about pushing *her* back against all those pillows even as he opened her personal favorite séance book.

Damn, the volume even had an organized table of contents which started with the header, *What is a séance?*

"Here we are." She plopped a pad and colored pen on the table, then stood there as if undecided what to do next. "Would you like something to drink?"

He eyed the empty wineglass. Yeah, a little libation to quell her nerves. Though why she had nerves after that fantastic experience between them in the truck, he wasn't sure. He plucked the glass off the table by the stem. "Wine would be great."

She scampered off into the kitchen, popping her head out once to say "Is Riesling okay? I only have sweet stuff."

"That's fine." She only had sweet stuff because she was so darn sweet herself, but his inner voice called out to her, *hurry up, hurry up*.

He glanced at the second heading. *Nonbelievers don't belong in your invite*. Well, hell. After what they'd done in his truck, he *was* a believer, and it was Opal's sensory perceptions he wanted to explore.

He hadn't heard the kitchen door or her feet on the light blue carpet, but he smelled her. Sweet Opal essence. She set two wineglasses on the table and sat at the end of the couch, too far away. Reading the next heading with his finger under the line, he considered ways to tempt her closer.

What you'll need to make your spirit comfortable. "Ah, here it is. Your shopping list." Flipping to the indicated page, he pushed the book a tad to his left so that she would have to lean over him to read it.

She sipped her wine and didn't lean over. "What's it say?"

"Candles." If he doled out the information piecemeal, she'd be forced to look for herself, her excitement eventually unbearable. And he wanted her excited.

"What kind?" she asked, pen poised, pad on her knee.

"Purple or violet." For something to do with spirituality. "But you have to have white, as well. Which supposedly helps avoid—" He stopped, smiled, then pointed. "What's that word?"

Jack held the book at such an odd angle, Opal was forced to stretch over him to read. "Weirdoes. It says the white candles help avoid contacting weirdoes from the other side." She backed off far enough to lock gazes with him. "Are you saying I'm a weirdo?"

He shook his head, trying to appear serious. "This is referring to weirdoes from the *other* side."

ALL OPAL'S NERVOUS tension suddenly melted away. Jack made her laugh. Jack touched her and made everything feel right. And he smelled wonderfully good, warm male flesh with the slight tang of sex from the truck. "You're making fun of me."

"I would never do that." He really needed to do something about his expressive eyes. They gave away his mirth.

"Then what are you trying to do?"

"I'm trying to get you to sit closer." This time his eyes expressed wanting something far more.

Opal slid along the sofa until her thigh brushed his. "Is this close enough?"

"No. Closer." He urged her with his gaze as well, his lashes incredibly long and his eyes incredibly brown.

"But if I move any closer, I'll be in your lap."

He smiled, a wide, white smile. "Yeah."

"But then I won't be able to read the book."

"I'll put it on the couch beside us."

"How will I write?"

He dropped his forehead to hers. "It'll be an experiment to see if it works. If you can't read, you can get…off."

"With an offer like that, how can I refuse?"

He grabbed the book, dumped it on the sofa, then urged her to straddle him with his hand on her butt. Her skirt slid up her thighs. Once she was in place, he leaned back against the pillows and sighed. "Yeah, that'll work."

It would work for more than making a list from her séance book. Already he bulged against her, and she felt a flood of heat and moisture inside. "Now where were we?"

He put his hands on her butt and hitched her closer. "We were on the candles and not attracting weirdoes from the other side."

"What's next?" She didn't care one whit what was next. She didn't even care that Jack wasn't a believer. She only cared that he kept his arms around her and never let go.

He shifted, rubbed against her, then rolled his head to the side. "Incense, frankincense and myrrh."

She wanted to purr and rub herself all over him. "That's what the three wise men brought." Or something like it.

"Sorry. My eyes aren't focusing properly. It's incense with cinnamon, sandalwood and frankincense. I knew there was a frankincense in there."

She pushed against him, creating enough room to put her pad on his chest to write. "Okay, got it. What's next?"

"My wine. I'm parched, and I can't reach it."

She set the pad aside and leaned back, stretching to reach the glass on the other side of the table. With each movement, she fit more tightly to him, clasping him harder between her legs. He braced her with warm, rough hands at her waist where her shirt had ridden up.

"Here. Have a sip." Her voice sounded oddly uneven. She held the glass to his lips and watched him drink. "What's next?"

"What do you want to come next?"

It most certainly wasn't another item to add to her list. "I want a taste of wine."

He took the glass from her fingers and held it up.

"Not from here—" she tapped the stem "—from

here." She stroked his lips with her finger, first the lower, then back along his upper lip.

He didn't need a second invitation. Tangling his hand in her hair, he pulled her down for a delicious, open-mouthed exploration, all sweet wine and hungry male. Then he pulled away.

"My turn to taste." He held the wineglass to her lips. When she was done, he nuzzled her cleavage at the same time he deposited the wineglass on the table. Then he snugged her close to his hips, held her face in his palms and tasted her. Devoured her with his tongue and his lips. This time when he pulled back, he left her dazed.

"What's next on the list?" she managed to ask.

He splayed a hand on the book and acted as if he were reading. "It says here we have to take our shirts off."

"I don't think that's right. I've never been to a séance where anyone is naked from the waist up." She could barely keep her hands from ripping off his shirt.

"It says it right here in black and white. And you want to make sure it works, right?"

"All right, just to make sure it really works." She peeled her shirt over her head and tossed it aside. "Your turn."

He pulled from the back, over his head, and threw the black shirt on top of hers.

His chest mesmerized her. Strong lines, defined muscles, firm abdomen. "You look like the Coke commercial," she murmured with awe.

He didn't react. Maybe he didn't get how beautiful he was. Instead he traced a finger along the lower edge of her bra. "What about this?"

"You undo it."

He stroked the front clasp, then deftly flicked it open. The lace clung to the curves of her breasts until he leaned in to nose it aside. The straps slipped down her arms and were gone. His lips caressed first one nipple, then slid to the other where he opened his mouth and sucked her inside.

Her head fell back and heat streaked down her center. She cupped the back of his head with both hands. No one had ever made her feel the way he did. At least for this moment in time, she couldn't think of anything she wanted more out of life than this, just this, his mouth on her, all his attention, all his strength.

He bit her pebbled nipple. She *was* psychic; she knew he wanted her as much as she wanted him.

"Oh, Jack. I've *never* heard of that being done at a séance."

He eased back. "I can see you haven't read through the whole book."

He skimmed up her legs beneath her skirt and palmed her butt with both hands, then his fingers snaked beneath the elastic of her thong panty and pulled it down. She rose to accommodate him until it was clear she had to climb off his lap for the rest of the delicate procedure. Once her panties were dispensed with, he pulled her more tightly against him than before, her skirt up to her hips and her center riding his arousal.

"Now what does it say?" she whispered.

His arm around her, he leaned over, pretending to read. "I'm supposed to put my hand between your legs."

"Why?" *Please, please, yes.*

"It's supposed to generate heat or something."

"I think I'm already generating heat."

He grinned. "I better make sure you're hot *enough*."

Sliding down from his grip on her butt, he trailed the crease of her hips, then glided his thumb along her center.

"You're right. You're very hot. And wet." He sucked her nipple once again into his mouth and tested her depths with his fingers. He found her clitoris with the pad of his index finger and popped the mercury out of her thermometer.

She clung to his shoulders, squeezing and molding to the rhythm of his slow strokes. She bit her lip, her hips rolled, her body tensed, strained.

He withdrew. Her nipple slipped from his mouth. "I think you're ready."

"I could have told you that. And you stopped too soon."

He looked up at her with an ingenuous gaze, the rat. "You want to follow the book, don't you? To get this just right?"

They'd done "just right" in the cab of his truck. How much more right could it get? More. Much more. "What does it say to do next?"

"It says you're supposed to…sheathe…my candle."

"Sheathe your candle?"

"Yeah. The purple one." He pulled her hand between them and caressed the hard ridge with her palm.

"But I don't have a…sheath."

He grinned. "That's what I thought. So I drove over to the all-night drugstore."

"Thinking ahead, I see." Maybe she should have felt bad that he'd planned the whole seduction. Then again, she couldn't have asked for a better plan. "I've got a patch, and a clean bill of health. What about you?"

"Clean as a whistle."

Opal put a hand to his cheek. "Then I don't want a sheath on your purple candle. I just want to feel you inside me."

AH, GOD. Jack squeezed her waist, her trust making strange emotions bubble up inside him. More than lust, more than passion. Something bigger. Like coming home without anxiety in his heart. It made him light-headed. *Opal* made him light-headed.

Yet she seemed to feel none of his momentous emotions as she leaned over to peruse the book. "It says we need to get completely naked for it to work." She started with his buckle, then the button on his khakis and finally the zipper. Rising from his lap, she tugged his pants and briefs down his legs.

He should have taken his shoes off when he came in.

Slipping away, she turned and bent to work off the offending articles, giving him a sweet view of her naked ass beneath the short skirt.

Okay, he was glad he hadn't taken off his shoes.

Socks, shoes, pants and briefs ended up in a pile on the other side of the coffee table. Then Opal slid back onto his lap where she belonged.

"Hmm, that's much better, isn't it?"

He put his head back, stretched, running his hands through his hair as he savored her. "If it got much better, I'd expire."

She snuggled his cock at the juncture of her legs, her heat surrounding him. There was nothing but the feel of Opal, her taste, the lightness of her spirit in his mind. He simply wanted inside her. He didn't give a damn whether she decided to have her séance or not. Not now.

She spread her hands. "Well, we're completely naked."

"You've still got your skirt on."

She pulled it higher. Sensation surged through his cock at the mere thought of being inside her pink, beckoning flesh.

"The book says it's okay to create a little naughtiness by keeping one piece of clothing on." She reached between her legs, took him in hand and stroked. Up, down, her own moisture on him giving the action a tantalizing slip-slide.

He wrapped his hands across her butt and reeled her in. She arched, wriggled, held his cock aloft until miraculously he slid into her depths. Ahh. They fit perfectly.

She felt like warm butter, her muscles milked him. He almost lost it right then. "Screw the book," he managed to mutter. "Just ride me like there's no tomorrow."

And she did. She rode him as if the sun wouldn't rise, as if the night would never end, as if this moment would make up for anything bad that happened in the future. Or had happened in the past.

He dragged her closer, inhaling her scent, guiding her with his hands on her hips.

"Jack, touch me. Put your finger on me."

Her arms were clasped so tightly around him, he could barely ease down between them. He felt the slide of his cock against his fingertips and the tight, wet bud of her clit. Moments later, she tensed, moaned, then threw her head back. Her muscle contractions were more than he could take, and his own climax shattered him to pieces.

In that wild moment, he knew he wanted more of this, more of Opal, more of her skin against his, her taste in his mouth. More of everything.

OPAL FELT BONELESS and weightless in Jack's arms. His breath fanned her hair and his arms crushed her close. He was deliciously naked and sweaty, still throbbing gently inside her. Sated and luxurious, she could have stayed on his lap forever except that her knees had started to ache a little.

Would he spend the night? She was nervous about asking. Why creating sex with a man was easier than asking him to spend the night was beyond her. It was like putting the cart before the horse. Or maybe it was fear of the wham-bam-thank-you-ma'am-gotta-go-now attitude that seemed peculiar to the male gender.

No. It was because men could be led around by their male appendage up until the point they got what they wanted. The rejection usually came afterward. When a woman asked them to spend the night.

Yet for all her doubts, a deeper sense of intimacy remained.

Jack stroked a hand down her back, leaving little sparks in its wake. "Can I spend the night?"

Wow. He'd asked. All on his own without any prompting. She didn't give him a moment to change his mind. "Yes." Then she hugged him a little tighter and asked, "Are those condoms you brought flavored?"

CHAPTER SIXTEEN

MY FINAL WORDS for My Loved Ones.

"If this is some suicide note meant to scare me, Nile, I'm not falling for it." Pearl was scared to death.

"It's not my writing," Nile said without inflection. "And it's not a suicide note." His voice dropped to a whisper. "It's worse."

She'd never gotten impressions from objects. Her talent lay in reading people themselves. Maybe it was merely intuition, a keen sense of body language, heightened observation. Now, she read the lines of Nile's body and thanked the Almighty that she couldn't zoom in on a single impression from the inanimate pieces of parchment.

"Read the article first."

Now she saw the folded slip of newsprint still inside the envelope. She didn't want to read. Her anger, swift to rise, was also hasty to rush out of her. All she felt was fear. Immobilizing. Yet she'd opened the monster, and its contents compelled her.

Unfolding the meticulously cut scrap of news, she saw the black-and-white photo first. A chubby-cheeked teen with dimples. The bloom of life glowed in her eyes, her round cheeks, the happy dimples and her smile. Anybody's child. Everybody's child. The apple of her father's eye. *Please, no, don't let this be.*

Pearl sucked in a breath against the sudden punch of words written below that sweet, happy face.

The Last Will and Testament Killer Claims Another?

The headline, with its question mark, beat against her temples. She glanced at Nile's impassive face, his dark eyes.

"Read it," he whispered.

She closed her eyes, their rims burning. Her churning insides fought against it, but she did what he commanded.

The body of Karen Elizabeth Richmond was discovered last evening by a local resident in a pond located on his 50-acre property just outside Lines, Michigan. The thirteen-year-old was abducted on May 15 on the street by her Lines home while riding her bike. At this time, the Police Chief will not comment on whether her drowning death was accidental nor on the possibility that the young woman could be the latest victim of The Last Will and Testament Killer, who has claimed four lives over the last year. The killer's distinguishing signature or modus operandi is forcing the victim to write a last letter to his or her loved ones. An anonymous police department source confirms the Richmonds received a letter the day before the body was discovered. The letter purportedly matched the girl's handwriting...

She couldn't read another word, couldn't take it. The article slipped from her fingers and floated to the carpet landing right side up, Karen Elizabeth Richmond's youthful, hopeful face smiling at her.

Her eyes blurred with unshed tears, her stomach clenched in agony, and God, she knew what those photocopied pages would yield. The sheets rustling in her trembling fingers, she looked to Nile.

"I was too late." His words were so simple, so devastating. They wrapped themselves around Pearl's organs and twisted.

A month ago, Nile had searched for Karen.

He pointed to the white pages Pearl had managed to hang on to. "Her parents got that in the mail. Her last words to them. I knew I was too late when I touched it."

She could barely breathe, just a tiny slurp of air to keep the spots from coming to her eyes.

"He made her write that before he…" Nile closed his eyes, his muscles going rigid.

Pearl had known that sometimes, many times, Nile failed. She'd known his failures tore him apart. But here was a face, a name. A *child*. He'd had to live with all those faces.

Now *she* would have to live with Karen's face in black and white.

She didn't read for Nile. She read because a young girl had spoken in her last few minutes of life, and Pearl was compelled to pay honor to those words.

To my Mom and Dad, I leave you all my love. I'm sorry for all the times I disappointed you. I did lots of selfish things, but I hope you can find it in your heart to forgive me and remember only the good stuff. Like how I always made you breakfast in bed on Mother's Day and Father's Day. You were the best parents. I'm glad that God gave me to you. I wish I didn't have to say goodbye this way. I wish I could have hugged you one more time.

To Andy, I leave all my love (there really is enough to go around) and my forgiveness for the rotten things you did to me. I know that's how little brothers are supposed to be. Sometimes I deserved your tormenting. And sometimes you covered up for me. Dad, I want to tell you right now that I kicked the hole in Andy's bedroom door, and it was my idea to fill it with the wood putty. So it's my fault the door warped and you had to replace it. Andy only let you think he'd done it because he felt guilty for making me so mad that day. So you can forgive him now.

And, Andy, I also leave you Scooter. Please play with him at least once a day. I know you've always said he was a yippy little barker dog when you wanted a German shepherd, but he's really very sweet if you give him a chance.

May God bless all of you and take care of you. And remember, I will always be watching over you, I promise.

Signed: Karen Elizabeth Richmond.

2:50 a.m. May 17.

Pearl didn't cry, she simply allowed the blurring moisture to overflow her eyes.

She could only imagine Karen Elizabeth Richmond's

horror and fear as she faced her inevitable death yet found the courage to give her family such beautiful, simple and selfless words. Pearl didn't dare open herself up to more, yet she knew Nile had lived the girl's despair, felt her heart beating in her written words.

"He drowned her like a rat."

The girl's terror rolled off Nile in waves. It had become a part of him, slithered beneath the folds of his ever-present coat, slipped between the buttons of his shirt and burrowed into his very marrow like a parasite.

"When they got the letter, I didn't tell her parents she was already gone. I couldn't." His anguish bled through the stiff, uncompromising words, in the clench of his fingers, the tightness of his lips, the rigidity of his legs, as if he were afraid he'd fall to his knees if he didn't lock down the muscles.

"Why did you want me to read this?" she whispered.

"Don't you know?" He mouthed the words as if sound failed him. Then he stepped forward, put his lips to hers, and suddenly his walls fell, his barriers crumbled and he opened himself completely to her.

A terrible darkness assaulted her. Images. All the terrible things Nile had seen. Darkness that dwelled in him, a deadly blackness that writhed and undulated like a wave crashing over her, tumbling her about, dragging her deeper, farther beneath the surface. It was like drowning. Terror seized her heart, and she couldn't kick her legs or flail her arms hard enough to reach that pinpoint of light above her. So close and yet so far. Water rammed up her nostrils like metal spikes, her lungs shrieked, her eyes bulged, blood vessels burst. Finally, panic, all-encompassing, plummeting, roiling.

She opened her mouth to scream and water gushed down her throat, clogged it. And she knew she was going to die.

"Welcome to my world, Pearl."

Her legs gave out beneath the onslaught. Collapsing to the floor, her fingers clenched spasmodically in the tufts of carpet. And then his thoughts, his emotions, his essence, all were gone from her, like a door slamming shut, a curtain closing or the last brick of a wall falling into place.

She couldn't open her eyes, yet she had to know. "Did you find him, the man who did this?" Her throat barely managed to let the sounds pass.

"The police tracked him. Not from anything I gave them. I'd already lost my gift. After I touched that letter, I…"

Tell me everything. God, how many times she'd said that. Begged for that. The terrible truth was, she didn't want to know anymore. Nile had been right. His life was more than she could bear. She couldn't force out the words. All she could say was, "I'm glad he's caught."

"Dead. He's dead."

She'd never before been glad for somebody's death. And she realized that was another piece of Nile's darkness, Nile's hell. Wanting the perpetrators to die. Horribly. Oh, the things he'd tried to shield her from.

"How long have you had to live with this?"

"Live?" The question was rhetorical; he sat on the chair beside her, his exterior so calm, but the inside, the part of which he'd given her the tiniest glimpse, lurked in his gaze. She knew now why his eyes resembled obsidian, as if the pupil and the iris didn't know where one began and the other ended. The black orbs truly were the mirror to his soul. And Nile lived in that darkness.

Nile lived experiencing the pain, horror, panic and death of all the people he hadn't helped.

He stroked a gentle finger over her forehead, back into her hair. "I've been this way since the first death I saw. Right after I turned thirteen. I never wanted this gift. I struggled against it for a long time. But in the end—" he tipped his head "—I gave in to it."

She leaned into the hand that cupped her cheek and closed her eyes. She found the courage to put her hand on his knee. He answered the beckoning touch, his fingers in her hair.

"I wanted to be an architect. I actually graduated from college with that goal in mind." The lines of his face smoothed out, leaving him expressionless. Dead.

He'd never shared the fact that he'd had aspirations of another kind once upon a time. He'd never shared details of his forced vocation. He'd simply gone away, sometimes for weeks at a time to God knows where, and when he came back to her, he came back…damaged, distant, more so each time.

She'd known what he did, intuitively sensed his anguish, but he'd left her for good before she ever got the chance to see inside his pain, to feel it for herself.

"Is that what it was always like for you?"

He steepled his fingers against her forehead, like some strange sort of Vulcan mind meld. "Yes."

A tear trickled down her cheek. "I'm so sorry. I thought I understood, but I didn't." She rose to her knees to cup his pale, hardened face in her hand. "I was angry because you wouldn't share, but I see how much you were protecting me."

"I didn't protect you this time." A ghost of a humorless smile touched his lips. "I thought if you felt what I did, my sight would come back." He stroked a finger down her cheek. "You always eased the burden before. Maybe you didn't know, but you did that for me. It was more than physical, Pearl, more than you can ever know. And I had this notion that if you saw everything I've seen, you could somehow help me *see* again." With a gentle brush of his hand, he pushed her hair back. "I'm sorry. I should never have done that to you."

He pulled a green pouch from his pocket, then spilled a strand of pearls into his palm. Frowning as he fingered them, he finally sighed with what sounded like regret.

"I exposed you for nothing. It didn't work. I haven't seen anything since the day I read Karen's words and knew she was dead." His nostrils flared and he puffed out a heavy breath, then poured the pearls back into their little pouch. "I still can't see."

"Then what can I do to help, Nile?" In his mass of jumbled feelings, she simply couldn't tell. Maybe she was too close to him, physically, emotionally. Maybe he didn't know himself.

He gripped her hand until she thought he might crush her fingers. "Nothing. Nobody can do anything. I'm not going to see again."

She drowned in the black emptiness of his eyes as he held her fingers to his lips, kissing them gently. Then he rose. She died inside knowing he would leave again, knowing she had to let him, and wishing she could have fixed everything for him. "Where are you going?"

He took the longest time to answer, the lines of his face impassive, his eyes bleak and unreadable. "To hell."

But Nile was already there.

IT WAS PAST TEN in the morning. Jack had encouraged Opal to lounge in bed with him. But no matter how many times he had her, it wasn't enough for him. Nor was it enough to distract Opal from her séance. Which was why they were now at her shop, closed for Sunday, collecting all the things she needed.

"Just put the book on the counter," she directed, "and read off what we'll need." They'd never finished writing up the list they'd started. "And do not tell me we need purple candle sheaths." The condoms had indeed been flavored, and Opal had been partial to the grape.

He turned to the marked page. "White, purple and violet candles."

She nipped through the beaded curtain into the back room. "You know, I didn't get my reading done last night. Or this morning." Was that a smile in her voice?

"If you hadn't been so obsessed with the grape condoms, you might have had time."

She popped her head out the door. "Me, obsessed? You kept begging me to taste-test every flavor." Then she was gone again.

Damn, she made him feel good. Not just the sex, but her smile, her laughter, her ability to enjoy life.

"I still think you should have your brother do the séance." He was glad she couldn't see the grimace of distaste on his face.

She came back with a box containing six candles and set it next to the book on the glass countertop. Her silky hair falling forward to hide her face from him, she answered him as she rearranged the contents of the box. "Julian has a duty to his viewers. That's more weighty than doing a favor for me." She was parroting what her brother and mother had said last night.

The only duty Julian Smith felt was to himself. Jack knew that from the hour he'd endured the guy's exalted presence. "Then how did he get away to fly up yesterday?"

"You know, I can't think properly about gathering everything we need with you asking me a bunch of questions." Which meant she didn't want to answer. "What else?"

"Incense. Cinnamon, sandalwood and frankincense."

She popped through the curtain once more. Hell, it was easier to just take the book and the box in there. It was a neat back room, shelves labeled for her stock, a small kitchenette at the far left, a Goodwill vintage desk with a computer against one wall. Opal was on her toes peering into a box on the next to the top shelf. He reached up to pull it down for her, the scent of incense sticks strong enough to make his eyes smart. She picked out what she needed.

"What about Pearl? Couldn't she help?"

"Pearl doesn't know how to do a séance."

Neither did Opal, but he didn't say that. She picked up the box, took it to the kitchenette's counter and set it down a little too firmly, jostling the neatly arranged contents. Why did she avoid looking at him, concentrating instead on filling her cardboard container?

All right, that was a stupid question. She didn't like what he was saying.

He took her elbow gently. "Come here." Guiding her to the desk chair, he sat, then patted his lap.

She scooped locks of her hair behind her ear. "We have to get going, Jack."

"Sit," he ordered.

She did, crossing her ankles and looping her arm around his neck.

"I just don't want you to be disappointed."

"You don't believe I can do it, do you?"

"Of course I believe. But it may not turn out the way you want it to. Just like…" He didn't finish.

"Just like my vision didn't turn out." She said it herself. "You know, Jack, if you don't believe, you shouldn't come with me tonight. It'll mess up all the vibrations."

"I do believe, and I'm coming with you." No way was he leaving her alone to deal with things that didn't go as she planned. "You're pouting." He kissed her lightly.

"I don't pout." She sighed and leaned her forehead against his. "Julian wouldn't help me. And I promised Victor. I have to do this for him. His wife died, and he misses her terribly, Jack. I've got to do something to help."

Despite her methods, her heart was in the right place. Which was another difference between Opal and his mother, whose delusions always centered around her own needs. He planted a kiss on Opal's cheek. "I." Another on her eyelid. "Will." The tip of her nose. "Be there."

"And you'll make sure you believe?"

"I'll do whatever you need me to." This time he touched his mouth to hers, running his tongue along the seam of her lips.

She opened her mouth to him, winding her arms around his neck and kissing him. His hand slid up her skirt to mold her body to his, her bottom bare since she wore only a thong. Her skin was soft, her hair fragrant, her kiss minty. She leaned back against his arm, her thighs parting slightly. He used the opportunity to glide to the front of her thong and skim his finger across her clitoris beneath the silk.

"Jack." She breathed his name into his mouth.

He couldn't tell whether it was a warning or a plea, but he snaked the elastic aside and slipped down to her opening. She was wet and warm, and his cock throbbed against her thigh. Whether he shifted her or she did it herself, he couldn't be sure, but all of a sudden there was room to push a finger inside her heat. He didn't stop kissing her, twining his tongue with hers to match the rhythm of his finger. He dipped her over his arm until her head rested on the edge of the desk and he had all the room he needed. Her clitoris begged for his touch, and she jerked in his arms as he rode the little nub.

She tore her mouth from his to gasp. He licked her throat. Her fingers pressed into his shoulder blade in answer.

"Come on, baby. Come for me."

Hot, wet, wanting, she went off in his arms, her body jerking against his, her breath panting from her lips. She flooded his fingers, the scent of her orgasm rising around them. He worked her until she whimpered, then her body relaxed. He held her, basking in the glory of her powerful response to him.

She opened her big blue eyes. "Is sex your way of pacifying me?"

"What?" He took his hand from beneath her skirt as she sat up in his lap, his fingers redolent with her heady scent. "Last night, as I recall, you were the one creating your own reality in my truck." The comment felt a bit like a low blow.

"That's true. But you came to my apartment with flavored condoms in your pocket."

Opal stood, wriggled her thong back into place and shimmied her skirt down as Jack watched. The orgasm had been wonderful, Jack's lips on hers and him calling her baby even better. But there was something wrong with this sex thing.

"You liked the purple ones," he said.

"That's not my point."

"Then what is your point? 'Cause I'm not getting it." He adjusted his pants over his still-very-there erection.

"My point is that just because I feel bad about something doesn't mean you have to have sex with me. I'm going to feel bad whether I have an orgasm or not, and I'm still doing my séance tonight."

"You think I was trying to make you change your mind about the séance?" He bore a wide-eyed innocent look.

She wasn't buying it. "I'm a big girl, Jack. I can take disappointment. I don't need you to kiss me like I have a boo-boo that needs fixing. I don't need fixing." It hurt that he thought there was something wrong with her, something that *needed* fixing. Something more than just gaining a psychic talent. That wasn't about fixing. It was about…realizing a dream.

He stared at her for what seemed like the longest time, his eyes unreadable, his expression intent. She had the feeling momentous things were going on behind that closed-off face.

Then, as if she'd switched a light on, or off, he tilted

his head and beamed her a gorgeous smile. "All right," he agreed—though to what, she wasn't quite sure. "But I have a boo-boo." He patted the bulge in the front of his jeans. "Could you please fix it by kissing it?"

WHEW. THAT WAS A CLOSE ONE. Opal almost had him pegged.

I don't need fixing.

Her words beat a drum in his mind, to the point where he didn't even give a damn that preparing for her séance had taken precedence over fixing his "boo-boo." She'd packed up her séance paraphernalia—what was so special about a white tablecloth anyway?—then they'd driven to Blue's, where Opal bullied her grandmother into attending the séance.

I don't need fixing.

After his mom died, he'd avoided women in need, but the minute Opal fluttered her eyelashes and whispered "help me," he'd started playing the same role. And he liked it. Found he'd missed having someone who needed him. He actually *needed* it.

Wasn't that a sorry reason for being with a woman. Yet, he'd spent so many years fixing his mom, albeit unsuccessfully, that he hadn't a clue how to deal with a woman in any other way.

Maybe that's why he'd glommed on to Blue's idea about keeping Opal's mind off things by using sex. If he couldn't fix Opal, there was always sex to take her mind off what was wrong. No, not sex. Making love. There had been nothing casual about what they'd done.

I don't need fixing.

With Blue at her séance, Opal didn't need Jack's independent verification. She didn't need him to fix her. So what the hell *did* she need him for?

Sex was now the bond between them, the cement that held them together. The idea terrified the bejesus out of him.

A sex bond was the easiest bond to break.

IN VICTOR'S QUIET HOUSE, Nile lay naked on his bed in the darkened room, the air-conditioning eddying over his body. Hours ago, he'd drawn the curtains against the bright afternoon sun. Its radiance had mocked him, forcing him to blot it out. A sliver of brilliance still shone through the curtain join as late afternoon faded to dusk.

Perhaps an hour ago, Victor had knocked on his door, calling out his name. Nile hadn't answered, letting the old man think he wasn't in. Victor's footsteps had faded down the stairs.

Nile played Tamara's pearls in his hands like a rosary as the soft voice of a meditation tape droned next to his ear, the recorder on his pillow. He'd never used tapes or other tools, had never needed them before. It was a desperate act, but now he'd grab at any device available.

But the pearls told him nothing. Without his extra perception, the world around him lay buried in fog. Two days he'd had the pearls in his possession, and he was no closer to finding Tamara than if he'd been Sergeant Guthrie, who had her listed simply as a missing person. He'd called Guthrie again, twice, and gotten the same answer. No leads. And Nile had none in his own search of the street.

Nile had never prayed. He didn't believe his gift came from God. Yet he prayed now. He prayed that

Tamara was alive—though his heart shrieked of her death. He prayed to regain his sight—though he no longer believed that would come to pass.

He prayed that Pearl would survive what he'd done to her.

He'd wanted to make love to her to lose himself in her sweet, young body, her caring soul. He'd wanted Pearl to push life back into him. He was like a vampire, sucking her life force. He'd done it from the moment they met. The attraction was instant. He'd *felt* the connection in his fingertips, his cock, his heart. Like an addict, he craved her. He hadn't asked her out on a date. He simply told her he wanted her, then driven her to his house and taken her on his living room rug. Afterward, when he'd filled his spirit, he'd given her pleasure. He drank from her and made her cry out with the intensity of her orgasm. But he always took his first. When he came back after a torturous trip, he went immediately to her. She recharged him. Gave him back his humanity. He took from her again and again.

God, he loved her still. It was a selfish love, but it was all he had. She had once been his salvation. Now he knew for sure he would be her death. Last night had been worse than anything he'd done to her before.

And despite the sharing, his curse had not returned. He was too far gone now for that to happen. After failing with Pearl, he now knew it was gone forever.

Unless Guthrie came up with something, Cecelia Whitley-Dorn would wait in vain for her daughter to return.

CHAPTER SEVENTEEN

DREAD SAT IN JACK'S BELLY like a load of cement. A séance with Grandma Blue, Pearl and Lillian. Another family gathering, though minus the asshole brother. Didn't Opal know the meaning of "been there, done that?" What was she thinking? This morning the guest list had included only him and Blue. Or so he thought.

He was afraid he might create his own reality right in front of them and spontaneously combust. And not in a good way.

"Oh, Dyna-mite, I need a boo-oost." Like a child, Grandma Blue singsonged from the other side of his truck. The old lady had finagled a ride with him, and Jack knew what was coming. Another discussion on the seduction of Opal.

He was in no way, shape or form going to tell Grandma Blue that Opal had already seduced him but good. He wanted more, more and *more,* and if that didn't show he was seduced out of his frickin' mind, he didn't know what would.

Blue pointed her neon pink muumuu-clad posterior in his direction as he rounded the truck. How many muumuu colors did she have? He planted a hand, pushed while she pulled and was rewarded with a fear-inducing "ooh" out of her.

"Why did I get stuck driving you over, Blue?"

"*Stuck* with me?" Settling the pink material around her, Blue gave him a look. Of course, he couldn't see it through her wraparound sunglasses—at least she hadn't done the eyelash extension thing again—but he could feel it boring into his forehead.

"I meant 'given the honor.'" He shut the door before she could make another comment. After he'd dropped her off at her rental car, Opal called midafternoon, conning him into picking up Blue. He was such a sucker, because at this point, he'd do anything for Opal.

Then she'd sprung the other surprise on him. Mom and sister would be there, too, something about needing participants in multiples of three. How was he supposed to fix things for her if her whole family witnessed the debacle?

I don't need fixing.

How had he allowed himself to become this involved? Two instincts warred inside him, the desire to run like hell versus the need to make life perfect for Opal. The fact that the battle within was so like the many years he'd watched over his mother scared the pants off him. He'd *failed* his mom. Guilt had been his constant companion in those days, and the worst guilt had been over wishing an end to the struggle. Jesus. There *had* been an end to it all. For a moment, the intensity of that thought trapped his breath in his chest.

"That's better," Blue said as if several minutes hadn't passed. Jack couldn't even remember what the hell he'd said to her. Not that Blue seemed to require a comment from him since she went on. "Now, the reason you're with me, Dynamite, is because I told Opal you and I needed to have a man-to-man talk."

He groaned. She bopped him in the arm. "Don't you dare groan at me, young man."

Starting the engine, he backed out of her driveway. "It's none of your business whether I got into Opal's pants or not." Dammit, he felt his face heat, which is exactly what he was trying to avoid by broaching the subject himself.

"I wasn't going to ask."

"Hah. You think you can lie to me because I can't see your eyes?"

"All right, I admit I was going to ask. And I'm her grandmother, so it is my business."

"She's twenty-eight years old. Her sex life has nothing to do with you."

"Her *sex* life?" Something about the term earned him a wraparound glare.

"She's an adult."

"Did you say *sex* life?" The tone implied something he obviously wasn't comprehending.

"Yes, I did say that, Blue. Now read those directions off to me." The only way to deal with the little woman was to keep strict control of the conversation. Letting his guard down even for a minute could open him to catastrophe.

"Get on the freeway. Now about her—"

"North or south?" Yep, retain control, steer all discourse.

"North. About Opal's sex life. I don't like the connotation."

Be vigilant, take control. "How far north do we go?"

"Atherton." She was quiet long enough for him to

merge onto the freeway, then she started again. "Sex life implies something mechanical, something merely biological."

There wasn't a damn thing mechanical or biological about the things he'd done with Opal. They were downright spiritual in nature. A communion. "I'm not talking about it, Blue."

"We're discussing philosophy here. Not reality."

"No philosophy discussions." He slashed a hand through the air for punctuation.

"Dynamite, you're being very difficult today."

Yes, he was, and barely maintaining control. Thank God they were nearing the Atherton exit. Blue was one tenacious bird.

"Can't we just be silent for a while?"

She harrumphed and hung on to the door handle as he took the turn at the bottom of the freeway ramp. "You didn't ask which way."

"I read the directions earlier, I know which way. And you should have told me as soon as I got off the freeway."

"Are you pissed at me, Dynamite?" All sweetness and innocence.

"Why would I be pissed off?" He planted both hands on the wheel, ten o'clock and two o'clock, then cracked his neck.

"Okay, since you can't handle sex, I'll change the subject. Turn left at the third light."

"I can handle it." What he couldn't handle was the idea that Opal might not need him for anything other than sex. He wanted to give her more.

"No, you can't handle it."

"Yes, I can," but his teeth were clenching up again.

Then, dammit, the yellow light came up on him too fast, and he slammed on his brakes to avoid going through on the red.

Blue peeled his hand off her chest. "That wouldn't stop me flying through the windshield, you know. And I am wearing my seat belt."

"Sorry."

"Well, since we can't talk about sex, let's talk about Opal's new car."

Ah, thank God. "Did she hear about the insurance settlement?"

"What difference does it make? She's still got to buy a new car. And I want you to help her get a good deal."

"She's capable of getting her own deal."

"It's a well-known fact that car dealers stiff women."

"Not the savvy ones, and Opal strikes me as being pretty savvy when it comes to finances." Witness for the prosecution, her freeloader family taking advantage of her financial skills.

"She's good, takes after me, but car salesmen…"

At the third light, he got in the left-turn lane. "Do not tell me you couldn't get the better of a car salesman."

"Well…" Blue trailed off again.

The light turned, so did Dynamite. "Blue, I am not going to believe it even if you swear to me."

Dynamite was a tough nut to crack. But Blue knew she *would* crack him. "I wasn't quite so opinionated in my younger days." She'd *always* been opinionated. And a fighter. In fact, one might have used the label bitch. And no smooth-talking, lying sack of bleep bleep car salesman ever got the better of her.

Some men, like most women, weren't cut out for the

car-buying jungle. Chester, God rest his frozen banana soul, melted the moment he stepped on a car lot. And that good-for-nothing spoonbender father of Opal's had to take his teenage daughters—namely Opal—with him to get a decent deal. Not that Blue intended letting Dynamite in on that. Jack needed to think he was needed.

"Dynamite, you can't let her down on this car thing."

"Blue—"

"This is it." A sweet Victorian. At least it would be sweet with some maintenance. The grass was overgrown and brown in patches. Weeds had sprung up in the beds. The flowers were all leggy. And the house could use a coat of paint badly. Their arrival, however, was enough to distract Dynamite. Or maybe it was the sight of Opal waiting on the sidewalk, her breasts popping out of her top and her legs exhibited nicely in skintight Capri pants. That girl knew how to dress like eye candy.

Blue refrained from raising her hand in a high five.

Things were moving along nicely. They'd made love, if that telltale blush on Dynamite's cute little cheeks meant anything. He was being neatly insinuated into their lives, the séance, car buying, let's see, there were all sorts of things that needed fixing at Blue's own house.

He was such a caretaker, she was sure she could get him to hang around indefinitely while Opal worked her many charms.

GOOSE BUMPS OF EXCITEMENT peppered Opal's arms. She'd dressed with Jack in mind. She'd dressed for herself, too. She loved her Capris and her strappy sandals. But the excitement bubbling inside her was born of her newest plan. The séance would work and instead of Jack needing to kiss her and touch her to cure her disappointment, tonight she could make love to him in triumph.

Her mother was seated at the head of Victor's dining room table. Not quite sure how that had happened, Opal still didn't bother to argue. Especially since Victor, on the opposite end, seemed to have no problem with it. He'd removed a leaf in the table. More oval than round, it would still suit Opal's purposes. The most important thing was that the participants create a circle.

"Ms. Smith, it's such a pleasure to have you here."

"Please, Victor, we don't need to be so formal, do we? Call me Ms. Fontaine." Lillian smiled sweetly as she snapped the folds from her crisp white napkin and laid it across her lap.

"My mother has worked with some of the greatest stars," Opal, seated at her right hand, said for her. Lillian was too proud to say it for herself.

"I think I'm gonna throw up." Grandma Blue ineffectually muffled the sentiment with her napkin.

Her mother glared. Jack put his elbows on the table, leaning over his plate. His thigh brushed Opal's, and she detected a slight smile creasing his lips.

The seating arrangements weren't perfect, top-heavy in the female department, but there was nothing to be done about it. She hoped the higher levels of estrogen in the room didn't have a negative impact on her séance. She'd placed Jack next to Victor on one side and Grandma Blue on the other. Opal figured having Grandma Blue and Jack as far away from Lillian as possible was paramount. Pearl, seated across from Opal, rounded out the numbers to an even multiple of three.

"The tuna fish sandwiches are wonderful," Opal said, easing the tension.

"I made them myself," Victor said. The pouches beneath his eyes indicated a sleepless night, but nevertheless he'd done an excellent job as séance host.

Her mother, still giving Grandma Blue her best evil eye, patted her lips with her napkin. "I've never tasted the like."

Lillian probably hadn't tasted tuna fish since she was a child sitting at Grandma Blue's scarred Formica table. Her tastes had risen with her station, or so she liked to say. But Mother knew how to milk an audience, even if it was an audience of one.

Victor smiled appreciatively, though there was a certain knowing look in his gaze. Opal was sure he knew how to milk his audience, too.

"But, my dear, you haven't touched yours." He tipped his head in Pearl's direction. "Shall I fix you something else?"

"Pearl's on a perpetual diet, Victor." Her mother waved her hand dismissively. "Please don't concern yourself."

"I'm fine, thank you." Meek, almost pathetic. Pearl's voice had that same defeated quality when Opal had talked to her on the phone just before noon. In fact, she wasn't quite sure why Pearl had agreed to come. Nile had to be the reason for her continuing despondency. Opal made a mental note to talk about it with her sister later. As soon as the séance was over.

As if her thoughts had telegraphed themselves to Victor, he cleared his throat. "Perhaps we should talk about the organization of our upcoming event this evening."

Since it was her show, Opal jumped in. "I've got

some candles and incense and other things I'd like to set out as soon as we're done eating."

"Your brother doesn't require that kind of paraphernalia."

Opal cringed. Julian didn't require anything but his innate ability to pick up emanations from the spirits surrounding people, but she really didn't want to have to explain about Julian in front of Victor. *Not now, Mother.*

"Opal's extensively researched the subject, Ms. Fontaine. I helped her last night, and I'm sure she'll do a damn good job."

Aw, Jack. What a guy. Her heart beat faster that he was once again willing to jump to her defense, not to mention his hand on her thigh stroking lightly.

Grandma Blue winked mischievously at him. Jack winked back.

"While some are busy researching—" disdain flattened her mother's lips and flared her nostrils "—others take action."

Her mother at her most pompous never failed to depress Opal, proving that in her mother's eyes, she could never be a tenth what Julian-the-Adored was. She'd never have enough psychic ability to incite a compliment from her mother. Except today. Today, Opal marveled that she actually felt…powerful. Especially after her trouncing last night.

It was because of Jack. Defending her. Touching her. Making love to her. Letting himself go in her mouth. Now that was power. That was trust. Sitting only inches from her, Jack gave her a much-needed confidence boost.

She turned his hand and laced their fingers on her lap. "Some actually research *and* take action, Mother. With spectacular results."

"Opal, you know nothing about how to conduct a séance." Her mother simply wasn't used to Opal taking charge, unless it was about restructuring the family—mother and son—finances when they'd once again overspent or gotten themselves into another misguided venture. Not that she wasn't happy to fix it for them. There was a sense of vindication in that.

"I know exactly how to perform the tea and cookie routine." She'd watched Julian do it any number of times.

"Tea and cookie routine?" Jack queried with a raised brow.

That had always been her favorite. "It's like having friends over for coffee and cake, tea and cookies, whatever. It's just that a few of the friends are from the other side." Yes, yes, why hadn't she thought of it before? Candles and incense weren't the only ways to invite a spirit to visit. "We need an extra chair."

Jack looked around the table. "And the spirit's supposed to sit in it?" His voice didn't exactly rise, but there was a definite alteration in his tone.

"Yes. Move closer to Victor and give me room." Extra chairs lined the wall next to the sideboard, and she dragged one to the table.

Jack's eyes shifted from her face to the empty chair and back again, then he edged his own seat closer to Victor's.

"I'm sorry, I don't have any cookies." Victor's hand on the table suddenly curled into a fist.

"How about ice cream instead of cookies?" Grandma Blue slyly suggested.

"Now *that* I have in abundance." Victor beamed at Grandma Blue. "Prudence loved ice cream."

In her excitement, Opal clapped her hands like a child. "Then it's perfect."

"Ice cream will melt." Having lost the limelight, her mother looked about ready to beat the table.

Grandma Blue narrowed her eyes. "The dead don't mind a little melted ice cream. In fact, Chester liked his that way."

"Well, we're not contacting Chester, are we, Mother?" Lillian quipped contemptuously.

Opal stepped in again before the tiff degenerated into a brawl. "What kind of ice cream do you have?"

For just a moment, something dark passed over Victor's face. His smile faded, the dance left his eyes, and his gaze lifted to the ceiling. "We have just about anything you want."

The poor man was thinking about his wife, it was obvious. Happy memories mixed with the sad, giving him that melancholy expression. Her heart lurched. Opal imagined Victor and his darling Prudence sneaking down to raid the freezer in the middle of the night, making sundaes and sharing loving moments.

She felt Victor's pain like a sharp stick through her middle, but she also saw the potential of ice cream and how well it could work with her newest plan taking shape. Which was really quite simple, of course. She needed a way to get Prudence to talk through her and ice cream might be the key.

"I like chocolate chip cookie dough," Grandma Blue blurted. She had this small problem with eating too much of the cookie dough before she baked the cookies.

It could, in fact, be called an addiction, and once she got started…well, it was a wonder there were ever any baked cookies to be had.

"Shouldn't you have vanilla?" Opal suggested, to avoid feeding the double addiction of ice cream and raw cookie dough.

She tut-tutted. "I can handle the hard stuff."

Victor winked, enjoying Grandma Blue's antics. Some of the darkness lifted from his eyes and the weight from his shoulders. "Chocolate chip cookie dough, it is." He scanned the group. "Any other requests?"

Opal looked to Jack. She had visions of hot apple pie topped with vanilla and whipped cream. That's what he made her think of. Lusty spice and smooth as cream.

"Pistachio," he said, his gaze on her low-cut, pistachio-colored sweater.

A flush rose to her cheeks at the image of Jack wearing nothing more than whipped cream.

Opal diverted her attention from her lustful thoughts by stretching across the table to pat Pearl's hand. Pearl seemed to need a lot of gentle pats these days. And a lot of endearments. Damn that Nile. "What'll you have, sweetie?"

Pearl fluttered her hands listlessly.

Opal made the decision for her. "She'll have chocolate. Do you have any caramel sauce?"

Victor opened his arms expansively. "Ask and you shall receive." His delight at the sudden turn of plans was telling.

"Victor, bring a bowl of Prudence's favorite, too." Opal knew just what to do. Ice cream was the way to draw Prudence out. Or rather in. Right into herself. She'd let Prudence speak through her. It was a perfect plan.

PRUDENCE'S MINT chocolate chip ice cream had melted in the bowl, but so far, no Prudence. Half an hour and still no Prudence.

Opal wanted to retch.

In desperation, she'd had Victor draw the drapes to blot out the setting sun. Then she'd brought out her box of supplies. The candles had been charged with peaceful energy by passing them from hand to hand around the table, and Opal lit the last of the incense sticks. She'd go the traditional route.

"Now we must all join hands and close our eyes. Remember not to break the circle of hands for any reason." Opal heard the faint tremulous quiver in her own voice. She should have stuck with the tried-and-true right from the beginning, candles, incense, darkness and chanting. But no, no, no, she had to go and try the tea and cookie routine, or in this case, the ice-cream routine.

Jack's warm fingers slipped around hers, and he squeezed.

Not all was lost yet. Jack still cared.

If only her mother's hand wasn't so cold. Opal wished she'd seated herself next to Victor, a true believer.

"Breathe in, then out, slowly. Three times. Clear your mind and get in touch with your senses."

Her mother sounded as if she was snorting. Or was that laughter?

With everyone's eyes closed, Jack raised her hand to his lips. He gave her strength and melted her heart faster than the ice cream had melted in Prudence's bowl. She would carry on.

"Beloved Prudence, we ask that you join our group."

She waited, holding her breath, then entreated Prudence three more times, slowly, gently, beseechingly.

Somebody hummed in time with her chant, someone who sounded suspiciously hoarse, like Grandma Blue.

Nothing. She didn't feel a wisp of cold air that would betray Prudence's presence. Nothing, darn it. "Prudence, if you are with us, please rap the table once."

Instead, Prudence rapped the dining room door frame twice. Opal shrieked, which was completely stupid. She might scare dear Prudence away.

The overhead chandelier flipped on. "Am I interrupting?"

Dead silence fell into the room. It was not the kind of dead Opal had been hoping for.

Pearl blanched, the color leached from her face, her eyes on something a few feet behind Jack's shoulder. Opal turned. Horror of horrors. Their intruder was none other than Nile Montgomery. She was so angry she almost forgot to take a breath.

How could he even *think* to be here after what he'd done to Pearl? Opal bounced to her feet, her fists bunched and ready to do battle for her sister. "You are vile, Nile Montgomery."

"Hey, that's a new one. Vile Nile. I like it." Grandma Blue tittered.

Opal ignored her grandmother in favor of squashing Nile with a menacing look. "We're in the middle of a séance. You might just have ruined Victor's only chance at contacting his wife."

Nile's weird, black-eyed gaze had Victor twitching in his seat. "Nile, my boy, I thought you were out for the evening."

"Yes, I can see that, Victor."

Victor wrung his liver-spotted hands. How did Victor know Nile? How was it possible?

"I've interrupted. Sorry. I'll take my leave." Nile's gaze passed over Pearl. She visibly shuddered.

Damn Nile for doing this to Pearl. Walking in and out of her life. Again. And damn him for not fighting back. Opal really did need to pound something right now. "You can't just walk away like that."

But he already had, his coat flapping around the edge of the dining room.

"Ooph." It was the most potent sound she could make.

Then she looked at Pearl. Her sister was staring at the empty doorway as if she'd seen a ghost. Well, they all knew it wasn't Prudence.

"I'm sorry, Opal, but I have to go now. Can you drive Mother home?"

And then Pearl was gone. That man had destroyed her sister, stolen her joy and her happiness. And now Opal didn't have participants in multiples of three to finish her séance.

As usual, Nile Montgomery ruined everything.

CHAPTER EIGHTEEN

OPAL TURNED a horrified questioning gaze on Victor. "What was he *doing* here?"

Jack noted that she couldn't even say the body-finder's name. Her fists clenched and unclenched at her sides. Her distress had grown exponentially from the moment her séance had failed to work. All Jack had been able to do was hold, squeeze and kiss her hand without breaking the circle.

The elderly man toyed with the spoon in his empty ice-cream bowl. "He's a guest in my house."

"You *know* him?"

"We've been friends for years."

"He doesn't have any friends."

Jack tried to pull her gently down into the chair. "Opal, it's all right."

He knew nothing was all right as she shook him off. "If you've known that horrible man for years, then you must know about Pearl. My sister." She pursed her lips. "You probably even know about my brother."

Jack didn't fully understand her hurt, but it was clearly written in her rabid eyes. He hated that there wasn't a thing he could do. Whatever made him think making love would offer any solace in the bad times?

"Victor." That's all she said, and finally took her seat again.

All semblance of kindly host, wise old man, or even needy husband slid from Victor Patell's face like watercolors in a rainstorm. "I tried your brother first. He wouldn't even take my phone calls. And his producers told me my story didn't make for good TV drama."

Yeah. What was one old man with a wife who died of cancer when Julian could have contacted someone who would provide much more drama for his television viewers? Someone who'd died a terrible death in a fire or an explosion or a homicide. Or by convincing herself she was Tinker Bell and trying to fly off the roof of her apartment building while her son was at work.

Blue was the one who jumped to Opal's rescue where Jack knew he was less than useless.

"That little weasel," Blue groused. "If I'd known the way Julian was treating the older generation, I'd have used his inheritance to blackmail him into staying another day."

What inheritance? Blue's furniture that had been around since the sixties or her wardrobe of brightly colored muumuus?

Opal's mother primly pursed her lips. "Mother, nobody cares about your will."

"Hah. The two of you think of nothing else."

Maybe the little lady *did* have money tucked away.

Opal held up a hand before they started a fist fight. "Victor, why didn't you tell me?" It was clear that in her mind, the elderly gentleman's omissions constituted lies. "Why did you pretend you didn't even know who Julian was?" Her voice rose with each question. "Why didn't you tell me you knew Nile?"

He hung his head. "Contacting Prudence didn't concern Nile."

"What about Julian? Why didn't you flat out ask me to get him to contact your wife?" As badly as she'd wanted to do it herself, she wouldn't have put her own needs above Victor's. If the old man had given her a chance. Opal was the most selfless person Jack had ever met.

Victor faltered. "I thought you might not speak to him on my behalf if you knew his producers had already turned me down."

It wouldn't have made a bit of difference to her, Jack knew. She'd reacted to the old man's emotions about his wife, and those were real. Jack turned to take her hand just as he had minutes before during the séance debacle. Instead of allowing his touch, she pulled free to clasp her hands in her lap. She was closed to him. So closed and hurt, his heart literally ached for her. The combined scent of incense and candles made his stomach roil.

Jack shoved the chair between them out of the way, putting himself once more within reach of Opal's thigh. He let his own rest against hers. This time she didn't shift away, though she continued to ignore him. In fact, she ignored everyone. Not like a petulant child so much as someone who had too much on her mind to pay attention to anything else.

Jack felt helplessly out of reach of her.

But there was something else bothering him, something about Victor Patell. "You know, it's awfully coincidental that you were on the same freeway at the same time when we had that accident."

Victor's head sagged on his neck as if he'd lost all his spine. "I don't know what was in my head. I just wanted someone to help me and no one would. And I couldn't go to Pearl, not after what happened between those two young people." His hand fluttered in the direction in which both Nile and Pearl had disappeared. "So I followed Opal looking for an opportunity. Any opportunity. Then I accidentally ran into her. Literally. And it was a sign that she was the person I had to speak to." He spread his hands in desperation. "Don't you see?"

No, Jack still didn't see the reasons for the lies. "All this just to contact your wife?"

Blue chose that moment to scuttle her spoon in her empty ice-cream bowl. "Leave the old geezer alone, Jack."

"Mother, don't be so rude."

Jack noticed Lillian only spoke if she had something to disapprove of.

Seated next to Victor, Blue patted his hand. "You don't mind me calling you an old geezer, do you." It wasn't actually a question. Victor shook his head. "I didn't think so. I lost my husband over twenty years ago, and I still speak to him to this day." She smiled, off in her own little world for a moment. "You don't have to have a séance to talk to your wife. Just…talk. She'll hear."

The voice that answered came not from Victor but from the doorway. "A séance to talk with Grandmother, and you didn't invite me?"

Someone was always sneaking up on them in Victor's house. Jack turned to the latest newcomer. They all turned.

A youth stood just inside the double doorway. No, not a younger man, closer to Jack's own age, with blond hair and symmetrical, unblemished features. A prettyboy type, so good-looking women would probably fall at his feet, but Jack just thought he looked…girlish.

"Darius." There was something off-key in Victor's voice that drew Jack's attention. "I mean, of course, of course, my boy, please join us. I thought you were out." The old man sounded falsely bright.

"You should have knocked on my door. You know I'd do anything to help you."

One corner of Victor's mouth twitched. "But I did knock."

"I was there the whole time." The answering tone came off sounding like an accusation.

"Oh, yes, I must have been mistaken." Victor's smile—a grimace really—looked smeared on, and it certainly didn't reach his eyes.

Darius returned the grin, and in the strangest way, that stretching of his lips chilled Jack right down to his bones.

"I hope you don't mind I shared your ice cream, Darius." Victor's fingers clenched on his thighs.

"Why would I mind?" A flicker in his eyes told Jack he did. "Introduce me to your friends, Grandfather."

Tension shimmered off Victor like a cloud. But he maintained his smile and did the introductions, if a bit too rapidly. "Opal, Lillian, Blue and Jack. They're all Smiths. Except Jack. He's a Davis." He fluttered a hand at the stranger in their midst. "And this is Darius, my grandson."

The way Darius stared at Opal crawled across Jack's scalp. His eyes got bluer, his smile wider, and Jack knew it wasn't mere friendliness. She was a beautiful woman, but there was something extra in Darius's gaze, something almost predatory, as if he wanted a piece of her flesh.

Opal felt it, too. Her shudder traveled along her leg pressed closely to Jack's.

There was something wrong with this Darius. Jack

didn't have to be psychic to feel the man's presence like a sharp fingernail straight down his spine. As Darius pulled a chair from the wall and placed it right next to Victor, Jack was thankful he'd already removed the seat that had separated him from Opal.

"So, dear Grandfather, tell me why you wanted to talk with Grandmother?"

Victor paled. "I miss her."

Darius put his arm around Victor's shoulders. "So do I, Grandfather, so do I. But that's no reason to become so despondent. She wouldn't want you to do that. And you know I'm here to help you in any way I can."

Beneath the weight of his grandson's arm, the old man seemed to shrink and moisture glimmered in his eyes.

Yet Jack had the suspicion the only person Darius wanted to help was himself.

Darius lowered his voice, as if Victor were the only one in the room. "Please, please, tell me what I can do to help. Mourning Grandmother for so long isn't good for you."

Wasn't grief natural, a process toward acceptance and moving on? Jack had done his own grieving, yet what he'd accepted was guilt. He didn't have a word of consolation to offer the old man.

Victor stared at his age-spotted hands now clasped on the table to hide the tremors shaking his fingers. Jack's heart went out to the old guy as a tear formed in the corner of Victor's eye, shimmered on his bottom lash, then slid down his cheek.

"I'm sorry. You'll have to excuse me."

Opal watched the old man go, his steps slow and defeated, with a mixture of guilt and sympathy dulling her eyes. Jack knew what she was thinking. The aborted séance had only made Victor's misery worse, and she blamed herself.

Darius heaved a great sigh. "It's been terrible for him, you know. I'm at a loss how to help. He gets worse every day. I'm afraid for his health." He twisted his hands yet the gesture seemed staged, as if he were trying to convince them of his sincerity.

Blue was uncharacteristically silent, watching Darius with an intensity that could have bored holes through a two-by-four. Lillian, obviously out of her depth with emotional displays, seemed to look at anything in the room that was inanimate. Supposedly being psychic, shouldn't she have felt some weird emanations from the guy? Yet, she didn't say a word. And if Lillian was out of her depth, then Jack had already drowned.

He knew only one thing for sure. The séance had made things worse for Victor. How was Jack going to help Opal get over the guilt of that?

WITH THE NIGHT almost upon them, two old geezers chatted as they packed up their fishing poles and gear and threw the last of their bait over the end of the pier. It had, at one time, been the main bridge spanning the lower Peninsula and the East Bay, Nile remembered. But progress had required something wider, something modern. Gulls flapped and dived to the water, snatching up tender morsels of dinner. Cars whooshed by on the new bridge overhead. Just beyond earshot of the old men, Nile took a seat on a wooden bench and gazed out over the water to the edge of the marshland.

Still prattling, the two old goats sauntered past him with their gear and a bucket of fish they'd caught. Nile wondered if he could be carefree enough when he was their age to while away his Sunday fishing. If he ever reached their age. He'd never imagined himself past forty.

So, Victor had contacted Pearl and her family. Why hadn't he gone straight to Julian? Nile hadn't revealed much about his relationship with Pearl, but Victor did know the supposed "star" of the family was Julian the Great, not Opal. What the hell did it matter why the Smiths had been at Victor's house? The only thing that mattered was Nile's own screaming lack of ability.

His pocket bulged, and he stuck his hand in his overcoat to touch the felt pouch containing the pearls. He'd fondled it often, hoping that the moment of revelation might come upon him unexpectedly, a moment when his guard was down, a moment when his subconscious ruled his conscious. A moment that didn't come.

His eyes misted for the parents, for Tamara, and when he turned his gaze from the setting sun, Pearl appeared through a blurry haze. He'd known she'd follow him. He'd seen her car in the rearview mirror and felt her gaze as she parked and watched him make his way out onto the pier. Now, the fading rays of sunlight made her glow, imbuing her with a halo. God, he loved her. If he'd been a different kind of man, he would have asked her to marry him the day he met her, then given her the first of many babies. But he wasn't a different kind of man, and the psychic curse their child might have to endure could never be the price of his happiness.

She walked the last few meters, her gauzy skirt billowing in the salty wind off the bay. Her blond hair bunched in her hand at her nape, she tugged at several strands sticking to her ruby lips. He wanted to taste them, taste her, lose himself inside her, inside the bliss, even if it lasted only a minute.

Too late for any of that.

She sat next to him, close, far closer than he'd expected, her knee brushing his. She exuded the scent of flowers and sunshine. A scent like the once-innocent Tamara might have radiated.

A fist contracted in the center of his chest. He closed his eyes, swallowed hard, as if the tip of a knife had somehow lodged itself in his throat. He would always take from Pearl, never give. "Help me," he whispered.

She took his hand, splayed the fingers and cupped his palm to her cheek. The touch almost undid him.

"I will help you. I want to more than you can possibly know. But that's what you intended when you had me read the letter."

"Yes. I knew you were too bighearted to turn away. But it didn't work last night."

She shook her head. "We're going to try again. We gave up too easily." She could mean the search for Tamara. Or that they'd given up too easily on their love. No, *he'd* given up too easily.

Oh, the softness of her skin against the tips of his fingers, his palm. Warmth radiated up his arm. He wanted to revel in it, to bury his face in her hair and drink in her fragrance until nothing but Pearl existed.

Instead, he reached in his pocket for the pearls, shivering as he touched the pouch. A pearl to unlock the mystery of a pearl. The universe was steeped in irony. Yet cold filled his bones, despite the lingering heat of the day rising off the concrete pier and Pearl's warmth seeping in through his fingers and his knee where she still touched him.

"You had these last night. Are they what you need help reading?"

He'd lost a moment in time, one second his hand was in his pocket, the next the pearls lay spilled at their feet without his having been conscious of movement.

"Yes. They belonged to Tamara."

"Why did you throw them down?"

He didn't know, not even remembering the act. "They fell."

She dropped her hand to her lap, taking his with it, still holding him, still infusing him with all her warmth. Then she bent to pick up the necklace, trapping his hand between her thighs and breasts. For a moment, he couldn't move, didn't want to move.

She cupped the strands in her palm.

Turning to him, her clear blue eyes soft with emotion, she let her gaze travel from his eyes to his mouth to the unruly hair he hadn't bothered cutting in months.

"I'll hold you while you read them, Nile."

He swallowed, wanted to beg her to never let go, but he kept his lips sealed. His need would only hurt her in the end, just as it had before.

"But not here," she added. "Come home with me."

Home with her. He wanted nothing more in this world.

"FAMILY COUNCIL," Grandma Blue directed Opal as they left Victor's house. "Drop The Mother off at home and come directly to Hank's Pizza Place."

So Jack would be part of the family council but Lillian, who waited out at the curb, her foot tapping impatiently, didn't make the grade. Not that they'd ever had a family council before.

"Hank's Pizza Place? But you just ate." Opal didn't know why she bothered asking except that it was something to say instead of losing herself in despair. Her séance had driven poor Victor to tears.

"Tuna fish sandwiches and ice cream does not constitute a meal. It's bread crumbs. I need pizza."

"But what are we family counciling about?"

"Opal, I will have Jack paddle your behind if you don't stop asking all these dumb questions."

"All right, Grandma Blue, you win." But Lord-love-a-duck, the way she felt right now, she did not want to be in the car alone with her mother.

And that conversation went something like this.

"Why in heaven's name did you think you could do that séance?"

What *had* she been thinking? Oh yeah, she *wanted* another colossal failure in front of Jack, and she *wanted* to make Victor cry. "I told you. Julian wasn't available."

"It was a disaster."

"Yes, Mother, I know it was." Before she'd made Victor cry. Even before Nile showed up. Long before Victor's weird grandson did. There was just something about that guy that gave her the heebie-jeebies. Maybe it was the way he stared at her mouth. His gaze actually made her lips hurt. She thought about asking her mother if she'd picked up any vibrations, but interrupting Lillian's rant with anything other than the topic *she* chose would only make it last longer.

"If anyone finds out about this, it will be a complete embarrassment to Julian."

It was a total embarrassment to *Opal*. But worse was the sense of despair she felt regarding Victor. She didn't truly understand his reasons for all the deception, but it was obvious he was in misery over his wife's death. And Opal had done nothing to help him. The poor man had actually cried. *That* was the worst. How could she have thought a séance would help him? No, that had been all about her own selfish desires and nothing to do with what Victor needed.

"No one will find out," she told her mother, as if Julian's embarrassment were somehow more important than Victor's crushed soul. That was the one thing Darius had picked up on. Victor was despondent. Opal didn't have a single idea how to help him.

"I can't show my face in this town again."

Oh puh-leze. Opal's fingers tightened painfully on the steering wheel. If she heard one more word out of her mother's mouth…

"You've disgraced us."

That was it. Opal couldn't stand it another second. Not one more. Combined with all the years she'd kept her mouth shut, played nice, and hoped one day she'd measure up, she wanted to scream. She just wanted her mother to shut up. "Mother, this isn't about you. And it isn't about Julian. This is about that poor man, Victor. He was crushed."

Her mother sucked in a deep, surprised breath, as if she couldn't believe Opal would relegate Julian's star status to a lesser position than an old man's grief. "If word of your stunt gets out, Julian's career could be tainted."

If Julian had agreed to do the séance, Victor and Julian would both have been saved. But for the great Lillian Fontaine, it was all about her son's renown. Forget about Victor's despair. Forget about Pearl's gift, which wasn't worth a mention, at least when compared to the incredible Julian Smith. "And you didn't even consider Pearl's feelings."

"Pearl? What has she got to do with anything?"

Trust her mother not to have seen the devastation Nile left in his wake. Opal glanced sideways at her mother's perfect profile. "You really don't know, do you?"

"You're speaking in riddles."

Opal realized she was. Her mother was fixated on stardom and reputation and didn't have a clue what went on in Opal's or Pearl's life unless *she* needed something. "Maybe you'll figure it out someday. But I doubt it."

"I refuse to be talked to this way."

"Well, you can walk the rest of the way home, if you want." Opal couldn't believe she'd said that, any of it. But though she knew she'd never change her mother, it felt good to have the words out. Really good. By the time she'd dropped off her mother—who hadn't gotten out of the car and walked the rest of the way home despite her miffed feelings—and driven back to Hank's Pizza Place, Opal had a totally different perspective on things.

All that mattered was helping Victor. Contacting his wife wasn't the way. It wouldn't bring her back. He needed grief counseling. She should have seen that right in the beginning. Now she *knew* what needed to be done.

Hank's was full and rowdy. The pool table at the back already had a ring of onlookers crowded around it, and the cheers competed with the big-screen TV blaring a rock video. Thankfully Jack and Grandma Blue had found a booth closer to the front of the pizza parlor and thus out of the noise a bit. The everything-on-it pizza was already on the table between them. Opal felt as if she'd lost the last half hour of her life as she slid into the seat next to Jack. He'd already put a large piece on a plate for her and poured her a frosty mug of beer. What a sweetie.

Oh, no, he'd given Grandma Blue a beer. Beer gave her gas, which Grandma Blue never tried to contain as a normal person would.

"All right, give her a hug and a squeeze and a kiss, then let's get on with it." Grandma Blue tucked into her first slice.

Jack squeezed Opal's knee beneath the table, then put his mouth to hers. Spicy and tangy. He backed off to change the angle, then came in for the real kiss.

Grandma signed the cross with her gnarled fingers. "No tongue, please, I'm still here, you know."

"I wasn't using my tongue. Be quiet and eat your pizza."

Miracle of miracles, Grandma Blue did just what Jack told her to do.

Jack rubbed his nose to Opal's. "Are you okay?" he murmured.

God, the man made her want to throw her arms around him and hug him forever. She'd never had anyone care about her feelings as much as Jack did. He anticipated how she'd react to something and did his best to compensate. Not that he could change the mistake she'd made with Victor. No, only she could do that.

"I'm fine," she said, while at the same time getting choked up by his compassion.

Grandma Blue looked up with a beer-foam mustache. "All right. Commiseration time is over. Now, about Victor."

"What about Darius?" Jack asked as he bit into the gooey pie of sausage, cheese, mushrooms and peppers.

Opal's mouth watered, and it wasn't eagerness for the tangy pizza sauce.

"That's a weird name for a kid. I don't like him."

Opal had to agree with her. "Darius gave off creepy vibes."

"Victor was afraid of him," her grandmother announced.

Jack cocked his head. "I thought you weren't psychic."

"I'm not. When I touched Victor's hand, he was vibrating." She gulped her beer, then slammed it down. "I think the reason he wanted to talk to his wife was about that grandkid. Advice from the other side on how to deal with that weirdo."

Jack scratched his eyebrow. "It's not our business, and I think you're reading too much into it. What Victor needs is a good psychiatrist he can talk out his grief with. The grandson's just…" He seemed to search for the right word, and Opal knew he thought the same as she and Grandma Blue did.

"He's a freak. I'm seventy-six years old, and I've got immense powers of perception you couldn't even dream of—" Grandma Blue shook her bony finger "—and I say there's something peculiar going on in that house. We have to do something."

Jack stared her down. "Well, I'm on my second life here, so when you add the two together, I beat you in number of years."

Opal dropped her jaw to stare at him. When had he learned to speak her grandmother's language?

But Jack wasn't done yet. "I say Victor needs someone to talk to. Without you butting in."

Grandma Blue put up her hand, palm out. "Talk to

the hand, boy. You ain't got nothin' on me. I was Cleopatra's mother."

Opal dropped her slice of pizza on her plate. Cleopatra's mother? Not. Grandma Blue said the only thing Lillian had ever been queen of was the bathroom. "Will you two stop trying to outdo each other? Jack, you know Darius gives off bad vibes as well as we do. And Grandma Blue, you know Victor's creepy grandson isn't the issue. Victor is crazy with grief over his wife. So now that Mother's out of the picture, we're going back to Victor's and give him our shoulders to cry on." They'd give Victor their own brand of grief counseling. "Grandma Blue, you tell him how it felt to lose Grandpa Chester, and how you dealt with the sorrow. I'll talk to him about Dad. And Jack—"

She felt Jack's withdrawal as if he'd actually moved to the far end of the bench. No, uh, mentioning Jack and his mother wasn't a good idea.

Grandma Blue belched softly—darn that beer. "That's the smartest thing you've suggested since getting arrested for prostitution." Then she grabbed another piece of pizza. "One for the road. Now wrap the rest up for Victor. Pizza is good for baring the soul."

Just then, the group congregated at the pool table cheered. Opal took it as an omen that they were doing the right thing.

"DRINK YOUR BRANDY, Grandfather. It will help your nerves." Darius leaned forward and tapped the bottom of Victor's brandy snifter. "Then we can talk some more about Grandmother and how you feel."

Victor sipped his second brandy, even if it was

making him sleepy. Darius had always been solicitous in his commiseration, but how could the boy truly understand the loss he felt? Yet his goal in talking with Prudence had been to find a way to feel closer to Darius, and, as much as he'd rather drink his brandy alone with his thoughts, this was an opportunity Prudence would have pleaded with him to take.

The Smiths and Jack had left, the house fell terribly silent, and Darius had followed him into his study. Usually Darius went out or closeted himself in his bedroom. Up there, he had the Internet, satellite TV, music and anything else he could need or want to amuse him. But tonight, despite the late hour, Darius had chosen to stay with his grandfather.

That had to mean something. Perhaps the séance had not been a complete and total debacle. Perhaps his breakdown could turn out to be a breakthrough between them. So Victor allowed Darius to fix him a brandy, then a second.

"When do you think Nile will be home?" Darius asked.

Was that the second or third time Darius had asked? Victor's mind felt fuzzy, and he couldn't remember. "Maybe not at all tonight." Nile spent his nights prowling San Francisco's Tenderloin and other Bay Area hellholes looking for Tamara.

"Good. Then we can have a nice talk. Tell me everything that's been bothering you, Grandfather. I feel we haven't talked enough during our few short months together. Tell me about Grandmother."

"She was my anchor." Sometimes, in his darkest moments, he thought what a blessing it would be to join her. But Prudence wouldn't want him to leave Darius.

"I know you want to be with her."

Had he said that aloud or had Darius merely guessed his state of mind? Sleep, so sleepy. Darius's face flickered in front of him like an ancient TV with a picture tube gone bad.

"Drink up, Grandfather." Darius once again tapped the brandy snifter, this time tipping it against Victor's lips.

"There, that's a good boy. Finish it all."

The liquid burned as it went down.

"You want to be with her, don't you? You're dying to be with her. Be with her." *Be with her. Be with her.*

The boy's voice was almost a chant in his head.

"I know how much you've missed her. In fact, I'm surprised you managed all these months. It's been absolute hell for you."

God. There was so much truth in that. But Prudence had something for him to do. Something to do with Darius. Victor was so tired right now, he couldn't think of it.

"And I'm sure that poor Tamara's disappearance weighed heavily on you. It must have made you relive the bad time when your own daughter disappeared. You must have had nightmares about the horrible years, all the memories. I'm surprised you didn't succumb to your grief in the first couple of days after Tamara vanished. I really thought you would."

Darius's words seemed like a replay of an earlier conversation. If only he could remember. Muddled, he felt so very muddled. With each sip of brandy Darius encouraged him to take, his confusion grew worse.

"It's too bad I went out after your dear friends left, I'll tell the police. I knew you were despondent over the failed séance. It was your last hope of talking with

Grandmother. You finally had to face that she was gone forever. But you refused to talk to me about it and even told me you wanted to be alone for the rest of the evening. I left the house because you asked me to, but I had no idea you would ever consider taking this way out. Perhaps if I'd been home, I would have been able to stop you. But really, I hadn't a clue."

What way? What are you talking about? Victor realized his mouth would not move to ask.

"Suicide is such a terrible waste. You must have hoarded some of Grandmother's leftover pills from her illness and taken them all with your brandy. I do wish I'd thrown everything out of her medicine chest. Your friend Nile will find you, but it will be too late. And I'll have to tell the police how I belatedly realized your greatest desire was to join Grandmother. If only I'd understood that before it was too late."

Please, please, I don't understand. But Victor was afraid just the same.

"I'll give you a wonderful funeral, then I'll bury you right next to her. After all, it's the least I can do after you were good enough to change your will so that I inherit everything when you die."

Darius leaned forward and tipped Victor's drooping chin. The boy's face blurred, sharpened, then faded again. Only his voice remained.

"It would have been so much easier if *you'd* killed yourself right after Grandmother died. Or when Tamara first disappeared. That's how I planned it should happen, anyway. But you didn't even think about suicide. Now, I'm forced to help you along. That wasn't part of my plan, Grandfather. You were supposed to take care of it yourself so I didn't get my hands all dirty like this."

He felt a tap on his nose that sent a burst of pins and needles across his skin, and his fuzzy brain cleared in a moment of understanding. How long had his grandson planned his death?

"It's really for the best, Grandfather."

Darius wiped off the brandy glass with a handkerchief, then carefully wrapped Victor's hand around it. Fingerprints. Victor was powerless to stop him, his limbs refusing to obey his mind's commands.

Surveying the scene, Darius smiled. "You'll be happy now. Isn't that the nicest gift I can give you?"

So death was his grandson's final gift to him? *Oh Prudence, where did I go wrong?*

Then he succumbed to the darkness.

CHAPTER NINETEEN

PEARL STOOD BEHIND Nile and pulled his black coat from his shoulders. Her apartment was still warm after the hot day, too warm even for Nile. She took the felt pouch from the pocket, then laid the jacket across the wing chair next to the sofa. She slipped the drawstrings over her wrist.

"Sit. I'll get you a brandy."

Pouring, she heard the soft whoosh of the sofa cushions as he sat, then returning to him, she curled his fingers around the snifter, and pushed the coffee table out of her way. She sank down on the carpet beside him, her skirt flaring, then settling.

"Drink," she urged.

Nile sipped, rolling the liquid around his tongue, then swallowed. She took the glass, putting her lips where his had been. The few drops of piquant liqueur burned her throat as it slid down. Then came the gentle lassitude of strong alcohol.

Fortified, she removed the bag from her wrist and dribbled the pearls into her hand. Rising to her knees, her thighs melding to his calves, she held out the pooled strands. "Put them on me."

Nile looked from her face to the necklace. His fingers

twitched, then finally he took it. Pearl gathered her skirt in her hands, then pulled herself to his lap, once more settling her skirt around her. She wore a scoop-necked silk T-shirt, leaving her throat bare. Nile looped the necklace around her throat, his fingers cold, then warming as they touched her flesh.

"Now what?" he whispered.

"Now, we're going to make love."

His eyes reacted even as she watched. The pupils widened slightly and the color, usually close to black, heated like magma. "Why?"

"It's the only time we ever communicated, Nile. When you were inside me. When you came." Then she leaned in and took his mouth with hers.

It had been so long. She hadn't been living since the day he left, but now life raged in her veins. She felt, smelled and tasted every stroke of his tongue against hers. The rough edge of his teeth. The firmness of his lips. The bite of brandy.

She pulled back to undo his black, collarless shirt.

"Sex is all we ever had between us, Pearl. I need more this time."

She unbuttoned the cuffs, then pushed the shirt off his shoulders. He leaned far enough forward to let her drag it down his arms and off. His skin was pale but his flesh solid, toned.

"We never had sex. We made love. And it was the only time I ever felt you were mine. This is the way, Nile. With you inside me and your arms around me, if you can't read the necklace then you'll never read it." She tore off her shirt, tossed it aside, then undid her bra and bared her breasts to him. She stroked a finger across her throat and the smooth pearls. "When you're inside me, you'll be inside the necklace."

Rising to stand beside him, she held out her hand. "Are you willing to try?"

In answer, he took her hand as she led him to her bedroom. She walked out of her skirt. It fell to the carpet by the door.

"Let me." Before she could bend and remove her cotton panties, he pressed his body to her back, slipped his fingers in the upper edge of the elastic and dragged them down her legs. His lips followed her curves, down, then back up. She'd missed his scent seeping into her mind, like cool rain on hot concrete or the perfume of a thunderstorm. Powerful. Elemental.

He pushed her to her knees on the carpet at the end of the bed. Tipping her head back, she rolled her back against his erection. He stroked a hand down her cheek, then cupped her chin and raised her face as he bent to her.

"How do we play this, Pearl? Fast, hard, slow, sweet?"

"All of the above." Still on her knees, she turned to unbuckle and unzip him. "First our mouths. I've missed the way you taste."

Once naked, he palmed her face, forcing her to look at him. "I love you, Pearl. I always have. I'm just not sure it's enough."

She cupped his hands in place, savored the feel of him. His fingers, cool when they'd first touched, were now hot. "If you believe, it will be enough. Just let yourself go."

He smiled, a strained stretching of his lips. "I think you just want to get in my pants."

"It's a good line, isn't it? I wonder if anyone else would fall for it."

"Looking at you like this, no man would dream of refusing."

"No more talking," she whispered, then bent to take him in her mouth. Oh, the salty taste of him, the clean scent of soap and flesh, the brush of pubic hair against her nose. Wrapping her hand around his length, she stroked his sack with her pinkie, then bore down, taking him all the way in.

Nile groaned and held her head to him, thrusting lightly. Her eyes watered with emotion. His taste in her mouth was so right, the fit of his cock between her lips so perfect.

Then he was lifting her to her feet, raising her until she was high enough to wrap her legs around his waist, and falling with her onto the bed.

"TASTE FOR TASTE," Nile murmured and crawled between Pearl's legs. There was nothing like the taste of her, the flowery scent of her hair, the feel of her smooth supple skin. How had he lived without this? Lived? He'd been dead, the walking dead. He took her clitoris as she'd taken his cock, swirling his tongue, then putting a finger inside her. Her tremble rippled through him as if it were his own. He dipped his tongue down to lap at her juices. Then he shimmied up her body and took her lips. Taste for taste. They mingled their unique flavors and became one.

He raised her legs to his hips and entered her like a man coming home after a terrible war. Her body took him, warmed him, filled him, completed him.

She had found the one way to reach beyond his panic. Need and want and love of her eclipsed the fear of what he would feel, see and hear when he touched the necklace. There was nothing but her. For the first time in forever, he wasn't afraid. He'd run away, now he'd come home. Instead of him taking, Pearl gave. Such a slight change in perception, yet a momentous switch in consequence.

He pulled her hips higher, closer, and buried himself deep. A slow easing back out, then home again, high again. Harder. Faster. And back to slow, sweet strokes. She entered his mind, rising like the bubbles in champagne, clouding his vision. Only the feel of her was real.

"Put your hands around my throat."

He rolled with her, pulling her on top to ride him. She leaned low, bracing her hands beside his shoulders. Breath pumping, her sweet pussy tensing, contracting around him, she pulled him closer to the edge of consciousness, the edge of reason. With his last measure of sanity, his orgasm pounding up through his cock, he coiled his fingers around her throat and the pearls along with her.

Power that only came with cataclysmic release flowed up and out and shot back in. And with Pearl's arms grounding him, Nile opened his mind.

Then the vision was upon him.

His eyes closed, Nile knew he lay in Pearl's bed steeped in her sweet, potent scent. Her hands stroked his chest, up, down, her touch centering him. But what he saw behind his lids was a dented street sign on the corner by an abandoned strip mall. Beneath his feet lay an expanse of fractured concrete, weeds sprouting from the fissures. The lights broken or the electricity long since cut off, the parking lot lay in darkness pierced only by moonlight. Boarded windows lined the ruined facade, the sparkle of shattered glass on the sidewalks beneath them. One moment he was on the outside, the next he'd floated through the doorway of the third shop from the right end. Here lay the bent spines of display shelves and smashed countertops. Leaves and other debris had been driven up against the walls, the carpeting rank with mildew and patterned with water marks from a storm that must have come through before the boards were put on the windows.

A padlocked door beckoned from the back corner of the shop.

His body tensed. A fist clutched his chest in a mighty grip, squeezing the air from his lungs. What lay behind that door struck terror into his soul. He grounded himself with Pearl's touch reaching from the real world into his nightmare vision. Her voice murmuring indistinguishable comfort words wrapped around his vital organs, soothing, drowning out his own inner voice screaming for him to run.

The scene changed again in the blink of an eye and now he stood right in front of the door. The padlock was shiny with newness and set firmly into the wood.

She was in there, Tamara, a broken, bloody doll-like figure. He knew it, felt it, screamed in agony with it. His mind and his gift had fought facing this moment, cleaving his soul.

Only Pearl had been able to put the pieces back together. And only with Pearl could he do what he had to do. Which was to open that door with his mind and bring Tamara home to her parents.

He floated through the padlock, the wood and finally

the layers of fear binding him. The stale, musty odor of disuse swirled in the long-abandoned concrete room.

A soft whimper filled the air and seeped into his mind. A lump in the corner materialized beneath the window, then morphed into a body. Hands and feet bound, mouth covered by duct tape, eyes swathed with a ratty, soiled cloth.

Then she wriggled against her bonds.

Nile arched, grimaced, then opened his eyes. Pearl's face filled his vision, but in his mind he still saw Tamara trussed up in that makeshift cell.

"She's alive," he whispered. His heart pounded so loudly, he couldn't hear Pearl's reply.

Her lips moved but all he heard was the wail of his error. "She's alive."

He'd almost let her die. If he didn't move now, she would die. "I have to call Guthrie."

Pearl took his face between her hands. "Don't you remember? You already did that."

He lay half on top of her, their legs twined but their bodies now separated. He couldn't remember turning with her to put her back to the mattress, nor the moment he'd pulled from her enveloping body. In his hand, the dial tone of her phone was almost shrill in the silence.

"You called him and told him exactly where to find her. He's on his way there now."

He had no recollection, no sense of the passing of time. There was only the rank smell of that improvised cell in his nostrils and Pearl's warm flesh against his.

She shook him. "Nile, come back to me. Now."

"I thought she was dead." He rolled away from her and sat up, pressing his fist to his chest. "I knew it inside." Not only had his gift failed, but so had his perceptions, his fear so coloring his thoughts that he'd been unable to consider any other possibility.

And she would have been dead, if not for Pearl.

Nile threw his legs to the floor, gripping the sides of the mattress until his knuckles turned white. His breath panted from his open mouth. He'd denied her for so long, but the truth was clear. Without her, his gift was nothing, useless.

She knee-walked to his side, then wrapped her body around him. "You've seen the worst your gift has to offer. And you've seen the best. You've found other people before it was too late. And now you've saved Tamara, Nile."

They had saved her together. The impact of that knowledge immobilized him, froze his vocal cords. Pearl didn't merely soothe the savage beast inside him, thereby giving him the ability to open his mind. She added power to him, to his gift. She allowed it to work the way the universe had intended.

She grabbed his chin and forced him to look at her. "You can't function because you blame yourself, Nile. For everything. You can't stop the evil other people do. But you can give everything you have to do what you can for the people left behind. That's *all* you can do, Nile."

He stared at her, her words almost nonsensical. He'd put the dark circles of sleeplessness beneath her eyes. But he'd also released in her a strength that hadn't existed six months ago.

She dropped to her knees on the carpet in front of him, running her hands up his thighs and nestling her belly to his legs. "Talk to me, Nile."

He blinked, swallowed, then drew in a deep breath and let it out slowly. And he came back to her. "Will you help me? Touch me? Hold me? Live through it with me?"

She didn't hesitate. "Yes."

The knots in his body, his bones and the tissues of his mind suddenly untangled, as if that one word from her was all he'd needed. Ever. He cupped her face. "You're the only thing that kept me sane yet I threw you away. You're my anchor to the real world yet last time it almost destroyed you." That's why he'd run from her. To save her from himself. "Can you do this with me again? Live with me? Love me?"

"What was killing me was that you couldn't take what I had to offer."

He saw that now. No, it was more. The truth of it beat inside him like the thrum of the universe. They were less than complete beings when apart, but together, they were more than the sum of their individual parts.

He pulled her closer, mouth to mouth, then uttered his truths. "I've dreamed of you all my life. I've loved you since the moment I saw you. You make me whole, Pearl."

"We make each other whole."

Then she kissed him, with the sweetest, lightest touch of lips he felt to his soul. His gift opened like a flower blossoming beneath the sunshine, and Nile finally knew what he had to do. Now. Tonight.

"I didn't see who did this to her, but I could sense a familiar aura having been in that room with Tamara. I know in my gut who did this."

The last time he'd listened to his gut, it told him Tamara was dead. Now he knew that for false. It was never his instincts that were faulty, but his fears that kept the truth from him.

"Where to?" Pearl whispered as if they were talking about something deeply intimate.

Which it was. They were talking about sharing their souls. "Victor's house. I need to touch something that belongs to his grandson." And find hard evidence against Darius that he could take straight to Guthrie.

"I didn't know Victor had a grandson."

He began to realize just how much of himself he'd kept from Pearl. His friends, his family history, his associations. Without intending it, he'd made her live on the fringes of his life. "I'll tell you everything you want to know."

She rose and held out her hand to him. "I'll go with you."

He took her hand, her heart and everything she offered.

"BUST THE DOOR DOWN, Dynamite."

"He can't bust down the door, Grandma Blue. That's invading Victor's house and privacy." They'd knocked several times. No one answered.

"Something's wrong in there." Grandma Blue put her hands militantly on her hips and glared hard enough to double her height. "Victor wouldn't have gone anywhere."

"He could be sleeping," Opal commented. Yet last night he'd still been awake way past eleven, and it wasn't that late yet.

"Nobody sleeps through five doorbell rings and my fist pounding. Now get that door open."

Instead of busting through the wood door, old and very solid, Jack simply turned the handle. And the door opened.

"See, what'd I tell you? If he's sleeping, he wouldn't have left the door unlocked."

"Victor," Opal called. No answer. The lights were on, but the house was as silent as the proverbial tomb. And eerie. Then she heard the clocks ticking, the house creaking and finally a weird banging she realized was water in old pipes. Sound layered upon sound she hadn't at first noticed. But nothing that signaled Victor's presence. Or that of his grandson.

Jack wandered into the hall, stopping at the stairs with his hand on the newel post, his head cocked like a dog listening for surreptitious kitty-cat paws or the opening of his dog food bag.

"This is creepy." Grandma Blue shuddered. She should have put on a sweater over her muumuu. But then Opal didn't think cold air caused the shiver.

She felt it, too, that skittering of little ants up and down her arms. Something *was* wrong.

All the doorways off the hallway were closed. The dining room was to the left, and when they were here earlier in the evening, the double doors on the right had been open. A study or library, Opal had noticed, with a big old-fashioned wood desk and lots of bookshelves lining the walls.

It was odd that the doors were now closed. She didn't close her inside doors except for the kitchen so that she could ignore the dirty dishes if she didn't have time to do them.

Her hands went to the pulls on each of the study doors and shoved them apart.

One lamp burned. A reading lamp. Victor's head sagged against his desk, his forehead resting on the blotter. Pink scalp showed through his thin white hair. Opal's heart shot to her toes and her blood to her ears, making them roar.

The elderly man had had a heart attack because she'd failed to contact his wife.

She might have screamed, except that was so TV-movie-of-the-week. Instead she just sort of hummed. Grandma Blue shoved her out of the way.

With a hand on the old man's wrist, she announced, "He's not dead. Call 911. Where the hell is his phone?"

Opal just gaped. Her cell was in her bag, but how did one call 911 on a cell phone? Was it the same as calling it on a regular phone? She was in a different city from her own home, so how would the dispatchers know?

Thank God for Jack, the quick thinker. He rushed past her and found the phone out of Victor's reach on the floor.

Why was it on the floor? There seemed to be too many strange things going on in this house.

And odd noises. Above her, somewhere to the left, the floorboards creaked. Not the same creak she'd heard when they first entered. Softly, then louder, not a settling, but as if someone practiced a stealthy walk to mask their steps.

That didn't make sense. Why would someone hide up there?

Nile. He was sneaky. Or it could also be the grandson. She had to let them know about Victor. That would make her feel less useless than hanging out in the doorway while Jack and Grandma Blue did all the important stuff for Victor. Yes, finding the grandson would make her useful.

Two at a time, she bounded up the stairs to the

second floor. There wasn't a moment to lose. Maybe whoever it was knew what had happened to Victor and called the EMTs already. Help might be on its way at this very moment.

At the top of the stairs she turned right in the direction of the sounds and ran smack-dab into a chest.

"Oomph." She almost bounced back onto her butt.

Cold hands gripped both her arms to steady her and warm breath fanned her face.

Darius didn't have a single expression on his face, at least not one that was definable.

He was such an odd character. He didn't smell bad. In fact, he had a distinct lack of smell…as if he were an apparition. And he set her heart thrumming as quickly as it had when she'd seen Victor's head lolled on his desk.

Victor!

"Your grandfather's ill."

Darius just looked at her. His head tipped to one side, still with his face devoid of expression. Maybe he hadn't understood.

"Jack's calling 911. Victor isn't moving."

Why was he still holding her like that, his grip a tad too hard, his fingers pressing into her flesh.

Then he shook his head, slowly. Sadly? "You know, I really shouldn't have gotten up this morning."

Huh? Okay, maybe he was in shock. She was certainly in shock. And Victor was *his* grandfather.

"I'm sure he's going to be fine."

"I'm sure he is, too." But he didn't look relieved by it, just sort of resigned.

She tried to wriggle out of his grasp, but despite his slight build, he had tenacious fingers. Like an octopus.

"We should go downstairs," she suggested. "And see how he's doing. Don't you think?"

He let go of one of her arms, turned and headed back toward the main stairs, pulling her along.

Except he didn't stop there. Instead, he moved straight along the hallway into the darker recesses of the house.

"He's in the study." She pointed back over her shoulder. "That way."

"I know exactly where he is. And it really aggravates me that I've got to change all my plans. That's what happens when you make last-minute changes. You don't have time for attention to detail and everything gets fucked up."

"Umm, okay." What the devil was he talking about? "But your grandfather's back that way." Thank goodness Jack and Grandma Blue were taking care of Victor, because Darius certainly wasn't worth a hoot in an emergency.

"Which is why we're taking the back stairs. So your brainless brawny boyfriend and the old lady don't see us." He slid his hand down her arm and grabbed her wrist.

Uh-oh. She dug in her heels.

Which didn't stop him at all. He threw open a door leading to a deep stairwell.

She opened her mouth, but he turned, slight but tall, like an ominous stark tree trunk in a terrifying nighttime forest. "Don't even think about screaming. If you give me any crap, I won't hesitate to kill you."

Her gaze riveted on the glint of gunmetal in a single stream of moonlight from the window at the end of the hallway. She didn't doubt for a moment that he would shoot her.

Her heart pounded in her ears. This couldn't be happening. Darius didn't even turn on a light to descend, and moving too fast, Opal almost lost her footing. She hung on to the banister with a death grip—oh, that really was the wrong thing to think right now—and gathered her wits against the dark, disorienting stairway and Darius's almost disembodied voice.

"You royally fucked up my plan for Nile to find him dead in the morning. It was supposed to look like suicide."

She had to admit she was a little slow on the uptake, which was the only explanation for letting herself be led along like a lamb to the slaughter—not to mention the gun—but most people didn't expect to find themselves dropped into a murder plot as if they were watching an episode of *CSI* or *Law and Order.*

"So I'm your hostage to make it out of here alive?"

Darius chuckled as he hit the bottom of the stairs and pushed through a door leading to the darkened kitchen. The skylight overhead let in a stream of moonlight that made the remainder of the room seem even darker. And a lot scarier.

"Yeah. A hostage. Or something like that. A hedge against any new screwups in my plans."

She saw the rest clearly reflected in his moonlit eyes. Once he no longer needed a hedge, he'd kill her.

"OPAL? WHERE THE HELL did that girl get to? Go find her while I stay with Victor."

Blue never failed to amaze Jack. And because of that he followed her orders without question. Especially since they went right along with his own thoughts.

"The ambulance will be here in a few minutes," she

said, shooing Jack with one hand while with the other she soothed Victor's hair as if he could feel it. "Go see what she's up to."

Jack was out the study door when she launched into a diatribe on all the things Opal could be doing.

"Like falling down the basement staircase, where the door slams, locks behind her and nobody finds her for three days after which she's shriveled from dehydration, if alive at all."

Blue was the biggest drama queen of them all, but her scenario still scared the heck out of him.

Now that they'd done everything they could for Victor and help was on the way, Jack's heart had reverted to a seminormal beat instead of a frantic pounding.

But where was Opal? He cocked his head. Not a sound from above. Earlier, he could have sworn he heard every creak and groan in the old place. Now, sinister silence.

Why had she wandered off? For that matter, why had she forced the séance in the first place? If she'd left well enough alone, would Victor be unconscious in his office, an empty bottle of prescription pills by his hand?

Hell, that was a shitty thought. He wiped it out of his mind.

The hall chandelier was on, but the lights were off at the top of the stairs. He left the front door open for the paramedics, after checking the walk and driveway on the chance that Opal decided the ambulance driver needed help locating the right house. Taillights disappeared around the corner at the end of the road, that was all. Jack climbed to the second floor. Flipping on lights and calling her name as he moved from room to room, he received no answer except a familiar churning in his gut that said Opal was in danger.

He found a back stairwell that led down to the kitchen. No Opal. He opened a door which turned out to be the basement stairs. Thank God she wasn't lying at the bottom.

He checked outside the back door. Which stood wide open into the night. He called her name. No answer.

The mournful wail of an ambulance siren sounded in the distance. Help was on the way for Victor, but Jack's gut was screaming. Just as it had the day he came home to find a crowd in front of his building and his mother not in the apartment.

Opal was gone, and something bad had happened to her.

CHAPTER TWENTY

"I HAD A FOOLPROOF PLAN. Where did it go wrong?" Darius shifted his hand restlessly across the dashboard of his richly appointed luxury car.

"So, like, what *was* your plan?" Opal decided Valley-girl ditzy was her best option. Especially since Darius had laid the nasty-looking gun in his lap after he'd forced her behind the wheel of his car. He had her cruising through quiet neighborhood streets, turning where he told her to turn. They were going in circles so that she didn't know where he was taking her nor how long she had before he did whatever he was going to do.

Should she risk grabbing for the gun? Sheesh. She should have taken one of those personal safety courses where they told you exactly what to do when a maniac had you captive in a car with a gun in his lap and you were doing the driving. She'd managed to hold the button down so the doors didn't automatically lock, and he hadn't said a thing about putting on her seat belt. Thank God the damn beeping had stopped. Darius wasn't wearing his, either, all the faster to jump at her if he had a mind to.

He shook his finger at her and slithered his eyes sideways to glare. "I see my mistake now. I gave myself too many alternatives. I should have stuck with one plan. I should have been patient and waited out the old guy. It couldn't have taken that long for him to die of natural causes. He's eighty-three, for God's sake, he couldn't live that much longer. In the meantime, I could have lived off his money." He gestured at the hood of the car he'd obviously paid for with Victor's money.

"And instead—" Opal lifted one hand from the wheel and spread her fingers "—you did what?"

"I didn't plan on *doing* anything. All I wanted was to urge *him* into suicide. But he just didn't get it. No matter what I said, he kept repeating that Prudence wouldn't have wanted him to kill himself. I kidnapped that little drughead Tamara, thinking her disappearance would tip him over the edge, reminding him of when my mother vanished. Even sending her parents the pearls should have had some effect on the old man. But noooo," he said with anger and derision, "he wouldn't let go. I swear, for an old guy who missed his wife like they were soul mates, he sure didn't seem anxious to be with her. I thought he'd think suicide was a great idea."

Lord. She couldn't quite fit together all the pieces of Darius's puzzle, except that Tamara was the name of the girl Nile was searching for. What she did see clearly was that Darius had a devious mind and was totally without conscience. If she was frightened before, he now had her bones rattling in her skin. "So tonight, you just helped Victor along?"

Darius glared at her. "Yeah. With all of you there to bear witness to the old man's despondency, I couldn't resist the temptation to use Grandmother's leftover drugs. It seemed like a perfect setup. All of you could testify as to how upset he was. But I've learned my lesson. Patience. Next time, pick a plan and stick with it. Don't deviate. Now what am I supposed to do with you?"

Well, gee, that was easy, at least in her mind. "You could let me go."

He compressed his lips. "Yeah right."

Opal's only hope was to lead him into thinking that *her* plan was *his* plan. "What's the point in adding murder to what you've already done? Isn't there a statute of limitations on kidnapping? If you can hide long enough, that'll run out and you'll be free. But with murder, they'll hunt you down."

He eyed her, and there was something about his smile that shuddered right through her body. Oh, God. He'd already committed murder, so what was one more? Not the girl, Tamara, please not that.

He waggled one finger at her. "You know, you're giving me an idea. Maybe I don't need to kill you yet. How would you feel about being a sex slave? Since you've ruined all my plans, I think you owe me some payback. I could make a lot of money off you. It could get me through this little rough patch since I've lost all Grandfather's money." He smiled at her like a raptor. "It's not so bad. You just do what they tell you to do."

He was taunting her. He had to be. Isn't that what maniacs did, taunt with the worst-case scenario and incite debilitating fear? "Umm, maybe we could try something else. I'm really good at finances. I could manage your stock portfolio." He wanted money. She could get it. Thank God he didn't know anything about Grandma Blue's money, or he'd be ransoming her.

"Too risky. Besides, I don't have the stake to start

with. No, sex slave is a better way to go. I have all the contacts. I swear, all you do is lay back and let them do what they want."

That sounded ominous. "*Anything* they want?"

He shrugged. "Some men like to cause a little pain. Or a lot of pain. But don't worry, you'd be an asset, so I wouldn't let them permanently mark you. Unless of course they paid me a lot of money for the privilege."

Opal shuddered again. He caught the reaction and grinned.

Okay. Ransom was a really good idea. Grandpa Chester's settlement money was the only thing Opal had to offer at the moment. "My grandmother is rich. She'd pay you whatever you think you could make off me as a prostitute."

"Are you talking about the hag in the muumuu?"

"She's not a hag."

He laughed. "Nice try. But I'm not buying it. I think you'd make a perfect sex-pain slave." Then he sighed contentedly as if he could see the very image in his head.

He probably got his kicks from someone else's degradation, pain and fear. Like a demon who lived off terror and got stronger with it. Oh, God, maybe he even got kicks off watching someone else do the killing. Like in a snuff film. As long as he got paid a lot of money to let it happen.

She imagined he could hear the frightened rush of blood through her veins. And he liked it.

She didn't need a vision to know what would happen to her, to feel it rumble in her belly and eat like acid at her bones.

Tonight, tomorrow or months from now, she would die a horrible death if she didn't do something drastic soon.

FOR VICTOR, all was being done that could be done, Jack realized. With her usual wacky ways, Blue had been extraordinary in the emergency. The paramedics had just finished loading him into the ambulance. Jack's worry, however, had magnified on a logarithmic scale. He'd been through the house top to bottom, including the gardens and garage, and there wasn't a sign of Opal. She'd simply vanished. Maybe she blamed herself for Victor's collapse, seeing it as a result of her failed séance, and was hiding somewhere in abject misery? Jack didn't think so, but it was a possibility. Helpless, he didn't have an inkling where to continue the search.

Which was why the sight of Pearl pulling up to the opposite curb in her white compact seemed like God or whoever was out there had thrown Jack a lifeline.

"What's going on?" Crossing the street, Pearl had the wide-eyed look of a frightened rabbit.

Blue flapped a hand at the paramedics closing the doors on Victor. "Victor's gonna be okay, but the boys think he ingested pills."

Ingested pills? From the looks of things, the pitiful old guy had tried to kill himself. A cop had shown up almost on the heels of the paramedics. He'd studied the prescription bottle on the blotter beside Victor and his look had indicated his conclusion. That same look also denoted his thoughts when Jack told him Opal had vanished. The police wouldn't be putting out an All Points Bulletin on her after a mere thirty minutes.

Finding her would be up to him and her family. He grabbed Pearl's arm. "Opal's missing. She was here with us, then she disappeared." Just freaking disappeared into an empty house. He didn't believe in psychic phenomenon, but Opal's disappearing act was inexplicable.

Pearl worried her lip with her teeth. "Where's Darius?"

"The little peabrain wasn't even here when we arrived," Blue crabbed. "Can you believe it? His grandfather is emotionally squashed flatter than a pancake, and the kid takes off for the evening. I'll say it again, there's something wrong with him."

On the other side of the street, Nile Montgomery climbed from the passenger door of Pearl's car, a cell phone glued to his ear. Hell, the least he could have done when he saw the ambulance was hang up. Finishing the call, Nile tucked the phone into his coat pocket.

When he reached her, Pearl grabbed his hand. "Victor took some pills, but he's going to be okay. Darius isn't here." She squeezed and looked up at the guy's dark, closed face. "And Opal's missing."

Something passed between them, communicated through touch and sight, then Montgomery spoke. "Guthrie found Tamara, but she's in bad shape and couldn't say who did this to her."

Tamara. Hadn't Opal mentioned the name? Yeah, the girl the body-finder was searching for. "Didn't you hear? Opal's gone." He snapped his fingers. "Just like that. You're supposed to find missing people. Find her." Damn. Jack himself should have done something besides running around like a chicken with its head cut off calling her name throughout the house.

Montgomery looked at him. The guy had the coldest

cutting eyes. Jack wondered if there was a soul lurking in there somewhere but doubted it.

"Darius took her," Montgomery said. "I sense it, even if Tamara can't say."

Jack's head started to pound. Though he hadn't appeared to be in the house when they arrived, Darius was the only logical explanation. Opal hadn't walked away on her own. Or had she? Maybe she'd gotten another of her "absolutely marvelous" ideas she *had* to act on immediately without a word to anyone. Shit.

"He stole Tamara and now he's stolen Opal," Montgomery added without a flicker of emotion. "I need to touch something of his to see where he's gone."

"Well, the door ain't locked," Blue piped up. "Get in there and do your stuff."

As crazy as it felt, the psychic guy was Jack's best hope. Jack followed, taking up the rear of the troop as if something might jump out at them before they made it up the stairs. Yeah. The big protector. Jack the freaking Giant Killer. Not.

Upstairs, like a homing beacon, Nile hit the first room on the right. When Jack crowded in, the guy stood in the middle, head swiveling from left to right. The bedroom had it all, an eclectic mixture of state-of-the-art and ancient, flat-panel TV, TiVo, computer on the rolltop desk, monster king-size bed with a riser to reach it, old-fashioned wardrobe rather than a closet.

Montgomery opened a bureau drawer. "His stuff's here."

Which meant he intended to come back. Didn't it?

Instead of reaching in to touch, the psychic guy closed the drawer and headed for the adjoining bathroom. Pearl went with him, his hand clasped in hers, inseparable. A large room with tile counters, pink-and-gray patterned tiles on the floor and rising to the wainscoting, a claw-foot tub with showerhead. Montgomery headed to the sink. He looked, tipped his head left then right just as he'd done in the bedroom. As if he heard voices or something. Then he picked up the abandoned toothbrush between his thumb and forefinger.

In the mirror, Jack saw his lids close, his eyeballs shifting back and forth beneath them. The weird movements sent a chill down his spine. Pearl sidled closer, hugging Montgomery's hand to her breasts. She leaned her head on his shoulder, watching him in the mirror, and stroked a hand up his back.

It was the most oddly intimate moment Jack had ever witnessed. He felt like a voyeur.

"Makes the hackles rise, doesn't it?" Blue whispered at his elbow.

He tugged the little lady from the room.

"Hey, I wanted to watch."

"Pervert."

She beamed. "I resemble that remark."

He couldn't bring himself to laugh as he usually did at her antics. Blue squeezed his hand. "She's going to be okay. Opal's resourceful. Sort of like me."

Which only increased his worry. Opal had a penchant for finding trouble. In this case, it was bad trouble. He couldn't deny that or throw it off as another of her harmless schemes.

"I should have watched out for her."

"Shoulda woulda coulda." Blue flapped her hand. "That girl's gonna do what she's gonna do and you know it."

Yeah, he knew it. But he should have anticipated her next move. He should have anticipated something. He'd learned that lesson the hard way with his mother, always try to figure out what their next move is going to be and nip it in the bud. He knew it, but with Opal, he'd allowed himself to be sidetracked by sex. Magnificent, momentous sex. But it had screwed with his perceptions.

Blue grabbed his arm and shook it. "Guilt is just another way of feeling sorry for yourself, and it's rubbish. Nile will find her."

He hated relying on Montgomery, on a skill he didn't believe in. Still, he concentrated on the low murmur of voices from inside the bathroom, but couldn't decipher the content.

Pearl poked her head out the door. "Nile saw where Darius plans to take Opal." She eyed Jack. "They have to cross the College Avenue overpass. We've already called Sergeant Guthrie to cut him off right there, if he can."

The overpass where he'd watched Opal trek back and forth.

Grandma Blue turned, muumuu billowing with her suddenly pumping stride as she headed to the door. "Let's roll. I'll drive. Pearl, you navigate."

Appearing behind Pearl, Montgomery snorted. "I'll drive *and* navigate. Blue, you'll sit in the backseat with Jack as quiet as a mouse."

Psychic army to the rescue. Jesus H. Christ. Jack knew he was as bad as they were. But he didn't have another plan. If Nile "saw" where Darius was going, then Jack was going to be fast on the man's heels. Right now, he didn't care how he got Opal back, he just wanted her back. Safe.

If they weren't already too late.

THEY WERE COMING UP on the College Avenue overpass. Where the nightmare had started the day she had her vision. The dash clock flashed 11:00 p.m. The road was deserted. Why couldn't there have been cops on the overpass looking for prostitutes? She merged to go up and over the freeway, cresting the hill at the top of the bridge. The light on the other side was red.

"There's no one around, run it."

"A cop might see me and stop me for a ticket." Braking, she slowed, readying for a full stop.

"Run it." The gun was no longer lying negligently in his lap but pressed to her cheekbone. His glare bored into her forehead like a laser.

Under cover of that stare, she slipped a hand from the wheel down to the side of the door, searching for the handle. He'd shoot her later. Or he'd shoot her now. Or he'd turn her into a sex slave. She wasn't going down without a fight.

Her fingers found the handle. The light turned green. "See. It's changed. Are you happy now?"

Then she yanked open the door and threw herself out. She landed, palm splayed, but if she'd done any damage, her body didn't react to the pain. Instead, she was up and running, the grind of the car's gears screaming in her ears.

He was trying to ram it into Park from the passenger seat.

"Move," she whispered.

The car came to a stop in the middle of the intersection. She headed back up the incline, away from him. Her breath sawed in and out. Her legs pumped. Then her sandaled foot slipped sideways. She tripped over the sidewalk curb, then tumbled to the concrete. Grabbing the fencing along the overpass, she tried to pull herself up, but her knees seemed too weak to hold her. Oh, God, she wasn't going to make it. Damn shoes. He was coming, the sound of his pounding steps behind her like an army of demons. She thought she heard sirens. Or maybe that was just the ringing in her ears.

Then flashing red lights crested the hill in front of her. The sirens screeched to a halt. Two cops jumped out of the car, yelling, then concealed themselves in the V of their open doors, their weapons pointed at Darius, which meant they saw the gun in his hand. With the wailing sirens and tires, she knew more troops had arrived in the intersection below at the other end of the overpass. They were surrounded.

But Darius could still shoot her in the back. On her knees, she turned against the fence, facing him head-on.

He'd stopped less than ten feet away from her, his head swaying from side to side, his gaze first on the police cars at the top of the rise, then on the others in the intersection where his car sat, its door open.

With cops at either end of the overpass, Darius had nowhere to run. *What's your plan now?*

She knew what she wanted, what she prayed for. If she'd never created reality before, she needed to create it now. She stared at Darius, concentrated on him, imagined the cells of his brain receiving her message. *The fence over the freeway, it's your only way out.*

In the blink of an eye, he was climbing, just as she'd wished him to. Up. Over. The fingers of one hand clinging to the chain link as he hung over the highway while with the other he aimed the gun straight at her, now from a mere four feet away.

"I'll blow her away before you can get me, and then I'll jump," he shouted.

Opal slumped back against the fence. His face was obscured by the links yet she felt the gun as if he had it jammed against her cheek. Her muscles seemed paralyzed, and she knew she couldn't rise to run before he shot her down.

Everything was doubled, tripled, smeared across her vision. Except for the fingers of his hand clutching the fence. He held on with only one hand.

Turning, the headlights of the police cars almost blinded her, but there in the wash of blue and red, she thought she saw Jack. She wished she could just melt into a sweet little dream where Jack was holding her in the front seat of his truck, yelling at her for being such a dope. *Please don't let me die.*

The fence rattled at the back of her head. She rolled until her cheek was pressed to the links and Darius's eyes met hers.

She'd screwed up his plans. Again. Payback time.

In his dark eyes, she saw her own death.

TIME STOPPED. Around Jack, everyone froze like players in a paused movie. Except Opal. She turned, and for a moment that went on forever, looked at him as if he were the only man in the universe. As if he were her salvation.

He would not let her die. He would not fail. Not this time. He swore to God to keep that promise.

Darius rattled the fence like a caged animal.

Let him fall.

With all the rage and fear filling his soul, a bellow rose from Jack's diaphragm and his immobilized limbs came loose. He charged like a maddened bull. A hand grazed his arm then fell away. The bridge shuddered beneath his stampede, and wind howled past his ears.

In headlong flight, his entire body weight crashed into the fence, his only thought to throw himself between Opal and the madman's gun pointed at her beautiful face. He would give his life for her and it would be worth it.

Darius startled, the gun jostled and his body slumped as if he'd lost his footing on the outer edge of the concrete. He opened his mouth, the pistol fell from his grasp and he grappled for a sure grip in the fencing. He didn't make it. In another timeless, endless moment, Jack watched as Darius's sweaty fingers slipped from the chain links to which he clung.

Then he was gone.

Jack didn't hear him scream. He only heard the screeching of tires. And the sound of the impact on the freeway below the overpass.

Time skipped, fast-forwarded, and Opal was in his arms. Soft, sweet, trembling, terrified.

He touched his lips to hers. They breathed life back into each other. "Don't ever scare me like that again."

"I won't." She hugged him close. Tight. Never ending, giving him as much comfort as he gave to her.

He heard the sound of rushing feet, voices, shouts

and more sirens. He didn't want to think about what lay on the freeway below or the memory of those fingers giving way one at a time. And him just watching, praying for the fall. He didn't want to remember that Opal had seen the sight a week ago. He only wanted to hold her for an eternity.

Her body warmth bled into his bones, his marrow, his soul.

"I'll never let you go again. I promise." He'd find a way to protect her. Even if he had to lock her up in his apartment. No, he'd give up his job so that he could watch her every moment of every day. "I love you, baby."

Then they were pulling her away from him, checking her for damage, asking questions. All he saw was her pale face and the residual fear lingering in her eyes.

He'd do whatever he had to do to protect her. Whatever. He'd made a vow he'd die before breaking.

CECELIA WHITLEY-DORN hugged Nile as if he'd given her heaven on earth. Hours after Opal's rescue, Pearl watched the exchange in the nighttime corridor of the hospital.

"Thank you," Mrs. Whitley-Dorn whispered, touching his cheek as if he were her angel of mercy. In the dim hall lighting, her blond hair looked dark, and tears smudged on her cheeks.

They were tears of gratitude. Nile had given her what she needed most in the world. Yet his stiff stance in her embrace proclaimed that blame rode his shoulders.

Pearl could hear his thoughts as if he'd spoken them aloud. He'd screwed up. The woman's daughter would have been home days ago if he'd dealt with his fears.

"She's going to be fine. She even agreed to go into a

drug rehabilitation facility." Mrs. Whitley-Dorn smiled and swiped at her cheeks. "Thank you," she said again, then her husband, George, took her arm, leading her back to their daughter's hospital room.

Nile watched them go with the same dark-eyed, soulless gaze he'd worn every time he'd returned to Pearl.

She touched his arm. "Don't you dare start blaming yourself."

Her words seemed to bring him out of his trancelike state. "All's well that ends well?"

"Yes, that's exactly what I mean."

For now, everyone was safe. Yes, Tamara had a battle ahead of her, but she would recuperate. Opal had been rescued unharmed. She was in Victor Patell's room right now, as were Grandma Blue and Jack Davis. With the way Jack kept Opal tucked beneath his arm, Pearl knew everything would be all right for her. Victor, too, would recover from the overdose Darius had fed him, but he would also have to deal with what his grandson had done. With the kind of man his grandson had become.

Sergeant Guthrie was still piecing it all together from the stories Opal, Tamara and Victor had told. Darius had been aware of Tamara's drug problem and had, in fact, been supplying her for the last few weeks. With the promise of more, he'd lured her away from home that Friday night, then stashed her in the abandoned mall site, drugged to the gills to keep her under his control. If, in despair, Victor didn't succumb to suicide within the next couple of days, Darius planned to kill Tamara, hoping that would drive Victor over the edge into suicide. Darius had delighted in telling the poor girl all about his plans for her. Thank God, he hadn't succeeded. That Darius's goal was getting his hands on Victor's money was obvious, but why he hated Victor to the degree his actions clearly indicated was as yet still a mystery.

But Nile was the one who needed Pearl the most now. She couldn't let tonight's events undermine what they'd shared.

She pulled him to the side of the hallway as a nurse pushed a cart past. "I love you." When he made love to her earlier, when he'd shared his worst fears, his nightmares, his gift, she'd known for sure they were soul mates. "You need me. You're not complete without me." She wasn't complete without him. "You said that. Don't take it away now."

He closed his eyes, pain riding his features. With a deep breath, he opened his dark, dark gaze to her. "I'm not going to run away again."

"I wouldn't let you even if you tried. I'd follow you to the ends of the earth."

He cupped her cheek. "You don't have to go that far. I'm not leaving again."

"But I have to watch you like a hawk so that you don't let yourself go under again. The world needs you, needs what you can do. And I'll be there to make sure you get through it." For the first time in her life, she felt truly needed. "You found Tamara alive. Don't you see how important that is?"

He placed his lips to hers and murmured, "I see how important it is." Slipping a hand beneath her hair, he anchored her to him. "I'll have doubts the rest of my life, but with you by my side, I will do what has to be done. Whatever that is."

He'd touched her with all the strength of his gift and she'd thought she would drown beneath the weight of his burden. Now she knew that without each other, they couldn't survive.

She hugged him close. "I'll never leave you. I'll always be here. Whatever we have to do, we'll do it together."

He hugged her back with everything in him, until she thought she would burst with the enormity of his touch.

"Together," he whispered.

"Together," she returned. It was a vow they made to each other that nothing would break, not even his self-doubt. "Take me home."

Wherever they went would be home as long as they went there together.

CHAPTER TWENTY-ONE

OPAL JUST WANTED to curl up in Jack's arms and sleep. The paramedics had cleansed her hand and pronounced her fit, but she was tired of answering questions, and there'd be more tomorrow.

A little while ago, Pearl and Nile had left Victor's room hand in hand. There was something different about Nile. Opal hadn't once thought about calling him names. Not after Pearl pulled her aside to tell her what Nile's gift had put him through. Opal hated to admit it, but maybe there was a downside to being psychic. Except that the return of Nile's gift had saved Tamara. If not for him, Darius would have died without revealing that the girl was alive. And Nile had saved Opal, too. Everything would have gone differently if Nile hadn't had Sergeant Guthrie send his men to the overpass.

Yes, they had many things to be thankful for. And *she* had Jack to be thankful for.

He stood at the far end of the room, watching Grandma Blue tend Victor, then he caught her eye. Opal flushed. He'd said he loved her.

All she wanted to do right now was go home with him.

But first, she had to apologize to Victor.

Be brave. She squared her shoulders and stepped to his bedside.

"The old fart needs his rest," Grandma Blue whispered, "so don't be carrying on, okay?"

"I'm not an old fart," Victor croaked, but there was a curve to his pale lips.

Grandma Blue was an avenging angel at his side. She would battle the forces of nature—or the nursing staff—to tend him. She was exactly what Victor needed after the terrible things that had happened.

Opal didn't feel guilty about Darius. Nile theorized that her "vision" was the result of various events coalescing around her. Victor had been following her. Tamara was kidnapped and Darius's evil intentions were like a vortex sucking her into its center. She was somehow destined to be on that overpass with Darius, and like a hiccup, the universe had opened itself momentarily to give her a glimpse of what was to come. Darius's demise, however, had been predestined by his own actions. If Darius hadn't done the things he'd done, he could have changed his own reality, created a better reality. But he'd been bent on a path of destruction. It wasn't her fault. It wasn't Jack's. He'd thought to save her by jumping between her and Darius.

What had been her fault was dinking around with trying to do the séance herself instead of forcing Julian to do it. She took Victor's hand. "I'm sorry about not contacting your wife. I was just thinking about my own needs instead of yours."

He squeezed lightly. "I should have told you the truth about why I needed to contact Prudence." He closed his eyes. "I don't know why I felt compelled to tell all those lies."

"There, there," Grandma Blue intoned. "For most people, lying's second nature. Why, I lie whenever it suits my purpose."

"White lies to preserve someone's feelings are okay, Victor." Opal didn't want him feeling guilty.

Victor laughed softly, as if he weren't capable of much more at the moment. "What a sorry bunch we are, apologizing and apologizing. If you forgive me for my little white lies, I forgive you for pretending to be psychic."

Pretending? It hit her like a punch right in her solar plexus. She *was* just a pretender. The universe's hiccup would probably never happen again. She could never be as talented as Julian. She could never even be like Nile, who Pearl had said absolutely hated his psychic gift. How could he hate it? Being psychic was all she'd ever wanted.

Now wasn't the right time to think about all the things she wanted to be. Victor was going to be fine, Tamara was safe, Pearl and Nile were happy, well as happy as someone as dark as Nile could be.

And Jack had said he loved her. That's what she needed to think about. She glanced at him as he mouthed the words, "Ready to go home?"

Oh, yes, she was ready. So ready.

"I forgive you, Victor. And thanks for forgiving me." She squeezed his hand one last time. "And Grandma Blue, if you're going to stay, then get a cot. Don't you dare stay up in that chair. Your back will be a mess in the morning."

Her grandmother straightened alarmingly considering her arthritis, and sniffed. "If you're saying I'm too old—"

Jack stepped forward then. "Of course she's not saying that, Blue." He kissed her cheek endearingly and Opal's heart melted. "She's just saying that you better not run the nurses ragged while you're taking care of Victor." Then he muscled in to squeeze the old man's shoulder. "Don't let her boss you, and we'll check on you tomorrow."

Grandma Blue was still huffing as Jack pulled Opal from the room.

"Well, I never, I'm not bossy, let me tell you…"

Then her voice faded away as Jack tucked Opal beneath his arm and whispered, "Let's go home."

JACK WAS TAKING HER to his apartment. It was like being offered the keys to his kingdom. Without having to ask, Opal knew he didn't take just any woman home.

Unlocking his apartment door, he tugged her inside gently by her uninjured hand. Not that the other hand was bad. Just a few scrapes that didn't even throb. Still, a little of his particular brand of TLC couldn't hurt.

Flipping the light on, he raised her hand, cradling it in his. "Does it still hurt?"

"Yes. It needs another kiss to make it better."

He obliged, lingering on the abrasion, then sucking the tip of her index finger. She closed her eyes. Ah, just what she needed.

"You must be tired. Do you want a cup of tea? Or some wine? A bath? Or do you just want to go to sleep?"

She wanted him to say he loved her again. Instead, she said, "Tea would be great."

He was off, leaving her side to rush to the kitchen as if he couldn't do enough for her. "Sorry about the mess," he tossed over his shoulder.

Then she saw his apartment. And knew exactly why he didn't have women over. He was a slob, a big, caring, wonderful slob. Pots and pans rattled in the kitchen as if he had to clear the stove to set a kettle boiling. Then the water ran. He probably had to wash a mug before he could make her tea. The table in the small dining area was a mess of soda cans, paper plates and one beer bottle, and three neat stacks of bills, each with a sticky note attached indicating the week payment was due. Construction trade journals and sport magazines obscured the surface of the wood coffee table in front of the sofa. The top of the TV sported a quarter inch of dust, but the picture of a dark-haired woman looking suspiciously like Jack was completely dust free. His mom. Opal's heart warmed, even as she took in the cast-off clothes covering the lounge chair and a laundry basket in the corner filled with wrinkled T-shirts and jeans.

After the immaculate condition of his truck, the state of his living room astonished her. And made her go all gooey with the ways she could take care of him. Jack needed her.

"I should have taken you to your place."

She turned to find him standing in the kitchen doorway, his hands stuck sheepishly in his jeans pockets, his eyes roving the disaster zone.

"Is your bedroom just as bad?"

"Worse." Then he brightened. "But the sheets are clean. I actually did laundry the other day."

She loved him. She knew it in the deepest pit of her soul. He wasn't perfect. But he'd risked his life for her. "I don't think I really want the tea."

"Good." He took three steps toward her. "Because I couldn't get the pilot to light. The stove is kind of old."

"Maybe you should tuck me into bed instead."

Two more steps. She could feel his gaze on her lips and his body heat reaching out to her. Then he cupped her cheek. "I'm sorry."

"I don't mind about the mess."

"I meant about tonight. I should have kept you safe."

She covered his hand, his warmth radiating through her arm. "I feel safe now."

"But I shouldn't have let you get away from me in the house. If I'd—"

She cut his guilt off with her mouth. He tasted of the mints he kept chewing in the hospital waiting room. He tasted of love and caring. He took her face with both hands and deepened her kiss, making it his. He alternately devoured then backed off to lick, coming back again, changing the angle, sweeping her away with him. His hands moved over her shoulders, down her arms, then around to her hips, pulling her close, holding her there.

She moaned.

"Did I hurt you?" There was an almost frantic note in his voice.

"No. Don't stop."

He kissed her throat. "I should let you sleep."

She arched her neck and closed her eyes to the feel of him against her, in her arms. "I'm not sleepy yet."

"But you need to relax." His fingers pushed aside her sweater, baring her shoulder to his lips. "You had a bad scare out there."

He did, too. And he was struggling to find a way to make it all better for her. She could make it better for both of them. "You're right. Relax me, Jack." She rubbed herself against him. He was hard. He wanted. She just had to make him let go.

Days ago—or maybe it was just yesterday morning, which did indeed feel like a lifetime ago—she'd accused him of using sex to mollify her. Now, she would use it to make him feel better. But she would call it lovemaking.

"A back rub?" was his whispered offer.

She slipped her hand between them, palming the front of his jeans. Then she eased away. "Not that kind of rub. Something better."

He dropped his hands to her butt, hauling her up against him. Burying his mouth against her hair, he found the shell of her ear and licked. Fire shot through her.

"Tell me what you want," he breathed against her ear. "Anything."

"This." She wrapped her arms around his neck and climbed his body. He put his hands beneath her butt, raising her until she could wrap her legs around his waist.

Good, so good, the feel of him right where she needed him. She let her sandals clunk to the floor, then squeezed her legs, closer, tighter, until there wasn't a breath of space between them. Jack groaned.

"You make me crazy."

"Good." She wanted to. She wanted to make him forget about Darius, about Victor, about feeling bad for anything at all.

At the entry to the hallway, he stopped, bracing her against the wall as he took her mouth, stealing her breath and her heart. Then one hand slipped between her legs. "Is this the rub you want?"

She wanted her tight Capri pants off. Now. She

wanted his jeans off. She wanted skin and hard male flesh. But more, she wanted… "Put me down."

He let her slide to the floor. "Don't stop, baby, not now." His eyes glittered, dark, hot, enticing.

She pushed him against the other wall, her hand on his buckle, then his zipper. "Remember what you did to me yesterday at the shop?"

His eyes widened, then his mouth quirked. "Yeah."

"Well, now it's payback time." The moment the words were out of her mouth, something skittered across her flesh raising goose bumps. Darius. Payback time. She almost put her hand to her mouth to keep from screaming. No. There was only this. Only Jack. Darius was gone, and it wasn't their fault. She dropped to her knees, yanking his jeans with her. Soft cotton cradled his bulging erection. Jack put his hands on either side of her face.

"Make me crazy. Please."

Somehow she knew he wanted much more. He wanted to wipe away bad images from his mind. She pulled him free and took him in her mouth. When he growled and his fingers tensed, she knew that for a little while there'd be nothing but this. Nothing but her mouth sliding down to take the length of him, her tongue stroking, laving the slit at the top, sucking him into a whirlpool of sensation.

He held her head, feeding himself to her, never forcing, letting her take only what she could handle. Opal struggled with the back zipper of her Capris. She wanted to be naked, open, ready for him.

"Hold on right here," she directed, wrapping his hand around his penis, setting a rhythm for him to follow.

Transfixed for a moment, she watched the slow and steady pump of his fist. Her breath caught in her throat, her panties turned into a sopping mess. There was something so incredibly sexy in watching him. He felt it, too. A tiny drop of come oozed from the tip. She tongued it off, lingeringly, savoring the taste. Then she licked her lips and raised her gaze to his.

"You look at me like that much longer and I'm going to come without you."

"Don't you dare," she ordered before maneuvering off her Capris and panties. Then she grabbed his hand and yanked him down on the hallway carpeting. "Come inside me. Now."

"Yes, please." He levered on one arm, pushed her legs apart and moved between them, testing her with a finger, stroking over her clitoris and drawing a gasp.

"You're so wet and ready. Opal…" He sucked in a breath. His eyes glimmered. "I love you so damn much. I wish I'd—"

She clamped a hand over his mouth, suddenly afraid. One more word and she might start to think he only thought he was in love with her out of guilt. Then she pulled him to her, feeling the thick slide of him inside her. He closed his eyes and rolled his head back.

"Yessss."

Oh, yes. "Just like that, please like that." Forever like that. She pulled her legs high and clung to his corded arms.

The rug burned her backside as he drove deep inside her. One moment she had every faculty, felt every touch, the slip of skin on skin, the rush of breath through her throat, the scent of his hot needy male sweat and desire, the crush of his weight on top of her. And then she was

gone, exploding halfway to the sky, with the echo
of his roar as he followed her.

JACK HAD TAKEN HER in the middle of the hallway with
half her clothes still on. When was the last time he'd
vacuumed? Christ. This wasn't what he meant to
happen. He'd wanted to coddle her in clean sheets, baby
her, stroke the fine hairs at her temple as she feel asleep,
not whomp her buns into the carpet.

"I'm sorry."

She opened her eyes. "You really need to stop saying
you're sorry."

Yeah. He just didn't know how else to make it up to
her. Sex wasn't enough. It wasn't even right. That was
all about him. But damn, when she'd gone down on her
knees, when she'd sucked him, then wrapped his own
hand around his cock while she took her pants
off…well, hell, he'd forgotten he was supposed to be
making her feel better. He'd thought only about burying
himself inside her and staying there for-freaking-ever.

He rolled off. "I'm too heavy."

"I like heavy."

Her pistachio-colored sweater had ridden up her
abdomen to just below her breasts. Her buns were
probably red and sore from the pounding he'd given her.

"Stop beating yourself up."

He was sure he hadn't said any of that aloud. But
he hadn't treated her the way she deserved. She'd had
a terrible night. He should have done so many things
differently. Yanking his pants up, he flopped back
against the carpet. He'd lost a lifetime out there. If
he'd lost her…

She flipped over on top of him, her hair falling across half his face. "Thank you," she whispered with that special Opalescent smile that damn near ripped his heart out.

"Don't ever do that again," he whispered, not meaning to but unable to stop himself.

"Do what?" She smiled, seductive, hot, enticing.

"Don't put yourself in danger like that."

The smile faded. "I didn't do it on purpose."

"I know that. But somehow it seems to happen." He captured her hand and placed it over his heart. "I can't take it."

"Poor Jack." She kissed the point of his chin.

She didn't see. She didn't understand. "I mean it. You could have been killed. No more crazy stuff, okay?

She pulled back, tipping her head. With the living room lights behind her, he couldn't see in her eyes what was going on in her head. "Crazy?"

"Well, not crazy. But this whole trying to be psychic thing. It's not real. And you only get yourself into trouble."

She sat up and reached for her pants.

He didn't want her to shut him out, not after the way she'd just let him in. But she had to understand. "I mean, look what happened on the overpass the first time. You got us arrested."

"You only got arrested because you slugged the cop."

"I did it to protect you."

She shimmied into her panties, then her tight pants. In response, he had to zip and buckle his own jeans.

"I didn't ask you to protect me."

"Yes, you did. You asked me out there in the first place to look out for you."

"I asked you out there for independent verification."

She rose and went back into the living room in search of her shoes. Or her purse. He couldn't let her go.

"Don't get angry."

"I'm not angry, Jack. I'm trying to understand what you're saying." She pointed her index finger. "You think I'm nuts."

"I didn't say that."

She sat down on the couch and put on one strappy sandal. "You said I needed to stop doing crazy stuff so that means you think I'm crazy."

"Well, hell, you have to admit the whole vision thing is—"

She held up a hand. "Don't you say it. Don't you dare say it. You don't want me if I am psychic and my family doesn't want me if I'm not." She shook her finger at him. "But you know what, I'm done with the vision thing. I never want another one. When Darius fell—" This time she stopped herself.

He ached for her. She'd never felt wanted. And no matter how *he* looked at it, real or delusion, she'd have to think Darius's fall from the overpass was her vision come true.

"And I suppose you think the whole thing was my fault because I ran upstairs by myself back in Victor's house."

"I didn't say that."

"But you thought it."

"No." Yes, he had.

The other sandal on, she stood up, narrowed her eyes and put her hands on her hips. "That's exactly what you thought. You think that what happened tonight was my fault. If I hadn't wandered off by myself. Why, if I hadn't insisted on the séance, Victor wouldn't have been so sad in the first place and—" her lip trembled "—the rest of tonight wouldn't have happened."

Dammit, he'd had a few of those thoughts back in Victor's house, but she made it sound like some crime he'd committed.

"Darius wasn't my fault. I didn't make him do those things. He did them on his own."

"I didn't accuse you of that. I never even thought it." But hell, his bitterness suddenly bubbled over. All the pent-up anger, fear and frustration he'd felt all night long, maybe since the day he'd met her. "But all you've done is get yourself into one mess after another since I met you. No matter how many times I tell you, you don't listen." His feet moved, pacing him back and forth, and his hands tunneled through his hair. He knew his anger had suddenly morphed into being about far more than Opal's actions over the past week, but he couldn't seem to stop himself. "I'm always cleaning up after your messes. But you don't learn. You just do it again. Over and over and I'm sick of it, do you hear? I can't take another damn moment."

"I'm sorry," she whispered.

"And don't say you're terribly sorry. You're always sorry. And you always do it again. And it's not my fault you're dead."

The word sucked the air out of the room. Sucked the life out of him. The anger, the pain and every other emotion, as well. He swallowed. "I didn't mean that." He'd meant every word. Only he hadn't wanted to say them to Opal.

"You did mean it."

But instead of an answering anger, he saw compassion in her eyes.

And he knew, he just knew she was going to ask it. He didn't know if he could stand it when she did.

"How did your mother die?"

He didn't know if he could stand answering the question, either. But after his outburst, he owed Opal an explanation. "Two years ago she thought she could fly like Tinker Bell off the roof of the apartment building we lived in. But she couldn't," he ended on a whisper. He didn't tell Opal about the years of looking after his mother yet never being able to help her. With what he'd already said, Opal could figure that out on her own.

"I'm sorry, Jack."

"She was sick in her mind. The last ten years of her life were pretty bad for her, especially when she wouldn't take her medication. I should have institutionalized her. But I thought I could take care of her." He'd failed.

She touched his arm. Warmth. He couldn't touch her back. "I'm so sorry, Jack. I wish you'd told me."

"It doesn't matter." Which was the damn stupidest thing he'd ever said.

"It does matter." She squeezed his arm until he was forced to look at her. "But I'm not like your mother, Jack. I don't need you to save me. I don't need fixing. I didn't create Darius the madman and I didn't make him do the things he did."

He closed his eyes and puffed out a breath of air. "I know you didn't."

"Maybe you do, but the next time I do something you think is dumb, you'll wonder all over again about me."

She was going to walk out on him. He knew by the shredding of his chest muscles around his heart.

"Either you want me the way I am, Jack." She tipped

her head, her blue eyes the color of a weeping sky. "Or you don't want me at all."

He wanted her to be normal. An accountant maybe. Even a salesclerk at a department store. Someone who worried about paying bills or buying a new car or putting on a few extras pounds. Someone who wanted to get married and have babies. Not the owner of a metaphysical shop with a medium, a tarot reader and a psychic-to-the-stars for family. Not to mention Blue.

Normal. He didn't know exactly what that was. Only what it wasn't. Opal was right. The next time she put on her wacko hat, he'd flip all over again.

It was better to just let her go. Because he couldn't take it if something bad happened to her.

She kissed him on the cheek, then shut the door, closing it on his heart forever.

OPAL DIDN'T START CRYING until she reached the elevator. Unlike her building, Jack's high-rise had interior entries and halls with new gray carpeting and fresh white paint. Her sniffles seemed to echo up and down the empty corridor. For a moment, she hoped he'd open his door.

But he didn't.

Her heart ached for him. His mother. How awful. She should have known something terrible had happened, especially when he got so angry with Julian. And she could just smack her brother for making that terrible Tinker Bell comment. He was an insensitive lout. But knowing about Jack's mother explained a lot of things. Why he'd needed to fix her and take care of her. Why he couldn't bear that her family was psychic. To him, that just made them all crazy.

But it also doomed their relationship.

Jack didn't love her. He said he did, but he couldn't. Because to him, she was just like his mother. She wasn't good enough for her family, now she wasn't good enough for Jack.

Maybe, in some ways, Jack had a good point. But not about certain things.

"Darius wasn't my fault," she whispered, as if she needed to hear it again. The universe had sent her into his path for a reason. She didn't know what that reason was yet, but she did know she wasn't to blame for the things he'd done.

The bell dinged and the door opened to reveal an elderly woman and a fluffy miniature poodle bouncing on the end of a short Flexi lead. Opal stepped inside and backed up against the opposite wall. The woman glanced at her watch.

God. Her stomach flip-flopped as the elevator dipped in descent. It was the middle of the night. Her hair was mussed and her clothes askew. She must look as though she'd just had a wicked night on the town.

"He's got irritable bowel syndrome, poor little boy."

The woman was talking about her dog and didn't even seem to notice Opal's attire. Her tan overcoat draped flannel pajamas, the pink bottoms peeking out beneath the hem of the coat, her feet covered in matching slippers.

"That's too bad," Opal offered.

"This is the third time we've been out tonight."

"You must be tired."

"Not really. I don't sleep much anyway." Her white hair piled on top of her head didn't look as if it had been slept on. "Did you have a fight with your husband?"

Well. That was blunt. Just like something Grandma Blue would ask. Opal wasn't sure what had happened with Jack, but the lady obviously saw something. Maybe the tears she hadn't quite wiped away. "He had a meltdown."

The woman nodded sagely. "Men are like that."

"It wasn't his fault," Opal felt obligated to say. "He's under a lot of pressure."

"And women always find excuses for them."

It didn't feel right letting this woman put the blame solely on Jack. "I'm not making an excuse for him. It *wasn't* his fault." Jack had only been doing his best to protect her. He just didn't understand that she didn't need protecting.

"Of course, dear." The woman watched the floor numbers ticking off above the door.

"No, really. I wanted…" What *had* she wanted? For Jack to make her feel good about herself. To accept her the way she was. To make her believe she was okay.

To make *her* believe.

The elevator hit the first floor, and Opal's stomach dropped.

"Must run, dear, before my baby loses control of himself." She rushed across the lobby to the double-glass entrance.

Opal didn't move. The elevator doors closed on her, then the car sat because she hadn't pressed a button.

She'd told Jack she didn't need him to save her or help her yet from the moment she'd met him, she'd been asking for exactly that. *Help me, Jack, just help me with this one thing, then I'll be okay.* She'd told him that he had to want her just the way she was, but all her life she'd sought to be what she thought *other* people wanted.

Every action he'd taken had been because he saw a helpless woman who looked and acted as if she needed fixing. Jack was right about everything. She'd gotten them both arrested because she wanted to prove she was psychic. She'd rushed up the stairs in Victor's house because she felt useless in the emergency. She'd wanted to prove she wasn't, at least not totally. So she could be good enough. Just as she wanted to be psychic to prove she was good enough.

Victor had said she was pretending. And he'd been right. She was pretending that if she found just the right thing, just the right gimmick, just the right *vision,* she'd be acceptable.

But what had being psychic brought the members of her family? What were the real intrinsic benefits? Julian, grand medium, didn't even care enough to help a desperate old man contact his dead wife. Her mother, "Psychic to the Stars," her sole purpose in life was to bask in her son's glory. Had being psychic made their lives better? More importantly, had it made them better people? The answer, sadly, was no.

What of Pearl and Nile? Tonight, and also the night they sat drinking tea in Opal's apartment, now that Opal thought about it, Pearl had said Nile hated the things he saw, that he struggled every day to deal with the gift the universe had given him. He *suffered* his gift. As Pearl suffered hers.

Being psychic made them who they were. But had it made them *better* people? It certainly hadn't made their lives easier.

She'd accused Jack of trying to fix her. But really,

wasn't she the one who thought she needed fixing. By searching for her psychic ability, she hadn't been realizing a dream, she'd been looking for a way to be accepted. As if there was something about her that was lacking. Something that needed fixing.

Opal pushed the elevator button for Jack's floor.

She was the person who needed to believe in herself the most. And she never had. Jack had been trying to fill the hole she'd created herself.

The elevator seemed to rise far faster than it had gone to the first floor, then the door opened with a whoosh.

Jack stood there with his truck keys in his hand. "I figured you'd need me to drive you home."

"Yeah." They'd come to his apartment together. "I'd forgotten." She'd been a ditz again. She searched Jack's face for something more than just a hero who wouldn't let a scatterbrain walk the streets by herself in the middle of the night. "I'm not really ditzy *all* the time."

"I know." Jack stepped into the elevator before Opal stepped out, then pushed the first-floor button.

THE CAR DESCENDED, and Opal's knees dipped for balance. She didn't hang on to him. Even without a smooth mirrored reflection, Jack could see her more clearly than he ever had. In the silvered doors, her wavery reflection was half a head shorter than his despite the heels on her sandals. Next to her, he felt ten feet tall. Her hero. Some hero.

He'd practically accused her of causing the whole thing with Darius. But the man was evil, a monster. Opal hadn't made him do the things he'd done. She'd been as much his victim as Tamara Whitley-Dorn.

Opal was ditzy sometimes, but she was lovable. She had the oddest methods, but she had a big heart. She could find trouble in the smallest cranny, but she wouldn't hurt a fly. She believed in psychic phenomenon, but she wasn't crazy. She knew right from wrong, reality from fantasy.

In short, she was nothing like his mother.

When he hadn't believed in Tinker Bell, her light went out and his mother had died. Just like the storybook. He didn't know if he could have done anything to save her. But he did know that granting the unconditional acceptance he'd always denied his mom was the most important thing he could ever give Opal.

"I was wrong," he said to her reflection.

She put her hand in his. "So was I."

He looked down at her. "You were?"

She stared straight ahead. "I went overboard with my vision thing. I took risks I shouldn't have. I got us in trouble, and I hurt Victor with the séance. I didn't mean to do any of that, but I did." Finally she looked at him. "I'm not psychic. I never will be psychic. And I'm starting to realize that's okay."

"Everything about you is okay, Opal." Just okay? "No, I mean everything about you is perfect. Whether you're psychic or not. You're perfect just the way you are."

She smiled then, and his heart missed a couple of beats. "Yeah. I *am*, aren't I. I don't need to be psychic."

He wanted to kiss her senseless, but she tipped her chin at him. "And what were you wrong about?"

"What Darius did wasn't your fault. You're not crazy. I had no right to make comparisons. You don't need me to take care of you or fix you. You don't need to change a thing. I know you can take care of yourself."

She turned and latched onto his arm like a limpet. "Oh, Jack. I do need you."

"Why?" He held his breath.

"Because you and Grandma Blue are the only normal ones in my family."

Her family. His heart burst. Yeah. He wanted to be her family. He cupped her chin, pulling her up for a kiss. "Next to your grandmother, *you're* the most normal person I know." In addition to being adorably quirky.

The elevator stopped, the doors slid open, and an elderly lady with an itty-bitty poodle climbed on without waiting for them to exit. He glanced at his watch.

"Irritable bowel syndrome," Opal whispered.

The dog or the woman?

After punching the button a couple of floors above his, the lady sniffed primly at the lovely limpet on Jack's arm. "I see you've succumbed."

He'd never seen her before, but the woman gave him a look that could slice off a man's privates. He remembered to punch his own floor before they went past it. He didn't want to be stuck on the elevator with the woman any longer than necessary.

Opal merely smiled. "He promised he'd never do it again."

"Hah. That's what they all say."

Then Opal looked at him, her eyes wide and lovely. "Oh, I forgot to tell you I love you."

"Yeah, you did forget."

The old lady rolled her eyes. "See, he's got you groveling."

"That's not groveling," Jack said, just as he went down on one knee. "*This* is groveling." He kissed Opal's hand. "Will you marry me and make me the happiest man alive?"

On Opal's other side, the old woman snorted. "I thought you said he was your husband."

"You just assumed. I never said that. And, yes, Jack, I'll marry you."

The dog yipped with the exact amount of enthusiasm Jack felt erupting inside him, and the doors opened to his floor.

"Quickly, quickly, get out. Ranger has to go again."

Ranger? That teeny-tiny thing?

Opal dragged Jack out of the elevator. "There's just one more thing."

"What?" Making love in the hallway of his apartment building?

"Grandma Blue is going to want independent verification that you're Dynamite before she'll let me marry you."

He grimaced, though it was hard to keep from smiling around Opal. "Don't tell me."

She twinkled like a shining star. "Yeah. Julian's going to have to do a séance."

Ah, God. Julian. That man would be his brother-in-law. "For you, sweetheart, anything."

"And, Jack, in case you don't get into the spirit, go ahead and fake it."

For her family, he'd fake it. For Opal, he'd *be* Dynamite.

CHAPTER TWENTY-TWO

IT WAS SEVEN O'CLOCK, Grandma Blue was in her bedroom "sprucing up," and Jack would be here any minute for the big séance. In another half hour, Grandma Blue's house would be filled for the big event, Julian, Mother, Nile, Jack, Victor.

Pearl plucked at a tiny hole in Grandma Blue's ancient sofa. "Nile wants to go up to Tahoe and get a quickie marriage."

Opal gasped. "Grandma Blue will have a fit."

"She's the one who suggested it. She told Nile she'd put the money he saved her on a wedding into a college fund for our children."

Children? "So you're not worried about that anymore?" Opal whispered. There was the whole cursed children thing that Pearl had been worried about.

"Our kids will be the most perfect little psychics ever born." Pearl shrugged. "Or not. I'll love them whether they can bend spoons, read minds, contact the dead or they're just plain wonderfully normal." A brilliant sparkle lit her eyes.

Opal realized she could never again call Nile a dirty rat bastard worm. Pearl was too happy. Besides, the not-a-worm-any-longer was starting to grow on Opal.

She'd actually seen Nile smile a few times in the last couple of weeks.

"What about you and Jack?"

"Jack's ready to go to City Hall right now." He'd already moved a bunch of his things into her apartment, and Opal loved having him come home to her at the end of the day. She'd even taught him to pick up after himself. Somewhat. "But I think we'll go for a winter wedding."

Pearl smiled. "I'm happy for you, Opal. I'm happy for me. You know, two weeks ago, I thought the world was going to end."

"It didn't." Darius had created havoc in their lives, but Opal was trying hard not to dwell on it. Sometimes, though, she saw his eyes just before he fell

Pearl tipped her head. "Do you think Darius was born evil or did the things that happened to him when he was a child turn him into a monster? Was his guardian ultimately the one responsible?"

Born or made? It was an age-old question. Taunting Tamara in her prison much as he'd taunted Opal in his car, Darius had revealed a lot of things, the most significant being that he was abused as a child. His "guardian"—who wasn't a guardian at all, but the man his mother was living with when she overdosed and died—sold him over and over to terrible men who used him for terrible things. He'd threatened to turn Opal into a prostitute, but that had been *his* nightmare.

But did it excuse what he'd done as an adult?

Darius's so-called guardian had eventually gone to jail for manslaughter. Darius went into the foster-care system. Right after getting out of prison, coincidentally a few weeks before Darius showed up claiming to be Victor's grandson, the man had been murdered.

Nile had provided a lot of answers as well. Victor had given him access to Darius's belongings, and Nile had spent hours "reading" each piece and putting together Darius's history as best he could. Darius had indeed murdered the man who'd tortured and sold him for sex. Shortly thereafter he'd started searching for his grandparents. It wasn't quite clear to Nile why Darius hadn't searched for Victor and Prudence before, but he sensed that the so-called guardian revealed some detail just before his death that instigated Darius's search. What did come across clearly to Nile was that once Darius learned he had grandparents, he blamed them for leaving him to that horrible existence. In his disturbed mind, he believed they should have done more to investigate their daughter's life the seven years she was away. If they had, they would have found him. For supposedly abandoning him, he felt Victor's fortune was his due, and he actually enjoyed watching Victor and Prudence suffer through her illness. He'd relished Victor's suffering once she was gone.

There was a lot more to learn about Darius, and both Nile and Sergeant Guthrie were still working on it, but Opal didn't believe they'd ever understand it all completely.

"Pearl, I have no idea what made Darius do the things he did, but let's talk about something else." *Please.* There were delicious smells coming from Grandma Blue's kitchen, they still had to set up the candles and incense before Julian arrived for the séance, and Jack would be here soon.

"I'm sorry." Pearl pressed her hand. Then she looked

past Opal, her eyes widened and her eyebrows disappeared into her hair in shock. "Grandma Blue, what are you wearing?"

Opal was leery of turning around, and when she did, she almost didn't recognize her grandmother.

"What are you two gawking at?"

She wore the loveliest matronly powder-blue dress Opal had ever seen. At least on Grandma Blue, who kept the muumuu industry afloat. The blue-white locks of her hair curled attractively around her face. And she wore makeup. Blue eye shadow, a light shade of blusher and pale pink lipstick.

"You look beautiful," Opal managed to murmur in awe.

Her grandmother flapped a hand. "So like you think I'm putrid the rest of the time?" She could be so Valley girl when she wanted.

"No, no, that's not what I meant. I just meant..." This was a dream. Or...oh my God, Grandma Blue had the hots for Victor and had dressed especially for him.

"Did you get the sausage rolls out of the oven?"

"The timer hasn't rung yet."

Opal and Pearl followed Grandma Blue into the kitchen, where she'd already bent down to check her precious rolls. "Now my hair's going to go all limp," she fussed as heat wafted out of the oven. "And you know what they say about going limp."

Opal didn't *want* to hear what they said about going limp. "I'll get it. You don't want to mess up your pretty dress."

"Do you think Victor will like it?"

Victor probably wouldn't recognize Grandma Blue, either. "He's going to love it."

"Is there something you want to tell us?" Pearl grabbed the oven mitts and pulled out the tray of sausage rolls.

"Whether I've slept with him or not is none of your business."

Opal stuck her fingers in her ears and squeezed her eyes shut. "You're right, so don't even bring it up in front of us." Then she cracked one lid and pulled out one finger. "But you have been spending an awful lot of time with him."

Grandma Blue sniffed. "I'm helping him get over his wife."

Opal did a windup motion. "And, and?"

"I think old folks should give each other comfort in the last remaining years."

This time Pearl did the windup.

"I've got a premonition he's going to ask me to marry him."

"Oh, Grandma Blue, that is so wonderful."

"Wonderful?" She snorted. "It's one massive amount of fuss, palaver and paperwork. Old people shouldn't commingle their assets—" she winked "—so to speak. And believe me, you grandkids will appreciate that when I'm gone."

"We don't care about mingling assets," Opal affirmed. "You and Victor are perfect for each other." Even that first day with Victor in her shop, she'd known Grandma Blue would adore him and his humorous turn of phrase. "Please don't send him away."

Grandma Blue grimaced, tipped her tiny nose and stared down it at Opal. Or up, as the case may be, but the result was the same. Astonishment. "Hello. Get a grip. I'm just going to tell him we should live together in sin. I've never done that before, you know. It'll be a whole new experience."

Lord. The universal plan for what had happened recently in their lives became clear. Nile found he couldn't live without Pearl, Victor and Grandma Blue would dance together through the twilight years.

And, amongst all the other souls roaming the entire earth, Opal had found Jack. Now *that* was creating her own best reality.

"HE FAKED IT," Julian whispered, all bent out of shape.

Blue dragged him into the kitchen out of earshot.

The boy was such a wuss when it came to being upstaged. And Dynamite's performance tonight had definitely upstaged him. Blue knew she'd made the right choice in picking Jack for Opal. Why, caring enough for Opal to play along with the game, the boy had obviously researched every detail of the real Dynamite's life and done a dynamite job of answering every question they'd put to him during the séance. Even the hard ones.

The best part was that Blue was the only one who knew for sure whether his answers were right or wrong.

"I mean, what if he's after Opal's inheritance?"

"Get a life, Julian."

"I'm just looking out for Opal's best interests."

He was looking out for his own inheritance. Grandma Blue raised a brow. "Charities," she singsonged. Julian got the hint and shut his mouth. "Now I want you to apologize to him for butting your oversize nose into that business about his mother."

Julian put a defensive hand to the offending append-age. "It is not big."

"Yeah, well, on the TV screen, you bear a marked resemblance to Jimmy Durante. Or Barry Manilow."

"Oh, my God. Why didn't someone tell me?" he said, touching his nose.

She pinched his arm. "Forget your nose. Now, about the apology?"

He sniffed righteously. "I was relaying a message to him."

"He didn't ask for any messages. So apologize. Or I'll give your share to the Society for the Prevention of Goldfish Abuse."

"There is no such thing."

She raised a brow. "There will be."

He rolled his eyes. "All right, I'll apologize."

"There's a good boy. Now give your old granny a kiss." She tapped a finger to her cheek.

He kissed her obediently, then oddly, he took her hand in his. "There *was* a spirit here tonight."

Blue's heart gave a little flutter. "Who?"

"Prudence."

She sucked in a breath. "Why didn't you tell Victor?"

"Because she said the message she had was for you."

"Well, come on, spit it out." There was a fifty-fifty chance Prudence would give her blessing or tell Blue to take a hike.

"She told me to tell you to take care of him for her. She really loved him, you know."

Blue smiled. "I know. And he loved her."

Julian tipped his head. "It's going to be hard for you to replace her. They had a very happy marriage. I don't want to see you get hurt."

She had the feeling the kid actually meant it. Miracle of miracles. Maybe there was hope for Julian yet.

"That's the really nice thing about being as old as dirt. Somewhere along the way you figure out you don't have to replace anyone. You just add on more years to the happiness that was already there."

"Grandma Blue, you scare me when you get so profound and philosophical."

"Julian, you scare me when you morph into a nice guy. Now go apologize."

"Faker, faker," he singsonged in a very good imitation of herself.

There. All's well that ends well. Opal wouldn't be mooning around about how she didn't fit into the family anymore. Pearl had finally seen the light and found Nile's missing link. Blue liked that boy, she really did. Now, the only lost cause in the family was Lillian. Blue didn't get her hopes up that her daughter would be making any vast personality changes in the near future.

Ah well, there was always Victor to make up for her disappointment in Lillian. There couldn't be a nicer old coot on the planet. Would have been nice if Prudence had deigned to speak to him and ease his mind about the whole Darius debacle. But Blue figured that was a lesson Victor needed to learn on his own, forgiveness, acceptance and moving on. Yeah, the universe still had lessons to teach old codgers, even if most of them thought they were too old to learn anything new.

And Blue, well, she was tired of having only Chester to snuggle up to in the middle of the night.

"SORRY ABOUT the misunderstanding at Opal's psychic-coming-out party."

Glancing over his shoulder as if making sure Blue was watching, Julian Smith held out his hand.

Two weeks ago, Jack might have walked away without acknowledging him. Or knocked his block off for messing with him in the first place. But Jack Davis was a new man. In fact, he was dynamite.

"Apology accepted."

They shook hands, though Julian had a foppish grip.

"I wish you and Opal all the best." Julian's lip sort of curled when he said it. "Welcome to the family."

"Thanks." Opal's family was his family now. Gulp. He was no girlie-man. He could handle it, and he did actually look forward to adding Great-Grandma to Blue's name. She'd probably smack him the first time he did it.

Speaking of the little lady, she clapped her hands. "Everyone, outside and gather on the front lawn."

Then she grabbed Victor's hand. There was something scary going on there. Victor no longer looked as deflated as an empty potato sack, and Blue, for the first time ever, or at least since Jack had known her, was dressed in something other than a muumuu. When she looked at Victor, she had that special little sparkle Jack recognized in himself when he looked at Opal. Which he did now, zeroing in on her on the other side of the living room.

She looked up as if they were psychically connected.

He raised a brow and gave a slight nod of his head.

She came right over and hung like a limpet on his arm. See, they *were* psychically connected. Sometimes, all he had to do was look at her, and she'd jump him.

She'd also helped him find out everything he needed to know about Dynamite Davis so that he could pass the test.

"What's on the front lawn," he whispered against her ear. Man, she smelled good. Sweet like candy. Hot like sex in a dark room or beneath a midnight sky. And something else. Like home.

"I have no idea what she's got planned."

"Hopefully not another test." Then they all trooped outside.

The floodlight over the garage was on, and with great ceremony, Blue shushed them, then pointed her remote opener and the garage door rose.

Someone gasped. Opal's mother. Or her brother. For some reason, they sounded very much alike.

"Oh, my God," Opal whispered.

"What?" He was missing something here.

"Dynamite, come here." Blue held out her hand.

He knew he wasn't going to like this, but he took her tiny hand in his. Then she used the remote to flip on the interior garage lights.

He couldn't believe his eyes. Inside sat a gleaming white classic Corvette.

"Mother, you can't." Lillian seemed close to hysteria.

"Of course I can."

"But Julian wanted it."

"Julian can buy his own. This one belongs to Dynamite."

Jack smelled Opal's sweet scent as she came up beside him, felt her warm hand slip into his, her body flush against him.

"I don't get it," he said.

Blue beamed. "This was Dynamite's Corvette. After I got Chester's settlement, I rescued it from a wrecker and had it completely restored."

"Chester's settlement?"

"I'll tell you later," Opal whispered.

"And since you're his reincarnation," Blue went on, "I'm gonna let you drive it."

"She never let me drive it," Julian groused.

"Touch it, Dynamite." They all followed him into the garage, Blue with Victor, Pearl with Montgomery, then a glowering Lillian and son.

And Opal, shining as brightly as the gleaming white paint of the Corvette.

"After Dynamite died, they found a Corvette in his garage," Opal said.

"It was a terrible scandal," Pearl added.

Jack raised a brow.

"He drove race cars for *Ford*," Blue snapped as if he should have gotten it right away. "He was supposed to *hate* Chevrolets."

"Faker, faker," whispered through the garage.

"But I don't care," Blue declared. "He loved this car."

"It's a beauty," Jack murmured with awe. "A '63 split-window Sting Ray coupe. They only made 10,594 of them." He couldn't say how the production number slipped into his mind.

"And he got some cool extras," Blue coaxed.

"Leather seats, power windows, Posi rear end." He glanced at his future grandmother-in-law. "You can't let me drive this. It's too special."

She jangled the keys. "Weekends," she said. "I don't want you dirtying it all up at work."

He pulled Opal along with him, their clasped hands caressing the split-window along the back. "327ci, 360hp fuel-injected engine. Sintered metallic brakes, a 36 gallon fuel tank, pin-drive wheels." He could almost feel that baby purr.

"What's a pin-drive wheel?" Opal asked.

"It's—" He wasn't sure. The special option had simply popped into his head.

"That's exactly what Dynamite ordered," Blue said, staring at him, her head tipped to the side. "The guys at the factory had records going way back. I even framed a copy of his order form."

It couldn't be. Nah. It wasn't possible. They were all staring at him. "It was just a lucky guess. Isn't that what everybody orders?"

Opal looked at him, her eyes wide. "You *are* Dynamite." He hoped he'd always strike that note of wonder in her.

"Will you love me even if I'm not?"

She put her hands to his face and kissed him. "Oh Jack, I love you no matter what."

He loved her so damn much that he'd be whatever she wanted him to be, her husband, her lover, Jack the Giant Killer and the reincarnation of a long-dead race car driver all rolled into one "Well, I am Dynamite, baby. And Dynamite loves you."

Blue smiled. Her face dropped ten years. And she jangled the keys. "Wanna take her for a spin, Dynamite?"

He smiled in return. "Well, she's a Chevy and not a Ford—" he winked "—but it'll still be my pleasure."

She tossed him the keys, then he ushered his lady into the other side and climbed behind the wheel.

His butt settled into the leather seat, the gearshift fit his hand like a glove, the wood-grained steering wheel beckoned and when he fired her up, the engine was like music.

Like a sound he hadn't heard in years and suddenly realized how much he'd missed. Except he'd never driven a split-window coupe, had never even sat in one. He was a truck kind of guy.

Nah. It couldn't be. Really. It wasn't possible. Was it?

"Jack, are you okay?"

He shook himself, then met Opal's welcoming, understanding, beautiful gaze. Okay? "More than okay."

"Then let's blast off, Dynamite."

Yeah. Blast off. Life with Opal was going to be sheer dynamite.

HQN™

We *are* romance™

Return to a world of magic and mystery in this captivating sequel to *The Forest Lord* by

SUSAN KRINARD

Enchanted blood flows in veterinarian Donal Fleming, who secretly hungers for the freedom to live like the animals he tends, unrestrained by civilized society. Until a chance encounter with the very proper Cordelia Hardcastle introduces both to a passion they'd never dreamed of, leaving Donal to choose between human love and the powers that, to him, are life itself....

Lord of the Beasts

In stores this October.

www.HQNBooks.com

PHSK139

HQN™

We *are* romance™

New York Times bestselling author

BRENDA JOYCE

**sweeps readers away with her newest
de Warenne family saga.**

Sean O'Neil was once everything to
Eleanor de Warenne—but since he disappeared from
his ancestral home, there has been no word, and even
Eleanor has abandoned hope, promising her hand to
another. Then, just before her wedding, Sean reappears—
and in a moment's passion, he steals another man's bride.

The Stolen Bride

Return to the captivating de Warenne family,
in stores this October.

www.HQNBooks.com

PHBJ184

HQN™

We *are* romance™

Three timeless stories from three unforgettable authors!

RACHEL LEE
MERLINE LOVELACE
CATHERINE MANN

A SOLDIER'S CHRISTMAS

Home is where the heart is seen at the front door

RACHEL LEE
MERLINE LOVELACE
CATHERINE MANN

Three bestselling authors of military romance have joined forces to bring you these emotional stories about finding holiday peace and love on the front lines.

Don't miss the mass-market paperback edition of this popular anthology.

Look for it in stores this October.

www.HQNBooks.com

PHXMAS155

REQUEST YOUR FREE BOOKS!

HARLEQUIN® *Presents*

PASSION GUARANTEED SEDUCTION

2 FREE NOVELS PLUS 2 FREE GIFTS!

YES! Please send me 2 FREE Harlequin Presents® novels and my 2 FREE gifts. After receiving them, if I don't wish to receive any more books, I can return the shipping statement marked "cancel." If I don't cancel, I will receive 6 brand-new novels every month and be billed just $3.80 per book in the U.S., or $4.47 per book in Canada, plus 25¢ shipping and handling per book and applicable taxes, if any*. That's a savings of close to 15% off the cover price! I understand that accepting the 2 free books and gifts places me under no obligation to buy anything. I can always return a shipment and cancel at any time. Even if I never buy another book from Harlequin, the two free books and gifts are mine to keep forever.

106 HDN EEXK 306 HDN EEXV

Name	(PLEASE PRINT)	
Address		Apt. #
City	State/Prov.	Zip/Postal Code

Signature (if under 18, a parent or guardian must sign)

Mail to the Harlequin Reader Service®:

IN U.S.A.	IN CANADA
P.O. Box 1867	P.O. Box 609
Buffalo, NY	Fort Erie, Ontario
14240-1867	L2A 5X3

Not valid to current Harlequin Presents subscribers.

Want to try two free books from another line?
Call 1-800-873-8635 or visit www.morefreebooks.com.

* Terms and prices subject to change without notice. NY residents add applicable sales tax. Canadian residents will be charged applicable provincial taxes and GST. This offer is limited to one order per household. All orders subject to approval. Credit or debit balances in a customer's account(s) may be offset by any other outstanding balance owed by or to the customer. Please allow 4 to 6 weeks for delivery.

Jennifer Skully

77104	DROP DEAD GORGEOUS___	$5.99 U.S. ___	$6.99 CAN.
77081	FOOL'S GOLD	___ $5.99 U.S. ___	$6.99 CAN.

(limited quantities available)

TOTAL AMOUNT	$ _____
POSTAGE & HANDLING	$ _____
($1.00 FOR 1 BOOK, 50¢ for each additional)	
APPLICABLE TAXES*	$ _____
TOTAL PAYABLE	$ _____

(check or money order—please do not send cash)

To order, complete this form and send it, along with a check or money order for the total above, payable to HQN Books, to: **In the U.S.:** 3010 Walden Avenue, P.O. Box 9077, Buffalo, NY 14269-9077; **In Canada:** P.O. Box 636, Fort Erie, Ontario, L2A 5X3.

Name: _____
Address: _____ City: _____
State/Prov.: _____ Zip/Postal Code: _____
Account Number (if applicable): _____

075 CSAS

*New York residents remit applicable sales taxes.
*Canadian residents remit applicable GST and provincial taxes.

HQN™

We *are* romance™

www.HQNBooks.com

PHJS1006BL